Wishful Thinking

S.P. Wilcox

ISBN: 0615726100
ISBN-13: 978-0615726106

DEDICATION

I dedicate this book to my husband and four amazing children.
Life is short, keep those you love close, and keep love unconditional.

ACKNOWLEDGMENTS

I couldn't have completed this book without the understanding of my family and friends. They thought I was a crazy person sitting at my computer for hours at a time and reading books until all hours of the night.

A special thank-you to my friend Heather Wenk. All I have to say is, thank God for our kids' Kindergarten class! Heather let me talk her ear off about the characters all summer long. She helped me find the characters' paths and kept my secret while I was busy writing this book, and she loves to read as much as me. To Penny Meyer who listened to me go on and on about this story. She gave me endless support and guidance in the more risqué parts.

To my niece, friend, and reading partner in crime, Nicole Lugo. I know reading is our addiction. Only you and I can understand this problem we have. Thank you so much for loving my book and your great idea to write the Prologue.

The story could not have been completed without the longtime friendship of Kim Looft. Without her in my life, I would have missed out on so many wonderful memories. Our friendship has spanned more than 30 years, never missing one important event in each other's lives.

PROLOGUE

"Sydney, please come to the party with me," Kendall begged.

I so did not want to go to this party. Kendall had met some guy taking an SAT prep class and wanted us to hang out with him and his friends. I was not interested; the party was across town with kids from a different school.

"Come on...I will owe you one, and you know his friend thinks you are super cute. Please, I need you to come with me. I don't want to go by myself," Kendall begged again.

"How does he even know what I look like?" I asked her.

"I showed him pictures of you on my phone and he has seen you on Facebook."

"Fine, but you owe me big time," I said completely exasperated.

Kendall picked me up at home and we headed to see this guy she was head over heels for. I fumed and bitched the entire way to the party. I was not in the mood to make small talk with a bunch of strangers, so help me if she hangs all over this guy and leaves me standing like an idiot there will be hell to pay.

Well we hadn't been at the party for fifteen minutes and where was Kendall? Yes, hanging all over this boy and leaving me to fend for myself. "ARGH," I fumed. This guy Kendall was trying to get me to indulge in is umm...to say the least...not my type. He kept following me around the party talking my ear off about who knows what. I asked Kendall about a million times how much longer we need to stay but she just ignored me.

Luckily, I saw a few girls I know and hung out with them until this weirdo finally leaves me alone. After an hour and half of hanging around this party, I am done!

"Kendall, can we please go?" I ask her.

She gives me a dirty look and continues on with her conversation. Oh, hell no, she is not going to ignore me like this.

"Umm, Kendall, can I talk to you for a minute?" I ask her.

She whipped her head around at me, "No I am not ready to go. Go have a drink and hang out with everyone, dance... go have a good time, but we are not leaving yet." She narrowed her eyes at me, telling me "you are stuck here until I am ready to leave".

I could feel my cheeks turning red and steam coming out of my ears. I walked outside, pulled out my phone and start looking through numbers to see who I could get to come pick me up. As I scrolled through the numbers, one jumps out at me...Trent. My smile grew wide and my heart rate picked up. I have had my eye on Trent since the beginning of the summer. School is starting soon and this is a good opportunity to get the ball rolling. I wouldn't mind starting out my senior year of high school with a boyfriend.

I hit his number and sweetly asked if he would come get me from this awful party. Fifteen minutes later I am getting into Trent's truck and we are headed to a party on our side of town. Trent has a red Toyota 4x4. It is over the top too big, but he loves it. And that is how it started. After that night Trent and I were inseparable.

Oh, did I mention that Kendall and I are not speaking to each other? She is pissed I bailed on her, and I am pissed she put her own boy needs in front of our friendship, making my relationship with Trent even more dependent.

School was starting in less than a week- senior year. Kendall and I had great plans for the school year, not to mention practically every class together. If we don't make up soon, this would be a long, long year.

"Hi, gorgeous, what do you want to do tonight?" My adoring boyfriend, Trent, asked me.

"Whatever you want," I say.

"Well, Dylan is having a party. How about we go hang out at his house, Sound good?"

"Yeah...sure."

I don't really care what we do as long as we do it together. I am so head over heels for this guy; I could care less as long as he is

2

holding my hand letting everyone know we are together. Trent would give me loving kisses, hold my hand, and whisper the sweetest things in my ear. We have been together for almost a month. Trent picked me up and we headed to Dylan's for the party. We are driving towards Dylan's when Trent pulls over at the park not far from the party.

"Sydney, I hope you know how much you mean to me. I can't imagine not spending every waking moment together. Once school starts, we will be able to see each other all day and after school." Trent is looking at me with those beautiful deep blue eyes.

"I know this year is going to be so great. I never thought I would be excited for school to start, but I am." I said with a giddy tone.

"So, you know we have been taking things kind of slow," he said to me in a gentle voice. It took me a minute to realize what he is talking about. Then the light bulb went off in my head and I started to get a bit nervous.

"Well, I...I am just not ready for that yet. I mean, I think about it too, but, we have only been dating for a month. I am just not ready." I told him. I am so nervous, I know guys want what they want, but I am not ready to give in to his needs quite yet.

"Oh, Sydney, I would never pressure you to do something you don't want to, but... I am falling in love with you." Holy shit... did Trent, Senior God just tell me he is falling in love with me? My heart is swooning.

"Well, no I didn't know... " I said as I leaned over to give him a kiss.

Trent pulled me closer to him in the cab of his truck and began kissing me from ear to ear, tickling behind my earlobes, making my heart pound. Strange sensations began pinging through my body. I am having feelings I wasn't used to as his lips moved over my neck and his hands caressed my breasts. I was beginning to pant. I pulled away from him.

"We should stop...our friends are probably wondering where we are, let's go to the party." I said to him.

"Of course, yes, let's get to the party," Trent said through clenched teeth.

I knew he wanted more, but not in his truck. I am not having sex with him in his truck.

We arrived at Dylan's walking hand- in-hand into the party. I walked around a corner with Trent following right behind me, and I smacked right into Kendall. Damn it!

"Kendall."

"Sydney."

The tension couldn't have been thicker between us. Right behind Kendall was Dylan. What the hell was going on here? I turned to look at Trent and he is smiling from ear to ear.

"Did you know about this? Did you know she is seeing Dylan?" I asked, my voice overtly loud and annoyed.

"Hello, I am standing right in front of you. Yes, Dylan and I have been seeing each other," Kendall stated.

Dylan said to both of us, "You two need to talk. We are best friends and you two are best friends. You need to resolve this fight you are having so we can move on as one big happy family." Trent was nodding his head in agreement with Dylan's statement. It wasn't a request from them, rather, a demand. They walked us to the backyard and sat us down face to face to work out our problems. After a few minutes of the silent treatment, Kendall and I both started apologizing and wishing we weren't both so stubborn. Realizing we were dating best friends had us even more giddy than usual. This just added to how great our senior year is going to be.

By the time school started a few days later, you couldn't tell where one of us started and the other ended. The four of us were joined at the hip. Every date, every moment, spent together. Our friend Heather was more annoyed than anyone. She told us it wasn't normal. I think she may have even warned us we were in over our heads, but we just ignored her.

I was so in love with Trent, and Kendall was just as in love with Dylan. Homecoming was coming up and we were super excited. The dress, limo, dinner, and all of the essentials were taken care of. We told our parents we were spending the night at another friend's house after the Homecoming dance and would be home Sunday morning. Trent and Dylan were able to reserve two hotel rooms, one for each of us. I couldn't wait to spend the night with Trent.

After the dance we headed to the hotel. Trent had planned everything out. He gave me a beautiful bracelet before the dance. He put flowers in our room, and had a bottle of bubbly chilling. When he opened the door to our room, he swept me up in his arms and carried me in, placing me down on the bed. Trent was very handsome, with light brown hair, deep blue eyes, a nice set of muscles, and stood a good head taller than me. I was giggling when he put me down on the bed.

Trent leaned down giving me a wonderfully long sensual kiss.

"Mmm…" I moaned into his mouth.

"Mmm…is so right. I could kiss you like this every day, but right now, I have so many other ways I want to show you how much I love you." Trent's words were making my heart pound and my body ache.

For the last few weeks he had been working my body up into a frenzy every time we made out. His hands would go everywhere and his words would fill my head with love and desire. I almost lost control a few times but he didn't let me; telling me he wanted to make our first time together special. I knew tonight would be the night and I wanted it so badly. I could feel my love for Trent radiating out of me and his love for me encompassing me as he unzipped my dress and continued kissing me.

"Sweetheart, are you sure you want to give this to me? We don't have to if you don't want to." Trent's words were emphatic and sweet with concern for my wishes.

"Yes…I want to give you this…I want you to be my first…I know you love me…I can't imagine it with anyone else." I barely squeaked out through our kisses.

Trent's tenderness was heartwarming. He helped me out of my dress as I toed off my heels. I was left in only my panties and matching strapless bra. He pulled my hands over my head and rained kisses all over my body. I began arching to him; my mind was lost in the sensation of his touch. After many minutes of relentless kissing and our hands all over each other, our breathing labored, our eyes met and I nodded my head yes, indicating my wish to continue to the next step.

Trent grabbed the foil packet he had put on the night stand, and covered his ample erection. I braced for what he had warned me might hurt. Our hips moved with perfection together. I am not sure if it hurt or not as I was lost in a world of love and passion brought on by my loving boyfriend whose beautiful eyes had me in a seductive trance.

I could feel a few small tears leak out of the side of my eyes, rolling down the sides of my face.

"God...Sydney, that was amazing, thank you for giving me this, I will hold this moment in my heart forever...I love you," Trent said as he kissed my tears and held me tight.

I snuggled up to him and we feel asleep in each other's embrace.

The next few months were wonderful. Trent and I continued on with our relationship, having as many stolen moments together as we could get. Over the holidays Kendall and I, along with our parents, went on a tour of the schools we had applied to for college. We made it home just in time for the big New Year's Eve party at the country club. Trent and Dylan thought we would still be gone when we surprised them at the party. I would say the girls hanging all over them in our absence were less than happy when we arrived, placing ourselves at their sides.

Our dear friend Heather pulled us outside onto the balcony a few minutes after we arrived.

"Listen, I don't want to be a downer, but you need to confront Dylan and Trent. Those girls were not just flirting with them; they have been seen with them all over town while you two were gone." Heather informed us.

I scrunched my eyebrows as my blood began to boil. Kendall looked pale as we turned our bodies in the direction of Trent and Dylan, who were standing with a group of our friends.

"What? I don't believe you. I am sure this is all a misunderstanding," Kendall blurted out at Heather.

Heather's eyebrows shot up, and she said, "Are you kidding me? I wouldn't make this up. You need to find out what is going on. I think they have been cheating on you with those girls behind your backs."

My body began to shake with anger. Why would Heather say such a thing? My heart was pounding out of my chest and I felt ill. Trent came outside and wrapped his arms around me from behind kissing my neck.

"I missed you while you were gone. Thank you for surprising me by coming home for New Year's Eve. I can't imagine not being with you tonight." My body was stiff during his embrace I pushed myself away from him. I turned my body around glaring at him with my mouth in a grim line and a scowl across my face. Kendall's stance was much the same as we glared at Dylan and Trent.

"You missed me?" I pointed my finger at him through squinted eyes. "You are such a liar! How long have you been cheating on me?" I yelled at Trent.

He looked shell shocked by my accusation.

"What...?" Trent replied in disbelief.

"Are you going to deny it? Heather saw you with those same girls all over the place while we were away. What do you have to say to that?" I seethed at him. I was light-headed from the emotions coursing through my body.

"Come here sweetheart, you don't know what you are talking about. I don't think Heather understands what she saw. Those girls are nothing...we were just hanging out. Nothing happened." Trent took my hands in his as he finished speaking. "You know I love you...I would never ever be unfaithful. Anyway you and Kendall were off doing who knows what on all those college campuses leaving Dylan and I behind. How do we know what you two were up to while out on the road?"

I looked up into his eyes; I could see the sincerity and love looking back at me. I could feel the anger begin to dissolve and my heart pitter pattering with love for him.

Heather stormed off furious with us, and we spent the rest of the evening with Trent and Dylan wrapped around us like blankets.

Over the rest of the school year we were just happy go lucky couples. We went to all the dances, school events, and spent more time together than we did apart. As the school year began to come to a close, and our high school graduation grew closer, Trent and Dylan became more and more possessive of our time. I just thought they were worried about what would happen when we left for school in August. My cell phone was constantly blowing up with text messages wanting to know my whereabouts. Trent would ask how long I would be out shopping or when I would be back from the movies. When I said I was going away for the weekend, he wanted to know exactly what time I was leaving, and exactly what day and time I would be back.

I thought he was just being loving and concerned about me. Kendall was receiving pretty much the same treatment from Dylan. We had an end of summer part at Kendall's house a few days before we left for college. Dylan and Trent were late, claiming they stopped to pick us up flowers to show us how much they loved us.

Two days later we were headed to Arizona for Sorority Rush. Kendall and I in her car, and our Mothers behind us in my Dad's SUV filled to the rim with all of our stuff. As we pulled out on to the highway, both of our phones began to ding like crazy. Kendall and I were deep in discussion about how Rush would be and how excited we were to be starting college. I pulled my phone out of the cup holder it was resting in, and saw text after text, email after email. I turned to Kendall with a strange look on my face.

"I have 5 texts and like 10 emails? Don't you think that is weird?" I said to her.

"Open them and see what they are," She said, and continued on with our discussion.

I opened the emails first; there was an email from Heather and nine more from some other friends.

Heather's email had an attachment. I read the message silently to myself as tears began to sting my eyes.

"Oh, hell Kendall, this message is from Heather and there are a whole bunch of messages from everyone."

"Okay… what does it say?" Kendall asked with trepidation in her voice.

I began to read the message out loud to Kendall, my voice was shaking.

"Hi girls, I know you are driving to school and are together while you are reading this. I tried to tell you on numerous occasions that Dylan and Trent were up to no good. You wouldn't believe me so I have attached photographic evidence to back up my claims. These pictures were taken last night before and after you said your good byes. Please don't forgive them. Start a new life at school, have a great time. Never look back. I love you both and will miss you terribly until you come back. Heather."

I hesitantly opened the attachments. My stomach began to flip over and my head began to pound with heartache. How could they be so heartless? All lies, everything they said were lies. Each picture was like a knife in my heart. Trent caught in compromising positions, sucking face with some girl. His hands holding her face with a wicked smile on his. Dylan's arms wrapped around another girl, licking up and down her neck. The photos were dated from last night, after they had said good-bye to us.

Kendall was about to have a panic attack as she drove down the freeway. I opened more emails and found pictures of more betrayals; some dated all the way back to New Year's Eve. Heather had warned us that evening but we didn't want to believe it. How could they do this to us? More photos from Spring Break and the weekend we went away for my sister's college graduation.

"Good God, we look like stupid girls. How could we have been so stupid?" I said to Kendall.

"How could we have not seen what was happening? All those times I thought he was being concerned about me. Shit, he was making sure he wouldn't get caught. I am so stupid."

I kept saying it over and over again. This was supposed to be a wonderful day; not the day my life came crashing down around me because my boyfriend, the one I loved, the one I gave my innocence to breaks my heart. Kendall couldn't even put two sounds together to make a single word. She was using all of her concentration not to let the car crash as we made our way to Arizona.

The text messages were just as bad. I think some of the photos actually came from the girls phones they cheated on us with. My stomach was rolling as bile came up into my mouth. I took some much needed deep breaths, as did Kendall. We discussed our options the entire way to Arizona. We didn't call anyone, not even Heather; and especially not Trent or Dylan. We were not about to give them one more minute of our time.

Kendall and I agreed, we had more important things to deal with first. We would not deal with this situation until after Rush was over. We stopped responding to all calls and texts from our "boyfriends" and I use this term only in jest because they are not boyfriends. They are the slimmest douche bags I have ever encountered.

Once Sorority Rush was over and we had pledged the same house. We made our way to our new dorm room together. It was time. Kendall and I looked at each other and sent out the final text, it was like the shot heard round the world. This would be the last time I wanted anything to do with Trent.

Saturday, 8:00 am: Sydney to Trent: Hi sweetheart, hope all is well. OH…YOU CAN KISS MY HOT ASS…YOU ARE

9

DUMPED! DON'T CALL ME...DON'T TEXT ME. Have a nice day!

CHAPTER 1

As I walked back to my dorm room, exhausted from finishing my last final of my freshmen year, I felt relieved. It was midafternoon and the sun was high in the sky, beating down on me as I headed to my room. Putting my key in the door I could already hear the giggling. Argh, my roommate Kendall, and her boyfriend Matt, had just finished finals this morning and were undoubtedly inside snuggling on her bed. I took a deep breath and opened the door-walking in I dropped my backpack on the floor, and of course they were kissing, I sighed.

"Seriously," I said, "Can you two keep your hands off each other for five minutes?"

"Well hello to you too... Sydney," Matt laughed out.

Kendall just sat up and said, "Sorry Sydney, we lost track of time!"

Kendall and I had been best friends forever. We'd gone to school together since the seventh grade and we knew everything about each other. We came to college together, pledged the same sorority together, and had lived together our freshmen year of college. Kendall met Matt in her Human Sexuality class, well not right away; she came home from class one day and said, "I think I am in love." After that it wasn't long before they met and had become inseparable. Matt was a year ahead of us, fraternity boy, one of the nice ones though. Let's just say Matt had become part of the landscape in our room. Kendall was not very tall, with brown hair, brown eyes, a perky nose, a personality to die for, super outgoing, and confident. Matt was tall and slender with fair skin and sandy blonde hair. They made a darling couple when they were not making out in our room 24 hours a day!

Kendall asked me, "So how was your last final?"

"Good," I said, "I am just glad it is over. What is our plan for tonight?"

We were heading home in the morning. I should say, I would be staying home for the summer and Kendall was just coming home for a few days. She was coming back to take summer classes and of course, to be with Matt. No surprise there!

Matt piped in, "We are having a party tonight at the house- you know, end of school year and all." Kendall and I exchanged glances and both said, "Sounds great, what time?"

"It's probably started already, but why don't you guys head over after you clean up and eat dinner." Matt headed out after that, and Kendall and I decided we were in need of power naps. After studying for finals the long night ahead of fun would require it.

After our much needed naps, we had dinner in the cafeteria down stairs. We showered and spent 30 minutes trying to decide what to wear. Although the days were hot already in May, the evenings tended to cool down just enough to make you question your fashion sense. Shorts, tank tops, and light sweaters and we were ready to go. I looked at Kendall; grinning from ear to ear she couldn't wait to see Matt again, as if they had been apart for months, when it had only been a couple of hours.

"Kendall," I said.

"Yeah, Sydney."

"Will you do me a favor tonight and not leave me standing like a dork while you and Matt hang all over each other? You are going to be here all summer with him. This is our last night before we…I mean I, go home for the summer. Come on, can we just hang out, all of us, and have a good time together?"

At the question and demand I had put out there, Kendall rolled her eyes at me, but agreed. I was in a much better mood now, not that I had been in a bad mood; I just didn't feel like making small talk with a bunch of Matt's fraternity brothers and pushing away their not so polite advances for the next 3 hours. I knew plenty of the guys in his Fraternity, not in an utmost and personal way, but enough to know which ones to steer clear of, and which ones were not threatening to my reputation. Plenty of girls would make the walk of shame between fraternity row and the dorms, but not me. I had, so far, eluded that moment. Heading over to Matt's fraternity house, I reminded Kendall of her promise to hang out with me and not spend the entire evening with Matt.

We arrived at the party with smiles on our faces. Matt and his friends were standing at a long table playing beer pong. It would be less than a minute before Kendall and I each had a beer in our hands in the customary plastic cup. Fraternity houses, no matter which one, were all the same and smelled like beer and sweat. Kegs were flowing, music was blaring, and there were quite a few people here. We drank just enough to relax and release the stress final exams put on us and have a good time, playing beer pong and then on to around of quarters.

Kendall and Matt ended up hanging all over each other and dancing a little. Neither of them were really much of a dancer. Mostly they swayed back and forth in each other's arms like love struck goof balls. I sighed and continued to dance with a few of my sorority sisters and some of the guys. As the night grew to a close for us, the party would continue on long into the night. We were heading out early for home, so we said our good byes and walked back to our room. We passed out, not from drinking but rather exhaustion.

After loading Kendall's car in the morning with our stuff, we headed out early before the desert heat made the six hour drive home worse. Going to school at Arizona State University was great, just far enough away from our parents to give us the freedom we craved, but close enough to get home without too much effort. My parents wouldn't let me bring my car to school for freshmen year, reasoning "you are living on campus, you won't need it". Of course they were mostly right since everything had been within walking distance to my dorm. As we drove home, we talked about how much fun freshmen year had been and all the people we had met, both the good and the bad ones. There was of course much talk about Matt and how fun her summer would be back at school with him. I wasn't dreading going home, but Kendall and I had never been apart this long. I wasn't worried about our friendship, it would just make for a different summer vacation.

When we left California for college last August, we had left behind serious boyfriends, who we would later find out, were not quite as serious about our relationships as we had been. The ex's, were best friends and thick as thieves. The knowledge of their betrayals had come to us through text messages and pictures. Cell phones were the demise of all. Our high school friends had sent us the images not long after we arrived for Sorority Rush last August. Kendall and I stopped returning their phone calls and text messages, and we didn't call or go see them when we had come home for the various breaks we got from school. We moved on- Kendall more quickly than I. Not for my lack of trying, there just hadn't been anyone that made the hairs on the back of my neck stand up with excitement.

Kendall dropped me off at home. I was tired from the long drive, but it was good to be home. Alone, I was here alone. No one was home. My Dad was away on a business trip, my Mom was at work, and my sister, who had already graduated from college, and was taking a year off to decide what to do next, was nowhere around.

My sister and I are polar opposites. She did well in school, dated the right boys, and was the perfect daughter. Long curly brown hair, blue eyes, the same height as me, and driven. I, on the other hand, have medium length blonde hair, hazel eyes, and stand almost 5'5". I was far from ugly, but I didn't see myself as anything special. School was not my favorite thing. I got average grades and was more interested in the social part of college life than the academic. I had seen my share of restrictions and being in trouble for not receiving good grades in high school.

I plopped down on the couch in the family room, turned on the TV, and was quickly taking a nap. I woke a few hours later to my phone beeping at me, there were 3 text messages. One was from Kendall saying she was having dinner with her parents and would see me tomorrow. The second was from Heather, asking if I was home yet. The third, I just erased not even reading it, once I realized who it was from. I sent Heather a text back.

Friday, 4:03 pm: Sydney to Heather: Yeah, I am home, what's up?

Heather was a friend from high school. She stayed home and was going to community college, working at a local yogurt shop, and was living with her parents. As soon as we graduated from high school, her parents sold their house and bought a house at the beach. Not right on the beach, but close enough for a nice view, cool ocean breezes, and terrible parking.

Friday, 4:05 pm: Heather to Sydney: Beach party 2night, come, plz come? Haven't seen you in months, it will be soooo fun!

Hmmm, could be nice to go to the beach tonight, my family would be home late and what was I going to do, sit here alone?

Friday, 4:07 pm: Sydney: Ok, give me directions, time.

Texting did have its advantages, got right to the point.

CHAPTER 2

I headed down to the beach, in my white Jetta, which was waiting in the driveway for me with a full tank of gas and freshly washed. I had put on jeans, t-shirt, and brought a hoodie sporting my sorority letters prominently across the front. I had also brought Heather an ASU hoodie, which she had been begging for all year. Finally I found a parking space; parking at the beach, even at night, was a pain in the ass. I took a deep breath, filling my lungs with the smell of the fresh ocean air. There is just something about being by the ocean that is so soothing.

Before I even knocked on her front door, she was opening it and hugging me with so much glee I thought I would fall backwards. We went inside and she told me about working at the yogurt shop, living by the beach, and her classes.

I asked, "So, who is going to be at this beach party tonight?"

She stopped in her tracks, turned around and said, "Sydney, don't worry, not one person you know."

"Great," I said with sarcasm, "Who am I going to talk to, if these are all your new friends?"

We were in her bedroom talking, Heather was gorgeous, wherever we went all eyes were on her with her long blonde hair, deep blue eyes, and long legs.

"I invited you here to get you out on your first night home with a different crowd, before you ended up caving and hanging out with you- know- who all summer just to pass the time!"

My jaw dropped, but I had no response. She was probably right. I would have been bored, picked up the phone, or innocently sent the "ex" a text, to see if there was still a spark. Thankfully, Heather was a step ahead of me.

Finally, I responded, "Good thinking, so glad you are in my corner! So, let's go to the beach," I said firmly.

It was still May, so the nights at the beach were cool. When we arrived, beach chairs in hand, sweatshirts already on, the bonfire was burning strong. The crackling of the wood and the smell was exciting. People I didn't know were hanging around talking, and a group of guys were playing a game of football not too far away. Heather introduced me to her friends, people from her work, and others from the beach community who worked in the local shops.

We put our chairs down in an open spot not too far from the fire, "Sydney, this is Russ, he manages the local surf shop," I shook his hand and Heather skipped away to hopefully get us a drink.

I was feeling a bit self-conscious being the new person in the crowd and not knowing ANYONE but Heather.

Russ, started on, "Hi, it is nice to meet you. Heather has been going on about you coming home for the summer and hopefully staying with her in her parents' beach house."

I tilted my head and squinted a bit, "What…huh," I replied, I must have looked completely lost because Russ started to laugh.

"Didn't Heather tell you?" Just then Heather arrived with a beer for each of us from the cooler on the other side of the bonfire.

"Heather, what is this about me staying with you down here for the summer? You know my parents are not going to let me do that," I growled at her.

"Sydney, it was just an idea. My parents are going to be gone for most of the summer and I just thought, maybe if you got a job down here, maybe your parents would allow it." She said all this with a big smile on her face.

"Come on," she continued, "It will be great. My parents are travelling and I don't want to be here alone. They are always working. Do you really want to be under your sister's watchful eye, with her lecturing you about what you should and shouldn't be doing?" I think she kept talking about it, but my minded drifted, maybe, if I found a job and could live rent free with Heather.

"Sydney are you listening to me? Did you even hear what I just said?"

"What?" I turned to Heather.

"I said, Russ is looking for someone to work part time at the surf shop."

I looked at Heather and then to Russ, "I don't know anything about surfing," I said.

Russ sighed, "Sydney, you don't need to know anything about surfing. Do you like clothes?"

Of course, I love clothes. What right- minded female didn't like clothes and shopping?

"Well...yes," I responded to him.

"Then you can have the job!"

"What? Just like that? You don't even know me and you are giving me a job?"

Russ said "It is not rocket science; you stock, fold, ring people up, and look cute all day just like you are. You start tomorrow at 3 pm, don't be late."

I was stunned. I hadn't even been home a day and had a part time job. Awesome! We sat down in our chairs, not too far from the bonfire. There were more people around us now. The guys playing football were walking up and a few sat down. I wasn't paying much attention and continued my conversation with Heather.

Heather went on and on about this guy she was dating, I was only partially listening as I gazed across the fire when the hairs on the back of my neck began to tickle and stand on end. I watched as he gripped his beer bottle with a strong, sun tanned hand. My eyes followed up his arm and even through the flames I could see strong muscles rippling beneath the thin t-shirt he was wearing. As my eyes continued up, I saw a strong jaw, big smile, deep brown eyes, and short dark brown hair, which looked freshly cut. Not too short though, just enough to put your hands through and tug a little. As I continued in my moment, his head turned and saw me staring. I didn't mean to stare, but he was just gorgeous. I had to pull my eyes away- how embarrassing. I knew I was blushing and when I got enough nerve to look at him again, he flashed me a strong smile and continued his conversation.

Oh my goodness, I turned to Heather, who was still going on about the guy she was dating. I interrupted her, "Who is that?"

"Who?" She asked.

"That guy... right there, directly across from us" Heather turned her head to look, "Don't look," I said, my heartbeat quickening.

"Well if I don't look, how will I know which guy we are talking about?" She laughed.

"Fine," I got all flushed again. "The one, grasping his beer in two hands in the grey stripped t-shirt."

She looked over at the group of guys and then back to me, "No way… don't even think about it Sydney. How is it you have a way of always picking out the bad boy in the bunch?"

I just looked at Heather with a strange feeling inside, what did that mean?

"What, why would you say that?" I asked her my voice laced with irritation.

"Didn't you learn your lesson with your "ex"? He was nothing but trouble, not that you and Kendall would listen to any of us. You two fell head over heels for those guys and they ended up breaking your hearts." She was right, but, the hairs on the back of my neck were on high alert and the strange sensation I was having throughout my body told me this time things would be different.

"Heather could see my eyes, dancing with delight, and thinking of all the fun this summer would bring. My mind raced off…this was going to be one fun summer. Heather rolled her eyes and shook her head.

"I am not getting involved, taking blame, nor introducing you to him, do you understand me?" she said.

"What?" I looked at her with a sad face.

"Oh no, don't give me that look. You are not going to convince me to introduce him to you, if you want to meet him, you will have to make your own introduction."

"I can't do that. You know how self-conscious I am," I said making a sad puppy- dog face.

"I don't know why you are self-conscious; every guy here, given a chance, would want you. You're every guys dream girl." I looked at her, she is nuts. "Well, then I guess you won't meet him. Believe me it is for the best cause he will only break your heart and ruin your reputation." With that I leaned back in my chair sipping my beer, I couldn't keep myself from peering at him over the flicker of the flames.

We toasted marshmallows over the fire and made some *s'mores*, eating the very gooey but yummy mess. I met a bunch of Heather's friends and then we headed back to her house.

Once back at the house I turned to Heather, "I don't know why you wouldn't introduce me to Hot Bonfire Guy."

What did she think was going to happen; geez I am only in town til mid-August, which gave me less than three months of summer vacation. I have to be back at school for Sorority Rush.

Heather spun around and with a straight firm face, "You DO NOT want to get involved with him, he is…" she paused, "Not good for you."

"Fine, forget about it, we don't need men to have fun." I continued, "It is summer, we are at the beach and we both have jobs, it is going to be great."

I went home the next morning, Saturday; Mom was up reading the paper and my Dad had not returned yet from his trip. My sister was still sleeping.

"Hi Mom, I have some great news", I said, and gave her a kiss on the cheek.

"You're very happy this early in the morning, what's up?" she asked.

"I found a job."

Looking at me over the newspaper, "Really, how is that when you have been here less than 24 hours and were out all night?"

I knew she was not going to be overly happy when I told her my plans, but hey I am over 18, have a part time job and a free/nice place to stay, what could she complain about?

Cringing I went on, "Well last night at the bonfire, Heather introduced me to her friend, Russ. He runs the surf shop by her house and is looking for some part time summer help, so he offered me the position." Before she could say anything I continued, "Heather has asked me to stay with her at her parents' house by the beach for the summer…so she won't be alone while they are off vacationing."

Looking straight in my mom's face, which was not so happy anymore, she asked me how much I was to be paid, did I have to pay rent, and how often would I come home to see them? My eyes wide, I could not even believe she was actually considering the information I just presented. I answered all of her questions.

After what seemed like an eternity, she grinned and said "That sounds like a great offer, you should definitely do it, and you will have a great summer living by the beach with a great friend."

This seems way too easy. There was the lecture about being safe, not partying too much, saving money, and still coming home to visit my parents. Still thinking this was way too easy, I headed up to my room. Thank goodness I did not unpack any of my stuff. I would just put it in my car and head back down to Heathers. Feeling completely excited, and pretty good about myself, I sat on my bed and relaxed for a minute.

When I looked up, my sister was standing in the door way, "What are you so happy about?" she snarled at me.

Ugh, I am so glad I am not going to be stuck here with Miss Grumpy Pants all summer.

"Well I am going to stay with Heather at her parents' beach house," is all I replied.

"For the weekend?" She asked.

"No, for the summer," I said and stuck my tongue out at her as I walked out my bedroom door on the way to the bathroom.

She followed after me yelling, "What! Mom and Dad are not going to pay for you to live at the beach for the summer!" feeling all proud of herself that once again she thought she had the upper hand. I laughed and advised Miss Grumpy Pants, "I already have a job lined up, I'm living for FREE at Heathers parents' house, butt out! This is none of your business anyways. You will be busy working and doing whatever it is you do with your friends."

I continued, "Besides, Mom already said yes. I am heading back to the beach now; I have to work at 3 today. So, gotta go, have fun here all summer!" I waved at her and headed to the bathroom.

Mom and Dad were fine with this whole plan and decided to take an extended vacation themselves. They would be leaving for a few weeks, leaving my sister by herself. She is 22 so she can be alone. No doubt she will have her very boring boyfriend come stay... eek!

So, not only did my parents allow me to go away to college when I was 17, not turning 18 until 3 months into college, they are letting me stay down at the beach for three months with my girlfriend. I headed down to Heather's again, but before I hit the road I sent out a text.

Saturday, 10:15 am: Sydney to Kendall: Staying @ Heathers for summer, got job. Come down 2night.

Saturday, 10:20 am: Kendall To Sydney: What??? Job??? Where???

Saturday, 10:26 am: Sydney to Kendall: Tell u 2night, work @ 3, surf shop by beach

As I began unloading my stuff at Heather's house, she came running out jumping for joy and screaming, "This is going to be the best summer ever! We have to get our work schedules the same. All the shops are open from 9 am to 9 pm."

Looking at her with my eye brows raised and a smile on my face. I haven't even started my new job and she wants me to demand certain hours. I was not about to walk up to Russ and tell him when I would and would not work.

"Let me see what my schedule will be first and then we can try and work it out so we at least have the same days off together. Anyway, if we are closed by 9pm every day, we still have the whole night to go out."

I arrived at the beach surf shop just before 3 pm. Russ was there ringing up some customers. The store had a very clean, beach feel. The front of the store was filled with bathing suits, shorts, tank tops, t-shirts, and hoodies. The back of the store had wetsuits, surfboards, and all that surf stuff, which I had no clue about.

Russ came over and greeted me, "Sydney, so glad you are here. Let me show you where you can keep your purse."

We walked to the back room; there was a small bathroom (not so clean), and a desk with phone, fax, and computer. There was also tons of back stock, and a few lockers. He showed me which locker I could use and I put my purse inside.

He held up two t-shirts, "Blue or black, small or medium?"

Looking at the shirts, "Small, can I have both? I mean if I am working every day, shouldn't I have two?" Wow, I can't believe I asked for both.

"Good point," Russ said. "Yes, you may have both. You must wear one of the our logo shirts to work every day, with shorts, mini skirt, or pants, got it?"

"Yes, sir," I said saluting him like a captain. I went into the bathroom to change into my work shirt. Russ, took me around the store and showed me everything. I would start today, folding clothes and helping customers, eventually learning the register over the course of the next week. Russ introduced me to two other employees, Rebecca and Mike.

As evening approached, Russ wanted to hang some new posters we received for a display. He yelled for me across the store. No customers were in the store so no one was offended.

"Hey Sydney, can you run over to the hardware store and get me some double sided poster tape?" I must have had a confused looked on my face because he handed me some money, walked me to the door and pointed me in the right direction.

Smiling, I said, "Ok, I will be back in a few minutes."

"No problem, when you get back you can take your break and get something to eat."

Food! I had totally forgotten about eating I was so busy helping customers and folding, and folding, and folding! I found the hardware store, which was right on the corner of the two main streets running through the very fun beach town I was now calling home Well, for three months anyway. I walked through the double front doors and was struck by the oddest feeling. The hair on the back of my neck was tingling. It was at the same moment when I saw a very tall, tan guy in jeans and t-shirt helping a customer pick out bug spray.

My heart started to pound in my chest and I felt a bit woozy, probably because I had not eaten since breakfast, but my heart and pulse had sped up. I tried to quietly pass behind him without him seeing me. I darted down the paint aisle, which is nowhere near where I needed to be. Holding my breath, I shut my eyes to regain my composure. When I finally relaxed, my eyes opened and standing next to me was Hot Bonfire Guy. My mind was aflutter. How did he get so close to me without me hearing him?

I looked up at him and he said, "Are you guys repainting something at the surf shop?" His smile was wide and his voice teasing. His voice was like liquid gold, flowing through my ears deep and sexy.

How did he know I worked at the surf shop and why would I be painting?

"Um, no I don't think so, why do you ask?"

"Well you are standing on the paint aisle in deep thought; do you need help finding a color?" I could hear the playfulness of his tone, but I am completely embarrassed "Well, no I guess, I am just...umm... can you tell me where double sided poster tape is located?" I blurted out like a total dork. He laughed, "Sure I will show you. So did you just start at the surf shop?" he asked.

I was following behind him, taking in the view, which was mighty fine, "How do you know I work at the surf shop?"

He pointed to my shirt, blue with black writing in the corner.

"Oh, yeah, I forgot I am wearing this shirt." Seriously, he must think I am an idiot.

He took me to the aisle where the tape was located and went off to help another customer. I quickly picked a few packages and headed to the checkout stand. Great, nice impression I have made on this guy. I have to get out of this store before I make a total fool of myself. I put the tape on the counter and of course, Hot Bonfire Guy was now ringing up customers. My day just keeps on getting better. He looked at me kind of funny, like he had seen me somewhere before.

"What?" I asked him, "Why are you looking at me like that? Do I have something in my hair?"

He laughed, "No, you don't, but you look familiar to me, have we met? Oh... I know, you were at the bonfire last night with Heather from the yogurt shop, right?"

Since there was no one behind me, I thought maybe I can redeem myself by having a normal conversation with Hot Bonfire Guy. I should find out his name so I can stop calling him Hot Bonfire Guy.

"Yes, I am staying with Heather for the summer and today is my first day at the surf shop. Sydney, my name is Sydney Stanton."

He smiled at me with a big, bright smile and I thought I might melt right in front of him like a popsicle on a hot summer day.

He nodded his head up and down, "Nice, sounds like you are going to have a good summer. We tend to have a lot of fun around here during the summer. I'm Grant Montgomery; it is nice to meet you Sydney." He stuck out his hand for me to shake it. As I reached across, I knocked over an entire container of those little hammers, argh, way to redeem myself, not embarrassing at all. As our hands touched, I felt a quick bolt of electricity fly through me, starting at my fingertips and making the hairs on the back of my neck jump with glee. I looked up at him, my eyes wide, I could feel my cheeks blushing. I wondered, did he feel it too, the electricity? As I walked out the front door, I turned and I waved good bye to Grant. He gave me a head nod with his smile broad across his face. Panic set in- I think I might have an anxiety attack, this was bad, very bad.

I was hitting myself on my forehead with the palm of my hand and mumbling under my breath. Thinking to myself, "What just happened?" The surge of excitement I felt go all through my body when we touched was beyond stimulating. I walked back to the surf shop, handed the tape to Russ, took my purse from the back room and headed to the yogurt shop for a 30 minute break.

Walking in, Heather greeted me with a very happy greeting, "Welcome to Galactic Yogurt, what I can get for you today?"

I started laughing, "Galactic Yogurt is that what this place is called? That's hilarious- where does the name come from?"

"Don't make fun. The owner's six year old son loves Star Wars, so Galactic Yogurt it is! It is out of this world yummy. What do you want to try?" Heather asked.

Well, what I really wanted was to know how Grant's lips might taste, but I was not going to bring that up because Heather was already on edge about me meeting him. I just couldn't stop thinking about him; his touch, the electricity, my mind was racing and so was my heart.

CHAPTER 3

I woke up on Sunday morning tired and out of sorts. I really hadn't had a good night's sleep since before finals, and with a new job, new living arrangements, and staying out late to hang with Heather's friends, I was exhausted. Kendall came down last night and spent the evening with us, and we hung out at the local pizza place talking and joking around. Kendall Martin would be heading back to school this afternoon. She said she was excited about summer classes starting on Monday, but really, I think she just missed Matt.

I had to be at work at 10 am and it was already 8:45. I still had to shower and eat, but at least work was walking distance away. When I went into the kitchen, Heather's parents were eating breakfast and gave me a big hug with "Good mornings" attached to them. Heather was making toast and brought me some as well.

Her parents had a quick announcement, "Girls we are heading out of town for a few weeks and you better behave while we are gone. No loud parties, no one in our room, and absolutely no boys spending the night," her Dad belted out.

"Of course not Daddy," Heather said.

I shook my head left to right, "Mr. Connors, I think you know us better than that. We wouldn't have boys spend the night," I said.

Laughing, he stood up and carried his coffee cup to the sink, "Girls, we were young once too, don't think we are complete fools. Just behave while we are gone."

Heather and I looked at each other, with big wide eyes and made funny faces as if to say yuck, ewe, too much information.

"So, we are not going to tell you when we are coming back in town, this will keep you two on your toes, to keep the house clean and boys out, do you hear me?"

After that speech, her parents went upstairs to pack; not knowing when they are coming back would definitely keep us on our toes.

I rushed to get ready for work, we headed out since both of us had morning shifts, "Hey let's go to the beach after work, what time do you get off?" I asked.

"3, I'll be done at 3," Heather yelled back to me as I headed down to the surf shop. The day flew by and at 3 pm, I was out the door, picked up Heather, and we walked back home to change. We walked in the house and it was very quiet. Stuck to the fridge was a note:

Girls, we will be gone for about 3 weeks or so, not giving you the dates...I stocked the fridge with all the things you like to eat, don't eat out every meal and don't just eat junk food. There is an envelope with money in it for groceries. Have fun we will call you when we land. Call us on our cell phones if you need anything.

Love you both, be good.

Jumping up and down in the kitchen, we opened the fridge and found it totally full; fruit, snacks, juice, good stuff. We ran to our rooms and changed into our bathing suits. I need a new one, first pay check, getting new suit! Grabbing all the necessary items for the beach; towels, sun screen, chairs, magazines, water, and snacks, we were set. Finally reaching the sand and burning our feet no less, damn I forgot how hot the sand can get, we set up our stuff. We walked down to the water to cool off. Sitting back down in our chairs, I put my head back and closed my eyes. A power nap at the beach- this is the life. It was probably close to 6 o'clock, when we packed up our beach gear and started to walk back home. The sun was low in the sky and beginning to set with a cool breeze blowing my hair. I felt a chill roll through me.

Talking about making dinner, we didn't notice a group of surfers walking next to us.

"Hey... Sydney," someone yelled.

I don't know anyone down here and who would know me, I looked up. My eyes grew wide, my heart got the nervous pumping feeling, and Heather was giving me the evil eye. It was Hot Bonfire Guy…I mean Grant, yummy! We stopped, so we could talk to them. Heather was shaking her head. I could see the look on her face, and trouble with a capital T was what she was thinking. Damn he looks hot; wetsuit pulled down just below his hip bone, surf board under his arm, hair a sexy mess, and his smile, no words come to mind about his smile…drooling, I think I am drooling. Don't even get me started about the six pack he is sporting.

"What's up Heather?" Another of the guys said as he put his arm around her neck and bumped her hip with his.

"Who is your friend?" He asked Heather.

Grant butted in, "This is Sydney Stanton," not only did he remember my name but my last name too! This is going to be interesting!

"Sydney, this is Curt, Curt, Sydney." She put her hand out in front of us as she gave introductions. There was also Carlos and Tucker, but they didn't captivate my attention.

"Hi," I said and waved a semicircle to the guys. I am such a dork. They smiled and invited us to have burgers with them for dinner.

Still with his arm around Heather, Curt said, "Well, we mean come over to our house and we can bbq some burgers."

Heathers face was beaming with joy, this must be the guy she was going on and on about the other night at the bonfire, the night she advised me against Hot Bonfire Guy, I mean Grant. What is going on here, I thought looking around this group? Heather could be all googlie eyed for this Curt character, but I can't even look in Grant's direction without her getting mad?

We agreed to come to their house for dinner, first stopping and dropping off our beach stuff at home. Heather and I quickly changed out of our swimsuits and into shorts and t-shirts. We grabbed some chips and soda for our impromptu dinner party and walked back over to their beach house. I say "dinner party" loosely based on the group of people we would be eating with. "Heather, is Curt the guy you have been going on about?" I asked with a suspicious tone.

"Yes, isn't he adorable? Did you see his eyes?"

"No, I didn't, but what is the deal you can have something with him, but I can't even look at Grant? Would you like to explain?"

"I told you why. I can't stop you from getting involved with Grant, but just be sure you go in with both eyes open. Don't be fooled by his charms, he has issues," Heather advised. I rolled my eyes as we walked onto the patio of their beach house.

Luckily, this group did not all live together. Just Grant and Curt, who live on the first floor of a house by the beach, and when I say by the beach I mean on the beach! The house was a gorgeous three story home with full view of the ocean. The first floor was right on the beach. It had lounge chairs, bbq, fire pit, 2 bedrooms, 2 bathrooms, small kitchen, family room with couch, table, TV, and every kind of video game you could think of. The second floor must be a private area, super clean, a great room with a giant kitchen, and amazing view. Third floor, we were not allowed to go to.

Curt and Heather went upstairs to the main kitchen to get the burgers, buns, some fruit, and cookies for dessert. Carlos and Tucker were sitting outside cleaning off their boards in the outside shower and changing into dry clothes. Grant excused himself to go change and by the sounds of it take a quick shower. I was feeling uneasy, just thinking about him taking a shower, my mind drifted off. I was lost in thought of Grant rinsing off in a steamy shower, wiping off the sand, and lathering up with some super yummy guy smelling body wash. Because one thing I know, this guy smells good, a mix of beach, salt, and him. My heartbeat kept getting faster. I was leaning on the kitchen counter, when Grant came around the corner from his room, wrapped in just a towel. His muscles were glistening from the water, his tan body was ripped, no tattoos, and no piercings. I don't think I have ever seen a guy with such an amazing body. I must have blushed, he looked at me with a smile and I think desire, that had me almost throwing myself at him. I turned away, trying to be cool, but he laughed under his breath, grabbed a beer from the fridge, and headed back to get dressed. I think he came out here on purpose to see my reaction. Well, he got a reaction out of me and I was ready to take off home, when Heather and Curt came back downstairs with all the food.

"Where are you going? They both asked.

Just staring at them, stuttering I said, "Outside for some fresh air, problem with that?"

The bbq was already on and Curt came out to put the burgers on it. I was sitting in a chair on the patio looking at the view, when above my head a bottle of beer appeared, held by Heather.

"Geez, you almost gave me a heart attack," I said.

Laughing at me, I turned to her, "Why is that you can go out with Curt, but I can't even look at Grant, are they brothers or what?"

"No they are cousins, their mothers are sisters." Heather continued, "This is Grant parents' house, and they stay here for the summer, so Curt comes with them to escape the heat."

What... escape the heat...oh my God, "Where are they from and how long have you known them, and how long have you been seeing Curt, and why can't I show interest in his cousin?" Wow, that was a lot of questions.

"Shhh...they will hear you, Sydney, keep your voice down."

I thought Heather was going to give me a lecture. So, here was the story, in hushed tones, she told me only the basics and said she would fill in the rest when we got home. The basics were, Grant's parents were very successful and lived in Arizona. They bought the house when he and his brothers were little; Grant is the youngest, 21. They have been coming out here, to the beach every summer. Now that they are older, their parents don't have to come as often to "babysit", so to speak. Curt comes with him every summer, Heather met them last summer, after her parents moved to the beach. She and Curt have just started dating. That was all the detail I could get until we go home. The guys all came outside and were talking about how great the waves were today.

I have no clue what they are talking about. Heather knew of course because she has been hanging around the surf crowd for a year now and understands. Grant sat down next to me at the very long table on the patio with his burger and beer.

"So, how was work today Sydney?" His voice so deep and inviting.

Feeling uncomfortable with all that male testosterone next to me I started to squirm in my seat. Could he tell he was making me blush and my heart race? God, I hope not! I had a full mouth of burger when he asked me the question. I hesitated and pointed at my mouth, as if to say, "mouth full of food, can't answer". He laughed and shook his head, yet again, embarrassing moment for Sydney.

After finally swallowing my food, I replied, "It was good, but I was glad to get off early enough to hang with Heather at the beach for a while."

Grant smiled and said, "Well I am glad I ran into you at the beach." He was glad he ran into me, what does that mean? That just made my pulse rush. I have never had this response to any boy in my life. Not that he is a boy... he is most definitely not a boy.

We finished eating and I was ready to leave, but Heather was nowhere to be found, I would have to head out without her. She and Curt had taken off on a walk, Carlos and Tucker had gone home and I was left with Grant. This was not good; I already was self-conscious enough in front of him. He was gorgeous, all tan, muscled, and a smile that was over the top dreamy. His hair was still damp from the shower and I so badly wanted to run my fingers through it. What am I thinking? I am out of control; my desires are taking over my brain. I better head home before I can't control myself. Good thing I didn't even finish my beer. Grant picked up my now warm beer and gave me a look like, "What you didn't finish it?" I shrugged my shoulders at him, but said nothing.

"Grant, thank you so much for inviting me for dinner, the burgers were great, but I am tired so I am going to head home," I said.

"What about Heather?" he asked.

"I'll text her and let her know." I started for the side gate as we were right on the patio by the sidewalk. It was only a short walk to the house.

He sidled up next to me, "Let me walk you to the house. I would feel more comfortable if you did not walk home alone."

"Really I am fine, I can walk by myself," I replied.

"Well I am not fine with it, I will walk you if you will allow me to," he responded. Taken back by his comment I did not want to hurt his ego or offend his obvious concern about me walking home alone. He grabbed my hand and we walked together. Once again a bolt of electricity was winding through my body. Did he feel the same thing? I wasn't about to ask.

We walked in silence for a few moments and then he stopped, turned to face me, put his hands on my cheeks and held me., Leaning in, he took a deep breath, smiled and said, "Sydney, you smell delicious."

"What?" I giggled.

Still very close to my face, he whispered it again, "You smell delicious," and with that I was over the moon again, my heart pounding out of my chest, my pulse racing, and my eyes looking down embarrassed by his more than forward statement and gesture. Taking a deep breath, I looked up at him, my lips moving up and his coming down, our lips barely touching I could feel his breath on my face. At 6'2" he towered over me, as our lips came in full contact, the kiss was moving, I was up on my tippy toes to reach him, I did not want to miss any part of this kiss. It was a deep warm kiss, our tongues moved in perfect sequence, I could do this all night. We slowly pulled apart and I blushed, he took my hand again and we continued on back to my house.

As we approached the house, I turned to him, "Grant, why did you kiss me like that, we barely know each other?" Quiet for a moment, he looked up at the stars in the clear sky and then back down at me.

"You know, your eyes twinkle like stars in the sky. The kiss? I couldn't help myself. I have wanted to do that since I first saw you looking at me through the bonfire the other night."

Did he just say that to me... my eyes sparkle like stars in the sky? I didn't know if this was a line he practices in front of the mirror, or is he for real? This only confirms how dreamy he is.

I tried to keep my composure, "Grant, the kiss was...um...great, but I am not looking for a one night stand and you seem like the one night stand kind of guy. I have no desire to spend the summer avoiding each other after one foolish night, not to mention, I just don't do that kind of thing."

Taking a step back, he looked at me like I had punched him in the stomach; obviously he wasn't used to being turned down. I actually was feeling quite proud of myself.

"Oh... um... yeah, I didn't mean to imply or make you think, I only invited you over to um..." he trailed off.

So, I finished the sentence for him, "To get into my panties!"

He started laughing, "You did not just say that! I can't believe you Sydney, you take my breath away."

Still not getting into my panties!

I walked up to the door, unlocking it, and he turned me around and with a serious, but mind altering, smile on his face, holding me by the tops of my shoulders said, "I don't know what you have heard about me, or think you know about me, but I am not what you think I am. I can feel the lightning bolt too and don't even try to tell me you didn't feel it. I see your breath catch, and your pulse race, each time we have touched by accident or on purpose."

I didn't say a word. I opened the door and began to walk in as Grant walked back down the path to the sidewalk, he yelled up to me, "Sydney!" I turned to see what he wanted, "I saw how you reacted when I came out in my towel, I know you feel the lightning bolt!"

With that comment floating in the air, he walked off and I closed the door and threw myself down on the couch. My mind day dreaming, what is his story, he is from Arizona, did he attend Arizona State University, does he have a girlfriend? Of course he has a girlfriend, did you see him, just thinking about him is making my mouth water! Heather is right, I should just keep my distance... trouble, he is trouble.

Monday morning rolled around, I am not even sure what time Heather got home last night but I didn't even hear her come in.

I went downstairs, "OMG, are you serious?" on the couch, Heather and Curt were snuggled up asleep under a big blanket.

CHAPTER 4

Are you kidding me? She warns me away from Grant, and now she is asleep with his cousin on the couch? Banging things around in the kitchen, Heather pops her head up over the family room couch, "What is going on in there?"

"Shouldn't I be asking you this question?" I responded.

"I am making my breakfast and heading to work, I have to be there at 9 for a shipment. But when I get off work, you and I are going to have a very, very long talk."

With that, I finished making my breakfast, ate, and out the door I went. Listening to them giggle was making my stomach turn. I was not doing this again, a whole semester of this with Kendall and Matt was enough, not the entire summer with those two.

I got to work just before 9, Russ was opening the door. He introduced me to a few other employees, Rick and Carla. Since I am the newbie, I get the joy of unpacking the new shipment. At least it kept my mind busy or else I would have been stewing all day about this morning's events. I am not even going to think about what happened between Grant and I last night. Finally lunch time, I was starving, since I never finished my oatmeal this morning, not a huge oatmeal fan unless of course it's in cookie form. Trying to eat better can be stomach turning. A sandwich, I need a good sandwich, chips, and some iced tea.

"Russ, where can I get a great sandwich and an iced tea?"

"Go to the Blue Moon Café, they have the best sandwiches around town," Russ advised.

Stomping out the front door, with money in my pocket, I was in a foul mood, muttering under my breath, people were looking at me as if I was a crazy person. Maybe I was, why am I so frustrated? I found the Blue Moon Café, looked over the cool menu written in colored chalk on a wall painted in chalkboard paint. I choose chicken salad on squaw bread, some kettle potato chips, and a giant iced tea with lemon. I waited at a table inside for them to call my number. My hair was up in a ponytail, black surf shop tee with blue writing, my favorite jean mini-skirt and Tom's on my feet. For what seemed like forever, they finally they called my number. Before I could grab the tray from the counter, Mr. Tall, Dark and Handsome was bringing it to me. When did he walk in? I was in such a tizzy fit with myself over Heather and *him*, I hadn't even seen him come in the café.

Walking towards me with a swagger of utmost confidence and a devilish grin, he placed my tray of food in front of me, "For my lady, your lunch is served."

That was very nice of him, what does this guy want from me? I told him last night, he had no chance, why is he being so nice? I was hoping not to have any more contact with him than necessary. "Thank you."

Sighing I realized they forgot the lemon for my iced tea. I got up and proceeded to the back counter, leaning over the counter my shirt started to ride up a little, I quickly grabbed the lemon and sat back down at my seat. Guess who was sitting with his lunch at my table.

Shaking my head, I said, "Make yourself at home at my table."

Wow that was sarcastic and not nice. Inside I punished myself for being nasty to Grant when all he was doing was sharing my table.

"Well someone is not a happy summer camper today," he replied to my snide comment.

Argh, I will have to apologize now.

"Sorry, I did not mean to be so rude, I'm just…annoyed with Heather today."

"Why, cuz Curt spent the night with her?"

"Well, yes, they were asleep on the couch. What if I would have come down in my panties or something."

"Then I would have been soooo jealous that he saw your panties and I didn't," he said with a crooked smile.

I completely blushed at his comment. Is this guy nuts, does he think he is going to win me over like this, not happening. I have been down this round with sweet talkers, who end up being heart breakers. In the background of the café I could hear some music playing, listening very hard I think it was Tim McGraw, totally changing the subject, I said, "Oh, I love this song, do you like Tim McGraw?"

"Tim McGraw, country music, yeah, I like some of his songs. Especially this song, you know the part where he sings, "it felt good on my lips.""

Rolling my eyes, I took another bite of my sandwich and a long drink of my iced tea. Grant was making me more frustrated trying to sweet talk me.

"Sydney, would you like to go have yogurt with me after work this afternoon?"

Knowing I was asking for trouble with a capital T and how very much it would piss Heather off, I said, "Yes Grant, yogurt sounds nice. I'll meet you there around 2 pm."

He obviously was not happy with my response because his eyes narrowed and brows furrowed a bit, "What?"

"I get off work at 1:30, I will pick you up at the surf shop and we can walk together to get yogurt," he said confidently.

"Fine, whatever floats your boat."

Did I say that out loud…snap I did, he was smiling at me, "Whatever floats my boat, huh, there are many things that float my boat, currently you, Sydney Stanton, float my boat."

Trying not to seem interested, we both finished our lunches. With his hand placed on the lower part of my back, he walked me part of the way back to the shop before he had to return to the hardware store for work.

Lunch with Grant, and the walk back to work with him, left me with a longing feeling which I cannot shake. What is going on with me? My stomach feels all knotted up, I'm flush and a bit sweaty. It must be the weather, maybe the sandwich was bad. As 2:00 grew closer all those feelings came racing back, stomach knotted, and heart racing with the anticipation of what was to come. I said good-bye to my co-workers, walking out the door, Grant was leaning against the back of the bench on the sidewalk I smiled when I saw his glorious face and I knew, it was coming, the fall, my fall was coming.

He smiled back at me with those amazing brown eyes. He had changed out of his work clothes and he was wearing board shorts, a tank top which showed off all his delicious muscles, and flip flops. I looked him up and down and my mouth slightly opened, my breathing changed, and I licked my lips.

Noticing my obvious delight, "Do you like what you see?" Grant asked.

Startled I said, "Well, what's not to like!"

Laughing he took me by the hand and we walked together to get some yogurt.

Walking in the yogurt shop with a smirky smile, I knew would drive Heather mad, I heard, "Welcome to Galactic Yogurt, would you like to try…"

She stopped mid-sentence, steam coming out of her ears; she saw Grant and me together, holding hands. I thought she was going to kill me with the daggers coming out of her eyes.

"What are you two doing together?" She asked through gritted teeth.

"Well, we ran into each other at lunch and Grant asked me out for yogurt after we got off work, what time do you get off today Heather, since we didn't get to talk last night or today?"

She knew she was supposed to tell me the deal with Grant and Curt last night, but since Curt had spent the night, I never got any of the details she promised.

Grant requested a cone with peanut butter and chocolate swirled together. I decided I had lost my taste for yogurt, Grant insisted, so I got a plain vanilla cone.

"Wow, you live on the edge with your flavor choices," he said to me. Annoyed with his comment I took my cone and we headed down the pier to finish our yogurts. Muttering again to myself, he looked at me and laughed as he ate his. I tried not to watch, but his tongue seemed to be doing a number on his yogurt cone that got my blood boiling.

"Why are you looking at me like that, Sydney, do you want to taste my yogurt, do you think it has more flavor than your plain vanilla selection?"

There were so many ways to answer his question, I turned to look out over the ocean and finish my cone. He came up behind me, wrapping his warm arms around me, holding me in front of him, leaning his chin on my shoulder, he started to nibble a bit on my left ear.

I turned to him ever so slightly, leaning to look at him, he just smiled and said, "I couldn't help myself, it was so enticing and you were licking your yogurt, I just had to nibble a little."

"Well don't, I don't want people getting the wrong idea about us."

"What are you so afraid of, why are you embarrassed to be seen with me?"

I don't know how to respond to such a direct question. So far, Grant had been nothing but nice and mostly polite accept for the obvious flirty conversations we were exchanging.

"I will be honest with you..." I said.

"Well I would hope so, why would you lie to me," he replied. I rolled my eyes at him.

"Really, can I finish without you interrupting me? You are very nice, handsome as all hell, and you make my heart race, but something deep in my core says, yes, you will have fun with him, maybe even the time of your life with him this summer, but when you go back to school or even before you leave for school you will get hurt and to tell you the truth, getting hurt by another guy is not on the top of my to-do list," there I said it, my cards on the table. How will he respond, I hope he just leaves me alone and we can just be friends.

Well my brain is telling me to run, but my heart wants to run right into his arms.

"What did Heather tell you about me and my cousin Curt?"

Not much really, "Just that you are cousins, your Mothers are sisters, and you come here every summer."

"So, why don't you want to spend time with me, why are you trying your hardest to fight our obvious connection? I didn't hear anything bad, disturbing, or life altering in the information you were given."

"Grant, Heather said you were trouble with a capital T! Why would she tell me that unless she knows something which she has not told me, and I know you are not going to tell me?"

"Look, Curt and I come out here every year, to escape the heat. As we have gotten older our parents don't need to take so much time off work and we can be here by ourselves. They only come on weekends, if that. We surf, bbq, and have a great time. No foul play, nothing funky, just a good time. I am not sure what Heather knows, or thinks she knows, but when you find out let me know."

And he continued, "Why is alright for her to date Curt and you can't be seen with me around town?"

That is the question I have wanted answered since last night. Since Curt was over this morning I was unable to obtain the answer. I really did not want to fight with Grant. I was enjoying his arms wrapped around me and the nibbling on my ear. How do I get him to do that again?

I felt dirty and sweaty from unpacking the shipment and work today, "I should really go home and clean myself up. Would you like to walk me home?" I asked him.

His eyes twinkled and did a little dance, "Are you sure you won't be ashamed to be seen with me?"

Laughing he grabbed my hand again, love it, and we walked back down the pier towards my house. As we turned the corner, he dropped my hand and quickly made his way around a large minivan parked on the street. Way off in the distance I could see a group of girls walking toward us, now I know what he is hiding, a girlfriend. I think my heart just cracked a little. Giving him the dirtiest look I could muster, I quickened my pace and was in the house before he could catch up to me, double locked the door and sunk to the floor.

Dropping my head in my hands, I let out a long frustrated noise, when I looked up Heather was standing in the kitchen, "I told you so" was the only thing she said.

Standing up, I looked her straight in the eye, "You didn't tell me anything," I said with frustration in my voice.

"I told you he was trouble, what did he do now?"

"Let me ask you something, why is Grant trouble with a capital T, but Curt is not?"

"Curt is the same age as us, 19, he is more innocent, doesn't use girls to fulfill his needs."

"How do you know Curt is so innocent? They're cousins; Grant could be a good teacher and have been corrupting him all these years, teaching him the ropes on how to get a girl to do whatever he wants." You could hear the frustration in my voice.

Heather rolled her eyes at me, "You don't live here all year long. This guy rolls into town for three or four months each summer, he has a different date all the time."

"You know this for a fact, you have witnessed it first hand, other girls have confided in you of Grant's wicked ways?"

We were yelling at each other now, standing in the kitchen with the big sliding doors open for anyone who was walking by to hear us. This was ridiculous; we were fighting over a guy, gorgeous Hot Bonfire Guy, someone I had only just met.

"You told me to make my own introduction, you said you wouldn't introduce me and be blamed for whatever happened. Do you remember that at the bonfire?"

"Yes," Heather replied.

"Well then, what is the problem? Heather, I am only here for the summer, I want to have a good time, and he is yummy, sweet and has been nothing but a gentleman with me. I am going to take my chance and see what happens."

Grabbing a beer from the fridge I went to sit down on a chair on the patio to relax, Heather joined me a few minutes later.

Placing her beer on the table between us, she asked, "Why did you come in the house all flustered, drop to the floor and put your head in your hands if Grant is such a gentlemen?"

I don't want to tell her, because it will only drive home her point some more. I take a deep breath, I tell her about walking down the pier, him holding me and the ear nibbling and then the dreaded walk home. She didn't respond right away, then my phone beeped, new text message, actually two new messages.

Monday, 4:05 pm: Kendall to Sydney: Made it back to school, classes suck, weather sucks, hot as hell, Matt great!

Monday, 4:06 pm: Sydney to Kendall: Glad u made it safe, beach fun, job good, heather frustrating as hell, miss you!

Monday, 4:08 pm: Kendall to Sydney: LOL!! U know she has ur back, have fun it is summer.

Monday, 4:11 pm: Sydney to Kendall: Trying to have fun, she is stifling my good times, with hot men.

Monday, 4:12 pm: Kendall to Sydney : Hot men, do tell...

Monday, 4:15 pm: Sydney to Kendall: Burgers, walk home, amazing kiss, lunch, yogurt ear nibbling warm arms. Heather bursting my bubble!

Monday, 4:18 pm: Kendall to Sydney: Take it slow, don't want to get burned again.

Monday, 4:21 pm: Sydney to Kendall: Like u took it slow with Matt?

Monday, 4:22 pm: Kendall to Sydney: Different, we are in love.

Monday, 4:23 pm: Sydney to Kendall: I think I am going to be sick...LOL.

Heather piped in wanting to know who I was texting. I told her Kendall, and I was just giving her the scoop of our recent activities. Who was this other text from, I didn't recognize the number?

Monday, 4:28 pm: New number: Sorry about earlier, I will explain later, can I come over?

Monday, 4:29 pm: Sydney: Who is this and how did you get my #?

Monday, 4:31 pm: New number: It's me Grant, I peeked at your phone, when you left it on the table at blue moon café today. By the way I loved the quick peek of your bare skin today.

Monday, 4:33 pm: Sydney: What?

I input his name into my phone so I would know when he was calling or texting me.

Monday, 4:34 pm: Grant to Sydney: When you reached over the counter to get the lemons for your tea, your t-shirt went up a little and I could see your bare skin between your low riding mini and shirt, delicious.

Monday, 4:35 pm: Sydney to Grant: Stop, you should delete that text, I wouldn't want your girlfriend to find it.

Monday, 4:36 pm: Grant to Sydney: I don't have a girlfriend, who said I do?

Monday, 4:38 pm: Sydney to Grant: I am tired Grant, going to shower and go relax.

Monday, 4:41 pm: Grant to Sydney: Shower can I join you?

Monday, 4:43 pm: Sydney to Grant: No, go away, spend some time with ur girlfriend.

Monday, 4:44 pm: Grant to Sydney: Argh...no girlfriend, can I come over?

I got up to go take a shower, still feeling grimy after my long day at work, fighting with Heather and Grant turning out to be the disappointment Heather said he would be.

"Who were you texting after Kendall?" Heather yelled from the patio as I walked to the bathroom.

"No one important," I yelled back. I went up to take a shower, turning on the hot water I undressed and left my clothes on the floor. Tomorrow there's no work, and I can do laundry. Wow, fun day you have planned I thought to myself as I climbed into the shower. I was washing my hair and deep in thought, when I heard a knock on the bathroom door.

"I'll be done in a minute." No response, I guess she went back down stairs.

As I rinsed my hair, I figured if I do my laundry tonight, maybe Heather and I could go to the beach in the morning and then come back have a late lunch, maybe bbq some chicken kabobs. Sounds good, I was starting to get hungry as I climbed out of the shower, thinking about tomorrow's meals when we haven't even had dinner yet. Shaking my head, I wrapped my towel around me, walking out in to the hall. I stopped dead in my tracks.

With a scowl on my face, "What are you doing here? And why are you standing in the hall waiting for me to get out of the shower?"

"Well, I was going to join you in the shower, but you locked the door so I couldn't get in," Grant said with his huge smile and arms crossed over his hard chest leaning on the linen cabinets.

"I don't have the patience for you and your lies. Get out of my way so I can go to my room and get dressed."

But he wouldn't budge, not until I said, "Fine what do you want to tell me? Can I at least get some clothes on for this conversation?"

"No, I have you exactly where I want you; you will listen to me because I know you don't want me to come to close to you, when all that is separating your hot body from me is that pink fluffy towel."

My jaw dropped open, did he just say that, he thinks my body is hot...no get a grip, remember he is not trust worthy. Find out what happened today, ask him.

"What is this about, Grant?"

"Today, when I dropped your hand and went AWOL behind the cars," I just looked at him, my hair dripping down my back, thank goodness I had brushed it before I came out of the bathroom, "Go on," I said. "Still waiting, do you have something to tell me, if not get out of the way so I can get dressed."

Frustrated with Grant's lack of courage to tell the truth, I tried to push him aside, but he grabbed me by my shoulders and there it was, the spark, it went spiraling through him to me or maybe it was the other way around. I don't know, but I couldn't take my eyes off of him. His hands began to slide down my arms towards my waist. Our eyes not breaking apart, our breathing was fast, my heart was thumping, I could feel him staring at my lips, my breasts ever so slightly coming up from the top of the towel. This was bad, very bad. I tried to regain my composure, but the heat between us was climbing, I could feel his body moving closer, his touch becoming more intense. I looked up into his eyes, I was drawn to him like no other man. Not my ex, no other date I had been on made me feel this way. I was losing control and I did not want to lose control with Grant, especially not standing in the hall with Heather, and I am sure Curt, not far away.

I took a step back, trying to get Grant to move away, but he wouldn't. He leaned down and kissed me. If I thought the kiss the other night was off the charts, this one was going to go platinum. He was holding me, one arm wrapped around my waist, the other at the back of my head. My knees were starting to buckle and I am sure if he was not holding me up I would have fallen to the floor by now. I was gripping the towel around me with both hands hoping it would not fall off.

When we finished kissing, gasping for air, I breathlessly asked him, "Why are you doing this to me, you have a girlfriend, I will never be the other girl. If you want to be with me you have to be honest with me and tell me what is going on, why did you bail on me today after I asked you to walk me home?"

No response, he looked at me with misty eyes, turned, and walked away. He walked out the door. He just left, what was this all about? I was even more annoyed, he had gotten me all hot and bothered more than once with no explanation. I was done; I would ignore all signs of him. Stomping to my room, I put on a cami and some shorts to go downstairs and make something to eat.

Heather was in the kitchen making quesadillas, guacamole, salsa, and margaritas. Yum, that looks good.

"Where is Curt?" I asked.

She just shook her head and said "He went after Grant when he left a few minutes ago, what happened up there?"

"I don't know. I tried to find out why he behaved the way he did today and he started to tell me then stopped. He got me all flustered and gave me this amazing knock your socks off, or in my case almost knocked my towel off, kiss. He wouldn't let me go get dressed until he told me the truth about today. But he never did, he just kissed me, got upset, and left." I so don't understand men at all, and people say women are dramatic.

I didn't want to talk about Grant anymore. We finished making dinner, sat down at the table turned on the TV, and watched the movie "Crazy, Stupid, Love" with Ryan Gosling, which seemed perfect for the situation I had had this evening. Neither of us had to work tomorrow, so we finished a pitcher of margaritas, or maybe it was two pitchers, locked up the house, and barely made it upstairs to bed.

CHAPTER 5

Two almost 19 year old girls, who together weigh less than some professional football players, should not drink two pitchers of margaritas. This is a fact. The sun was streaming through the blinds in my room, let me rephrase… screaming at me through the blinds. My head was pounding from the drinks. I felt like I had been run over by a Mack truck. I didn't hear any noise from Heather's room. I slowly, very slowly, made my way out of bed and to the bathroom. No wonder she was not making any noise, she must have been sick in the middle of the night and passed out on the cool tiles of the bathroom floor. I didn't want to wake her, so I went to the bathroom downstairs, then grabbed some ice water and couple of aspirins for my head, and came back upstairs with some for Heather. She was waking up when I entered the bathroom again.

"Morning sunshine," I said, laughing under my breath.

I gave her the water and aspirin. We both headed downstairs for some much needed caffeine. Not coffee drinkers yet, we popped open two cokes and sat down on the couch.

I could hear my phone beeping at me. I must have left it on the table last night. Not remembering exactly because of all the drinks. I had five new texts. Scrolling through; my parents, Miss Grumpy Pants aka my sister, Kendall, Russ and ugh…Grant. Not wanting to deal with any of them in my current hangover state, I put the phone down and closed my eyes for a nap on the couch. When we both woke a few hours later, hangovers mostly gone, we had some breakfast, or maybe it would be considered lunch. Then we grabbed our beach gear and headed out. Tanning was the plan.

We set up our stuff, laid back in our chairs, sunglasses on, and people watched for the rest of the afternoon. We could see a lot of guys surfing pretty far out, but couldn't really tell who they were. A few minutes later, a group of girls came up to us, stopping to say "hi" to Heather. She introduced me to them, but I was not really paying close attention to them; I was watching the guys who were surfing.

The girls started to walk away when the surfers made their way out of the water. Of course, it was Curt, Tucker, Carlos, and Grant. Not that I was surprised, I should have known by the way my eyes were attuned to his body out on the water. Curt kept walking up towards our seats, but the other three stopped to talk to the girls who were waiting for them where the water breaks on the beach. Curt put his board down, leaned over, and kissed Heather.

"Argh, I'm going for a walk," I said.

Heather just giggled and I was barely out of my seat before Curt sat himself down in my chair. Standing there watching these beach bunnies flirting with Carlos, Tucker, and Grant, my temper started to boil. Grant was standing in between Carlos and Tucker, who were fine looking guys, but Grant just stood out. He was tall, tan, a million watt smile, and had a strong jaw with stubble growing around his chin. I had to shake my head; the girl with a short blonde bob hair cut was gently pulling down the front of Grant's wetsuit, pressing her hand on his wet chest. I think I might be sick, not wanting him to see my annoyance, but it was too late, I could see his eyes watching me over the girl's shoulder, quickly I turned to walk down the beach.

I walked away as nonchalantly as I could without running. I was in the clear. I didn't want to look back just in case he was watching, and I didn't want to give him the satisfaction. I took a deep breath and continued down the beach along the shoreline. The beach wasn't too crowded yet, it is still early in the season, and school wasn't out for the kids. There were still plenty of people here, just not as busy as high beach season would ultimately be. Just as I started to relax and stopped muttering under my breath about getting all upset with the girl touching Grant, or Grant allowing himself to be touched by Blonde Bob Beach Bunny Girl, the thoughts began to swirl around my brain again. Uggh, I stomped on, I just need to forget about this guy, focus on work, and having a fun summer. "You are only going to be here until mid-August, don't get yourself caught up in something that you will not be able to control," I told myself.

I could feel it then; eyes burning through the back of my head, my insides stirring with heat, and those pesky hairs on the back of my neck tingling. Don't turn around Sydney, keep walking…but I didn't. I stopped pretending to look out at the boats sailing by.

Walking up, with confidence oozing out of his body, he said "Sydney, didn't you hear me calling your name?"

I turned and looked up at him his eyes filled with desire and frustration.

"No!" I snapped back at him and turned to keep walking, he grabbed my elbow before I could get away.

I looked down at his hand on my elbow and then up at him with disgust. I jerked my arm away, not wanting him to touch me, knowing the electricity that was between us.

"I can't do this, just leave me alone," I told him.

"You can't do what, you can't be my friend, I can't walk with you down the beach and talk, get to know you better?"

He looked at me with a sad face, totally trying to manipulate me to give in to him, allow him to walk with me.

"Why? I am not going to fall all over you and let you have your way with me and then discard me like yesterday's news. You still haven't even told me about yesterday," I said with complete exasperation.

Dropping his head, "Look, I behaved like an ass to you yesterday, more than once, but I…I have never had this feeling before. You make me crazy; the look in your eyes when you are looking at me, the way you tilt your head, the way your hair moves when you walk."

Squinting my eyes at him and shielding the sun with my hand, my mouth was hanging open yet again. I shook my head in astonishment, where is this guy from, his words make me melt. I continued to walk down the beach letting the waves wash over my feet, Grant following. He came up to me. I could tell by his movements he wanted to hold my hand, but he didn't. He kept his hand as close to me as possible.

My heart was fluttering in my chest; this guy was making me have feelings for him.

I started to talk, "I am only here for the summer and then I'm going back to school. I don't want or need complications that will make my life turn upside down. If you want to be around me you have to be honest even if you think it will hurt me or embarrass you."

Not that I believed Grant would be embarrassed by anything, I went on, "I am interested in getting to know you better too. You intrigue me with your bad boy image, surfing abilities, and the fact that you work at the local hardware store, when money seems to not be a problem for you."

"But..." he said.

"But, you have to tell me about yesterday. Why did you drop my hand and run away?"

"You know the girls who came up to us on the beach a little while ago? Well, the one with the short hair, I took her out a few times last summer, but I was not interested enough to continue seeing her. But she thinks I still like her and she wants another chance."

"So, you bolt away to avoid talking with her and then today you let her touch you in such an intimate manner? You make no sense. I told you, I didn't want complications and Blonde Bob Beach Bunny Girl is a complication."

Laughing at me he said, "Gina."

"Whatever her name is, if she is going to be an issue than this," waving my hands back and forth between us, "whatever it is, can't happen."

As we continued to walk, he asked "What do you mean when you go back to school; I thought you were from here?"

Stopping for a second to pick up a seashell, I responded, "I am from here, not the beach but I grew up about 30 minutes away, I just finished my first year at Arizona State University. I have to go back in the middle of August for Rush, Sorority Rush."

"So, you're a sorority girl... hmmm, I have known a few sorority girls in my day," with a wide smile he continued, "Well, just so you know I am only here for the summer too. I have to be at school in September for classes."

Assuming he was kind of a beach bum and lived off his parents, or whatever trust fund account they had set up for him, I was surprised.

"Classes? What? Where do you go to school?" I said with shock in my voice.

"What - did you think I just surf all year? I just graduated from college and I'm going to get my MBA at Yale. Classes start in September."

Wow! Gorgeous, athletic, smart and possibly nice, is this my dream guy? I doubt it, second guessing myself, what does he want with me. Without much effort he quickly scooped me up in his arms, starting to walk in the cold water.

With my hands gripped around his neck, I started to scream and kick my legs, "Grant, don't even think about it. If you throw me in you are going with me, I am not going to let go of you."

The twinkle in his eyes gave him away; it was as if I could see what he was thinking and feeling through his eyes. He didn't want me to let go, that was his plan. As he tossed me, not letting go of him, I cringed, the water was colder than I had anticipated. He had his wetsuit on so he didn't care how cold the water was going to be. When we came up from under a wave, our foreheads touching he leaned in and kissed me. No hesitation, not a long kiss just enough to make me tingle.

My nipples were hard as ice and when he looked down at my breasts as they rose and fell from the excitement he ignited in me, he grinned salaciously at me, "Someone is excited," raising his eyebrows up and down.

I jumped out of his arms and hit him on the shoulder, not that I could possibly hurt him. "You are so mean Grant Montgomery, you will pay for this later," I told him.

"That is what I am hoping for," he replied, running after me as I walked back to my beach chair and towel.

"Let's go out tonight?" He asked. "Just the two of us," he continued "We can go for a drive down to Laguna Beach and walk around or maybe even watch the sunrise together."

"Sunset you mean," I said.

"No, I meant sunrise."

Shaking my head at him I grabbed my towel and tried to dry off, I was freezing from the cold water. As I wrapped my towel around me to cover my shivering body, he came up and was rubbing his hands up and down my arms to help me warm up.

"I am glad you covered yourself up, I don't want anyone else seeing your hard nipples except me!" he said softly in my ear so only I could hear.

I completely flushed and pushed him away, "I am going home for a show…"I cut myself off mid-sentence because I could see the delight in Grant's eyes.

"Great, let's go get cleaned up, first you and then me, or we can shower together Sydney, you decide," he said. I just walked away not even wanting to respond to him.

I could hear him laughing behind me, and Curt and Heather say in unison, "If you hurt her, you are in deep shit."

"I am not going to let that happen, she is different," I could hear Grant yelling back to Curt as he ran to catch up to me.

His house was right in front of us as we both reached his patio at the same time.

"Why don't you wait for me out here, I just need to wash off my board and wetsuit in the outside shower, and then we can go in for that shower we discussed."

"You discussed it, not me," smiling as I spoke, "How about you clean up at your house and I will clean up at mine? Then you can come pick me up."

Not that a shower together wasn't tempting, I just was not about to get naked with a guy after only knowing him for less than a week. Anyway, looking at him, standing in the outside shower, washing off his board and wetsuit, his rock hard abs, perfect arm muscles, tan body was too much, wearing a low riding bathing suit. I can't compete with him.

"Sydney, can you help me for a second before you take off?" he called.

I walked over with trepidation in my heart, "Sure, what do you need?"

His surf board was clean leaning on the wall, his wetsuit was clean hanging on a hook, as I approached, and he pulled me into the warm water with him. Luckily this shower was hidden on the side of the house, where no one could see us.

With his arms wrapped securely around my lower back, I knew there was no escape plan. He lowered his head to mine, our foreheads touching, my breathing picking up, my mouth slightly open. What was he doing to me? I could feel his heart pounding, his breathing deepening. He leaned in and there it was, the most amazing kiss, our tongues dancing together, reaching up my hands finally running through his wet hair tugging ever so gently at the ends. I could feel the lightning bolt running from the feel of his lips on mine to the end of my toes, not missing my middle, my hips started to move and his arms pulling me closer, we were both letting out small moans of delight. This was going to be an interesting evening.

He pushed me up against the wall, water still falling over us like rain. I tried to stop but, I couldn't. The feel of him holding me against the wall with his body was unnerving. His lips continued to torture me, leaving my lips, heading to my jaw line, down my neck and around my ears. He was good at this- seduction. My body was climbing and filled with anticipation. He continued down my collar bone towards my breasts. Only wearing my bikini, he moved one triangle aside and cupped my breast with his hand, bringing his lips to suck on my nipple until it was hard. Using his other hand he repeated this maneuver on the other nipple. It was the middle of the day and Grant was going to make me come in his outside shower, without much effort, I must add. He continued to caress my breasts and suck on my nipples until I couldn't breathe. I was so still from the feelings moving through me I didn't know what to do. I put my hands on his upper chest to push him off of me. This was too much. He turned off the water and I grabbed my towel, wrapping myself up, he turned back to me.

"Sydney, we are not done yet, let me show you how good we are together, come with me," he said. Holding out his hand for me, knowing I shouldn't, but I did anyway.

I put my hand in his and let him lead me to his room. Shutting and locking the door, he kissed me again as I leaned against it.

Looking around his room, he pulled me away from the door. I saw a king size bed. Really, did he need a king size bed? A walk-in closet, bathroom on the other side of the room, dresser, and an armoire open with a big TV. Clothes were thrown all over the place and on his night stands, a few books and iPod docking station with his iPod in it. The walls were light blue and gray, a few framed surfing posters hung on them. I guess he wasn't expecting guests, or maybe he just didn't care. His room is a mess.

Still holding my hand, "Sydney," I looked up at him, his eyes had darkened and his gaze was all consuming. Filled with desire he pulled me close to him.

Our bodies were still moist from the shower we had been under on the side patio. I wanted to tell him no, but his touch consumed by body. I could feel myself, I knew I was wet between my legs and he was going to know it soon enough. I could see his erection and feel it beneath his shorts. Backing me towards his king size bed, I could feel the edge of the bed on the backs of my knees. He sat me down, our eyes not parting. His hands came up to my cheeks and he held me there kissing me, as if I was the only one for him, that his kisses would be mine forever.

He left me for a second, turned on his iPod, and music started to fill the room around us. Not sure what was playing, I remember hearing a sultry country voice come through the speakers, singing about how he needed something to do with his hands. How appropriate for what Grant was about to do with his hands.

"Grant, we shouldn't be here together, we barely know each other," I told him. No response, "This is a mistake I should go home," still no response.

He walked back to me, leaning down he kissed me again. That was my undoing, the kisses he gave me so filled with desire, love or lust not sure, but as if we were made for each other.

"Sydney, you think too much. Let me show you what you do to me, you are making me want things, I never thought I wanted before, until meeting you. I think we have a special connection, I agree we just met, but there is ..."

Without finishing his sentence he came over me pushing my back down on the mattress, his body felt amazing as he lay on top of me. My hands immediately ran through his hair and then down his back, my nails lightly scratching him.

He groaned, "You drive me mad, I want to take you in my arms and make you come."

Not knowing how to respond, I kissed him this time. Not allowing his lips to leave mine.

"All you have to do is tell me no once I will stop. Do you understand Sydney?"

"Yes," I could barely get the small word out.

The music was playing and our hands were all over each other, the tension from the flirting and the kissing had us both wound up tight. I could feel his hardness on my body as he leaned over me. My bikini top was off me. When did that happen? Grant was still in his board shorts. He flipped me on to my stomach without much effort, he began massaging my shoulders, kissing down my back; his hands were touching me gently. I was beginning to relax, his hands slid around my side and down my back, he rolled me over on to my back. He was holding each of my breasts massaging, feeling me, making me moan with desire. His kisses were like lightning bolts coursing through my veins, sending signals of lust all over my body. His hands, his lips moving down, his hands were massaging my inner thighs, my hips were moving, craving more, wanting his touch.

I let out a groan, "Oh, that...feels so good," I said softly.

He just smiled at me, continuing his exploration of my body. One hand still massaging my breasts the other hand was moving down. He was unrelenting, he kept on until my back arched and I cried for more.

There was a knock on his bedroom door.

Curt yelled, "Is Sydney in there with you Grant?"

Shit, shit, shit, they must have heard us. I didn't think we were making any noise and the music was still playing.

"Yeah, she is here with me," Grant yelled back.

"Okay, Heather was looking for her," he said.

I sat up, "We should really go out there, I don't want them thinking we are doing what we are doing in here."

His brows furrowed, "They already think that," he laughed.

"Are you regretting your choice, Sydney, to let me show you how good we are together?"

I blushed, "No, I just don't like the idea of people listening to us when we are you know...together."

"You're so cute when you are embarrassed, no one could hear us, although your moans were getting pretty loud," smiling and laughing at me, I smacked his shoulder.

"I was not being loud, was I?"

"You may not have been able to hear your own moans, but I did. Look how hard I am for you, you turn me on in a way no other girl ever has, I want to be inside you."

Another knock on the door, "Sydney, I am heading back to the house to change, do you want to come with me?"

I looked at Grant, his head hanging down in frustration, "Umm, yeah, I will be right there, give me a minute," I said.

I hopped up off the bed and grabbed my bathing suit top quickly putting it back on, wrapping my towel back around me.

"Sydney, don't go. Stay here with me, we can go have dinner and then finish what we started. Or finish what we started and then have dinner."

His eyebrows raised, his yummy lips making a sad face.

"I can't, I don't like when my friends bail on me for a guy, and I don't want to do that to Heather," I said.

"Fine, can we still go have dinner, pizza? The local place is pretty good, we could go there eat and take a walk on the beach, maybe get a yogurt. I loved watching you eat your cone," he said.

"Okay, but the four of us," I told him.

"Yes, the four of us," he agreed.

I leaned down and gave him a kiss, "See you in a little bit," I said. And with that I was out the door.

I left Grant with a hard-on, I am sure he would take a cold shower, not that I thought that would help, but it might cool him down for a while. I need a cold shower too… man he has me on fire for him.

Heather and I both took showers and were standing in the bathroom together, putting on make-up. Heather started in on me, "You know you are going to get hurt, he doesn't know how to be in love, or monogamous, for that matter."

I looked over at her while I was putting on my mascara, "I just want to have a fun summer, I'm not looking for a husband or even a boyfriend for that matter. Can you not worry about it? I learned my lesson with Trent and I am not going to fall in love with him. We both have to go back to school at the end of the summer. He will be in New York and I will be in Arizona. Nothing to worry about just let me have some fun."

Heather eyed me wearily, "I know you, look at Kendall, she is already in love again, she and Matt are inseparable, just like when we were still in high school. You four were together all the time, I am just saying to be careful."

I had finished my make-up and faced Heather, "I know you are concerned for me and for Kendall, but this is not high school. We are not as immature and easily fooled by men or our hearts. It will be fine, let's go have a good time tonight."

CHAPTER 6

When we came downstairs from getting dressed for our pizza date with Grant and Curt, we found them sitting at our kitchen table drinking some beer.

"Well make yourselves at home. Oh…I see you already have," Heather said sarcastically.

I was wearing jeans, with a fitted t-shirt and my wedges, hoping to appear a little taller next to Grant. Heather had on a cute red strapless summer dress and some strappy summer sandals. Both guys were wearing shorts with polo style shirts and flip flops. Grabbing our purses we headed to the New York style pizza place down the main street. I love living down here, I haven't had to drive my car since I got here.

As we were walking, I could hear my phone beep from inside my purse, no doubt that would be Kendall wanting to know what was up with Hot Bonfire Guy. Curt and Heather walking ahead of us, Curt's arm was wrapped around Heather's neck and she had her hand in his back pocket. Grant put his hand out for me and I happily put my hand in his.

He whispered in my ear, "Are you still feeling the same euphoria as when you left me earlier?" I blushed, why does he like to see me squirm?

He continued, "You know you left me in a lot of pain, definitely blue balls, that wasn't nice!" I looked up at him; even though I had wedges on, I still wasn't as tall as him.

"Sorry," was all I could say. I didn't even want to say I will make it up to him, cuz he would hold me to that, not that I wasn't willing too, but Grant was more man than I could handle, I think!

We reached the pizza place, not crowded on a Tuesday night. We ordered a large pepperoni and a pitcher of beer. Grant ordered at the counter, no need for ID's I guess. Grant poured us each an ice cold beer, Coors Light, I believe.

While we were waiting for the pizza, Curt and Heather went to play air hockey, I turned to Grant, "How old are your brothers?"

"How did you know I have brothers?"

"Heather told me, so ages?"

"Ethan is the oldest, he is 28, lives in Texas, with his wife, and they are expecting their first child in January. He works in some high profile law firm. Noah is 24, lives in Arizona, not married, and works for a hotel management group. Actually, Noah is coming out this weekend. Is that enough background information for you Miss Stanton?"

I smiled and laughed, "For now!"

"Do your brothers surf too?"

Grant. Sitting next to me. Turned in his seat and holding both my hands in between his said, "Sydney, why are you so interested in my family?"

"I just like to know peoples' backgrounds, it helps me understand who they are and what makes them tick."

He smiled wickedly, "You know what makes me tick, Miss Stanton, you do. And if our pizza doesn't get here soon I might take you in to the bathroom and have my way with you." I giggled and shook my head at him.

Our pizza finally arrived, we finished our first pitcher of beer and were working on the second one, when guess who comes in for pizza…Blonde Bob Beach Bunny Girl, along with her two friends, and some guys I didn't recognize. This should be interesting. Not letting go of my hand this time, we continued our conversations without appearing to notice the group's approach. The girls stopped over to say hello. I wouldn't actually call it saying "hello" it was more of the way this girl was attempting to stake her territory with Grant. Rolling my eyes, I excused myself to the bathroom. I did really need to go to the bathroom, after a pitcher of beer, who wouldn't?

When I came out of the stall, I went to wash my hands, but she was blocking the sink, purposely. "What do you want?" I asked.

"You listen to me, you may be Heather's friend, but you are not going to come down here for the summer and steal my man right out from under my nose."

I tried not to laugh, but it just came out with a snort and high pitched squeal, "Your man, huh? Does he know he is your man? I don't think so, let's go out and ask him, shall we?"

After washing my hands, I opened the bathroom door for her.

She didn't move, "That is what I thought, you don't scare me Gina, and he is not your man, he is mine!" With that I walked out laughing, my heart racing, not usually one to be so confrontational. I can't believe I just called him "my man." I was falling for him in every way and I didn't even see it coming.

When I finally got back to our table, the three of them were staring at me, knowing Gina had followed me into the bathroom.

Heather, not afraid to ask, "So, anything happen in the bathroom, does she need medical attention?"

No medical attention needed except for her heart being crushed and stepped on like a bug. "Umm…no I think she will recover," I said.

Grant asked, "What did she say to you or better yet, what did you say to her?"

"She tried to mark her territory, her territory being you, I explained to her that you were in no way "her man" and when I asked her to come out here with me to ask you about it, she wouldn't even move."

Curt and Heather laughed and started talking about going to the fair in a couple of weeks. I leaned in closely to Grant, whispering in his ear, "I told her you were mine, because after I get you home tonight you will be!"

He looked at me with devilish delight and said "Drink up, we are out of here!"

I couldn't finish my drink fast enough for him. He was pulling me out the door, telling Curt we would catch up with them later. We were heading back to his house I assumed, based on the direction we were going. I was out of breath, from him pulling me so quickly along the sidewalk. Geez, I would be all out of breath before we even got home.

Reaching his beach house in record time, he was kissing me before he even had the key in the lock. As the door opened from the inside, his lips on mine and our hands all over each other, standing in the door way was his brother, Noah, I believe. He was, just as gorgeous as Grant, but without the tan.

"Hey brother, what is going on, he smacked him on the head. Don't you know you should open the door and come inside before you start making out with a girl?"

"Noah, what are you doing here, I thought you weren't coming out til the end of the week," Granted uttered.

"Well my company sent me out a few days early to check out a new hotel property we might be taking over, so I thought I would surprise you and I would say based on your entrance you are surprised."

Laughing at Grant and me being completely embarrassed, and a tad bit tipsy from the beers, he walked towards the kitchen. Grant said, "Next time don't surprise me, just text me with the information ahead of time."

Standing in the kitchen, sipping his beer, Noah looking amused, with the obvious situation at hand, and said, "Grant, are you going to introduce me to your very beautiful friend?"

Grant, not happy with the new situation, "Noah this is Sydney Stanton, Sydney my brother Noah."

"Hi," I said, Grant pulling me outside to the patio, sitting me down in a chair, turned on the fire pit. Grant went back inside to get beer or yell at his brother, I wasn't sure which. I could hear muffled voices from the inside but couldn't make out what was being said. I pulled out my phone to see who had text me earlier. Looking at the screen, realizing it wasn't Kendall as I had thought, and quickly deleted the unread message.

Grant and Noah came outside to the patio, each grabbing a chair. Grant handed me a beer, "Are you cold?" He asked, "Would you like a blanket?"

"I am fine, the heat from the fire pit is keeping me warm, thank you though," I replied.

I was wishing we were inside wrapped in the blankets on his bed, which this afternoon had been so very inviting.

"So Noah, how long are you staying?" I asked. Grant smiled at me wondering the same thing.

Noah finished his swig of beer, "Do you mean right this moment or how many days?" Grant said, "Both."

I almost spit out the beer in my mouth, this conversation was so funny.

"Don't worry little brother, I will go upstairs to my room, in a few minutes. I have an early meeting in Santa Monica, so I will be out of your hair early and all day. Just try to keep it down tonight, I don't want you two keeping me up all night with your exploits!"

I knew my face was turning beet red with that comment. I watched Noah suck down the rest of his beer.

He leaned down to Grant, "Nice job, she is hot, does she have a sister?"

I started to laugh, "I do have a sister, but I don't think she is your type."

On that note, Noah said good night, "Hope to see you again Sydney."

With Noah gone, Grant sitting in his chair, he raised his hands patting his lap, indicating he would like me to sit with him. I slowly got up from my seat, and sauntered over to him straddling him on the chair. I leaned back and finished my beer, arching my back so my breasts were right in front of his mouth.

He leaned in and bit my nipple through my shirt, "Ouch," his hands coming up under the front of my shirt and moving one hand around my back, sliding it down the back of my jeans.

"No panties?" he whispered.

I smiled wickedly, "I told you, you would not get into my panties, I never said anything about my jeans!" He started to laugh and lifted me up, still straddling him, carrying me with my legs wrapped around his waist to his bedroom.

His room was all cleaned up when we entered, I guess he knew he would have a guest this evening, or at least was hoping for a guest. He sat me down on the edge of the bed leaning over to kiss me. His breath was hot, my pulse was rushing through me, and he pushed me up the bed and lay down on his side next to me. Running his fingers along my arms, across my stomach, and down the sides my thighs, goose bumps running along my skin. He turned to his night stand and turned on his iPod, music was surrounding us.

"I am not really a fan of thumping hip hop music," I said.

"Don't worry it is a mix playlist, it will change, I think your favorite Tim McGraw is coming up."

My eyes were looking down and I couldn't help but notice his large erection in his shorts.

"See something interesting down there?" he asked me. I licked my lips, his breathing hitched.

"Everything about you is interesting, but right now, I feel bad that I left you high and dry this afternoon." I said.

Pushing Grant down on his back, I got on top, straddling him. I leaned down and kissed his lips with slow methodical kisses. My hands in his hair, I moved my lips down around his chin along his jaw line and sucked on each earlobe just enough to feel his hands tighten around my thighs. Scooting down his body I began to lift his shirt up, exposing his chest and ribs, tan and completely mouthwatering. He raised his back a little to help me remove his shirt over his head, tossing it on to the floor. I began giving him kisses along his chest, sucking gently on each nipple and continuing down passed his belly button. I could feel his erection between my legs bulging in his shorts and the feel of his hardness through my jeans. I knew I was wet, but first I wanted to give him some of the pleasure he had given me. I was unbuttoning his shorts and pulling down his zipper, and as I pulled off his shorts, I found him commando style. Looking up at him, he was propped up on his elbows watching the expression on my face.

"Looks like I am not the only one not sporting underwear tonight," I said as I salivated at his body.

He just laughed and continued to watch. He had taken his flip flops off before we left the patio. I finished pulling off his shorts and tossed them to the floor as well. The site of Grant completely naked in front of me was making me a tad dizzy. His features were out of this world hot, it was not fair for one person to be this fit and handsome all at the same time. All that surfing does a body good.

I took the full length of his erection in my hand, leaning down I licked just the top of him. He groaned. I laughed under my breath and continued on my quest. He was spectacular; I put as much of him in my mouth as I could. Holding him with one hand and fondling his balls with my other hand at the same time. The sounds coming from Grant were enough to make me come, with all his moans and "oh mys!" I licked up and down below the crest until his hands were twisted in my hair.

"Sydney, I am going to come, I don't think I can hold on any longer," he mumbled to me. "God this is so good, your mouth is amazing, what you are doing with your tongue, don't stop," he said.

I wasn't about to stop. My libido was in complete over drive, watching him come undone in my hands was a glorious feeling, the control I had over him right now almost had me climaxing with him.

I could feel his erection throbbing in my mouth, he was ready to come, "Oh my God, Sydney," he yelled out.

He came hard in my mouth for what seemed like an endless amount of time. I swallowed, licking my lips at him.

Grant pulled me up to him holding me on top of him, with his strong arms wrapped around me.

Kissing my cheeks, "Where did you learn that trick with your tongue? Wait I don't want to know, forget I even asked. The thought of you being in someone else's arms makes me...never mind I don't want to talk about it."

I was surprised by his emotions towards me, we had only known each other a few days and already he was feeling things for me, I knew it.

Smiling down at him, I asked, "What do you want to do now? Do you want to go dancing?"

Maybe not dancing, the look on his face said no dancing. "I wasn't planning going out again this evening," he said.

"Oh, ok, I have to work in the morning, do you want to walk me home?" I asked.

"Sydney, I don't want you to leave, we are not done yet. I don't have to be at work until 3 tomorrow, so I have all night." What did he mean? I started to squirm.

He flipped me over on to my back, laying his hard body on top of me, resting on his upper arms; I could feel his erection on my stomach.

I looked up at him, "What...I can't get enough of you," he said, with a grand smile.

He started kissing my neck, tickling me behind my ears, I giggled.

"What, are you ticklish behind your ears?"

"Yes, very," I whispered.

"Good to know." He continued on down my neck with his kisses., He smelled so yummy, my hips started moving, and I could feel the electricity between us igniting. He removed my t-shirt with flawless skills and he had my bra off without much effort. He was kissing my belly button. He took a drink from his beer and filled my belly button with the icy liquid. Dipping his tongue inside it and slurping it right back up.

"Delicious, you and beer- two of my favorite things," he said.

He unbuttoned my jeans, slowly lowering the zipper and kissing his way down my lower stomach, as he pulled the jeans from my body. My desires for him were over whelming me, if he doesn't take me soon I may not survive. His seduction of me was impressive, not missing a beat. He cupped my sex with the full strength of his hand, holding me down with the other.

My hips were starting to grind against his hand, "Hold still, Sydney, I want to look at you, your body is beautiful. Where have you been hiding yourself from me," he said in the sexiest tone I have ever heard. His hand began to play with my sex, inserting not one but two fingers inside of me.

I gasped, "Oh… oh… I want you Grant."

"You will have me once I am sure you and I will come together," he said.

"I don't think I can last that long, take me now," I demanded.

"Sydney, just a few more minutes, you won't come until I am inside you, do you understand?"

"Yes, yes, I won't… come, til you're inside me," I recited.

The next few minutes seemed to go on forever. His fingers should be registered as deadly weapons, maybe include his lips and tongue too. Finally, I heard foil tearing, Grant rolled a condom on himself, and then he was on top of me, "Ready?"

I gave him a dirty look and said, "I was ready ten minutes ago!"

He thrust into me, I screamed out not in pain but in joy. He was so hard, his erection was filling me, I was ready to explode in ecstasy. He pulled out a little and thrust inside me again.

"Don't let go yet Sydney, I can feel you tightening around me, you feel amazing, nothing I have ever felt before, like you were made for me."

"I can't hold on, I am going to…" and he thrust again, this time not leaving me he was relentless with slow pushes, pushing me over the edge without stopping.

"Now, together," and with that, I let out an "Oh… my God Grant, don't stop, it feels so good."

I could feel myself releasing, it was as if I was floating above my body, I have never felt something so raw and beautiful. Grant let out a long groan with his last thrust into me. He was coming inside me as I was relishing in his movement causing my orgasm, holding my head in both his hands.

He leaned his head forward onto mine, "Sydney, are you okay? That was indescribable," he panted, with hard breaths; he was trying to steady his breathing.

We lay together in his bed for a long time, eventually Grant stood up, "Would you like something to drink," he asked me.

"I would love some ice water, if it is not too much trouble," I replied.

"Be right back," he said. He walked out to the kitchen; I lay still in his bed. Wondering how all this came to be. I was drifting in my thoughts when he came back in to his room.

"Do you always walk around naked?" I asked.

He looked at me and smiled saying "Only when the girl I just had mind blowing sex with asks for some ice water." I laughed and he handed me the drink.

It was just what I needed, I set the glass down and said, "I should really go, I have to work in the morning and I am sure you have things to do…" Before I could finish my sentence, Grant was on top of me again kissing me all over.

"You can't be ready to go again, can you?"

"Well no, he let out a sigh, I just like being with you, you make me feel alive."

Not exactly the reaction I expected from him. He seems more the type to love them and leave them.

"Sydney, would you spend the night with me? I want to hold you while we sleep," he said.

My eyes got wide, "Are you sure, you want me to spend the night with you?"

"Sydney, we just had the best sex I have ever had and I think you will agree, we have something special here, I want to wake up with you in my arms." I gave him a big hug.

"Do you have a t-shirt I can sleep in?"

He raised his eyebrows at me, "You want to sleep in a t-shirt? I sleep naked, but whatever floats your boat," he said laughing.

Opening his dresser, he pulled out a very worn out t-shirt and tossed it to me. I looked at it before putting it on; it had worn out fraternity letters on it, from being washed probably 100 times. "Shut up, you're a fraternity boy," I started to laugh, almost falling off the bed, "Wait a minute, this says Arizona State University on it, you graduated from ASU? Why didn't you tell me?"

"You didn't ask," he replied.

"I told you I went there and was in a sorority and you said nothing. This is the same house Kendall's boyfriend is in, I have never seen you around the fraternity house or at any of the parties, how come?" I asked.

"Sydney, this was my senior of college, I moved out of the fraternity house after my junior year, I lived in apartment off campus and I needed to keep my grades up to get in to Yale. Way too much partying goes on at the house."

I was stunned; I didn't even know what to say to him. I had never seen him around campus; I guess he was probably taking classes on the other side away from the liberal arts buildings. It was a big school, it was possible to have never seen each other.

I got up to use the bathroom, still dumbfounded by this recent news and my body was still tingling from the earth moving orgasm Grant had given me. I looked at myself in the mirror in his bathroom, I like this t-shirt, I may have to forget to give it back, it is so comfy. When I came out of the bathroom, Grant was not in the room. I needed to get my purse, so I walked out to the kitchen, the shirt I was wearing went past my knees so I was not afraid of showing anything in case Curt or Noah happened to be around. I want to send Heather a text, so she wouldn't worry when I don't come home tonight.

Walking down the hall towards the kitchen, I could see Grant leaning on the kitchen counter, with his back to me drinking some water. Just in his boxer briefs, no shirt. My heart skipped a beat. He put his glass down just as I jumped up on to his back. Putting my arms around his neck, his hands instinctively, came backwards wrapping around my waist so I wouldn't fall off of him. I gave him a kiss and he whipped me around plopping me on the counter. Standing in between my legs, Grants hands started moving up my thighs under the long t-shirt.

I grasped his hands, "No," I said.

"Why not?" He smiled wickedly at me.

"I need to find my purse and text Heather so she knows I am not coming home tonight. Are you sure you want me to spend the night, I have to be up early for work?" He sighed at me, not releasing his hands off my thighs.

"Yes Sydney," I love when he says my name, it rolls off his tongue with pure desire laced through it. He continued, "I am going to get up early to surf, so I will wake you before I leave and walk you home, and then head to the beach, I told you I want to wake up with you next to me." He is so dreamy, there has to be a catch, I thought to myself.

"Okay, do you know where my purse is?" I asked.

"I think it is on the bar stools, wait here, don't move…" he said pointing his finger at me, "I will get it for you."

Not moving I sat on the counter watching him retrieve my purse, carrying it to me, he sagged to one side laughing as if the purse just was sooo heavy. I laughed at him.

"What do you have in here?" He asked as he handed my purse to me.

"You know girls have a lot of stuff, lip gloss, wallet, sunglasses, keys…" I kept on going, he was just looking at me.

I reached into my purse, pulled out my birth control packet, opened it taking one from the case, popped in my mouth and washed it down with the water Grant had left on the counter. His mouth dropped open, "What ? You're on the pill, I didn't have to use a condom… nice… I think I just got hard again."

I laughed tipping my head back a little, "Yes I am on the pill, I am not about to get pregnant. Yes, you still have to use a condom, I don't know where that thing of yours has been and I don't want to get an STD." He was standing in front of me again between my legs. He grabbed my chin, tilting my head up to look him in the eyes.

"Sydney, I don't have any STD's, I never have," he said with a serious look on his face.

"That is fine, I believe you, but we are still using a condom, we barely know each other and this is not an exclusive relationship," I told him. He dropped his head. He knew I was right but I don't think he liked how blunt I was being.

Hopefully that discussion was completed. He was still standing in between my legs, his hands creeping up my thighs again.

I hit his hands, "Wait a minute, I need to get my phone," I said. I took my phone out of my purse; I could see I had a few missed text messages. Starting to scroll through:

Tuesday, 7:35 pm: Kendall to Sydney: What's up, miss you! How is HOT BONFIRE GUY?
Tuesday, 8:05 pm: Mom to Sydney: Call me
Tuesday, 9:11 pm: Heather to Sydney: Where r u guys?

Seeing the next message, I made a grumbling noise and said "seriously…" and pressed delete. "What?" Grant asked.

"Nothing, I love technology and all but, it is annoying sometimes, you know what I mean?"

He looked at me strangely, he started kissing my neck and nibbling on my ear, "Stop I need to respond to Heather."

Tuesday, 9:28 pm: Sydney to Heather: Spending the night with Grant, b home early, have 2 work @ 9 am.
Tuesday, 9:36 pm: Heather to Sydney: k, b careful, Curt sleeping here!
Tuesday, 9:37 pm: Sydney to Heather: k, c u in AM.

My phone beeped again.

Tuesday, 9:39 pm: Mom to Sydney: Problem, call me. You must b at work, ran into someone today and u r going 2 b mad at me. Sorry. Call me.

Shit, I thought, I have to call her, I looked at the time 9:40 pm, kind of late I will call her in the morning, no, she just sent this text, I will call her now. I pushed, Grant away and hopped off the counter.

"I have to call my mom," I told him.

"Right…now?" He looked at me with those gorgeous eyes.

"Yes, it will only take a minute," I said.

I walked out on to the patio for some privacy.

"Hi, mom, what's up?"

"Hi, honey, how are things going, you having fun and being safe?" She asked.

Sighing, not wanting to say yes, just had wild sex with a hot guy, I only met four days ago, "Yes everything is great, your text said there was a problem, what's going on?" I asked.

"Well, I didn't want to tell you in a text message, plus it is far too much to type."

Goodness would she just get to the point, Grant was walking towards me and just watching him swagger to me was making me body crazy for him, again. I was smiling at him. She was talking but I really wasn't listening because Grant was next to me now, taking my breath away with his hard body. I put my hand on his bare chest, putting one finger up, indicating for him to wait a minute.

"Wait, what did you say?" I was distracted by him.

"Mom...what? You accidently did what? I thought I made it perfectly clear last fall that..." I turned away from Grant, so he couldn't see my face before I continued.

"Mom, our relationship was over a long time ago and I don't want him knowing I am back in town, even if I am down here."

I knew Grant couldn't hear my mom's side of the conversation. But I started to tense.

"Honey, it was an accident, it just slipped out, I ran into his Mom at the country club, she was asking me if you were home for the summer, I didn't see him sitting on the couch, before I knew it, I just blabbed you were back in town, but I didn't say where you were."

"So, he doesn't know where I am living or working, are you sure?" I asked.

"Yes, I am sure. But..." she paused for a moment.

"What, but...what?" I snapped at her.

My mom went on, "He got up from the couch and you know he is so adorable, he came up and gave me a hug and kiss and said how much he misses you, maybe you should give him another chance."

"Absolutely not Mom, he was cheating on me before my feet were even out of the state," argh, I grunted, "Mom, I have to go, have to get up early for work, are you leaving tomorrow?"

"Yes," she replied.

"Have a great trip, see you when you get back," I said.

"Ok, darling, again I am sorry, love you," she said.

I pressed end on my phone. Dropping my hands to my sides and lowering my head, Grant came up behind me put his hands on my shoulders, kissed my ear, "What's wrong, Sydney?" He turned me around and could see the tears in my eyes.

"Nothing, I don't want to talk about it," I said not looking him in the eyes.

"Well it must be something, you are all tense and look very unhappy."

"I will be fine, my Mom, she just forgets things sometimes, and never mind," I smiled and looked up at him.

"I like when you wrap your arms around me and kiss my neck, let's get back to that," I said to him. Knowing anything sex related would distract him from my obvious concern.

"I know what you're doing Sydney, but I am more than happy to kiss your neck again. You can tell me what is wrong when you're ready, I am not going to press you for information."

He took my hand and kissed it, not just kissed it but licked along the knuckle line so seductively, I could feel my wetness starting to move down my inner thighs, since I had no panties on. He led me back to his room, shutting and locking the door behind him.

CHAPTER 7

I could hear water running in the bathroom, what time is it? I opened one eye and looked at the clock 5:00 am, is he crazy! I rolled over on my side, hoping to fall asleep again. My body feeling a bit achy from last nights and this morning's more than fulfilling encounters with Grant. Just thinking about how he had woken me up in the middle of night with an erection so hard, I had to gasp for air when he slid inside me without warning. Believe me, no complaints here, it was off the charts good, he was off the charts good. He came out of the bathroom naked, looking for something. I didn't want him to know I was awake, taking in his naked body sent shivers through my body and I must have giggled a little because he turned and jumped on the bed.

"You are awake, I thought you might be," he said, leaning in to kiss my cheek.

"Put some clothes on, please," I whispered. Not fully awake my voice was still in sleep mode.

"Why, I am in my room, alone, with my girl, getting ready to go surfing," he said with playfulness in his voice. "Do you know how to surf?"

"No," I said.

"What...I bet you have never even tried," he said all excited.

"No, never, no one has ever offered to teach me, are you offering?" I asked him.

69

He looked at me with his amazing knock your socks off smile, "It would be my honor to teach you to surf, my lady," he said, bowing like a servant to me.

I laughed at him, what a goofball.

He smacked my butt, "Now get up hot stuff and come watch me surf."

"Are you crazy it is 5:00 am, I am not getting out of bed yet!" He turned to me and jumped on top of me with all his weight.

"Okay, I won't go surfing and we can stay in bed and I will rock your world for a second time this morning," he said smiling and moving his hands down between my thighs.

"No, no, I will come watch you surf, let me get dressed, do you have a tooth brush I can use," I asked.

Laughing and moving about his room to get ready, "Look in the drawers in the bathroom, if you don't find one just use mine," he said.

"Wow, such an intimate gesture," I said.

He looked over his shoulder at me pulling on my jeans, "I think what we did this morning is way more intimate that you putting my tooth brush in your mouth!"

Laughing and shaking my head, I went to get ready, while he headed out of the bedroom. He was waiting for me on the patio, looking at the waves.

I could see how excited he was to go, "You're wearing my sweatshirt," he said.

"Is that okay, it was on the chair and it is cold out here at 5:30 am?" I asked.

He just smiled, took my hand and we walked down to the water.

He was carrying his board, wetsuit already on, "I like seeing you in my clothes," he said.

I sat down on the sand while he headed out to surf. There were a few people running along the beach, supposed to be good exercise. I watched him paddle out, pulling my knees up and wrapping my arms around my legs. I rested my head on the tops of my knees, waiting to see him ride some waves. My eyes slowly closing, still tired from lack of sleep. I must have dozed off. I felt a hand on my shoulder, I was startled and looked up.

The sun was up and shining in my eyes, using my hand to block the sun, it was Curt.

"Good morning, Sydney, you know they make beds to sleep on," he said laughing and walking into the water.

"What time is it?" I yelled.

"Around 7:30."

I got up stretching, my arms way above my head, I walked back to Grant's to get my purse and walk home to get ready for work. Before heading home, I sent Grant a text.

Wednesday, 7: 40 am; Sydney to Grant: Thanks for last night and this morning! Loved, watching you surf. Work today 9-3.

When I got home, Heather was still asleep. I took a nice hot shower and brushed my teeth again. After getting dressed, I went downstairs to have breakfast. Heather was awake sitting on the couch, watching a rerun of "Friends" and eating a bowl of cereal.

"So, how was your night?" She asked, looking for details.

I must have been smiling from ear to ear, I felt great, two orgasms in less 24 hours, this summer was going to be great, I thought to myself. I laughed and began making some toast and washing some grapes in the sink.

"Well?" Heather asked, with raised eyebrows.

"How was yours?" I said to her, not wanting to give away any details from my evening.

Before she could answer, I said, "Oh my God, I talked to my Mom last night, you are not going to even believe what she did." Heather turned to me with the spoon in her mouth.

"What?" She said with a mouth full of cereal and a weary look.

I told Heather about my conversation with my blabbermouth Mother.

"Seriously, thank goodness my parents are away," she said.

"What are you going to do?" She asked walking to the kitchen with her empty cereal bowl.

"First off, we need to load the dishwasher with everything in the sink," I said laughing.

"Nothing. Trent doesn't know I am staying with you, though I figure he will think something is up when he doesn't see me or Kendall in our usual places around home. As long as we stay away from my parents' house, we should be alright. Since they are leaving today on vacation, I won't need to go up there at all."

I left for work, trying to push thoughts of Trent from my mind, and focusing on not falling asleep. I might need to start drinking coffee if I am going to keep up this pace. Shaking my head I walked in to the surf shop, Russ was at the register and Rick was already helping some tourists with renting surf boards.

"Morning," I said, heading to put my purse in the back room.

"Morning," they both said to me.

"Did you have a good day off?" Russ asked when I came up to him at the register as I typed in my employee code to track my hours.

"Yes, it was great," thinking if he only knew, I smiled.

"What, is that look on your face?" He asked. I have a look on my face? Great, my facial expressions always give me away.

"Nothing, what are my tasks for today?" Hoping to change the subject.

"I am going to train you on the register, so I don't have to ring everyone up all the time. You're a smart cookie, you will be fine." Once again my expression giving me away.

Russ trained me on the register all morning and by lunch time, I was ringing up customers with no help from him.

"Sydney, why don't you take your lunch when Rick gets back, he should be back in a few minutes, okay?" Russ said.

I nodded my head, yes. Rick came in a few minutes later, I went to get my purse, and check my phone.

"I will be back in 30 minutes," I clocked out and was out the door, grabbing my phone to see if Grant had responded to my morning text.

Wednesday, 10:45 am; Grant to Sydney: Working from 3-9, lunch? Did u use my   toothbrush?
Wednesday, 12:15 pm; Sydney to Grant: Yes to both!

I turned to walk to the Blue Moon Café, my favorite sandwich shop. Leaning against a convertible was my hunky guy. I smiled at him, he began to walk away from the car, which I hope was his, he walked to me, picking me up and kissing me on the lips.

"Wow, I like this," I said. "

"You like what?" He asked.

"You waiting outside my work for me and greeting me so sweetly," I whispered in his ear. I heard his phone beep. He pulled it out of his pocket and laughed.

72

"What?"

"I just got your text," he laughed.

We held hands and walked to the café together. Sitting down at an outside table, eating our lunch, it was a beautiful day. Heather walked up and ended up joining us for her lunch break as well.

"Sydney, what time do you get off work today, do you want to go to shopping?" Heather asked.

"I get off at 3, I will meet you at the house and we can go from there, I am not driving, I don't want to lose my parking spot," I told her.

"No problem, I will drive. What are you and Curt up to tonight?" She asked Grant.

"Um, I have to work til 9, Curt gets off at 7, I haven't thought that far ahead, right now, I feel like I need a nap, I didn't get much sleep last night," he said. I almost choked on my food, knowing exactly why he needed a nap.

We finished our lunches, Grant went to take a nap, kissing me good bye. Heather and I walked in the other direction to the surf shop and yogurt shop.

"Sydney, he sure seems into you, I have never seen him kiss a girl in public during daylight." Feeling my insides warm and relishing the feel of his lips still lingering on mine, I could almost taste him, as I licked my lips.

I hadn't responded to Heather's comment yet, "Oh shit, you are already falling for him, I can see it in your eyes and the crazy smile you have on your face. Sydney, you better be careful," she warned.

"What is up with you and Curt?" I asked trying to deflect attention away from me and onto her.

"He is great, all cute and cuddly, sweet, honest, and the nice body he has going on is a definite plus," she said giggling.

"Who has it bad, I think you are head over heels for this guy, when did you start seeing each other?" I asked.

We were standing in front of the surf shop, almost time for me to go back in, "Tell me quickly, I have to go back to work," I said.

"We met last summer and kind of did the flirty thing, but by the time we were starting to become friends he left for school and he just got back here last week, so last week I guess," smiling as she finished her sentence.

"I want to hear the rest, see you at the house in a couple of hours," I told her and we both went back to work. The afternoon flew by, I didn't check the time all afternoon, the shop was busy all day. The next thing I knew it was 3:00, I left work and headed home. I was tired. Heather came home a few minutes after me and we headed over to our favorite store to pick up a few things. On the drive over Heather continued her story about Curt.

"So anyways, we just sort of picked up where we left off last summer, the flirty thing and all, but the first kiss was the best, the months of waiting for him to come back, and then not knowing if he would still be interested. I mean, we would text back and forth, but him being so far away at Berkley, I was not about to carry on a long distance relationship."

She was nuts, she had be carrying on a long distance relationship with him, just as friends. "So, did you guys, you know, seal the deal last night?" I asked her.

"Sydney, you did not just ask me that, I don't screw and tell!" She said laughing hysterically. "And you," she asked me, "Did you seal the deal with Grant last night?"

"Not only did I seal the deal last night, but this morning as well," I said as I got out of the car. Walking into the store, I know she wanted more details, but I was not about to talk about it, as we shopped. We got the necessities: shampoo, cokes, cookies, sunscreen, and then went past the intimates section.

We both stopped, looked at each other with big smiles, "Yes, I am looking."

"Are you?" I asked Heather.

"Looking, yes, but not necessarily buying!"

It may be a discount store, but they have some cute stuff. I found an adorable satin set, black and pink, scalloped hem cami, low cut v in front, has triangle cups, lace at the neckline and tap shorts covered with matching lace around the top edges.

"I am getting this number here," I can't wait to wear it, thinking to myself, Grant is going to be all over me when he sees me in this outfit.

Heading home, delighted with our purchases, Heather picked out a purple and black satin slip, which I am sure Curt will have no problem taking off of her.

"So, what do you want to do tonight, it is only five o'clock? We could bbq something and then see what is happening in town tonight," she said to me.

"Umm, I think I am good with a chicken salad, I don't feel like grilling tonight, let's eat one of those pre-made salads your Mom left us and then I need a nap. I don't have to be at work until two tomorrow, so we can stay out a little later tonight, but I won't be able to make it through without a nap," I told her.

"Sounds great, I work at one tomorrow, then we have a plan," Heather said as we drove home.

Pulling in the garage, we headed into the house put away our stuff, pulled out the chicken Caesar salad, ate on the patio listening to the waves crash on the beach. After cleaning up we each went to our rooms for power naps. Lying down, I grabbed my phone:

Wednesday, 5:35 pm; Sydney to Kendall: Hey, how is Matt?

Wednesday, 5:36 pm; Kendall to Sydney: Well, it is about time, where have you been?

Wednesday, 5:37 pm; Sydney to Kendall: Work, Hot bonfire Guy (Grant), store.

Wednesday, 5:40 pm; Kendall to Sydney: Matt is good, tell me about HBG!

Wednesday, 5:42 pm; Sydney to Kendall: Not much to tell, spent the night with him!

Wednesday, 5:44 pm; Kendall to Sydney: What, r u nuts? U just met.

Wednesday, 5:45 pm; Sydney to Kendall: So, there is something different about how I feel when I am with him.

Wednesday, 5:47 pm; Kendall to Sydney: Argh, I can't leave u alone, u r going to get into trouble w/him.

Wednesday, 5:49 pm; Sydney to Kendall: Have a little faith in me, no I am not, having fun, it is summer. He graduated from ASU, he was in Matt's house. C, what u can find out about him.

Wednesday, 5:50 pm; Kendall to Sydney: Alright, I will ask Matt what he knows.

Wednesday, 5:51 pm; Sydney to Kendall: taking nap, super tired, no sleep and full day of work, going out 2night. Miss you.

Wednesday, 5:51 pm; Kendall to Sydney: Miss you too!

I fell asleep in a deep sleep, dreaming of my hunky guy working at the hardware store, lifting heavy boxes, muscles flexing and sweat dripping down his neck, wetting his t-shirt. I woke up in a sweat myself, wow that was a nice nap and a good dream to go along with it. I walked to the bathroom to shower, but Heather was already showering.

"Let me know when you are done, thanks," I yelled through the door. Relaxing on my bed, I pulled out my phone, should I text Grant, I don't want him to think I am being clingy. Well I am going to text him anyway.

Wednesday, 7:00 pm; Sydney to Grant: Hey, hope work is good. Lunch was nice. Heather and I going out 2night, want to meet us?

Not exactly expecting a response at all, I was surprised when my phone beeped.

Wednesday, 7:05 pm; Grant to Sydney: Was wondering when you would text me, get me anything @ store? Where r u 2 heading 2 2night?

Wednesday, 7:05 pm; Sydney to Grant: I didn't know you needed anything @ store, but I did get something for you! Not sure where we r going yet, someplace to hangout and dance would be fun.

Wednesday, 7:06 pm; Grant to Sydney: Is it chocolate? Can I eat it? U guys should go to the Captains Club on Ocean Ave.

Wednesday, 7:07 pm; Sydney to Grant: Do you luv chocolate? No, it is not chocolate, can you eat it, I guess in a way!

Wednesday, 7:08 pm; Grant to Sydney: I do luv chocolate, hmmm...not chocolate, what does it taste like?

Laughing at what he was texting to me, him having no idea what I was talking about, or maybe he did know what I was talking about.

Wednesday, 7:09 pm; Sydney to Grant: I don't think I know what it tastes like...maybe you, can tell me later!

Wednesday, 7:10 pm; Grant to Sydney: I am so lost, what are we talking about here, I will be off work in 90 minutes.

Wednesday, 7:11 pm; Sydney to Grant: Meet us @ Captains Club, getting ready.

Wednesday, 7:12 pm; Grant to Sydney: Can't wait!

We finally finished getting ready, "So, Grant suggested we go to the Captains Club, have you been there before," I asked.

"Oh, good suggestion, it is Wednesday right? $2 drinks from 8-10 and there is a local band playing tonight."

We were out the door a few minutes later. Grant and Curt were meeting us at the Club after they finished work and changed. Not that it matters what they put on their bodies, they would look hot in potato sacks.

Walking to the club, we noticed the streets starting to be busier with tourists, closer to the end of May now.

"ID's ladies," the bouncer at the door requested.

Entering the bar was like a time warp, the place needed a makeover badly. All kinds of Navy stuff hung on the walls, the walls looked like they were made of wooden ship planks, pictures of Navy ships, anchors, nautical themed stuff everywhere. The bar sat in the middle of the club, with a bartender on each of the 4 sides, there were a few waitresses taking orders. We found a table and then noticed Russ from my work, and a couple people from Heather's, and we went to join them instead of sitting by ourselves.

We had already shown our ID's (fake of course), so when the waitress came over, we didn't have to show them again. I asked for a margarita on the rocks, Heather requested her favorite, she was difficult, "Can I have a Pinnacle Whipped Cream vodka on the rocks with orange juice," she asked the waitress, "If you don't have Pinnacle then I will just have a margarita on the rocks."

I looked at Heather and shook my head, the band had not started playing yet, so it wasn't too loud. It was only 8:15 pm, the club was starting to get busier, and the band would be on at 8:30 pm. Grant wouldn't be here for quite a while. The waitress brought us our drinks.

We bumped glasses, "Here is to the best summer ever!" We both said in unison.

Russ ordered a round of tequila shots for our table. Once the shots arrived, we were all going to do them together. Russ handed us each a shot, passed the lime wedges around, and the salt. I licked my hand in between my thumb and index finger, and poured the salt over where I had licked.

Russ said, "On the count of 3...1, 2, 3!" holding our shots in our hands, licking the salt, downing the tequila and biting the lime. I shook my head, wow that was good, we were all laughing and having a good time. I could see Heather looking at her phone reading a text, I looked at her as if to say, who is it from?

"Heather," almost yelling at her. "Who is the text from?" I asked. My stomach was beginning to twist with anxiety, I could tell by the look on her face she wasn't happy. The band was warming up, some kind of cover band they would be playing a mix of different music from other bands. It was getting really loud inside the club. She handed me her phone.

Wednesday, 8:20 pm; Trent to Heather: hey heather, what's up, haven't seen you around, want to hang out with us 2nite @ dylans place?

I could feel myself become light headed, I felt ill. Heather took her phone from my hands and pointed towards the restrooms. We excused ourselves and went inside.

"Sydney, you look like you are going to pass out, are you okay?"

"No, I am not okay, are you going to respond to him?" I asked.

"I wasn't planning on responding, do you want me to?" Heather asked.

"God no, I don't want him to know where we are, does he know where you live?" I asked.

"I don't believe so, I have not seen him since last summer when you left for school, at your party," she said.

"Okay, then we should be fine, just delete the message and I don't want to worry about it," I told her. I was worried; if he was texting Heather out of the blue then he was trying to figure out where I was hiding myself.

"Let's go get drunk," I told her.

"I think we are already on our way in that very direction," she said laughing on our way out of the restroom.

We went back to our table and there was another round of tequila shots waiting for us, thanks to Russ.

I gave him a kiss on the cheek and said, "Just what the doctor ordered, perfect." We did the tequila shot ritual again. We were feeling no pain, the band was playing, "I Am Sexy And I Know It." So, out to the dance floor we went. I have no idea what time it was or how long we had been dancing. I was having a great time, we went back to take a break, we ordered two more margaritas and sat down to finish our drinks. We were asked to dance by two very attractive young men and headed to the dance floor with them.

The music was loud and the beat was great, not even sure what the band was playing. Our dance partners had left Heather and I by ourselves, but we didn't care. Dancing can be such a release. I was feeling more than happy. Not having seen Grant and Curt come in to the club, they had been watching us from the bar. Taking a few shots and having some beer, unwinding from the day of work and probably trying to catch up to the buzz we already had.

I was dancing, not paying attention to anything, with my eyes closed moving to the music. The hairs on the back of my neck started to tingle, as two large hands touched my hips, lightning shot through me, he wrapped his arms around my waist, leaning my back on his chest my head falling to his shoulders, I kissed his neck.

"How did you know it was me?" he said into my ear.

Slurring, "Because my body gives me a special signal when you are close and your touch makes me cream."

He spun me around, gazing into my eyes, "Sydney, don't tease me, I have missed your touch all day."

"All day, huh... well maybe we should go home and you can see what I got for you," I slurred again.

"Are you drunk?" A scowl on his face.

"No, not yet, but I am feeling mighty fine," I said laughing.

Pulling me from the dance floor, he was obviously not happy with my intoxicated state.

"Are you mad or something...Grant," I slurred again.

He sighed, "I am not mad, I just don't like seeing you so drunk, when I am not here with you."

"You're here with me now, oh my protective man, we just started...doing whatever it is we are doing and you're getting all possessive on me," slurring again.

Rolling my eyes at him, "Sorry, I...I mean...we, Heather and I were just having some fun, come and dance with me. I like the way you move, it is like you are making love to me on the dance floor," trying not to slur my words.

I was desperately trying to pull him to the dance floor with me, but he wouldn't move. So, I dropped his hand and grabbed some other guy's hand and pulled him to dance. If Grant didn't want to dance with me I would find someone else too. He didn't own me, I could dance with whoever I please!

I was dancing with some random guy, not really wanting to and trying to keep his hands off me. Heather said, "Who are you dancing with?"

I looked at him and then to her and shrugged my shoulders putting my arms up and shaking my head to tell her I didn't know. I had no idea where Grant was, Curt was next to Heather dancing. Next thing I know, I see Grant storming towards me, I smiled and put my arms around his neck.

"You're drunk and going to get yourself in trouble, I am taking you home."

That was the end of my evening. He was so mad at me, he walked me home unlocked my door and put me to bed. *That was it!*

I woke up in my bed, alone. I think it is Thursday, but my head is hurting and I am not quite sure. I looked at the empty bed and sighed. How did I get here, recalling the events of the night before. I laid back on my pillow. I remember going into the Club, margaritas, tequila shot, another margarita, shots and then more drinks. I sat straight up in my bed, muttering to myself... Shit, Grant is pissed at me. I got out of bed, put on some shorts because all I had on was my camisole. After using the bathroom, I went downstairs, I could smell coffee. Great -were Heather's parents back already, it hadn't even been a week. Nope thank goodness, but Heather was up and decided we need to become coffee drinkers. She poured me a cup added some French vanilla creamer and stirred it for me.

"You look awful," she said to me.

"I feel awful too," I said holding my head in my hand and sitting down at the kitchen table.

I took a hesitant sip of the coffee she had made, "Hey, this is pretty good."

I finished my coffee, "What happened last night, how did I get home?" I asked her.

"Grant," was all Heather said.

"He is mad at me, I know he is mad, shit, now what do I do?"

Heather didn't say anything, she was making French toast and scrambled eggs for breakfast. Smells delicious and would help my queasy stomach. I didn't bring up the text to Heather, not wanting to worry about it again. But thoughts of Trent and his heartbreaking betrayals were lingering in the back of my mind.

"I am so glad I don't have to be at work until 2:00, I think I will take a nap when I am done with breakfast," I said.

I cleaned up the breakfast mess, since Heather had cooked. I went back to lie down on my comfy bed. I looked at my phone, no new messages today, just a few from last night. Sagging back, a little sad, I scrolled through the messages from last night.

Wednesday, 9:00 pm; Grant to Sydney: Getting off work, be there in a few minutes.

Wednesday, 9:15 pm; Grant to Sydney: Are you still at the Captains Club?

Wednesday, 9:22 pm; Grant to Sydney: Never mind I see you on the dance floor.

Wednesday, 10:05 pm; Kendall to Sydney: Coming home in 2 weeks for weekend.

Wednesday, 11:17 pm; Trent to Sydney: I know you are staying somewhere, just let me see you.

Shit!

Wednesday, 11:25; Grant to Sydney: I know you were drunk tonight, I just want to keep you safe, probably better if we keep our distance for a while.

DOUBLE SHIT!

Now my head really hurts, along with my heart. I have known him for less than a week and was already upset and wanting to keep his distance. The fall, my fall, I have already fallen for him.

Not really crying, just a few tears gliding down my cheeks. I thought to myself, I just wanted to have a fun summer, no complications, no binding ties. Then along came Grant who put my heart and libido spinning out of control. Not sure if he was at work or not, I would send a text apologizing for my drunken behavior. Hopefully, he will be willing to forgive me and we can still have some fun together.

Thursday, 9:25 am; Sydney to Grant: Thank you for taking care of me and bringing me home safely. If I offended you in some way, I am sorry. I didn't mean to get so drunk. Can we

take a walk on the beach together after I get off work tonight at 7?

I fell asleep after I sent the message, my alarm went off at 12:30 pm, feeling much better I went to get some iced tea before heading to shower and go to work. Checking my phone for a response from Grant, none. My day at work dragged on. Russ was questioning me about where I had run off to last night and did I have a good time? I wasn't in the mood to talk. I was missing Grant, the sound of his voice, the way he smells. Geez, I need to get a grip! Finally, my work day was over, I dragged myself out the doors. Grant was sitting with his head down, rubbing his forehead, in deep thought on the bench in front the surf shop. I started to get a little flutter in my stomach, nervous as to why he was here, did he come to see me, was this the final brush off, my mind racing out of control.

A little nervous, I said, "Grant," he looked up at me with a weary smile.

He stood up, I started to walk to him. He put up his hand, saying to stop.

"What, did you get my text?" I asked.

"Yes, I got it," he said.

"Do you forgive me, I am so sorry, I behaved terribly. I shouldn't have gotten so drunk, I should have left with you when you asked me to."

He looked sad, almost betrayed in some manner. I didn't understand the look on his face.

"Sydney," he started, "I am not upset that you were drinking, although, you need to be careful who you choose to dance with, I guess I just didn't expect you to get so out of control last night and when you wouldn't listen to me, about taking you home, I just wanted to carry you out of the club over my shoulder. I knew it was not my place to do that to you."

Grant looked relieved for telling me how he felt, but I could tell there was more.

"I am so sorry," I started to say, "You do have the right, you're my friend, well I mean we are more than friends at least for the summer anyways, right?"

"Look, I am going away for a few days with Noah, let's see how we feel when I get back," he said to me.

"Oh…um, okay, sure, no problem," I stuttered. "See you soon," I walked away feeling worse than I did this morning.

As I turned the corner to pick up Heather at the yogurt shop, I could see he had deliberately taken the long way home so he didn't have to be near me. I waited outside for Heather to finish her shift, sitting at the table with my head down, resting on my folded arms.

She came out, "Are you alright, you look bad, still have a hangover?" I just looked at her with damp eyes and shook my head.

"I messed it up already, I haven't even been here a week, I find this amazing guy and I messed it up," I said.

Heather put her arm around me, we walked back to the house, grabbed some tea and sat down in the lounge chairs out on the patio. Trying to relax, Heather asked me what happened. I told her about the club last night, the message from this morning, and our conversation outside the surf shop a little while ago.

"First off," she said, "Grant, Curt, and Noah are all going surfing in Santa Barbara this weekend. Second, you didn't mess it up, Grant is insecure, and third, I think you are missing the big picture here."

I am so confused. Grant, insecure? I would never believe it, he has more self-confidence then anyone I know. Big picture what big picture?

"What are you talking about, I am so lost, what?" I said to her.

"Look there is a lot you don't know about Grant, he has trust issues," she said.

"What, don't we all, it is not as if Trent didn't break my heart after I gave him everything," I reminded her.

"Sydney, I know, I was there, I remember, but…Grant, well his situation is different, he has to be the one to tell you, not me, it is not my story to tell," Heather said. What? I am so confused.

"Alright, my head is starting to hurt again, you are making no sense to me at all. What did you mean by the big picture? What is the big picture?" I said with an annoying tone in my voice.

"Trust issues, Sydney he has trust issues, I think he saw the messages on your phone when he took you home last night," she said.

"The messages, they were all from him, where is my phone, let me look through those messages again," running to get my phone out of my purse.

I came back and sat down next to Heather on her lounge chair.

"Okay, three messages from Grant, one from Kendall…and, damn, one message from Trent, shit," I said.

I looked at Heather, "But I didn't, I can't control when he sends me messages, I don't even want him to send me messages, I don't want anything to do with Trent," I sighed, this is ridiculous.

Heather looked at me, "Okay this what I know…Curt, said when Grant got home last night he was furious, mumbling on about how you had given him all this shit about having a girlfriend and then confronting the blonde bob girl at the pizza place, but the whole time you were hiding a boyfriend."

I fell back on the lounge chair, my head hanging over the side, "Trent isn't even in my life and he is causing me problems, is it possible to block a number from calling or texting you? I am calling my cell phone carrier!"

Heather was laughing, "Good idea, why are you just now thinking of it?"

We both started to laugh, "When are they leaving for Santa Barbara?" I asked.

"I am not sure, want me to text Curt?" she asked me.

"Yes please, if they haven't left yet I want to go talk to Grant," I said with a hopeful smile.

"Wait…don't send the text yet, are you telling me, the big picture is the trust issue thing or is there more?" I asked.

"Too late, I already sent the text to Curt," Heather said.

The big picture, still waiting for the big picture information.

"Okay, according to Curt, Grant has not allowed himself to fall for a girl in a long time, not since the trust issue event occurred. Yes, he has had girlfriends and gone on many dates. But Curt says he has not seen him with the look he has in eyes in a very long time," I tried to interrupt her but she put her fingers over my lips so I couldn't talk, she continued "You know all this information is coming through Curt, so don't tell Grant you know any of this. Anyways, Grant never gets upset when his dates/girlfriends dance with other guys, doesn't pay them much attention at all. Until you walked into his life, Curt says he has only seen him this way with one other girl and she broke his heart."

Quickly, covering her mouth with her hand, "Shit, I just spilled the beans."

CHAPTER 8

Grant, Noah, and Curt had left to go surfing in Santa Barbara on Thursday afternoon and would be gone for a few days. I wanted to talk to Grant before they left, but they were already on the road by the time Heather sent out her text to Curt.

I had to work the day shift Friday-Sunday, so at least I would be busy. I was glad to know he wasn't around and I wouldn't have to worry about running into him in town, not knowing how he felt about me. Why I am so upset that he is mad at me, why does he feel betrayed because of the text from Trent? We are not in an exclusive relationship, not boyfriend and girlfriend. Why was he being so sensitive and possessive of me? What is his big secret? I need to call Kendall about this, had she found anything out about him.

Friday, 8:15 am; Sydney to Kendall: Did u find anything out about HBG?

Friday, 8:35 am; Kendall to Sydney: Do you know what time it is? I don't have class until 11 am. No, not really.

Friday, 8:36 am; Sydney to Kendall: What does that mean? Anything...

Friday, 8:37 am; Kendall to Sydney: All Matt knows, is HBG, graduated in May, doesn't spend too much time at the house anymore, rarely comes to parties/formals and has not had a serious girlfriend in a looong time! Although, he did make a strange face when I asked about him.

Friday, 8:38 am; Sydney to Kendall: Ok, thanks for ur help, by the way Trent is lurking around trying to find me which means Dylan is looking for you too.

Friday, 8:39 am; Kendall to Sydney: BIGGEST MISTAKES OF OUR LIVES!

Well, I was no better off than I was 15 minutes ago. No new information!

First thing I need to do today is find out how to block a number on my cell phone. I spent the next 30 minutes on the phone with my cell phone carrier, they explained how to block an incoming number. Okay, I can cross that off my "to-do" list for the day. Trent is officially blocked from my phone! Next orders of business, go to work, make it through the day and do it all over again until Grant comes back in town. I want to work this out with him. Friday was super busy at work, but I didn't mind, Heather was at work too, by the end of the day we were exhausted. We headed home then went down to the beach to relax. It was almost June, where did this month go? It was crowded today, I guess people coming down here for weekend getaways.

Minding our own business, reading a book in the sun under our umbrella, well I was reading a book, Heather was flipping through a magazine.

"Why don't you read one of my books, you will like them," I told her. "Do you have 50 Shades of Grey?" she asked.

"Of course," I handed her the first book, "I forgot to tell you I blocked Trent on my cell phone, oh great, look who is coming." The disgust in my voice couldn't have been missed.

Out of the corner of my eye coming down the beach I could see blonde bob beach bunny girl.

"I am proud of you, good job blocking Trent, what... Ugh," when she saw who I was commenting on.

Blonde Bob Beach Bunny Girl had no problem walking right up to us, with her little group of thugs. I rolled my eyes at her and continued to read my book.

"Hey Heather, we are having a party Saturday night, you and your friend want to come hang out with us?" Gina asked.

Heather looked up at her, "Gina, you know her name. Where is the party?" I must have whipped my head around too fast to give

Heather a dirty look for even considering going to this party because my neck started to hurt!

"It is at the Yacht Club, 7:00 pm tomorrow night, summer dress attire. No flip flops," she said. I rolled my eyes again, yacht club? That sounds so boring I thought to myself. Gina blabbed on "DJ, open bar, yummy food, and gorgeous men. What more could we ask for," she laughed. "Hope both you and Sydney can make it," walking away they waved like we were BFF's.

My brows were furrowed when I turned to Heather, "Are we even going to consider this invitation?"

"Well, do we have anything better to do? Do you want to sit home moping about Grant, feeling sorry for yourself?" Well now I had no choice, we had to go.

"Well I don't have a thing to wear, let's go shopping," I said. We were gone, took our beach stuff back to the house, and we were walking through all the shops by the beach looking for something fun to wear to the party.

After an exhaustive search we each found a cute summer dress to wear, Heather found a strapless navy blue maxi dress, with stripes running through it. I found a maxi dress with very thin straps going over my back, with different color stripes running through it. We both had wedges to wear we were set.

Saturday morning, we both were at work all day, super busy. Saturdays were always super busy. I did get my first paycheck. I hadn't heard from Grant since before he left and I didn't want to call or text him while he was away. He was obviously still upset with me, but until I could talk to him face to face, there was nothing I could do. I went down to the Blue Moon Café to pick up the lunch I had ordered for Heather and I, we sat outside the yogurt shop to eat. We talked about how busy it was and how hot it was today.

"So, have you heard from Curt since they left?" I asked.

"Yes," she said.

"What is with the one word answer, can you elaborate?" I totally bit her head off.

She sighed and said, "They are coming home sometime today, I don't know when, and I think you should wait for him to call you." Rolling my eyes, I was doing that a lot lately.

"Great, now I will be anxious the rest of the day, looking at the door and my phone to see if he is around, this sucks," I said.

She started laughing at me until I gave her the evil eye, which only made her laugh harder.

"What happened to, *I am not falling in love, not looking for a boyfriend, just a good time girl?*" she said to me in a very snarky tone.

I gave Heather a sad face, "She was never really here."

"Oh, what happened to her?"

"I was trying to fool myself, I knew the first time I saw him over the bonfire, he was different, the feeling I got when he looked at me, and the way the hair on the back of my neck stood up. I just didn't want to admit it to myself, I can't even believe I am admitting it now. I have only known him a week and I miss him like we have been going out forever. I promised myself after what happened with Trent, I would not allow myself to have those kinds of feelings again, at least not for a very long time." Heather's eyes were very wide, she started to clear her throat like she was chocking.

"Are you alright, are you chocking," I asked with concern.

Her eyes were looking over my head, trying to get me to turn around. I didn't move, I was frozen unable to move any part of my body... shit. Someone was behind me. I was pretty sure it wasn't Grant because I could always feel his eyes on me and the tingling of electricity when he was near.

Before, I could get myself to turn around, they were sitting down at the table with us, Trent and Micah. Could this day get any worse, well yes it could, if Curt and Grant showed up. Micah and Heather had dated on and off our senior year of high school, but had never been as serious as Trent and I. Well, thank goodness I have to go back to work.

I hopped up from the table, "Got to go, see ya," I said.

"Not so fast, I have been waiting for you to come home from school, only to find out you have been living down by the beach with Heather," Trent growled at me.

I could see by his demeanor he was not happy, not that his happiness was my concern anymore. He was holding onto my arm, not letting me go. Heather was up from the table too.

Russ came out of the surf shop, "Is everything alright out here, Sydney?" he asked.

Trent dropped my arm, "Yeah man, just catching up with my girl," he said, I almost got sick on the sidewalk with that statement.

"I am not your girl, not in a long time, and not ever again," stressing the tone of disgust in my voice.

I turned to walk in to the surf shop and go back to work. Heather was already at the yogurt shop.

Russ said, "I suggest you boys find someplace else to hang out!"

When Russ came back inside the surf shop, he could see I was visibly upset.

"Sydney, who was that guy? He is an ass."

"Tell me about it."

"Do you want to talk about it?"

"No not really, ex-boyfriend, cheated on me, I dumped him without blinking an eye, wants me back, enough said," I walked away to go wash my face in the bathroom. When I came out, the store was super busy, Saturday afternoon by the beach, always crazy!

I clocked out and was really not in the mood for this big party tonight at the yacht club with Gina and her friends. I knew Heather would insist we go out, not wanting to sit home on a Saturday night. I looked out the front windows to see if Trent or Micah were still hanging around, no sign of them- good. I walked to the yogurt shop to get Heather and we walked home to go get ready for tonight. It was already 4:00 pm, I needed a power nap, shower, and I would be in a better mood. Hopefully!

We were home relaxing, I could hear Heather's phone beeping like crazy. Mine was silent.

"Heather, your phone is blowing up, can you please check it. How many messages do you have?" She was laughing walking to look at her phone which was charging on the counter.

"Wow, 12 new messages, I am popular today," she laughed.

Scrolling through her messages, she turned to me, "Well, umm, one is from Curt saying they were stuck in traffic by LAX and not sure how long it would be before they were home. 11 of them were from Trent."

"What? Delete them, don't read them, seriously Heather, just delete them," I told her fear gripping my words.

"Ok, ok, I am deleting them!"

"You need to get his number blocked," I told her.

Shaking my head, knowing something bad was brewing, I went upstairs to take a shower, double checking all the doors in the house to be sure they were locked. We showered, did our hair, make-up, dressed, and we were out the door. We decided to take Heather's mom's car tonight, a white convertible sports car, this car was hot, and I have to say we looked good in it. With our new dresses on, we drove to the party.

We arrived fashionably late, not wanting to be on time. We drove up to the valet then headed inside, I was feeling a high case of anxiety.

Heather looked at me, "Calm down, we are here to have a good time."

I just smiled, she was right, we are at a private club, we're safe. We walked in, the music was great, the bar was open, and the guests were having a great time. Everyone from around town was here, we each got a margarita, our drink of choice this summer and one tequila shot, just one. We walked out on to the patio, the moon was high above the water and the ocean looked breathtaking. We stood next to each other, "1, 2, 3," I said. We tipped back our shots, the tequila warmed me as it slid down my throat. I was starting to relax, sipping our margaritas, I got the strangest feeling. Only one thing or one person gives me this feeling, the hair on the back of neck was standing on end, my heart was beating faster and my pulse was speeding up.

I turned around- Grant had just walked out on to the patio. In classic navy chinos, a crisp white button down, open a little on the top, and loafers. I could tell he was freshly showered his hair glistening from the patio lights. Curt was behind him coming out the same door, looking just as handsome as Grant. Heather and I stood still. They were walking towards us, drinks in their hands, I swallowed hard as he made his approach. I am not even sure if I am breathing, it seemed to take forever for them to walk to us. Curt got to Heather first, he grabbed her, dipping her back and smacking her on the lips with a big kiss, she giggled at him.

Grant came right up to me, looking down at me, he put his drink on the table next to us. I couldn't move, I was frozen. He took my face in his warm hands, holding my head still, he leaned in and gave me a kiss that made my toes tingle. The electricity was there, I could feel it again moving from our lips coursing through my body and his. I didn't want him to let go of me, not ever. He pulled me closer, wrapping his arms around my waist.

"I missed you," he whispered in my ear. "I am sorry, I shouldn't have left mad, but being away from you made me realize how happy I am when I am with you. I know we only have the summer together... I want to spend all my time with you."

A tear dropped down my check, he kissed my tear, "I... don't know what to say," I whispered back.

"Don't say anything, kiss me instead," he said, so I did.

The four of us went inside, sat down for dinner together, Grant didn't let go of me. He was either holding my hand, touching my back, touching my shoulders, giving me sweet kisses, whispering in my ear, it was wonderful. I was floating on top of the world. Nothing was going to upset me tonight. When the DJ called everyone out on the dance floor, we were more than happy to oblige. We had a rocking time, we danced all night, I didn't drink too, much not wanting to have a repeat of the other night at the Captains Club. Around 11:00, Grant said he was tired and asked if we could head home together. You know I agreed, we hadn't been together in a few days and I wanted to be alone with him.

We went and told Heather and Curt we were leaving, we would see them back at our house.

As we walked to his car, he pulled me in close, "Did I tell you how beautiful you are? You look gorgeous tonight and you smell like heaven," Grant said smiling his wicked smile at me.

I blushed at his words, "No you didn't, but thank you for your compliment."

"I don't think you realize how beautiful you truly are, all eyes were on you tonight."

"Don't be silly," I said blushing again.

"Do you want to go back to my house or yours?"

"I don't care, I just want to be with you," I said.

On the way home, I had an uneasy feeling we had unfinished business to discuss, not wanting to ruin our evening, I tried to keep my mouth shut, but I couldn't.

I started, "Grant, I want to tell you something, I know you looked at my text messages the other night. I want to talk about the one you read from Trent."

"Sydney, it is okay, you don't need to justify your actions to me."

"Justify my actions- I am not sure why you would say that, let me just clarify a few things, before we have any more misunderstandings."

"Okay," he said, we were holding hands in the car. I took a deep breath.

"Trent and I went out my senior year of high school, I was in love with him, well I thought I was in love with him. I gave myself to him. I thought he loved me, I thought we had something special. I was blinded by what I thought was love. When I left for school in August, I hadn't even put my feet on the ground in Arizona and I was getting all kinds of messages on my phone; pictures of him with different girls, picture's dated well before I left for school." I took another deep breath and continued, "I was too busy to deal with it right away, Sorority Rush taking place as soon as we got to campus. I was totally consumed with picking the right house so once that was over I had to deal with him during the few days in between Rush and classes. I knew he had made a fool out of me, cheating on me right under my nose. I dropped him via text message the least emotional way possible, and I have never looked back."

"I never respond to his messages, I don't return his calls, and I have most recently blocked his number from my phone. I have not seen him since last August, well, until he showed up in town today, looking for me. I don't know how he found me, but he has," I stopped talking.

My eyes were huge, waiting for a response from Grant. I could see the colors of his eyes had changed. Great- he is mad at me, I am honest with him, and he is mad at me.

"Why did you tell me all this, Sydney?"

"Because I don't want there to be secrets between us, I want us to be honest with each other so we don't waste the precious time we have together over miscommunications or misunderstandings."

We pulled into the garage at his house, once inside, we were still sitting in the car. I was nervous, my heart was racing, my breathing was unsteady, and I was thinking I may hyperventilate at any moment if he doesn't say something. He turned to face me in the car, it was dark, but I could see his eyes, they were hard, darkened, and looking for courage.

"What is it Grant… just tell me, if you don't want to be with me I will understand, I won't be happy but I will respect your decision," I said softly. I most definitely would not be happy.

"Sydney, it is just you have been so honest with me I think I owe you an explanation for my actions the last few days."

Now he took a deep breath, "When I was attending ASU, I pledged a fraternity my freshmen year, moved into the fraternity house and was by all means your average college guy. I went to parties and dated, until I met Ashley. She was everything I was looking for, we started dating at the beginning of my sophomore year of college. She took school seriously, liked to party, and was what I thought was my perfect mate." Hearing him talk about this girl, was making me sick, my stomach was doing flips. I don't think I want to hear the rest of this story. He continued, "We got serious very quickly, by the end of the school year I had given her my fraternity pin, you know, one step before engagement," he looked at me.

"Yes, I know what it means, please continue."

"Well, she even came out here to the stay with me for part of the summer. When we went back to school in August before our junior year, she told me she was pregnant. I was shocked; I couldn't believe it, we had been so careful, she was getting the birth control shot. I went to my parents, told them what was going on and they were fully supportive."

"So are you telling me you have a child, is that what this is about?" I was seriously going to be sick. I heard my phone beep, Grant was breathing heavily, I pulled my phone out. It was Heather. "Let me just check her text, I want to hear the rest of this story, I just want to make sure she is okay."

Saturday, 11:25 pm; Heather to Sydney: Don't go back to the house, Trent's car parked in front, we are heading your way.

My eyes got wide, when I read the text, "SHIT!" I said.

"What's wrong," I could see the concern on his face when he asked.

"Heather and Curt are heading here from the party, they just drove past our house, and Trent is parked in front waiting for us. What should I do?" I asked Grant.

"Nothing, you're here with me, we will figure it out tomorrow," he said. We were still sitting in the car, he leaned over and kissed me.

"Let's go inside, I think we could both use a drink. Do you have to work in the morning?"

"Not until 11:00 am," I told him.

"Good, let's go have a drink and spend some time together, I want to see what you have on under your dress," he said his eyes moving over me and licking his lips.

I was watching Grant, his Adams apple moved up and down as he sucked down his beer. My mouth was open and I was running my tongue along the tops of my teeth. He was so handsome, he looked delicious in his clothes, I couldn't wait to run my fingers along his chest.

I walked up to him and untucked his dress shirt from his pants, I put my hands underneath his shirt, onto his stomach, he cringed, "Your hands are freezing from holding your beer."

I continued moving my hands, "You know Curt and Heather are just a few feet away on the couch," I just smiled, my hands continued to travel down the outside of his pants, I could feel his hardness, his erection was filling my hands.

I looked over my shoulder at our friends, "I am going to bed... good night," I said I took my beer with me and headed to Grants room.

CHAPTER 9

We were alone, in Grant's room, he shut the door and locked it. He walked over and turned on the music, dimming the lights.

"Did you take your pill?" He asked me.

"Yes, of course, but you're still using a condom," I said.

He leaned in and kissed me, "I have missed your lips, Sydney, I missed your ears," kissing me on each, "I missed your neck," kissing all around it.

He gently pulled me towards his bed. He took my beer from my hands and put it down on his dresser. He slowly untied the back of my dress, letting the straps loose. He was kissing my collarbone and pulling down the straps over each shoulder. Before I knew what happened my dress was pooling on the floor at my feet. I was wearing a strapless all black sheer teddy under my dress, with strappy high heels, that made my legs look long and sexy, he left my high heels on.

"Sydney, did you wear this for me? How did you know I would be at the party tonight?" As he walked in a circle around me, I could feel his eyes drinking me in, I was feeling a little self-conscious but I knew he would like it.

Biting my bottom lip, I said, "I was hoping you'd come to the party."

"You look…out of this world amazing…delicious," I heard him breath in and the sound of his tongue smacking on his wet lips… "I could go on, but I would rather show you what you do to me," he said, he held my hand and helped me walk over my dress on the floor.

He finished walking me to his bed, he laid me down resting my head on the pillows. "You so are hot, in your black teddy on my bed, Sydney, and you are mine," his sultry voice making me swoon.

I had wanted him for days now, I could feel myself wet between my legs. My heart was pounding out of my chest and he was cool as a cucumber. His eyes were dark, burning through to my soul. I could barely swallow; he was kissing me down the front of my teddy, stopping to cup each breast, pushing the teddy down, and sucking hard on each nipple until they were hard.

I was arching my back with desire, "Please Grant, I want you, I want you inside me," I pleaded.

"Not yet," he said.

He was torturing me with his tongue on my nipples. His hand was slowly moving down to my sex. He gently massaged my clit through my teddy, moving the thin fabric to the side, he drew his fingers through my wet folds.

"You're so wet for me, I love it," putting his wet fingers in his mouth, tasting me.

"I love what you are wearing, but right now, I want to see you naked," so I took off the teddy.

He continued his exploration of my body, kissing his way down. His head was between my legs, using his broad shoulders to push my thighs further apart.

I couldn't watch, "Grant, don't, I have never umm..." I trailed off as his tongue was sliding through me, with one finger inside me, I was about to lose my mind. He was relentless, his tongue was licking, and sucking on the bud of clit.

I was moaning out from the pleasure he was giving me, "Your taste is divine... like honey and coconuts," he drawled and smacked his lips together.

I couldn't hold on, I was ready to explode.

"Grant I can't hold on, I am going to come," I moaned out.

"I want you to come," he pushed two fingers inside of me and took one last hard suck on my clit and with that, rockets were exploding around me, bright lights were filling my eyes, he had pushed me over the edge with desire for him.

I was breathing hard, I could feel him gently taking my high heels off, dropping each one to the floor. He was next to me now, he kissed me hard, I could taste myself in his mouth.

"Your taste is so sweet, I have never tasted something so pure," he whispered in my ear.

I could feel his erection on my stomach, he was ready.

"I am going to take you now Sydney, do you want it hard and fast, or slow and loving," his voice moving through me, pushing my need higher.

I could hear, the rip of the foil packet, "I don't care, I just want you inside me," I demanded.

He rolled on the condom. Moving over me, my anticipation was growing.

He slowly entered me, making love to me, "This is slow and loving, Sydney, do you enjoy this?" I could feel the full length of his hard erection inside of me, filling me, it was the best feeling, I had ever felt. Connected to him, we moved in fluid motion, "Or would rather have it hard and fast?" his voice so low so deep. He thrust into me pushing me up the bed.

"Hard and fast," I responded breathlessly.

He was talking, "I can feel your walls wrapping around me tightening on me."

He was thrusting harder, I was thrusting back, he was giving me his wickedly sexy smile, "Keep your eyes open, I want you to see the look on my face when I come inside you," he said.

My body was still high from a few minutes ago, when he had me coming using his tongue. My climb up to ecstasy was not going to take long, I was almost there, I was screaming out his name, I was arching my back, begging for my release.

"Sydney, come with me," he groaned. As if on command, I was gone, my body was shaking from his words, the orgasm was out of this world, I couldn't see or feel anything but him, coming inside me, with his final thrusts, gasping for air, he was saying my name over and over.

He was still inside me, leaning over me, trying to regain his composure;, I was still flying high, my body not ready to come to earth. This was the best feeling, it should be bottled and sold for top dollar I thought to myself. A huge smile was beaming across my face. He slid out of me, cold air hitting me where he had been. He walked to the bathroom and disposed of the condom, flushing the toilet, and washing his hands. He came back to the bed, pulling me close to him, holding me. My head was resting on his shoulder just below his neck.

"Sydney, I know we haven't been seeing each other very long, but I don't want you to see anyone else...I want this relationship to be exclusive, just you and me, no one else, is that alright with you?"

"For me it already was," I said back to him with my smile still beaming across my face.

"Great," he pulled me on top of him. Kissing me, "So, was the black teddy your surprise for me from shopping?"

"Nope!" Giving him a sly smile.

"Is there something else?"

"Yes," I said with my eyebrows raised, "You'll just have to wait," I added.

We fell asleep with my head on his shoulder. When I woke up I was lying next to him, he still had both arms around me. The sun was not up yet, but I could feel him squirming in the bed. I tried to roll away, but he pulled me back next to him.

"Where are you going?" He mumbled.

"Nowhere, just trying to give you some space to stretch out," I whispered, since I wasn't fully awake yet.

"Do you want to go surfing with me?"

"No, it is 5:30 in the morning and we just barely went to sleep," I growled.

"What do you want to do then?" He smiled wickedly at me.

"Sleep," I turned on my side, so my back was to him...bad idea.

Oh snap, I thought, as his hand came around my front and was cupping my sex, "Oh my God, are you hard, I can feel you on my back. It is 5:30 in the morning, you're crazy!"

"You make me this way Sydney; naked, sleeping next to me all night, and then turning over so I could see your perfect ass, you're so wet, is that what I do to you?" As his fingers plunged inside me.

"Yes, that is what you do to me," not looking at him when I said it.

This is an embarrassing topic, I went on "You don't even have to touch me, when I can sense you in the room, my breathing changes, my nipples start to get hard, my body is turned on by you, I cannot believe I just said that out loud."

We made love again, taking me from behind this time. My body was spent. I couldn't move, my legs were hurting and all I wanted to do was sleep. He went to get a drink and came back with some aspirin and water for me.

"This will help," he said handing me the pills.

"You are so sweet, I am a very lucky girl," I said, smiling and swallowing the pills. "Can we go back to sleep for a while?"

"Nope," he said, hitting me in the ass. "Get up, I am going surfing and you are going to watch me."

I started to climb out of bed, "Fine, but can I sit in a beach chair and watch with a blanket over me, it is so cold this early," my request lingering in the air, while he walked to brush his teeth.

"Whatever your heart desires," he said, closing the bathroom door behind him. I only had my dress to put on from last night.

"Hey, I don't have anything to wear," I sat back down on the bed and flopped backwards, waiting for him to come out.

I think I must have fallen asleep waiting for him, I was all curled up under the blankets when he came out of the bathroom.

"Did you fall back asleep? Geez," he laughed.

"Hello… I need some clothes, I have no under wear, nothing."

He laughed again, he rummaged through his drawers, handed me a pair of sweat pants which were way to big and one of his t-shirts.

"I guess I am going commando style," I said.

"Hmmm…" he got that look again. I ran into the bathroom to brush my teeth and do something with my out of control just had sex hair before he could catch me.

I was giggling to myself, "Hurry up," he yelled.

I came out of the bathroom, giant sweats, t-shirt, hair on top of my head like Pebbles Flintstone.

"Where is your sweatshirt I had on the other day, I like that one?" I asked.

"It is on the couch, let's go," he said, pulling me by the hand. I grabbed the sweatshirt and a blanket from the couch, got the beach chair from the patio, while he got his board.

I plopped down in the chair close enough to the water to see better, but not close enough to get wet. Grant had given me a kiss and was paddling out to surf. Seriously, does this sport have to be done so early in the morning? Coffee, I will need large amounts of coffee to make it through the day. I was impressed with Grant's surfing skills, I watched him surf all morning. Curt was out on the water now, where was Heather, she must have stayed asleep…lucky. I couldn't keep my eyes open, my lids betrayed me and I feel asleep leaning back in the beach chair. I have no idea how long I had been asleep. I could feel light drops of water, hitting my face, I awoke flustered, not knowing where I was, Grant was leaning over me from behind the beach chair, dripping his wet hair on my face. Damn he is hot!

He leaned down, laughing to himself, "Good morning," he whispered kissing my forehead. "I'm starving, let me make you breakfast. I know you must be hungry after the workout we had together," he said, pulling me out of the chair, I slapped his chest.

"Stop… someone might hear you," I chastised him.

"Who, the seagulls?" he laughed. We walked back to the house, he was rinsing off in the outside shower.

I pulled out eggs, bacon, butter, and milk from the refrigerator. I was already cooking the bacon when he came into the kitchen with only a towel around his waist.

"Don't get too close to the stove, I don't want you to burn your perfect set of abs with bacon grease," I warned him.

"Would you take care of me, if I was hurt," he asked.

I started to laugh, "Yes, I would be your wet nurse!"

The things that come out of my mouth sometimes, it is as if my brain was not attached to my mouth. He just raised his eyebrows at me, smiling, stole a piece of bacon, and ran off to get dressed.

"What kind of eggs do you like?" I yelled to him.

"What kind can you make?" He came back dressed in his work clothes.

With one hand on my hip, I glared at him "Rude, you don't think I can cook… your wish is my command, your highness," I bowed in front of him.

"Scrambled eggs would be great, can I have toast too?" he requested.

I nodded my head yes, "butter and jelly?" I questioned him with my back to him as I was cooking the eggs.

"Butter and jelly, we may have to try that later and not on my toast either," he said, looking super-hot, drinking some milk, I could see his throat moving up and down in his neck swallowing the milk.

He was sitting at the breakfast bar.

I just rolled my eyes, "On your toast, yes or no?"

"Yes both, and I said I wanted to make you breakfast, but this is nice too!"

"Anything for my man," I placed a full plate of food on the counter in front of him.

"This looks great, aren't you going to eat?" he asked me.

"Yes, I will sit right there," I came around the counter and sat down next to him.

He finished his food in about one minute, I looked at him with my mouth open, "I was starving!"

He rinsed his plate in the sink and came back around the counter to me. He turned my bar stool, so we were face to face, shimmying himself in between my legs. His arms leaning on the counter behind me, like a trap.

He looked longingly into my eyes, "Sydney, I have to be at work in 30 minutes, but I need to finish the story I was telling you in the car last night."

It was 7:30 am, "I will be off work at two pm, what time do you finish work today?" he asked.

"I am off at five."

"Can I pick you up from work and we can take a walk together?" he asked.

"Yes…I would like that," I smiled and leaned up to give him a kiss. I finished my breakfast and cleaned up the mess in the kitchen while Grant finished getting ready for work. I only brought my purse with me as he walked me home, I left my clothes from the party in his room.

Grant walked me to my door, lifting my chin he gave me a long kiss and said "Until we meet again, my sweet."

I was giggling at him, as he walked away down the street to work. I went inside the house, leaning against the door as I closed it. Taking a deep breath and smiling, I headed to my room for some much needed sleep, setting my alarm for 10:00 am, giving me two hours to sleep before I had to get ready for work.

My alarm sounded at 10:00 am, I was so exhausted, the house was quiet, nice maybe a few moments of peace. Heather must still be with Curt. I walked down to the kitchen to make some much needed coffee, which is my new best friend. Waiting for the coffee to brew, I leaned back against the counter, smiling thinking of my new man. My new man for the summer anyways. A strange feeling inside me made me sad, we only had the summer together, this sucks. Tomorrow is Memorial Day and my day off, I hope Grant has tomorrow off, I doubt it though with my luck.

I was on cloud nine, getting ready for work, having a snack before I left. I opened the front door to leave and was startled by someone sitting on the porch, head lowered, holding something. My stomach started to churn from disgust- it was Trent. Trying to walk by him, he stood up. I was standing on the top step standing very still, he was below me.

Looking up, "Hi... Sydney."

"What do you want, Trent?" I asked with hatred in my voice.

Handing me some flowers, "These are for you."

"Take them back, I don't want anything from you," I said. I could feel myself getting mad, my face starting to turn red, and my eyes starting to have poison arrows in them.

I pushed passed him to get away before anything else was said.

"Sydney, I screwed up, I ruined our relationship, it is all my fault," hanging his head down after he finished his confession.

I took a step towards him but stopped, "I appreciate the fact that you have come here seeking forgiveness, but I just don't have any forgiveness for you. You took my innocence, you broke my heart, and made me look like a complete fool. Not just a fool for trusting you, but for giving you all my love. You were cheating on me before I had even left for school, you had no regard for my feelings then, and you still don't know."

I really did not want to continue this conversation, I was going to be late for work. I was done being his girlfriend last year, I had put him behind me and moved on.

But he wouldn't let it go, "Sydney, please give me another chance, let me show you how I have changed. I did all the things you said, but I was stupid, I did not know how good I had it with you... until I didn't have you anymore."

I turned away from him, my frustration building. I looked back at him, he looked defeated, good; and he deserved to feel like crap.

"This is my life Trent and I am not going backwards. You are my past. I am not the same girl who left you last summer and I won't allow myself to be hurt again, especially not by you, it is still over, go home and just leave me alone," I told him.

I left Trent standing on my porch, flowers in his hands. "I am woman hear me roar!" I thought to myself as I headed to work...what a dork I am.

Work was out of control busy. My phone, tucked in my back pocket of my jean shorts, was beeping at me all day. Finally, getting a break for a few minutes, I checked the messages.

Sunday, 11:15 am; Grant to Sydney: Last night was off the charts HOT.

Sunday, 11:28 am; Grant to Sydney: R you ignoring me, I can't get the sight of you in ur black teddy on my bed, out of my mind...

Sunday, 12:05 pm; Grant to Sydney: Want to go to Angels game tomorrow night? R u out there?

Sunday, 1:12 pm; Grant to Sydney: Seriously, the thought of you moaning my name is making me crazy.

I gasped when I read his last message, he did not just put that in a text! What if someone else read his message?

Sunday, 1:21 pm; Sydney to Grant: Been super busy @ work, my 1st chance to look @ texts, stop, u r making me blush.

Sunday, 1:22 pm; Grant to Sydney: Yogurt after work, don't forget.

I didn't have a chance to respond, Russ was yelling for me to get my ass back to work and stop texting. Yikes, I thought, I have never heard Russ yell before. It was if people just came to the beach with no bathing suits or shorts...what was wrong with tourists? By the end of my shift, I was restocking all the bathing suits. Well, we were having a sale, maybe that had something to do with how busy it had been.

Grant came into the surf shop looking at the new wetsuits we had just gotten in stock. I was finishing hanging up the bikinis and cleaning out the dressing rooms. "Hey, how was your day?" I asked him.

"Better now," as he gave me a peck on my cheek.

"I am going to talk to Rick about these wetsuits, just let me know when you're done okay, babe?" he said and grabbed my ass. Did he just call me babe and grab my ass? I hope no one saw him. I just have a couple more things to do, the sandal and flip flop display looked like a bunch of wild animals had been at it.

As I cleaned up the display, I was watching Grant talking to Rick, he had plaid board shorts on, a faded t-shirt and flip-flops. I tell you this guy oozes masculinity, muscles in all the right places, smells like a dream, and his hair, just perfect. I was biting my bottom lip, when he turned and caught me staring at him. He just smiled at me with a twinkle in his eye.

"Ok man, just let me know when you get it in," he said to Rick as he walked, rather swaggered to me.

"Are you done my dear?"

I giggled, "Yeah, let me clock out."

We stopped by the Yogurt shop, talked to Heather for a few minutes, and headed down the pier eating our yogurts. I got mine in a bowl this time, eating it with a spoon not wanting to incite Grant's hormones anymore than I already did. We walked to the end of the pier and stopped on bench to sit down.

"What did you do after work?"

"Went home and took a nap, I was wiped out from the surfing and you having your way with me all night," laughing as he finished his comment.

I playfully smacked his arm, "Stop, people will hear you," I was blushing.

"Stop worrying about what other people think, geez, you are hypersensitive," he said.

"I am not, I just don't want other people knowing how hot you make me," I said, pulling my spoon upside down through my mouth, so you could see my tongue, licking the yogurt off.

Grant's body shook for a moment and he adjusted himself. I was laughing at his reaction to watching me eat my yogurt.

"Anyways, I need to tell you something," I said kind of seriously.

"Well I need to finish my story first," Grant replied.

"I really want to tell you this before we get all caught up in the drama that is apparently your life," I said.

He raised one eyebrow at me, "Drama," he said.

"Yes, drama!"

"Fine, Lady Sydney you have my attention," he put his arm down, in a bowing gesture, giving me clearance to speak.

"You are so weird," shaking my head at him.

"Okay, so when I left my house this morning…umm…when I opened the door…umm…" I was stuttering on my words.

"Sydney, just spit it out," Grant said, I could tell he was getting annoyed with me.

"Okay, Trent was sitting on my porch, holding flowers, begging for forgiveness, asking for another chance. There, I spit it out, are you happy now?" I took a deep breath after my long statement.

No he was not happy, his hand crushed the cone holding his yogurt. His hands were in fists his knuckles going completely white across the tops. He got up and put his cone in the trash can, walking back his jaw was tight, and his shoulder muscles were tense. I could see him trying not to get upset. His breathing was still steady, that was a good sign. Sitting back down next to me, my eyes were wide, waiting for him to say something, anything. I couldn't stand the silence, so I started, "I told him, how much he hurt me, how I was no longer the girl he knew, that it was still over, that I had moved on and he should just leave me alone."

Grant turned to me, his eyes a little softer now, his fists unclenched, I could see the stress he was feeling slowly leaving his body.

"Did you really tell him that," he asked.

"Yes, you asked me to be your girl and I am your girl," I said. Smiling he grabbed my cheeks and gave me an outrageous kiss.

"Do you think he got the picture, is he going to leave you alone?" he questioned me.

I turned away not wanting him to see the concern in my eyes, "I hope so."

CHAPTER 10

Grant and Curt both had morning shifts at the hardware store on Monday, Memorial Day. Heather had to open the shop and would be home before lunch. I lay in bed for most of the morning, doing a little laundry, calling my mom, and looking at Facebook. I only had A Facebook account so I could see what everyone else was up to. You know the people you didn't want to talk to or hang around with, but still wanted to know what was up in their lives? I very rarely updated my Facebook information.

We were going to the Angel's baseball game tonight. Noah had left the tickets for Grant before heading back to Arizona. The game was at 7:05 pm and his flight was at 6:00 pm, so we scored. I guess Noah's meetings went well and they had a great time surfing together. Heather came home and we decided to go get our toes done, a pedicure sounds nice, relaxing, some serious girl time. I picked out a bright shiny blue polish and had the manicurist paint silver bubbles on top of the blue, stepping out of the box a little. Heather picked bright yellow and had white flowers painted on her big toes. She was way more wild about these things than me.

"Hey, I will be 19 in a few months, I don't want to be stuck in a rut already," I told her. Heather laughed, "Yeah, you're getting so wild in your old age." We left the nail place and headed home. We were leaving at 6:00 pm because the drive up to the stadium could be brutal, the 55 freeway was a traffic jam every day.

Grant and Curt picked us up at our house. Driving up, me in the front with Grant, and Heather and Curt in the back, thank goodness the 2nd row had captain' s chairs or those two would have been all over each other. Curt and Heather were in a heated discussion about I don't know what, probably her bright yellow toes.

I looked at Grant, he takes my breath away every time I see how handsome he is, "Umm, you never told me the rest of the story, you know Ashley."

He gave me a sideways glance, "I know, I promise I will, but now is not the time," as he looked at our companions in the back seat.

"Whose car is this?" I asked.

"It is mine, my graduation present from my parents," he said. A brand new Grand Cherokee Laredo, with every feature available, sleek silver with black interior, very hot.

We pulled in to season ticket holder preferred parking, nice, I thought to myself. Who is this guy I am seeing, I am in awe of him? We walked to our seats, right behind home plate, on the Club Level, did I expect less?

"How did Noah get these tickets, these seats are awesome?" I asked Grant as we were sitting down.

He just smiled at me, "You're so sweet Sydney," giving me a kiss on the lips.

"What?" I said.

"My parents have season tickets to the games. Well, not the whole season- we share the seats with a couple of other families, but we always get the tickets when the Angels play the Yankees," he said with a hint of excitement in his eyes.

"Do you like the Angels or Yankees?" I asked.

"Yankees, of course," he said.

"What…you're a traitor," I said laughing.

"Look my parents are originally from New York and this is my Dad's favorite team, it is how we grew up, die-hard Yankee fans," I just looked at him, I hadn't noticed him sporting a Yankees Jersey with the name of some player on the back. I looked at Curt he had one on too, Heather and I both had on Angel's T-shirts.

The sun was setting and the game was super fun, we had hot dogs, peanuts, and beer. Every time the Angels hit a home run, fireworks were set off, it was great. The fans were cheering and people around us were very nice. However, I did notice a few of the girls around us staring at Grant, whispering about him. He didn't even give it a second thought, as if it was common place for women to stare at him all day long. Seriously, I am not sure how much more of this I could take.

I wanted to yell, "HEY STOP STARING, HAVEN'T YOU EVERY SEEN A KNOCK YOUR SOCKS OFF HOT GUY BEFORE!"

Grant was looking at me funny, while my crazy rant was going on in my head.

"Babe, what is going on inside your pretty little head?" he asked, tapping his finger on my head.

I must have blushed, because he started laughing at me and I think I heard a snort come out of him.

"Did you just snort at me?" I asked.

He kept laughing, "You just look like you were having a conversation with yourself, that's all," he said.

I crossed my arms in a small huff. He pulled me against his side using both arms, "What were you saying to yourself?" he asked.

"How do you know I was talking to myself?"

He gave me that all knowing look, "Because I could tell, your eyes were focused on something and your smile had faded." I was really going to have to learn to keep my thoughts and emotions off of my face.

The game was finally over, I don't think I have ever sat through all 9 innings of a baseball game, Angel's won, 9-8. Grant and Curt were grumpy the whole way home because the Yankees lost.

"Seriously, are you guys going to be upset all night over this, it is just a baseball game," I said.

Well you would have thought I said something outlandish, "Just a baseball game," Curt yelled from the back seat, "Are you kidding me, Grant you better talk with your girlfriend and explain to her, it is never just a baseball game!"

The only thing I heard was the "GIRLFRIEND" part, I like it! Everyone was laughing and we pulled in the garage at Grant and Curt's house.

We climbed out of the car, Grant came around and grabbed my hand.

"Would you like to take a walk on the beach, you can wear my sweatshirt?" he asked.

I nodded my head yes. We were walking down the beach, it was dark, the light from the moon was shining on the water. Grant twirled me around like a ballerina, I was giggling. The water was gently breaking on our feet as the waves went in and out.

"Thank you," I said.

"For what?" he asked.

"So many things, the game tonight, understanding about Trent, and making this summer really great," beaming at him, my eyes were locked on his.

I put my head against his chest and he played with my hair.

Whispering in my ear, "I should be thanking you, you have thawed my frozen heart and made me feel things I didn't know I still could, I think about you all the time. What you are doing, what you are wearing, what you are thinking about. I can smell you on me when we are apart and my mouth can remember how pure you taste." I looked up at him again, leaning down he kissed me.

He took my hand and we went back to his house. We were quiet, not saying anything, the only sounds as we walked were coming from the ocean moving back and forth. There was a small wall surrounding the patio in front of Grant's house. He sat me down on top of it, tilting my chin up to meet his lips, my breathing was picking up, my breasts were beginning to heave with desire, and the lightning bolt shooting through me was like nothing before. This time, this kiss he was giving me took me down, I was completely head over heels for him. The hard fall I had been trying to avoid, had crept up on me without warning. The kiss had me gasping for air, maybe it wasn't only the kiss, maybe it was my heart jumping out of my soul.

We went inside straight to his room, Heather and Curt were in Curt's room, I could hear her giggling, and his muffled voice. Grant had already turned on the music when I came out of the bathroom with just my Angel's T-shirt on. I had taken my shoes and jeans off, you could see just a hint of my black panties from under my shirt. Grant walked over to me, I was leaning against the door jamb. Smiling seductively at him, I was more than ready for him, my insides were excited, not to mention how excited my other parts were.

"I will not allow you to wear this Angel's shirt in my presence any longer," ripping it off over my head. My breathing was getting faster, he was being so intense, making my desires explode.

My eyes were still focused on him, "I like this bra and the panties are nice too, first time I have seen you wearing any," he said, licking his lips.

He pulled his Yankees Jersey off, showing off his hotter than hell upper body. I took a deep breath and moved closer to him, touching his chest with both hands. My hands moving up and down, and my tongue licking his chin, tasting the salt on his neck, I took another deep breath, filling myself with his scent. He was holding onto the door jamb, I unbuttoned the top of his shorts, pulling the zipper down, moving my hand inside to feel him.

I pulled down his shorts with one hand while I stroked his enormous erection with the other hand.

He was gasping, "Sydney, you don't have to do this," he said.

I didn't respond, I kissed his neck again. I slowly dropped to my knees, opening my mouth as much as I could, I took him inside my mouth, deep throating him as far as could without gagging. I moved my head and back forth, not letting go of him using my lips as a clamp, so he could not escape.

I could hear his moans from above me, "Yes, your mouth is undoing me... don't stop" he said.

"Deep throat my dick again."

"Harder, move faster... use your tongue like the other day," his hips were moving, his hands were holding my head and grasping my hair.

I could feel it he was ready to come, "I am going to come, swallow it... swallow it all," he said.

With one last thrust into my mouth, he was groaning, "Oh, yes, Sydney, Oh, God, you are the best."

He was still using the door jamb to steady himself, I was brushing my teeth, with my own toothbrush that I had brought over. He was smiling from ear to ear, completely satiated by my performance.

As I put my toothbrush down, he pulled me over to him, licking a little toothpaste off the corner of mouth, "minty," he said. I just smiled at him.

"Happy?" I asked, knowing full well he was very happy.

"No," he replied, with his sexy smile.

"No, I just gave you the most amazing blow job and you're not happy?" I crossed my arms and took a step back.

He grabbed me and said, "I know you are wet for me, let me taste you again and then I will be really happy." He picked me up and put me over his shoulder, my panties not really covering my ass very well, he smiled and I felt his tongue lick me.

I giggled, "That tickles."

He sat me down on the edge of his bed, the light coming from the bathroom hitting me only across my panties. The music was playing behind me, I could hear Enrique Iglesias and Pit Bull singing "I Like It." He laughed when he heard the song playing, slowly pulled off my panties, I lay down, but he pulled me up.

"Watch me," his voice demanded.

"I don't want to, it is embarrassing."

"I love your body, Sydney, you shouldn't be embarrassed, let me make you feel good," his words melting me from the inside out.

"The light is shining on you, I can see everything," spreading my folds open with both hands, and pushing my thighs wide with his elbows. He pushed one finger inside me and I let out a moan, he was moving his finger inside me, pulling my wetness out, coating my sex, pressing into my clit. He pulled out his finger and when he thrust inside me again, he used two fingers, I was moaning with delight.

"Sydney, look at me I want you to taste yourself," he took his fingers dripping with my juices and put them into my mouth. I laid back on my elbows, dropping my head back. My chest arched up, his fingers were moving inside of me again, his tongue was sliding up down my wetness. I was climbing so high, my hips were starting to grind, his fingers left me, and I could feel him insert his tongue deep inside me.

"I could have you every day like this, I am so hard for you," he said.

He stood up quickly, I could hear the foil packet ripping, he laid down on the bed, pulling me to him. He was lifting me on top of him, he was so hard, as he lowered me on to him. As he entered me, it was pure bliss the feeling I had, every inch of him, no space untouched. This was beyond my own desires, I was grinding on him, my body moving back and forth, he was pinching my nipples, make me groan from the pleasurable pain.

"I am going to explode," I told him.

"Make me come!" I yelled.

"Not yet, a few more seconds, I can't believe how good you feel," he moaned.

"I can't hold on, Grant," I screamed his name over and over, as my orgasm took me over, he was moving me back forth with his hands.

"Sydney, oh God, Sydney, I think I am in love with you," he said.

We were covered in sweat from the intense workout we were having. I fell on top of him, my heart racing, my head spinning from the rocket launching orgasm he gave me. I was panting, he was still inside me, holding me with both arms to his chest, his breathing still sporadic.

I didn't move off of him for a few minutes. Eventually he got up to dispose of the condom and I got up to get some water. I ran back into his room holding two bottles of water, naked.

"Did you just run to the kitchen naked?" he asked, with an unhappy look on his face.

"I forgot we weren't here alone until I heard noises coming from Curt's room, sorry," I said.

He just shook his head, I climbed back into bed with him, putting the cold water bottle on his chest.

"Hey, that is cold!," he screamed. I laughed and drank almost half the bottle in one drink. He looked at me with raised eyebrows, "Parched?"

"You could say that," I said, smiling at him.

I didn't have to be at work until after five tomorrow and Grant had the day off, so we stayed up talking. I didn't bring anything up about Grant's statement of love while we were having sex. Things get said it the heat of the moment, no need to torture myself.

"I am really not in the mood to hear the rest of the story, I just have one question… is Ashley still a part of your life, do you see her on a regular basis?" I asked. It was a valid question.

Grant answered without hesitation, "No, I haven't seen her or had any contact with her in almost two years." Thinking to myself, that is good sign.

"So, what do your parents do, this is a beautiful summer home, they must be very successful," I asked.

Grant smiling, said, "My Dad started a hotel management company before I was born and just has a great business sense, and my mom she is a doctor."

"What kind of doctor, is she?" I asked.

"She works with high profile athletes and celebrities, she is a therapist."

"Oh." I didn't know what to say.

"She started out just working with the athlete's at the University, helping them learn to deal with the stress put on them, then her name got around and the Cardinals and Diamondbacks started sending her clients," he said.

"So, does Noah work for your Dad?"

"Yes he does."

"Is that what you are going to do after you finish at Yale?" I asked.

"Probably, I am not sure."

"Did Noah go to Yale, too?"

"Yes, but Ethan went to Harvard Law School."

"Why the east coast, why not go to school closer to home?" I asked him.

"We all did our undergraduate programs at ASU, that was the deal our parents gave us, they said we had to do our undergrad programs at ASU and then they would allow us, which means pay for us, to go to school on the east coast for graduate school. My parents both went to NYU that is where they met. Then they moved to Arizona after they were married. We were all born in Arizona."

"Miss Stanton, you sure ask a lot of questions-my turn," Grant said, "so, do you have any siblings?"

"Yes, one sister; she is four years older than me, she already graduated from college, working full time trying to decide what she is going to do with her life, but I think she is just waiting for her dorky boyfriend to pop the big question, next question," I said.

Laughing Grant asks, "What do your parents do, wait let me guess, school teacher and post man," he says laughing.

I scowled at him, "You are so far off; my Mom is a Judge in Superior Court and my Dad has a consulting firm. Their schedules are very busy, so I was surprised when they decided to go on vacation for a couple of weeks."

I drank some more of my water, we were still cuddling under the covers.

Running my fingers along the muscles of his stomach, "What is your favorite color?"

"Blue," he said.

"What is your favorite color?" he asked.

"I don't have one, I tend to like yellow."

"Will you miss me when you are in New York, freezing your ass off?" I said, rolling on top of him.

"Freezing my ass off, that is not nice Miss Stanton, let me see how you like this cold water bottle touching your nice ass," he said, I screeched when he put the bottle on my bottom. I was laughing so hard tears were coming to my eyes.

"I am done talking, lets' make out," he said.

I am not sure what time it was when we stopped talking or for that matter what time is was when we stopped kissing. I had fallen asleep with him holding me, it was so nice. I felt safe and warm in a place I didn't want to leave, and I knew I didn't want this to end.

CHAPTER 11

June was here, there were tourists everywhere, the local kids were almost out of school and the beach was busy all the time. Surprisingly, the weather had been beautiful, not too over cast, warm afternoons with sunsets you only see in pictures. We were all busy with work. Kendall decided not to come out until the fourth of July, which was in the middle of the week this year. Not that any of us got the day off, because our shops would be so busy.

Thursday, 10:15 am; Heather to Sydney: lunch?
Thursday, 10:21 am; Sydney to Heather: yes, where? Slice
Thursday, 10:23 am; Heather to Sydney: perfect, noon?
Thursday, 10:24 am; Sydney to Heather: perfect, c u soon.

I met Heather at the pizza place for a slice and soda. We had barely seen each other in days, our work schedules were off, and we were spending most of our free time with Grant and Curt.

"Hey, it is nice to see you for a few minutes," she said to me. Hugging like we didn't see each other every day at home, it was just that we hardly got to talk without one of our hunky boyfriends being around.

"I can't believe June is half over, I mean, it feels like I just got here yesterday. Thank you so much for making me stay down here with you for the summer," I said.

"I am just glad things have been working out, I mean we haven't seen Trent or anyone for weeks, and you and Grant seem to be perfect for each other, don't you think?"

"Perfect, I don't know? I think it is the freedom of knowing there is no long commitment tied up in our relationship, I mean I will be gone in two months and he will be in New York; no real strings. no real heartbreak I guess."

We finished eating and were relaxing before we had to go back to work. We were discussing my relationship with Grant and the fact that a long distance thing would never work. She had the same issues with Curt since he would be going back to Berkley in the fall.

"You know you were wrong about Grant, not being good for me, he has been sooo goooood for me, in more ways than you know," I said.

"Eeew, too much information," Heather said. I just started laughing hysterically. We went back to work and the day passed at a snail's pace. I was anxious to get off so I could stop in to see Grant at work.

Thursday, 4:01 pm; Sydney to Heather: Stopping to see Grant @ work, b home in a few.

Thursday, 4:03 pm; Heather to Sydney: k, ask if they want to go to Captains Club, 2nite.

Thursday 4:05 pm; Sydney to Heather: k.

I was standing in the door way of the hardware store texting, when I heard someone say, "Excuse, me." In a high pitched annoying voice.

"Oh I am so sorry…" I started to say, but when I saw who it was, Blonde Bob Beach Bunny Girl aka Gina, I didn't feel the need to finish my apology.

"Have a great day," she said in her fake voice.

My lip went up with disgust as she left the store, what was she doing here anyways? I could feel my neck tingling, I knew Grant was not far away. I started looking for him up and down the aisles, finally finding him stocking some shelves.

He was up on a ladder putting boxes of paint rollers away, "Hey handsome, you look like you could use a break, come down and I will buy you a smoothie next door," I said.

No response, his muscles were tight and he had a scowl on his face. Great, things had been going so well, what could have happened? I hadn't even seen him since Monday, he had been surfing with Curt all day yesterday.

"Are you coming down to give your girl a kiss or what?" I asked.

No response, I hate the silent treatment. I stood there waiting for a few minutes. Seriously, I was not going to hang around waiting all day, until he decided he wanted to tell me what he is mad about.

"Fine, I am heading home, Heather and I are going out tonight, to the Captains Club, if your mood changes, please join us, if not don't come," I said to him. Still no response.

I walked home muttering to myself, about my one-sided conversation with my boyfriend. Heather was watching TV when I came in and I started banging things around in the kitchen.

"What happened, did you guys get in a fight?" she asked me.

"I am not sure. I went to see him, found him on a ladder, asked him if he wanted a smoothie and he wouldn't respond to me. Then I asked him to come down and give me a kiss- still no response. Argh," I grunted. "So, I told him what we were doing tonight and to meet us if his mood changed and I left, I didn't see Curt so you might want to text him."

"I will text Curt and see what he says," Heather said.

"I am going to lie down outside for a few minutes and try to relax. I don't know why he gets me so mad sometimes," I muttered under my breath.

"I know why," Heather yelled at me, "Do you want me to tell you why?" she asked.

"No!" I was trying to relax. I could hear Heather's phone beeping everytime she got a text, she must have gotten about 10 in a row.

Then I heard her talking on the phone, "No Curt, he needs to come talk to her about it, we didn't know anyone was listening to our private conversation, no don't hang up on me. Do you really think that? Well then you and your cousin should just stay home tonight!" she yelled in to the phone.

She came stomping outside to me, furious her hands clenched into fists, and she was talking through her teeth like her jaw was broken.

"What was that about? I have never heard you two yell at each other, not mad yelling anyways," I said, half joking.

Heather starting yelling, "Well, it seems when we were having lunch today Gina and her friends were sitting in the booth behind us and were listening to our very private conversation. Gina went and told Grant what we were talking about, and Grant told Curt, and now they are super pissed at us."

I sat up on the lounge chair, I could feel the anger brewing inside me, "That is why… I ran into her leaving the hardware store today, when I went to see Grant. She had just gone in to sabotage us, she was all "have a nice day" in her super sugary sweet bimbo voice. Oh my God, she enjoys making my life hell."

Now what? What was our plan here? I know Gina took everything out of context and only told Grant what she wanted him to know about the conversation, the parts to make Heather and I look bad. We had a discussion about trust and communicating, so there would be no miscommunications or jumping to conclusions without all the facts. Unless this was his way of getting out of our relationship before we got in too deep. I didn't want things to end this way, but if he was unable to communicate truthfully with me, what could I do? I did what all girls do, I stewed about it. I went for a run on the beach which would make me feel a little better.

When I got back from my run, laying back on the lounge chair, my feet hanging down, I pulled out my phone. I will text him and put the burden back on him.

Thursday, 6:03 pm; Sydney to Grant: I understand Gina eavesdropped on a private conversation today. She took info out of context. We should discuss. Unless this is your way of getting out of this relationship. U let me know.

No response. We were heading out to the Captains Club. Thursday night there was no entrance fee, and there was a DJ, so we could dance and have a good time, or try to have a good time.

Thursday, 9:00 pm; Sydney to Grant: I don't do the silent treatment game, so if you care about me at all come to the Captains Club tonight. Your failure to respond to me on more than one occasion leaves me with only one conclusion…

Walking to the club I showed Heather the text messages I sent Grant and his failure to respond, she thought I was being too harsh, I didn't.

"He is not playing fair, I put all my cards out on the table for him, I told him everything about me, my relationship with Trent. I told him to communicate with me and he is acting like a middle school kid, I just won't have it and I won't put up with it," I said.

"Well, maybe he will come to the club tonight and you two can hash this out then, can we try to have some fun, let it go for tonight, please," she begged me.

"Why aren't you upset with Curt," I asked.

"Oh, I am. I am just planning on taking it out on him in another way, like withholding sex." We were both laughing as we walked into the Club.

The bouncer no longer carded us since we were coming here once a week since the beginning of the summer. It was already crowded, the DJ was playing, "Call Me Maybe," and people were dancing and having a good time. I saw Rick and Russ from the surf shop, so we headed to their table. I could feel the hairs on the back of my neck start to tingle and eyes burning through the back of my head, but didn't see him. I knew he was here. We stopped by the bar to get a couple of drinks, looking around, I still couldn't find him. The bartender gave us our drinks and we headed to the table. The music changed, "Tongue Tied" was playing by Grouplove.

That is when I saw him on the dance floor, moving, hands on her hips, pulling her into him, she was laughing, putting her finger in her mouth, she looked right at me, as if to say, "I told you he was my man." Her head falling back laughing he was kissing the base of her neck.

I was furious, why would he do this? I pointed Heather's head in the direction of the dance floor, "And you thought I was being too harsh, I feel sick, I thought he actually cared about me, what I fool I am," I said. My stomach was churning inside, I hadn't felt this bad since the whole Trent episode seeing him with other girls.

Curt came up behind us, putting his hands on Heather's shoulders, "I am so sorry. I shouldn't have listened to what Grant said, and I should have asked you first."

He leaned in and gave Heather a kiss. "I know, I am sorry too," she said smiling at up at him.

"We have a problem though," she pointed to Grant dancing with Gina.

"Shit, I am sorry Sydney, I just went to the bathroom, she must have lured him to the dance floor, I will go get him," Curt started to move.

I grabbed his arm, "No don't. Grant is a big boy, he made his choice," I said with a tear coming down my cheek.

"Sydney, he has been drinking, don't hold it against him, go to him, tell him you're here," he said.

"No, he is kissing her neck and his hands are all over her, I can't do this again," I said.

"I am just going to finish my drink and head home."

"Absolutely not. You are not going home to flop around the house feeling sorry for yourself, you are going to stay here and have a good time," Heather said.

"It is summer, you are beautiful, every guy in this club is after your hot body, now let's have some fun," she said.

"Fine, but I will not be held responsible if either one of those two ends up needing medical attention," I told them.

"Don't worry, I will keep him on the other side of the club," Curt said. Just then a round of tequila shots arrived;, lick, salt, shot, lime. Here we go, the night went on like this, beer and many more shots. When I finally stood up to go to the restroom, Heather following, we were cornered in the hall by Gina.

I was feeling pretty happy after all the drinks we had, so Gina's presence was not annoying me too much.

"So," she seethed at me, "Whose man did you say Grant was? Not yours, he was never yours." Laughing she started to walk away from me, I grabbed her arm, holding on pretty tightly.

"You know Gina, you can have him, you can have my sloppy seconds any time," I said.

I went into the bathroom, so mad at myself for saying that, that is not how I felt at all, it made me furious the way he was touching her and allowing her to touch him.

"I should go home, I am drunk, I am going to make a bigger fool out of myself than Grant has already made out of me tonight," I laughed.

"Did that even make sense?" I continued.

When we left the bathroom, Grant was leaning on the wall with his arms crossed, glaring at me. I just walked by him as if there was no one there, just the wall. Heather was pushing me out to the dance floor and away from any fight that was brewing between Grant and me. Drunk as hell, I thought two can play his game, "Neon Hitch" was playing and it was hot, I scanned the room for the hottest guy I could find, well Grant was the hottest guy. So, I found another hot guy, next to the bar, I went out on the dance floor and started to move to the music, Heather was not far from me dancing with Curt. I looked this guy right in the eyes, and seductively mouthed "Come dance with me," and I used my finger telling him to come to me. He walked straight up to me pulling me into him cupping my ass and we began to dance. I knew Grant was watching, I could feel his eyes burning through my soul and the hairs were in full blown salute all over my body.

When the dance was over, I thanked my partner and excused myself to rejoin my party. A few minutes later my dance partner, sent over a round of drinks for our table. Tequila shots of course. He walked up and began massaging my shoulders, introducing himself to me it was so loud I could barely hear him. We did our shots, I thanked him again and he went back to sit with his friends. A few minutes later I saw Grant walk over to him.

Grant was telling him something, the guy pointed at me and then smacked Grant on the back, I could read his lips, "Thanks man thanks a lot!" he was saying. The guy turned around and never looked at me the rest of night.

I stood up and announced, "I am out of here, I've had enough bullshit for one night!"

I walked by the guy I danced with, "What did that guy say to you about me," I slurred out.

"He said not to bother with you, that you were just a tease," I was so mad.

Not that I wanted the guy after me, but really, Grant was being ridiculous. I walked by Gina and Grant, his back was to me and she was sitting on his lap. She gave me a dirty look and I walked right up to them.

Loud enough so Grant would hear me, "You know Gina, Grant has no control, so I hope you know how to get yourself off, because he won't be able to do it for you," I started laughing and was high tailing it to the door.

Grant must have thrown Gina off of his lap, because he caught up to me in record time.

Spinning me around, his eyes cold as ice, "What did you say?" he yelled at me.

"Let me go, I don't even know who you are, the guy I know would never have betrayed me the way you did tonight, dancing with that bleached blonde, making me look like a fool, who are you?" He let me go and I walked out of the club. I was running home, as fast as I could.

Heather and Curt were right behind me coming into the house. "What happened, what did you say to them?" Heather asked.

"He started it with the silent treatment," I am so going to have a hangover tomorrow, "Then hanging all over Gina, making me look like a fool and do you know what he told the guy I danced with, that I am a tease, can you even believe him?"

Curt grabbed my shoulders, "What did you say to him and Gina?"

I made a face like it was bad, both of them looked at me like I was a child, "I was mad and hurt, so I said something about him not being able to bring her to orgasm and she would have to pleasure herself, or something like that."

He deserved it after his behavior tonight. Curt looked at Heather, he grabbed her hand, "Heather let's go to bed and Sydney don't be surprised if he shows up here later, you two are so ridiculous, just face the facts and you will be much happier."

"What, what does that mean? I hate it when people talk in riddles to me," I yelled at him. They just went upstairs to Heather's room.

I lay down on the couch watching TV, with a bag of chips, nothing tastes better than chips when you have too much to drink. I put my head down and the next thing I know my head felt like someone is banging on it with hammer over and over and over again. Geez, I just feel asleep, I am not ready to get up yet. I turned over and put the pillow over my head, but the banging continued. Wait, I sat up, it was not my head, someone was banging on the front door.

"Hold on," I yelled. I was looking for my phone, to see the time. Damn, 1:15 am, who the hell is at the door, my vision was all blurry from sleeping and alcohol. Does that say 10 missed messages, I was walking to open the door, my heart started to pound as I looked at the phone. All the messages were from Grant.

"Who is it," I asked through the door, there was no way to tell through the little peephole.

"Sydney, please open the door, it's me Grant."

Shit, shit, shit. What did he want at this hour?

I opened the door in a huff, "What do YOU want?" I said in the bitchiest tone I could muster.

"I need to see you, I need to tell you I am sorry," slurring his words at me. He tried to hug me and hold me but I pushed him away.

"You smell like her, get off of me, I am tired Grant, go home, we can talk tomorrow." I was trying to shut the door, but he pushed his way in. I stood by the door, hoping he would leave. My heart was aching for him, I just wanted to throw my arms around him, tell him how much he meant to me. But I couldn't.

I closed the door, since Grant was already sitting on the couch with his head back on the cushions. I was thinking a bit more clearly now, since I had stopped drinking hours ago and slept a little, and I mean a little. By the time I walked to the couch, Grant was passed out. I put a blanket on him and went to my room to go to sleep.

When the morning came, the light was shining in to my room. I sat up, dropping my head into my hands, last night had been a huge disaster. Was Grant still a sleep on the couch? I tipped toed downstairs, I could hear him snoring, and he was out cold. I went back upstairs and packed an overnight bag. I left Heather a note:

Heather,

Going to my parents for the night, I will be back for work on Saturday. Text me when you get up.

Luv, Sydney

I snuck out of the house as quickly and quietly as possible, I didn't want to wake Grant and have to discuss last night again. He made his choice. Driving to my parents' house, my eyes filled with tears and I could feel the tears falling down my cheeks. How could he come to me after being with her, I could smell her on him. How did I allow myself into this position again? I guess I didn't learn my lesson well enough after Trent.

It didn't take very long to get to my parents' house, there are not many people on the roads at 5:30 am. My parents were still on vacation, thank goodness, this way I didn't have to explain why I was home. My sister was home and, her bedroom door was closed. Eew, I hope her boyfriend wasn't here.

I lay on my bed, closed my eyes, and slept until my phone started beeping like crazy on my dresser. It was 2:00 in the afternoon when

I got up. I staggered to my phone completely exhausted from the night before. I looked to see all the missed texts. I deleted the first 10 messages from Grant, I did not even want to read them.

Friday, 9:15 am: Heather to Sydney: Where are you?
Friday, 9:17 am: Heather to Sydney: Never mind found your note, call me.
Friday, 10:00 am: Grant to Sydney: Where are you? I need to talk to you.
Friday, 10:11 am: Grant to Sydney: Plz, call me, I am soo sorry.
Friday, 10:35 am: Grant to Sydney: I know I broke your heart, call me.
Friday, 10:49 am: Grant to Sydney: Damn it Sydney, please tell me, r u ok, I will come to where ever u r.

I couldn't read any more of his messages, my heart was breaking.

I went downstairs to get a drink and some aspirin, hoping not to run into my sister or her boyfriend. Thank goodness the coast was clear, oh rats not so fast, they had gone out for a run and were heading back to the house, I could see them coming up the walk. I ran upstairs, trying to avoid them. I decided to call Heather.

She answered on the first ring, "Hey," she said.

"Are you alone?" I asked.

"Yes, Curt took Grant home, he is a mess and I don't just mean a hangover. He went looking for you when he got up this morning and was furious when he figured out were gone."

"Well, I just need to get some perspective and I can't do that down there, you know what I mean."

"Yeah I totally get it, but Sydney you have to come back, you can't just run away, you will be back tomorrow for work, you are going to have to deal with this and figure it out."

My nose was starting to run, I could feel the tears threatening to drip down my face.

"I just…I just don't know what to do, why would Grant behave that way, take Gina's word over mine, not even letting me tell him what was really said, it's like he wanted to believe her, so we would be over," I said to her.

Heather had to leave for work, I told her I would be back in the morning. For now, I was just going to lay by the pool in the backyard and not worry about it. I slept the rest of the afternoon, no one bothered me. I got up and showered around 6:00 pm, there was nothing to eat in the house. So, I took a drive to get a burger, I could have gone to the country club but you never know who you might run into. I was waiting at the light to turn left, almost home, so far so good. I could see him out of my peripheral vision; Trent had pulled up to the light next to me to go straight. Crap-o-la, was what I thought, maybe he won't notice...highly unlikely. He honked his horn and pointed to pull over by the grocery store. I shook my head NO, tapped on my watch, not that I was wearing one, but pretending one was there.

I took off to my parents' house, opened the garage and pulled in closing the garage door behind me. Seriously, if he comes and knocks on the door I am going to go ballistic. I was tip toeing through the house, what was I doing, I am safe inside.

And there it was- the knock on the door, I yelled through the door, "Go away, leave me alone, I don't want anything to do with you."

I looked through the peephole, my heart skipped a beat, it wasn't Trent it was Grant. I looked like hell, I am not even sure if I washed my face or brushed my teeth today. My adrenaline had kicked in and my heart was beating out of my body.

Not sure if I should open the door, but I did anyways. He was standing there, shoulders hunched a little. I had never seen him like this lost, confused, frustrated.

"What do you want, Grant?" I asked.

"Can I come in?" he asked.

"No, you cannot," I said. I was trying very hard not to be a bitch, but I could feel the heat inside me beginning to boil over, remembering his behavior yesterday and last night, taking her word over mine.

"Will you come out and talk to me?" he asked.

"Fine." I closed the door, and sat down on one of the chairs on the porch, not the bench, I didn't want him getting too close to me. I didn't say anything, I figured he had hunted me down to tell me something, I would wait for him to speak...nothing of course. I stood up to go back inside.

He grabbed my hand, as I headed to the door. The bolt of lightning went coursing through me, warming my entire body.

"I know you feel that when I touch you, because I feel it too, every time...I am sorry," he said.

"You are sorry for what...Grant?" I asked.

He started, "I am sorry I wasn't honest with you about Gina, I am sorry I haven't told you the story with Ashley and I am sorry I gave you the silent treatment yesterday."

"What about your behavior at the club? Are you sorry for how you broke my heart by being with Gina, coming to my house at 1:00 am, with her scent on you?"

My voice was getting louder and more vengeful. "Are you sorry for giving me the cold shoulder, for touching her, holding her, kissing her in front of me? Are you sorry for letting her sit on your lap in front of all our friends and allowing her to kiss you all over, making me look like a fool?" He was sitting in the chair, legs open and he didn't say anything he just dropped his head.

I could see tears in his eyes when he looked up at me, he was still holding my hand.

"I know... I fucked it all up, we have something amazing, something I have never had before and I just let my past get in the way of my future."

"Grant I don't know what that means, but I can't do this. You don't trust me and I obviously can't trust you. I am still going to be living with Heather, but I would appreciate it if you would just stay away and leave me alone." He got up visibly upset by what I had said.

"I understand what you are telling me, but I am not happy about it, not happy at all, it is not what I want, I will leave you alone because that is what you want," he said it so sadly like I was the one who had broken his heart. Grant left and I went back inside.

I ended up driving back to the beach late Friday night, the traffic in the morning could be a bear. When I came in the house, Curt, Heather, and Grant were all sitting around the kitchen table eating pizza, assuming I wouldn't be back until tomorrow. Heather gave me 'the look', Grant turned and jumped up.

"Umm, Sydney, will you please talk to me, just give me another chance, I don't want to spend the rest of the summer without you being a part of it. I don't know what to do, how can I get you to forgive me?" smiling at me with his sexy bedroom eyes.

126

I just tilted my head "I don't know, I just don't know, I can't," I stopped. Heather and Curt were just sitting there watching this drama unfold in front of them.

"Continue on," Curt said.

Curt yelled at Grant, "Dude just tell her, stop being a chicken shit, and tell her!"

"Tell me what, I can't handle any more bad news, what is it?" I asked.

It was like the flood gates of his mouth opened and he didn't shut up.

"Sydney, I didn't have sex with Gina, I didn't do anything with her, not last summer and not this summer. I didn't enjoy her touching me, I only did it to make you mad because I was so mad at you for what you said at the pizza place, which I didn't talk to you about, I just assumed the worst and now you hate me. I acted like a fool, I embarrassed you at the club by pretending to be with Gina."

Curt yelled again, "Chicken shit... whimp... tell her!"

Grant yelled back, "Shut. Up. Curt."

He grabbed my hand and took me outside to the patio. We were sitting on the big couch, he was holding both my hands in his looking down.

"Jesus Grant, what is it? Did you lie to me about Ashley, are you still in touch with her do you two have a child together, what is it?" My voice was cracking and tears were threatening to give me away.

He started talking again, "Ashley? No, none of those things you said. Let me tell you about her, I told you I loved her or thought I did and believed in my heart that she loved me. She told me she was pregnant with my child."

"I was ready to give up everything for her, I was not going to go to Yale, I would have gone straight to work for my dad after graduation. We were going to live with my parents so they could help. We were supposed to get married after the baby was born. But the baby came early, really early and while in the NICU, the blood tests showed some genetic disorder. When I asked my parents about it they said we had nothing like that on our side of the family. My Mom had an amniocentesis when she was pregnant with me since she was over 35, her test came back clear which raised a serious red flag, for me."

"When I questioned the doctors they said this particular genetic disorder was carried through the birth father's bloodline and if my mother's amniocentesis was clear then there was no possible way I could be the father of this baby. I was devastated, the women I loved and the child she had been carrying was not even mine. They did a blood test to be certain. She had lied to me for months, she had sex with someone else before I came back to school for junior year." I just looked at him, tears were falling down my face.

"What happened to the baby?" I asked.

"The baby didn't make it."

"Ashley's betrayal has made me, for better lack of terms, gun shy. I follow with my head, never my heart, because I thought I was following my heart with her and I ended up getting my heart crushed on so many different levels."

I really didn't know how to respond to what he just shared with me. It was a heartbreaking story and I truly had empathy for him. But I wasn't Ashley.

"I just don't know what to do here. Grant, you just told me you don't follow your heart you only use your brain to protect yourself from getting hurt again. I totally understand, but I followed my brain all year at school and I was miserable, never allowing myself to get close to anyone because I didn't want to get hurt again. And then I saw you holding your beer by the bonfire and I couldn't take my eyes off of you, you made every part of me tingle with excitement and I didn't even know your name. I am not Ashley and I am sorry for what she did to you, but I shouldn't be held accountable for her actions. I have given you no reason not to trust me."

I looked away, he was still holding both of my hands, and my tears were flowing again, dripping down my face. "I have been following my heart with you from the first night I saw you. When we shook hands in the hardware store and the electricity sparked, I knew we would be different. I know from the lightning bolts that course through me every time we touch, I know... I love you."

"Did you just tell me you love me? I didn't think you would ever say that to me, after how I have behaved. I love you too, Sydney Stanton. I love you too."

He kissed me with his entire being. I could feel my body begin to shake from his touch, I was so happy.

"Well, just to be clear, I did say it first and don't tell me it doesn't count because it does," a smile as big as a ship across his face.

Curt yelled, "Did you tell her yet man, we are dying to know?"

We walked back into the kitchen where Heather and Curt were still sitting holding hands and being all giggly with each other.

We were all exhausted and headed to our rooms to go to bed, "Can we sleep here tonight? We always sleep at your place."

He hopped up on my bed and wiggled his eyebrows at me, "Come to bed my love, I have something to show you," he said laughing.

I made a funny face, "That sounds disturbing, don't ever say that to me again!"

CHAPTER 12

June was turning out to be a very hot month, temperatures were over 85 degrees everyday and that is very warm for the beach. People everywhere were trying to escape the heat of the inland cities. The yogurt shop was packed all the time, everyone and their brother needed new summer clothes, so the surf shop was busy all day everyday and the hardware store had people in and out all day too.

We didn't see Gina for a very long time and I think she was more embarrassed of her behavior that dreadful night at the club than we were. The four of us; me, Grant, Heather, and Curt were together all the time. Grant was trying to teach me to surf, but I was always too scared to stand up on the surf board. However, Heather was the perfect student, Curt had no problem teaching her, she was almost ready to get her own board and try it alone.

I had introduced Grant to my parents when they came home for a few days, my parents are super overprotective and were wary of his intentions. I tried to explain to them that we were just having a fun summer and not to worry so much. My sister almost passed out when Grant walked in the house, I mean, his good looks will stop you in your tracks every time. Tall, lean, tan, muscles in places I didn't know you could have muscles, and he is sweet as pie. This guy was a godsend, too bad it was only for the summer. We had dinner with my family and my Dad asking Grant a million personal questions would only be the beginning of the embarrassment.

It was almost the Fourth of July, Kendall and Matt are coming out for a few days and are staying with Heather and I at the beach. I can't wait to introduce Kendall to Grant, and Curt of course.

"Honey I'm home, where are you?" I could hear Grant calling for me.

"Oh darling, I am out on the veranda, please join me," I yelled back to him in a snooty voice. I was laughing when he came out on to the patio.

"You are such a dork," I said as I jumped up to kiss him.

"Mm mm…you smell good, new shampoo?"

"No, I just got back from the beach."

"You smell like heaven, salt and sand, two of my favorite things," he said. I put my hands on my breasts and pushed them towards him.

"I thought these were your two favorite things," I said mockingly. Not a good idea to tempt your man.

He was pulling me in to the house, "Wait, let me rinse off in the outside shower, so I don't get sand in your bathroom."

I was wearing one of the many new bikinis I had bought at the surf shop. I walked to the side of the house and turned on the rain shower. I was only under the water for a minute, when Grant came up behind me. He had taken off his shirt exposing his sexy body, he wouldn't let me turn around to touch him.

"This is not fair," I said. He had a bottle of body wash with him. I heard him squeeze some into his hands and he begin to wash my back up and down, massaging as he went. He went from my shoulders, lathering up my entire back, down to the backs of my feet, stopping at my inner thighs. I gasped as his hands washed around the edges of my bikini bottom. His hands went back above my shoulders, coming down around my front, he massaged my breasts through the bikini top, lathering everything in his path. His hands glided down my abdomen, and he cupped my sex through the bikini, rubbing over and over again, making the bikini rub over my sensitive spot until I was moaning in his ear, "I want you."

"I haven't finished washing you yet," he whispered in my ear.

He continued his torturous pleasure attack on me, lathering my feet, legs, knees and then back to my inner thighs. He was in front of me now, I had moved up against the wall and the water was still falling over us. I needed the wall to help support me, my legs already felt like jelly from the desire he was filling me with. He took the handle of the shower and was rinsing me off, he lifted the edge of my bikini bottom away from my body and was shooting the hot water down, and the sensation was spectacular. I was licking my lips wanting him to take me right here in the outside shower.

My hands began to reach for him, but he grabbed both wrists together and put my hands high above my head. I was already completely ready for him, my body was arching to him, I wanted him to continue touching me, but he had other plans. I could feel my climax burning through me just waiting for its release. I could barely get enough air in my lungs to keep me going. I was so hot, I could see his erection through his shorts, I knew he was ready.

"Grant please, just take me here, I can't wait any longer," I was pinned against the shower wall, his waist pressing against mine, and I began to grind against his bulging erection trying to get him to give me what I wanted. He lifted one of my legs and wrapped it around his waist, he released my arms and at the same time untied the string on my bikini bottom. My bikini fell to the bottom of the shower. I went to unzip his shorts, but he grabbed my hand stopping me.

"Not yet."

Leaning in and kissing my neck.

"Undo your bikini top," he said. I did that too and it fell to the shower floor. He leaned in kissed by breasts, licking each nipple until I thought I would come just from his touch.

"I want to see you touch yourself, Sydney, show me how you pleasure yourself," he said with a sultry tone.

"I don't... do that, I have never done that."

"Then show me what you want me to do to you."

He leaned in and kissed me hard, "Once you show me what you want, I will give you what you want, do you understand, but I don't want you to come until I am inside of you."

I nodded my head yes in agreement. I love when he gets all dominant and possessive of me in the bedroom... or in the shower. I took my hands and gently cupped my breasts, playing with my nipples, pulling on them to make them hard.

"Holy hell, you are so hot Sydney, I may not make it inside of you," he swallowed hard and moaned.

My back was arching more with my longing for him, he had me so wound up. I thought I might explode any second. My body was making moaning noises, my obvious pleasure from the feelings I was having. I kept one hand playing with my nipples and slowly moved my other hand over my belly button and down my lower stomach, I took his hand in mine and pulled them both through the wet folds of my sex, then I took both of our fingers and thrust them in his mouth and then into mine. My hips were moving, grinding on him. I grabbed the back of his head and pulled him down to kiss me, I kissed him with such force I bit his bottom lip just a little.

I knew with those moves he wouldn't remain in control much longer, we slipped in through the side door and headed right for his room. I hadn't even closed the door to his room before he was putting on a condom and pushing me back up against the wall, lifting my leg, he thrust inside me, penetrating me, his erection filling me, my sex clamping around his enormous erection.

"Oh...God... Sydney, I am ready," with one last thrust, my world burst into a million beads of light around me, I had climbed so high while outside, my orgasm was swirling around me, my body was spinning from the explosion. Grant was holding onto me, still pushing into me, and making manly groaning noises of complete satisfaction.

He picked me up and carried me to the bed, putting me down he kissed my lips, "Sydney Stanton, you rock my world every time, I love you." He walked into the bathroom and came out jumping on to the bed. I was under the covers, half into never, never land.

"I love you too, my hot bonfire guy," I whispered in his ear. We took a long nap together, holding each other while we slept.

I was not fully awake but I could hear footsteps upstairs, lots of footsteps. Then I could hear someone calling for Grant and Curt. The voice was getting closer.

"Grant wake up, someone is calling for you," I was pushing him to wake up.

"Answer my phone then," he said.

"Not on your phone, from inside the house, someone is calling for you, get up!"

He jumped straight up and listened.

"It is just my parents," he said sitting back down all relaxed.

"What- your parents? When were you going to tell me they were coming!" I barked at him.

"I told you they were coming out for the first two weeks of July," he gave me one of his raised eyebrow looks. "Didn't I tell you?"

"No you didn't tell me. Now I am naked standing in their sons' bedroom and I have never even met them. Ugh, nice impression this will make."

Grant was smirking at me. "Put your clothes on then," he said. He was so cool about stuff like this, never getting uptight or embarrassed, and I was totally freaking out.

"Dude... my bikini is on the bottom of the outside shower, go get it for me and then I will put on a pair of shorts over it, and one of your t-shirts, hurry up."

"Relax, my parents know all about you and they are fine with us having sex."

I looked at him like he was nuts, am I hearing him correctly?

"You talk to your parents about our sex life? This is weird, you're nuts," I told him.

"Just put on a pair of my boxer shorts and t-shirt, you can say your suit was all sandy so you left it outside, they will believe that. It's not as if they don't already know how hot I am for you," winking at me.

"This is a very odd conversation, can you move any faster?" I yelled at him in a hushed tone.

I was in the bathroom getting dressed, if you can call going commando under your boyfriends clothes dressed.

I could hear the knock on the door and the door opening, "Grant, didn't you hear me calling you?" his mother asked.

"Sorry mom, Sydney and I fell asleep, I have been teaching her how to surf and we were just wiped out," he told her.

"Well, where is she? Your father and I can't wait to meet her."

"She is in the bathroom, we will be up in a minute," he said.

"Oh, your brothers will be here later today or tomorrow, I can't remember what they said."

She walked out of his room. I came out of the bathroom and rolled my eyes at him. I punched him in the arm.

"Shit Grant, you could have given me some warning your whole family was coming to town."

I tried to make myself look like I hadn't just woken up from an 'I just finished getting some loving with your son nap'.

"Sydney stop fussing, you look beautiful, you always look beautiful, even when you're snoring you look beautiful," I punched him again.

"Ouch, stop doing that," he said.

"Okay, fine" I said, "lead me into the lion's den; your parents are going to hate me."

"I love you, they will adore you, Noah already told them how great you are, let's go meet the lions," he roared at me.

"You are in so much trouble for this fiasco!"

As we headed up the stairs, he gave me his wickedly sexy smile and said just before we entered the main kitchen upstairs, "I love when you say I am in trouble, it means good things are coming my way." Holding my hand we took the last step around the corner, into the main kitchen.

CHAPTER 13

Not having spent much time on the main floor of the Montgomery's beach house, it took me a minute to take in the perfectly decorated surroundings. The main floor had a huge kitchen with breakfast bar, and a long table with chairs on three sides and long bench on the fourth side. There was an enormous fireplace in the center of the family room and a very large sectional couch. There was a large TV over the fireplace and the sound system was playing soft classical music. The glass sliding doors to the balcony were open with the ocean breeze flowing through the room. The walls were finished in Italian plaster in beautiful earth tone colors.

Grant's parents were standing in the kitchen. Mr. Montgomery was leaning on the granite counter facing us, Dr. Montgomery was standing in between his legs, his hands holding her at her lower back, and she was looking up at him talking in a hushed voice. I saw his head come up as we entered the room and the twinkle in his eyes when he looked our way.

He kissed her cheek and said "Corinne, Grant and Sydney are here."

She turned around in his arms, I could see her taking in our approach. We were still holding hands walking into the kitchen.

Mr. Montgomery, moving away from the counter, came right up clasping Grant on the back and giving him a bear hug, "Son, you look great, the summer is doing right by you," he said.

"And Sydney, it is a pleasure to finally meet you," he said giving me an unexpected hug.

"It is nice to meet you too, Mr. Montgomery," I said.

"Sydney, please call me Kevin, Mr. Montgomery is my father."

"Um, okay Kevin," I said hesitantly. Grant took my hand, he had already greeted his mother and she was finished kissing his cheeks.

"Mom, this is Sydney Stanton. Sydney this is my Mom, Corinne," he introduced us.

I put my hand out to shake, "Sydney, you are just beautiful, the pictures don't do you justice," she said, giving me a hug "and please call me Corinne."

"Um, okay," I said.

"Why don't we all sit down for a few minutes and get to know each other. Would anyone like something to drink?" his Mom asked.

"Grant, Kevin, would you like a beer, water?" she asked, walking to the fridge.

"Yeah sure," they both said.

Grant looked at me, "Sydney, are you thirsty?"

"I'll help you Dr. Montgomery," I said.

I went in to the kitchen, "Corinne, please honey, call me Corinne. Would you like some water or a soda, this fridge only has beer in it," she said giving Grant a funny smile.

"Sorry Mom, we have soda down stairs, we just keep the extra beer up here."

I handed Grant and Kevin their beers and sat down on the bench next to Grant. Putting my phone down on the table, I was waiting for Kendall to call to tell me when they were less than 10 minutes away. I opened my water and took a long drink. I could feel Grant's hand on my thigh under the table.

Dr. Montgomery came and sat down at the table across from us with Mr. Montgomery next to her.

"So, we understand you are living with your girlfriend Heather for the summer, and working at the surf shop. Heather and Curt, are they still dating?" she asked.

Grant said, "Yes Mother."

"Just confirming before your Aunt and Uncle arrive, where do your parents live?" she asked me.

"Well my parents live about 30 minutes north of here," I replied. Great this was an inquisition, trying to figure out my intentions with their son. Their son who had already been burned once, which they knew all about.

"So, why aren't you staying with them during the summer, are they divorced?" she asked.

"*Mother*... that was forward," Grant said giving her the eyebrow furrowed look.

"Grant it is fine, no my parents are not divorced, um, well, when I came home from school for the summer I came down to visit Heather, and Russ, who runs the surf shop, offered me the job, and it is just easier to stay down here then drive back and forth, especially with gas so expensive, Heather would have been living alone all summer while her parents were off travelling the world," I said in one long breath. I could see Grant getting annoyed with his parents, he must have known there were more questions coming.

"Sydney, what are you plans? Are you going to continue working and take classes at the community college?" his father asked.

"Dad, I told you, Sydney is only here for the summer. She just finished her freshmen year at ASU, do you have short term memory loss or something?"

"Oh, yes, that is right, I forgot, sorry son. Do you have a major yet?" he asked me.

"No not yet, I am still undeclared. I am not sure what I want to do when I grow up," I said smiling.

Grant started to get up, "Okay," he said, "I think that is enough questions for one sitting, you guys have two weeks to ask Sydney all you want to know."

"Wait a minute," his Mother said, "sit back down, we won't ask any more questions. Let's just go over a few things now that we are in town. We know you two have become very close and probably have your own routine. We are fine with you guys spending the night together here or at Sydney's house. We just have a few concerns," she said.

I was squeezing Grant's hand under the table completely mortified by the conversation we were having with his parents. I could feel my face turning red. His father was sitting back in his chair, one hand around the back of his wife's chair, the other holding his beer, taking a drink he winked at Grant. Grant just smiled and shook his head. His Mother continued, "We are happy that you two are having a great summer together, we just want to make sure you are taking precautions and not having unprotected sex," my mouth dropped open, I closed it fast, I didn't want her to see me so shocked by her bluntness.

Grant said, "Mom, she is on the pill and I am using a condom every time, is that good enough for you?" I turned to look at him with my mouth dropped open again. Now I know my face is bright red.

"Also, Sydney you should keep some clothes here so you don't have to wear Grant's clothes, I mean that is fine once and a while but, like today, I am sure you would feel much more comfortable in your own clothing." My eyes got so wide I thought I would die of embarrassment right here at the table. Thank goodness my phone started buzzing, I looked over to Grant, he was shaking his head and taking a drink of his beer. Saved by my phone I thought to myself.

"Excuse me, I have been waiting for this call," I grabbed my phone and walked out on to the balcony.

Before I answered the phone, I could hear Grant saying, "Jesus mother you are going to scare her away, do you have to be so forward and blunt. Geez, she is not used..."

Answering my phone, "Hello," I said.

"Hey, Syd, we will be at the house in less than 10 minutes," Kendall said.

"Wow, you guys made great time," I said back, but my voice was shaking.

"What is wrong, are you okay?" Kendall asked.

"Yeah, I am fine. I just finished meeting Grant's parents, this is a great story," I said.

"Okay, I will be home to let you guys in, you remember how to get to the house?" I asked.

"Yep, see you in a few, bye" and I hung up. I was leaning on the balcony railing looking at the ocean, Grant came up behind me putting his hands down on each side of mine on the railing.

"Sorry," he whispered in my ear.

I put my head back on his shoulder, "Your mother gets right to the point, she doesn't mince words, has she always been this way?" I asked.

"Well yes, her work, raising three boys, and the drama from the Ashley incident, she just puts it all out there not wanting any false pretenses or misunderstandings," he told me.

His parents came out on to the balcony where we were standing.

"Sydney is everything okay?" Mr. Montgomery asked.

"Oh yes, my girlfriend and her boyfriend are coming in town from Arizona for the Fourth of July and they will be at my house in a few minutes. I should probably be heading home," I said.

Both his parents gave me a big hug and walked off talking about going to Costco to stock up on stuff.

"Oh kids, make sure you take the evening of Saturday the 14th off and all day Sunday, we have a surprise for Sydney, and let Curt and Heather know to do the same," his Dad said as they continued to walk upstairs.

"What is that about?" I asked Grant.

He just smiled and said "I have no idea."

I smacked his chest, "Yes you do... tell me."

"I can't, you heard my Dad- it is a surprise."

Just then Noah walked through the side door by the outdoor shower, yelling up to us on the balcony, "Hey lovebirds, does this belong to either of you?" he said holding up my very skimpy bikini. Seriously, could I have been more mortified.

"Oh my God, I thought you went and picked that up," I said hitting Grant's chest again.

Grant and Noah were both laughing.

"I have to go. Do you want to walk me home and meet Kendall and Matt?" I asked him, walking down stairs to get my flip flops and keys.

"Will you be mad if I just walk you home but don't stay? I would like to visit with my parents for a little while before I have to go back to work."

"No not at all," I leaned up and gave him a kiss on the lips. "Why are you going back, you worked this morning?" I asked.

"I told the owner I would come in to close up for him."

I got home a few minutes before I heard Kendall and Matt drive up. I had opened up all the windows in the house and the guest room, and I was waiting for them on the patio. Kendall came running up, so excited to be here, Matt was in awe of his surroundings.

"This is awesome," he said.

Kendall and I were hugging, jumping up and down, "I am so glad you are here, we are going to have fun," I said to them.

"Are you guy's hungry? Let me show you your room, Heather is at work, she should be home in about an hour."

I took them upstairs to the guest room, "Come out to the patio when you are done getting settled and help yourself to anything in the fridge." Today was Monday and they would be here until Thursday, the Fourth of July was Wednesday.

I was lounging on the patio waiting for them, thinking over my introduction to Grant's parents. I had never met parents who spoke so openly with their children about sex and relationships. His parents were different but in a good way. Kendall and Matt came down and I told them the whole story about meeting Grant's parents.

"Wow, I can't imagine my parents or yours talking like that," Kendall said laughing a little.

"I know, right? It was bizarre," I said.

It was only about four in the afternoon, "So do you guys want to go to the beach, what do you want to do?" I asked.

Matt said, "I think I am going to take a nap, I am tired after the drive, and cramming for summer finals."

"Can we go do a little shopping in town? I need a new bikini," she said.

"Of course, we can go to the surf shop and you can use my employee discount, and we can stop to say hi to Heather, let's go," I said.

She looked at me funny, "What?" I asked.

"Are you going to change or are you going to walk around in Grant's boxers all day?" she pointed to my clothes.

"Oh, crap I forgot, I will be right back."

We walked down to the shops on the main street, talking nonstop the whole way. She told me about shadowing the current Rush Chairman and how much work there is to putting on Rush, it sounded overwhelming. Next year Kendall would be Rush Chairman so it was a good experience for her. She talked about her classes and how ridiculously hot it is in Arizona.

"You know, you have to be back at school in mid-August," she reminded me.

"I know, why are bringing it up?" I asked.

"Because you just seem so happy here. You're not going to drop out and stay here with him are you?" She said with concern in her voice.

"Why would I do that? He is leaving for Yale in September and I am not going to drop out of school for any guy, not even if I love him."

"What? You love him?" Kendall shrieked. "You have only been together for like a month," she said shaking her head at me.

"I know but he is different, he makes my heart skip a beat, and you don't even want to know what he does to the rest of my body," I said giggling.

She scrunched her nose at me, "Gross Sydney, you are just gross." We entered the yogurt shop laughing, Heather let out a high pitched screech when she saw us walk in. She came around from behind the counter hugging Kendall.

"I will be off in a few minutes, you guys want anything?" she asked.

"No," we both said.

"We will be at the surf shop, Kendall wants a new bikini," I said saying the word bikini real slowly.

We shopped the rest of the afternoon. Kendall was on a mission and was giving her credit card a serious workout. Heather caught up with us at the bookstore.

"Have you guys read the 50 Shades trilogy yet?" Kendall asked.

"Of course, I finished all three books in less than a week, but Heather has been slacking and not reading, I think she is only reading the kinky parts and then acting them out with Curt," I said laughing. Heather just stuck her tongue out at me.

"Yikes, really," she turned to Heather.

"You are such a bad girl."

"You guys are mean," Heather stomped off. We were all laughing. We left the bookstore.

"Kendall, do you want to meet Grant?" I asked, "He is working at the hardware store right now.

"Hell yes, let's go," she said. We walked down the street laughing and talking.

Gina walked by us, "Hi girls," she said in her bitchy voice.

"Hi Gina," Heather said with a bitter tone.

"Who was that, she is umm, she looks like a slut?" Kendall asked.

"She is," Heather said laughing.

"We'll tell you about her later," I said.

"Tell me now, you know I love a good story," Kendall demanded.

"We can't, we're here," I said.

I knew he was close to me because I had that tingling sensation running through my whole body. I said hi to the girl at the checkout stand.

"Do you know where Grant is?" I asked.

"Yeah, he is helping Mr. Watson pick out paint colors for his granddaughter's playhouse. Do you want me to page him?" she asked.

I shook my head no and headed to the paint aisle with Heather and Kendall. Grant was in a deep discussion holding up paint color samples trying to help Mr. Watson decide what color to choose, when the three of us came walking up.

Mr. Watson's jaw dropped open as he looked at the three of us and then to Grant, "You are a lucky young man," he said. I think Grant blushed, what- was he actually embarrassed? This is too funny, I couldn't resist so I walked up closer and said, "Hey boyfriend," giving him a long kiss.

Mr. Watson just hit him on the back, took his paint samples and walked away mumbling, "Yeah, one lucky guy."

We were all giggling except Grant, he said, "Did you enjoy embarrassing me in front of Mr. Watson?"

"Well… yes… yes, I did," I said. "Grant this is Kendall, Kendall this is Grant." They shook hands, we all talked for a minute and then he was called away to help a customer.

He smacked my butt, and said "See you later hot stuff. Heather, Curt is in the back if you want to see him."

I just shook my head and walked away, "He is so weird sometimes," I said. We walked to the back of the store to introduce Kendall to Curt.

Heather chimed in, "Kendall get used to it, they are like this all the time, hands all over each other, whispering in each other's ears, it is so annoying."

"Really, annoying huh, not as annoying as hearing you call out 'Curt…oh God Curt…don't stop,'" I said.

Heather and I were rolling, Kendall not one to talk about her sexual antics, rolled her eyes and said "Can you keep your private stuff private?"

"Kendall, loosen up we are just joking around. You mean you don't call out Matt's name in the throes of passion?" Heather asked.

"I am not sharing," she said.

"We will find out over the next few days, the walls in the house are not made of stone you know," I said, and walked off to get a drink at the Blue Moon Café. Kendall was texting Matt to meet up with us and have dinner. The three of us were sitting, have a cold drink, talking about what we could do for the next few days.

"Okay, I have to work the Tuesday morning and Wednesday morning shifts, but I will be off both days by two. Heather has the same schedule as me. So you and Matt will be on your own. The Montgomery's are having a big Fourth of July party, so we will head over there in the afternoon, you know the usual; bbq, bonfire, beach football, and then the City shoots off fireworks around 9:00 pm, sound good?"

"Do I have a choice?" Kendall asked.

"No, not really," I said. Matt walked up then and we headed over to the pizza place for dinner.

We were eating pizza, talking, and having a good time. I was kind of missing Grant because I knew he would have enjoyed this evening. I pulled out my phone and sent him a text.

Monday, 7:30 pm: Sydney to Grant: Hey, missing you having pizza with everyone, coming over tonight?

Monday, 7:35 pm: Grant to Sydney: Miss u 2! Umm, Ethan coming in 2nite, surfing early, work @ 10. C U, 2morrow, ok?

Monday, 7:39 pm: Sydney to Grant: no problem, c u, after work, around 5, luv u!

Okay, not seeing him tonight would be different, but with his whole family in town how could I blame him. We finished up and headed home. Curt was sleeping at home too, since his parents were in town for the holiday. Man that house must have at least six bedrooms...big house.

By the time we got home it was late and I was tired, we were all tired. I had to work at 9:00 am, so I headed to my room to go to sleep. Heather went to her room, and Kendall and Matt stayed up lounging on the patio by the fire pit, and listening to the ocean in the distance.

CHAPTER 14

Heather and I both woke up late, getting a very good night's rest since neither of our men spent the night, keeping us up until all hours. We ran out of the house like crazy people not wanting to be late for work. Tomorrow is the Fourth of July and shops in town were going to be busy. I got to work on time, started my usual routine; stocking shelves, helping customers, and various other duties. I was behind the counter looking for the price gun when I felt it, my tingling sensation, I looked at the clock on the wall- 9:50 am, I thought he had to work at 10:00 am. I slowly stood up and he was leaning on the counter with his back to me, damn I am so good, I knew he was here.

In a deep kind of gruffly voice I said, "Umm, excuse me is there something I can help you with?"

He didn't turn around to look at me.

"Yes, I am looking for that HOT girl that works here, she usually has on a fitted black t-shirt, short shorts, and high top white tennis shoes, blonder hair, and hazel eyes, do you know her? You know sometimes, if she moves in just the right way, her shirt rides up and you can see just enough of her bare skin to give you goose bumps."

Then he turned around and smiled at me. I came around from behind the counter, I slid my hands up his tight chest letting them rest right on his pecs and said, "I missed you last night," giving him the most seductive look.

"Don't start teasing me I won't be able to make it through the day."

"I know I can feel my favorite part of your body getting hard," I whispered in his ear.

He looked down at me, gave me a kiss, and was out the door to go to work, but not before he smacked my ass, and said "See you later hot stuff."

"Ouch," I said. Seriously, he needs to stop doing that. I was rubbing my bottom where he smacked me.

Russ walked out from the back room, "You know we have video surveillance in here right?" He asked me.

"So, are you implying I am stealing from you?" I looked at him with an annoyed face.

"Absolutely not, I just want you to know, cuz we all just watched your little encounter with Grant on the monitor set up in the back," he said walking away laughing.

I think I was getting used to all these embarrassing moments, because I was not fazed by that in the least. The morning was zooming by as customers were in and out the whole time. Then I heard Grant's mom's voice as she came in to the store.

"Sydney?" I heard her call my name.

"Hi Dr. Montgomery, how are you today?" I said.

"Dear, *please* call me Corinne, why do I have to keep reminding you? This is my sister Courtney, Curt's mom."

"Hi," I said, shaking her hand.

"Courtney and I are looking for some new swimsuits for this little vacation we are on, do you have anything for us old ladies?" she said half laughing.

Courtney smiled and said, "You're older than me, so I am not an old lady." I just smiled not wanting to laugh and offend either one of them.

I took them over to the higher end suits; "What sizes? Do you like underwire? What style are you looking for?" I asked.

Believe me, these ladies were in good shape, not body builder shape, but I hope I look that good when I am their age.

"Sydney, you just pick stuff out you think we will like and set them in a dressing room for us while we look around," she said.

"Sure no problem," I said hesitantly. I could see Russ watching me I was all flustered waiting on my boyfriends' mom and his aunt. I got them all set up, they had picked out all kinds of clothes to try on;

dresses, shorts, and tank tops. They were in the dressing rooms trying on suits.

"Sydney, do you think Kevin will like this bathing suit?" she asked like I am her BFF.

"Umm… don't you think Courtney's opinion would be more fitting?" I asked.

"Don't be silly dear you're a young woman, tell me what you think."

She opened the door, wow she looked good.

"You look great, yes he will like it," I said.

Corinne pointed at her breasts, "Oh, Sydney listen, these are not real. I had them done after Grant stopped nursing, they were saggy and all," she informed me.

I let out a nervous laugh. Wow, too much information, she is definitely very open. They each bought a couple of new suits, shorts, tank tops, sundresses, flip-flops, and a pair of flats.

They were set, "Thanks honey for all your help, and by the way, we are really happy you and Grant are getting along so well. He deserves to be happy and it seems you are the one making him happy. Have a great day, see you at house for dinner, don't forget to ask for the 14th and 15th off," she yelled as they walked out the door.

"So, that was an interesting shopping trip," Russ said to me as I leaned against the counter.

"Interesting being the key word," I said.

"Russ, can I have the 14th and 15th off?" I asked him.

"Yeah, just send me an email and I will put it on the calendar."

"Thanks." I pulled out my phone.

Tuesday, 11:05 am: Sydney to Grant: Hi, ur mom and aunt just in here, bought out the store. Ur mom is very very open. Think they are headed ur way, good luck.

Tuesday, 11:07 am: Grant to Sydney: they r walking in the door. Do I want to know, what she said?

Tuesday, 11:08 am: Sydney to Grant: probably not!

Tuesday, 11:09 am: Sydney to Grant: got the 14th and 15th off!

Kendall and Matt stopped in on their way to lunch to see if I could join them, but the shop was slammed. I didn't take a lunch and Russ ordered pizza in for all of us since no one could leave for a break. When my shift finally ended I was wiped out. I sat down on the bench outside the shop to rest for a few minutes and wait for Heather.

We walked home and plopped on the lounge chairs on the patio.

I asked Heather, "Do you know what time we are supposed to be over there for dinner?"

"7:00," she said.

"Great, it is already 5:30, I was hoping for a nap and shower, guess I will skip the nap and take a shower. Have you met Curt's parents before?" I asked.

"Very briefly last summer, but we had just met and nothing had happened between us yet, it should be interesting tonight with both families together," she said.

"Does Curt have siblings?" I asked.

"Yeah... older brother...younger sister."

"You should see the bathing suits their mom's bought today, sexy, you know Grant's mom had her boobs done," I said.

"How do you know?" Heather asked laughing.

"She told me today, she is way open, talks about sex, nursing Grant, my Mom would never talk about that stuff, she is a breath of fresh air," I said.

"You're just head over heels for Grant, so everything about him is great in your eyes," she said. I gave her a nasty look and took off to take a shower.

I yelled downstairs, "Hey make some margaritas so we can be a little more relaxed when get to Grant's later, thanks."

We all got ready; me, Heather, Kendall, and Matt. We had a couple of drinks and then headed over to Grant's for dinner. The house was full of people, Grant's parents, Noah, Ethan and his wife, Curt's parents and his younger sister. We have spent a lot time over here, just not on the second floor with Grant's entire entourage. All the introductions were made, but when Matt and Grant were introduced I got the feeling they had met before. They were on the balcony talking and Grant has his arm on Matt's shoulder. I couldn't hear what they were talking about. This should be a more interesting evening than I had already anticipated. Heather was getting the inquisition from both Grant's mom and Curt's mom. I just laughed, walking with Kendall to where the guys were on the balcony.

They stopped talking as soon as we were in ear shot, the only thing I heard was Matt say, "she is going to find out so just come clean with her."

"So," I asked, "do you two know each other from the Fraternity House?"

Grant spoke right up, "Yeah, I remember when Matt came through Rush, we really wanted him to join the house and lucky for us he did."

I gave Matt a sideways glance, knowing he knows something he is not sharing with me or Kendall.

"Hmmm...I still don't understand why I never saw you around the house, you mean to tell me you didn't come to any parties this year, I find that hard to believe," I said with an I don't believe you look on my face and sound in my voice.

Grant, "I was there...maybe *you* just didn't notice me...maybe you were too busy dancing, drinking, or flirting with boys." He pulled me to his side and kissed my forehead.

"I am pretty sure I would have remembered seeing you there, you're hard to miss or forget," I said.

Kendall, "Yeah, why don't I remember seeing you...?" she looked over at Matt, but he was looking out at the ocean.

"Well Sydney, I think our men are hiding something from us, you might as well tell us before we figure it out," Kendall said to them.

Matt just kept looking at the water, "I have no idea what you guys are talking about," he grabbed Kendall's hand, "let's take a quick walk before dinner," he said.

"Wait, let me get a drink," she said. They took off, I could see them bickering a little bit, and I wondered what was being said.

Grant was leaning over the rail of the balcony looking at the water.

"How was surfing this morning?" I asked.

"Great, Dad, me and Noah went, it was fun."

"Your Dad surfs too, that is so cool," I said, putting my arms around his waist and leaning my head on the outside of his shoulder. He put his arm around me.

"So, what did my Mom have to say today?" he asked.

"Oh, she told me how she had her boobs done after you were done nursing!" I said, smiling really big waiting for him to squirm, he did just a little.

"I swear she has no filter, she just can't keep some things private."

"Your parents are great, different but great, mine are so conservative, very old school."

"Do you and Matt have a secret you don't want us to know about? I mean were you two lovers or something?" I asked him.

He turned and started tickling me, "Stop… everyone is watching us, come on what is it?"

We were still standing on the balcony by the railing, "You promise me you won't freak out or anything, promise me?"

"Okay, I pinky promise," I said. We linked pinkies and didn't let them go.

"I did go to the parties, but would never stay long, had to study and all. But, well… umm,"

"Oh gosh, you are such a chicken, how bad could it be?" I asked.

"I knew who you were even before the bonfire night," he said with a 'the jig is up' kind of grin on his face. I took a step back from him, our pinkies still intertwined.

"What? I had never seen you before the night of the bonfire, no parties at school, not walking on campus, no classes," then a flash came through my mind, huge lecture hall tons and tons of students. In my mind I could see him in the last row of the class, Biology 101.

"I can see your mind telling you a story, little tidbits coming back to you," he said to me.

"Were you in my Biology 101 class? Oh my gosh…you would sit in the very top row by the door. Why are you just telling me this now?" I asked, my head tilted to one side not understanding.

"I took the class to fulfill a credit I missed freshmen year or I wouldn't have been able to graduate," he said.

"So were you ashamed cuz you were a senior taking a freshmen course?"

"No don't be silly, I wasn't ashamed, I didn't care." He swallowed and I could see his Adam's apple moving up and down.

"Then what was it?" I asked.

Scratching his head, he said, "I noticed you the first day of class, your hair caught my attention, the way it moved when you walked in to class, and how you squirmed in your seat. I couldn't keep my eyes off of you, but I couldn't figure out who you were. Not until I saw you talking to Matt one night at a party. I pulled him to the side and asked him about you. All he would tell me was your name, and that you and Kendall were friends and roommates."

"So, why didn't you introduce yourself to me, you are not shy, and well maybe this could have been going on for much longer already?" I said with a sad look in my eyes. I was bothered by this new information.

"I don't know why, probably a bunch of reasons which make no sense now, but that is the story, are you mad at me?" he asked. I wasn't mad, just disappointed, all the missed time we could have had together.

"No I am not mad, just sad, I guess. We could have had so many more memories together and since memories are all we are going to have, I want as many as possible," I said looking away, I could feel a single tear drop rolling down my face. I wiped it away before he could see me getting upset.

"Dinner is ready!," his Dad yelled from the kitchen. Homemade lasagna, salad, and garlic bread- it looked and smelled delicious. We sat on the patio downstairs, the six of us.

I was sitting with my plate of food in front of me. I was picking at my food barely eating it, lost in my own thoughts. I could hear Matt ask Grant if he told me when they went to get some beers, "Yes, I told her," he said.

"Is she mad? She has a temper, you know," Matt said.

Grant laughed, "No she is not mad, I know I have seen her temper, not pretty!"

Kendall asked, "Plan for tomorrow, what is the plan?"

Heather and I both had to work, Curt and Grant had the day off, Kendall and Matt were going to hang out at the beach.

"After you two are done with work, we can all meet up here for the festivities, around 4ish say," Grant said.

"I think I am going to surf all morning with my Dad and Brothers. Curt are you in?" he asked.

"Yeah, Matt you want to surf with us?" Curt asked him.

"I don't know how to surf, but I will come out and watch," Matt said.

I looked over at Matt, "You know they start surfing at 5:30 am."

"I will come out and watch, just not at 5:30 in the morning," Matt said laughing.

I stood up, "I will be right back," I said and walked in to the house. I was lying on my back on Grant's bed just staring at the ceiling. Heather and Kendall must have followed me in the house, because they jumped on the bed about two minutes later.

"What are you two doing in here?" I asked.

"Are you alright?" they both asked.

"Yeah… why?" I responded, not very convincingly.

Heather asked me, "You barely ate your dinner and you seem sad, out of sorts, usually you are stuck on Grant like glue and making googlie eyes at him all night. So what's up?"

"Is this about him not telling you he knew who you were at school?" Kendall questioned.

"What?" Heather barked out, "I am lost, are you saying Grant already knew who she was before she moved down to the beach."

"Yep…that is what he told me tonight."

"So, what is the problem?" Heather asked, "Obviously he has been into you way before he became Hot Bonfire Guy."

I couldn't put into words the sadness I was feeling inside, it was like, my happiness had been ripped out, and depression had been spread through me without my permission.

I told them, "I am not sure, I just want to crawl under the covers and sleep, I feel so sad inside. Maybe it is the knowledge that in a month from now I will be getting ready to go back to school and all this will be over. He will leave me and go to New York, get his MBA, meet some other girl and fall in love with her and it makes my heart ache. Knowing now, that if we would have met in January or something, I would have had an extra five months with him…" I wasn't able to get any more words out, tears started to run down my face and I felt sick. "I don't want to talk about this, I am going to fix my make-up and I'll meet you back outside in a few minutes."

They left to go outside I went into the bathroom and sat down on the edge of the bathtub trying to regain some composure.

I heard a knock on the bathroom door, "Honey, are you okay? Grant is looking for you," his mom said. Great, she would read me like a book and ask me 100 questions. I was not in the mood to be analyzed by my boyfriend's mom.

I opened the door for her, "I was just fixing my hair and make-up," I could feel her eyes taking in the less than happy expression on my face.

"Sydney, are you sure you are okay, you look pale, are you not feeling well?" Concern marking her face.

"I am fine, just not used to such a big family I guess," I said totally fibbing to her.

"Sydney, anytime you want to talk I am happy to listen and help you through whatever it is that is obviously making you so sad," Corinne said.

"Now smile, you have a lovely smile, it lights up the room, and I know it lights up Grant's heart."

I gave her a hug, tears coming to my eyes again and my nose beginning to run, I could barely speak, "Thank you, you are very sweet, I am sure someday, whoever Grant ends up with will be very happy to have you in her life."

She pulled me away from her, keeping her hands on my shoulders, my tears were flowing down my face.

"Honey, why are you crying, did Grant do something to upset you?" she asked.

I couldn't talk I just shook my head no.

"Why did you say someday I will make another girl happy, how do you know you are not that girl?" she asked, the look on her face just like Grant's eyes scrunched furrowed eyebrows.

"I will be back at school in August and he will be in New York and everyone knows long distance relationships don't work. I still have three years of school and don't even know what I want to do with my life and everything will be over between us soon, I just… my heart already breaking at the thought of not having Grant in my life." I looked up at her, tears rolling down my face, "Sorry, it just all came out."

"Sydney, take some deep breaths and then we can talk," I did as she asked and felt a little better.

"Are you okay to talk with me for a few minutes?" she asked.

"I will talk and you will listen," she went on, "I know you and I just met but I have lived a lot longer than you have, there is one thing I know, these things have a way of working themselves out. Maybe you will break up, maybe you will be able to do the long distance thing, a lot of things can happen, don't let yourself get caught up in the 'what ifs'," putting her fingers up to make air quotation marks. "Enjoy the special connection you two have together, don't worry about what will come in a few months, enjoy what you have now and don't worry about the future, you will just give yourself an ulcer and end up sitting on the edge of every tub in every party you go to being sad."

She wiped my face with a tissue, kissed my forehead, pulled me up and said, "Smile!"

"Now we are both going to be in trouble because by now everyone is probably looking for us." We came out of Grant's room together and went upstairs to the main floor, when we entered the room all eyes were on us.

Grant came up to me, "Are you alright, what happened?"

"Nothing your mother and I were just talking," I said.

"Are you sure, Mother what did you say to her?" he asked with a harsh tone.

"She didn't say anything, I am fine, everything is fine."

Mr. Montgomery walked over to his wife, and hugged her, she put her head down on his chest.

"What is wrong?" He asked.

"We can talk about later, in private, nothing to worry about, just some much needed girl talk is all," she told him.

Grant was holding me, "Would you like to take a walk, just the two of us down on the beach?" he asked me.

"No, how about shots, I could use a shot, will your parents be upset if we do shots?" I asked him.

He laughed, "That bad huh, bring on the Patron!" he yelled out, and with that everyone was up and standing around the breakfast bar.

Mr. Montgomery and Grant's brother, Ethan, set up shots first all the girls went and then the boys. The first shot went down smoothly, warming my throat on the way down and calming my nerves. The second shot had me loosening up, and by the third shot, the music was blaring and everyone was having a good time.

"You know you have to work at 9:00 am? Don't drink too much more or you won't be able to get up and go to work," Grant whispered in my ear as we danced to some song on the radio.

I just smiled at him, threw my arms around his neck and kept dancing. Around 11:00 pm we headed home, all six of us. We ended up having a great time, and thank goodness Grant was helping me walk because I was having a problem putting one foot in front of the other.

He took me upstairs to my room, undressed me, and was tucking me into bed.

"Aren't you staying with me tonight?" my words slurring as I spoke.

"No, sweetheart, I am going surfing very early tomorrow, but I will call you to make sure you are okay, I am setting your alarm for 8:00 am, that gives you an hour to get ready, I love you, sweet dreams," he kissed me and I think I was asleep before he even shut the door.

My alarm went off on my iPod, reaching across the bed to turn it off, I was feeling for him in the bed and then remembered he didn't spend the night. Surfing, something about surfing. I dragged myself from my bed to the bathroom, mumbling about Patron and not doing this anymore. I bumped into Matt in the hallway and then went to get ready for work. Turning on the shower to warm up the water, I washed my face, brushed my teeth, and hopped in. Stepping out of the shower, I saw a note stuck to the mirror, it just said, "Good morning Sydney, I love you!" I smiled, that was the best start to my day.

I was giddy after that, I got dressed and went downstairs, they were all hung over, Matt had headed down to the beach to watch the guys surf. Kendall was watching TV, I made some toast and filled my cup with coffee and creamer, and sat down on the couch next to her.

"How are you feeling this morning?" I asked in kind of a loud obnoxious voice. Her head turning, she gave me the evil eye, not saying anything.

Heather, was barely moving as she came in to get some coffee, "Holy cow, they can throw a party over there, I wonder what tonight will be like," she said.

"Oh my gosh, it is the Fourth of July, I totally forgot, crap it is going to be ridiculously busy at the surf shop today, damn tourists," I said laughing to myself.

"You're in a good mood, considering you were all weepy last night before your three shots of Patron," Heather said.

"Yeah, what did you and Grant's mom talk about before the shots started flowing?" Kendall asked.

"Nothing, I just told her how I felt about Grant and how much I was going to miss him when the summer was over."

I left for work before Heather; since she woke up late I didn't want to wait for her. The surf shop was packed all day: flip-flops, tank tops, and sunscreen were flying off the shelves. Grant stopped in to check on me after he was done surfing. He brought me some lunch and an extra-large iced tea with lemon, my man is so thoughtful. He left to help get ready for the party this afternoon. He mentioned something about making water balloons for an after dark water balloon fight on the beach. I just couldn't wait to be done for the day. I wanted to get into my bikini and head to the beach to relax, and play in the water a bit.

I was so happy to get home and change into my bathing suit. I grabbed my gear and headed down to find Matt and Kendall on the beach. I set up my stuff, and finally relaxing, texted Grant.

Wednesday, 3:00 pm: Sydney to Grant: Just got to beach, hanging with M&K, come join us.

Wednesday, 3:05 pm: Grant to Sydney: almost done helping set up b there in a few

The beach was crowded of course, people were everywhere, playing football, frisbee, playing in the water. Grant came up a few minutes later and sat down in his chair next to me.

"Are you hot, want to go in the water with me?" I asked.

"I would love to go in the water with you," wagging his eyebrows at me. I stood and was stretching my body, he grabbed me and threw me over his shoulder, I was kicking and screaming, yelling at him.

"Don't you even drop me in the water, you will be in trouble!"

Instead of dropping me, he tossed me in and I was thrown under the wave, when I came back up, I grabbed his hand and pulled him in the water with me. I was laughing and hitting him at the same time. He pulled me up and fixed my suit, using what little material there was to cover me up.

Smirking at me he said, "Do all your suits have to show everyone what is mine?" I just laughed and dove under the next wave. He came right up beside me. We played in the water for a while and then went back to sit down.

"Do you two have to have so much PDA, it is gross," Kendall asked.

I just laughed and leaned over and gave Grant a rather inappropriate kiss for the beach, but I didn't care, seize the moment! We headed up to the house, Heather and Curt were sitting on the big couch talking about their day.

"Hi," I gave her a big hug.

"Yuck, you're all wet, go change," she said.

I took Grant's hand, I leaned up and whispered in his ear, "I really need to shower, will you help me?" I asked.

His eyes got big, he looked around, and everyone else was upstairs.

"Hey tell Kendall and Matt to get changed and bring sweatshirts back, ask Kendall if she can grab my red sweatshirt out of my room, please and thank you," I said to Heather.

I had dropped an overnight bag off in Grant's room before going to the beach earlier.

We went to get ready for tonight's party. I shut and locked the door to Grant's room, he was sitting on the edge of his bed. I walked over and turned on the music. I took his hand and led him to the bathroom, I turned on the shower and closed the bathroom door. I didn't take my eyes off of him, he was standing in just his low riding board shorts, with his hands on his hips watching me. First I undid the string around the back of my bikini, and then I undid the string around my neck, letting the top fall to the floor. I could hear his breathing deepen and then a small gasp escape, when the suit hit the floor. I pulled both side strings of my bikini bottom at the same time, so it would fall away in one swoosh. It did! His reaction was exactly what I was hoping for, his eyes darkened and the desire which spread across his face made me start to cream.

I walked up to him and removed his board shorts. His erection was outstanding, I wrapped my hand around him, stroking him up and down, and kissing his neck and chest, until I was lowering myself to my knees. I eased his hard length into my mouth and I could taste just a little cum on his crest. He let out a very masculine groan of pleasure. His hands were grasping and twisting in my hair.

"Sydney, your mouth is so good... this is so good," I was using my mouth as a vice, sucking him hard, I wanted him to come in my mouth.

I was filled with pleasure, I could feel my wetness dripping between my legs. Lost in thoughts of his pleasure, I felt him moving back and forth, thrusting in my mouth. Then he stopped, lifting me up he put me on the edge of the counter.

He ran his fingers through my wet, very wet, sex, "God, you are drenched for me. I want to taste you again."

He was below me licking me like candy, darting his tongue in and out of me, "I want you, I need you inside of me, I want you to make love to me because you love me," I rasped out to him.

My heart was pounding, my head was spinning from the electricity between us. I could feel the orgasm waiting to course through my body.

"Not yet, I am not done tasting you," he said. The bathroom was steamy hot from the shower and the need from our bodies. He sucked on the bud of my clit and my fingers dug into his shoulders. I was moaning for him, my back was arching.

"I am not going to last, hurry," I said. He started opening drawers looking for a condom.

"I don't care- I am on the pill and I love you, make love to me," I said.

There was no hesitation, he took his hardness and plunged right into me, thrusting inside me, I was screaming from the sensation.

"Don't stop, harder," I said, biting my lip to stop myself from screaming in ecstasy.

"Sydney, I don't ever want this to end, you are heaven I can't get deep enough into your body, it is never enough," he said in my ear.

"Don't leave me, I need you, I want the look on my face when I come inside you burned into your memory so you never forget me, watch me," he cried out.

"Come now," he said.

The words burning through my soul, his body holding me tight on him, my sex clamping around his hardness, "I won't leave you, ever," I said.

My body was shaking from the pleasure and he was still thrusting inside me, kissing me telling me how much he loves me. We just held each other as the waves of desire pulsed through our bodies as if we were one, until our breathing steadied, we pulled apart just enough for him to see the tears in my eyes.

We stepped into the shower and washed each other- not saying a word, just smiling. I was completely happy, this man he warmed my soul and he held my heart in his heart. I would hold on to all the memories, not letting any of them go. He was washing my hair and kissing my neck.

"I adore you, do you know that," he told me.

"I know," I said. We climbed out of the shower. Wrapped in towels, we left the bathroom and went to get dressed. I was sitting on the edge of his bed. Grant was sitting on the opposite side of the bed, sitting on the edge. I could feel him crawling across towards me. He gently pulled me down on to my back, so we were face to face but upside down looking at each other.

I giggled, "What are you doing?"

"I want to see you from every direction, tell me what is wrong," he asked.

"Why were you crying after, I made love to you?"

I didn't want to tell him why I didn't want him to know how much I was hurting, already missing him before we were even apart.

"Sydney just tell me, no secrets, remember?" he began to get tears in his eyes.

"I just, my heart, I just don't want this, what we have to end," I put my hands over my face, not wanting him to see my tears.

"Don't cover your face, I want to hold you until you feel my love wrapped all around you," he said to me.

Apparently, we were missing in action for a very long time, because when we finally emerged from Grant's room all smiles and holding hands, Matt, Curt, Ethan, and Noah, clapped and cheered for us that we had finally returned to the party. I just rolled my eyes, they were all fist pumping like little boys, and I went over to be with my friends.

Kendall just shook her head at me, but not Heather, "Well, that must have been some fun, are you sure you weren't acting out scenes from that book!"

"How long were we gone?" I asked.

"Long enough for everyone to question your whereabouts," Kendall said.

"Oh well, seize the moment is my new mantra."

Dinner was being served upstairs, standard Fourth of July stuff, burgers, dogs, salads, watermelon, and ice cream sundaes for dessert. Super yummy. When we went upstairs, the music was all 1980's nostalgic, Tone Loc, was blaring through the sound system, singing "Wild Thing," it was hilarious. The Montgomery's and Curt's parents, the Wilders, were dancing together.

Grant and his brothers were covering their eyes, yelling "It burns, make it stop, stop dancing!"

We filled our plates with food and sat down at the table on the balcony. The table is long enough to seat everyone.

"After dinner, we are going to play the dice game LCR, left center right, everyone know how to play, it is $3.00 to play, we play one round and then football on the beach or water balloon toss, whatever you kids want to do," Corinne said.

There were probably ten different conversations going on during dinner; talk of baseball, the upcoming college football season, music, cars, the usual stuff.

I was starving, I had finished everything on my plate and as I stood up to help clear the table, Grant took my hand and kissed the back of it, there were a few "awe how cute are they" from around the table. Kendall, Heather, and I were clearing the table and carrying dishes back to the kitchen.

"Should we put the ice cream and stuff on the table or do you want to wait until later?" I asked Corinne.

"No, here girls take all this stuff on the tray and take it to the table. Sydney and I will bring the rest," she said to Kendall and Heather.

"No problem," they said back to her. Great, I thought, just when I had my tears under control.

"Sydney, please help me load the dishwasher, would you Honey?" she said so sweetly.

"Of course," I said. She was putting food in storage containers, going on about food poisoning , and we could nibble on all this later after fireworks when everyone is hungry again.

"Are you feeling better today?" she asked me.

"Yes, thank you I am, I have a new mantra, seize the day," I told her.

"I like it and I am proud of you, remember what I said I am here if you want to talk. Did Grant tell you our surprise yet?"

"Umm, no," I told her.

"Okay, he wants to tell you so I don't want him to be mad at me, so my lips are sealed," she said.

"Okay."

Everyone was eating ice cream sundaes when Corinne and I came back to the table. Grant asking, "Do you want me to make you one?"

"No, I don't want a whole one, can I share with you," I asked.

"I don't like to share my ice cream, but for you I will make an exception!"

We played LCR while finishing up dessert. It took forever with so many people but Ethan's wife ended up winning. We headed down to the beach to play football, there were still quite a few people, but it had thinned out enough to have room for the game.

We split into two teams, basically if you were a couple you got split up. So Grant and I were on opposite teams.

The tension around us during this game was out of control. The men were yelling at each other, getting up in each others' faces. It was a bit unnerving, I thought we were playing a friendly game of football, I didn't realize family honor was involved. I was on Ethan's team, he was the quarterback, I was supposed to catch the football and make a touchdown.

"Are you nuts, you know I can't outrun Grant or Noah," I told him in our huddle.

Ethan said, "Suck it up and do it Stanton!"

I just shook my head. I come from a family of girls, no boys, they take this stuff way to seriously. I heard "hike" and I was running as fast I could go, I could see the ball coming towards me, I caught it I actually caught it!

I was so excited I didn't see Grant and Noah barreling toward me, but when I did I screamed, "Oh Shit!" I turned to run, but Grant just took me down by my legs, pinning my hands above my head he stole a kiss. Then he jumped up and high-fived Noah, "Yeah man, no mercy," they said.

I just laid there laughing, he stuck out his hand to help me up.

"You will pay for that later, Montgomery," I said giving him my squinty eye look.

We played until we were out of breath, dropping to the sand. Next up was the water balloon toss. We each had a partner and stood about an inch apart tossing the balloons back and forth as we walked backwards until, we were yards apart. Then the toss became a fight; water balloons were flying through the air, trying to soak each other, it was super fun. I showed no mercy on my boyfriend, I hit him I don't know how many times, until he was on his back in the sand.

Hands up in the air saying, "I surrender, I surrender."

He pulled me down on top of him, hugging me, and laughing, "You will pay for this later," he said while biting my ear.

"I am counting on it," I said.

I jumped up and ran away, throwing my last water balloon at Heather!

I heard her yell, "Damn you Sydney!" The bonfire was going to be on the beach and I ran inside to get my red sweatshirt with my sorority letters on the front. I brought Grant his Arizona State University sweatshirt and we snuggled-up in front of the fire.

It was close to 9:00 pm, the fireworks would be starting in a few minutes, I love fireworks. "Grant, when is your birthday?"

"March 11th".

"When is your birthday?"

"In the fall."

"I didn't know there was a new month called "fall" on the calendar- is that before or after November?" he said sarcastically.

"Not nice, October 11th," I said.

"You are so young, you won't even be 19 for three more months," "Don't tease me," I said, crossing my arms in a huff.

"I am not teasing you, it is the truth."

"Well Kendall is five days younger than me," I said.

"Hey, don't bring me into this!" Kendall yelled.

"When are you going to tell me what we are doing on the 14th?" I asked him changing the subject.

"It is a surprise, you will have to wait, but do you have a cowboy hat and boots, and you will need to pack for one night," he said to me.

"Very intriguing," I said my mind was trying to figure it out, I had no clue. The fireworks started and I went to sit in Grant's lap.

The firework show was spectacular. By the time it was over I was almost asleep in his arms.

"Do you want me to carry you to bed or do you want to walk?" he asked me.

"I can walk, can I spend the night with you tonight?" I asked him.

He looked down at me in his lap. His broad smile spread over his face.

"I assumed you were spending every night with me." I kissed his cheek.

"Hell, yeah," I said back to him, with a very happy smile on my face.

CHAPTER 15

The Fourth of July holiday had been so fun, everything was perfect. Kendall and Matt left early the next morning to head back to Arizona. Ethan and his wife Jessica, went back to Texas for some big case Ethan was working on. Grant and Curt's families were staying in town for a few more weeks. The beach was packed everyday now that school was out and tourist season was in full swing. It was hard to get a day off, so I am glad we all asked for the 14th and 15th of July off before the high season was upon us. Time was passing faster than I could ever remember.

I was getting ready for work and I hadn't heard from Kendall since she went back to Arizona, it had been almost a week since the Fourth of July. I was putting my make-up on, my phone was on the bathroom counter, when I heard beep, beep, beep. Texts.

Tuesday, 12:15 pm: Kendall to Sydney: Hey, been busy, miss u, don't forget to get a black dress for preference night/pledge presents formal.

Reading her message, I thought, oh crud, I completely forgot.

Tuesday, 12:16 pm: Sydney to Kendall: miss u 2, thanks for reminding me, totally forgot. Anything new to report?
Tuesday, 12:18 pm: Kendall to Sydney: no, hot as all hell here, miss beach, u r lucky

Tuesday, 12:20 pm: Sydney to Kendall: LOL, have work, talk 2 u soon

Tuesday, 12:22 pm: Sydney to Heather: Hey need to go shopping, r u free 2nite.

Tuesday, 12:25 pm: Heather to Sydney: no, how about 2morrow, am.

Tuesday, 12:26 pm: Sydney to Heather: k, where r u?

Tuesday, 12: 27 pm: Heather to Sydney: in my room! LOL

We both walked out in to the hall and were laughing, "I thought you left already," I said to her.

"Me too. What are we shopping for?" she asked me.

"I need to get a black formal for sorority stuff, which Kendall just reminded me about, should we go to the mall?"

"Yeah, I think the boys are going golfing with their dads tomorrow, so this will be perfect. Should we ask Corinne and Courtney to join us?" Heather asked.

"No," I said, "I don't want to shop all day with their mom's asking us a million questions." "Come on Sydney, they will make it interesting, you never know what we might find out about them, and they will be so touched by our invitation, pleasssee."

"Fine, lets' leave early for work so we can stop by their house and asked them," I said. We hurried to get ready, I threw my work ensemble on, which was pretty much all I wore since I worked every flippin' day.

We walked into the house through the bottom floor and started up the steps to the main floor. I could hear Corinne and Courtney talking and laughing at the kitchen table.

Standing on the stairs, I called up, "Corinne, it's me Sydney, and Heather is with me. Is it okay if we come up?" I asked.

The laughing continued, "Of course, girls, please come up."

"Well this is a nice surprise, Grant and Curt are at work, what's up?" they both asked.

I looked at Heather and then back to them.

"Well, Heather and I are going to go to the mall tomorrow to do some shopping and we wanted to know if you two would like to join us, you know a girls day out?" I said with a smile on my face.

They both clapped their hands, "Oh, yes, we both love to shop, that would be very nice, thank you for thinking of us," Courtney said.

"What time?" Corinne asked. I thought for a minute the boys would be leaving to golf around 8 am and wouldn't be back until late in the afternoon.

"How about we leave around 10:00 am? We can shop, have lunch, and then shop some more," I told them.

"We will be ready," Courtney said.

"Okay, we have to leave for work, have a great day," Heather and I said as we left the house.

"See, they are so excited, it will be fun," Heather said.

"See you later," I told her as I headed to the surf shop for the day. When I walked in, the surf shop was packed with customers, I never even made it to the back room to put my purse away, I just shoved it under the counter. I clocked in and started ringing customers up on the other register, the line to pay was ten people deep and I could see the frustration on their faces.

Russ looked at me, "I am so glad you are here, it has been like this since we opened!" I just smiled and continued working. It finally slowed down a few hours later.

I left to go get an iced tea at the Blue Moon Café. Grant was walking out as I was walking in.

"Hey, gorgeous," he said to me, leaning down and giving me a kiss.

"Excuse me, do I know you?" I said, giggling as he pulled me into him, wrapping his arms around my waist.

He whispered in my ear, "Yes, I know you, you have a beauty mark just inside of your bikini line."

I leaned my head back laughing, my face a little flushed from his intimate words.

He released his arms, he was holding a cup, "Sorry babe, have to get back to work, see you tonight," he said and started to walk away but not before he smacked my ass hard and said "See you later, Hot Stuff."

Damn him. I jumped a little, I yelled at him, "Stop doing that, now my ass is going to hurt all day." He just looked back at me smiling from ear to ear.

The rest of my work day flew by, I was late getting off work because one of the girls called in sick. I didn't get home until after 9:00 pm. I was thoroughly exhausted, I was so glad to have tomorrow off. Heather and Curt were sitting by the fire pit on our patio relaxing and listening to music. I went outside and sat down across from them. When I sat down, I must have let out a huge sigh.

"Wow, that was a huge sigh," Curt said.

"Oh sorry, I am so tired, we were slammed all day and I had to work late, I just need a few minutes of down time," I said.

"Is Grant coming over?" I asked Curt.

"I don't know, he was fiddling with his Jeep when I left to come over here."

Tuesday, 9:15 pm: Sydney to Grant: just got home, coming over here?

Tuesday, 9:25 pm: Grant to Sydney: I am already here.

I looked up and he was walking on to the patio from the street. My smile getting really big, he lifted my legs up and sat down next to me, letting my legs rest across his lap.

Holding my hands and kissing my knuckles, he said, "I hear there is a girl's marathon shopping event tomorrow?"

I smiled and turned my head a little, saying, "Are you mad we asked your mom's to go shopping with us?"

"Why would I be mad? I am just glad I don't have to go with them, you two don't know what you have gotten yourselves into, our Moms can shop all day, and I mean all day," he said laughing.

Curt starting laughing too. "Yeah, you two are going to need a vacation when are moms are done with you," Curt said.

I stood up a while later and took Grant's hand, "I am ready to go to sleep, and I think I need to have at least eight hours of rest to deal with your mom tomorrow."

In my room, we got ready for bed, I went to the bathroom to wash my face and brush my teeth. Grant was already all cozy under the covers when I crawled in to the bed next to him.

I snuggled right up to him, "My mom said she and my aunt will pick you guys up in the morning, so still be ready by 10."

"Sounds good," I said. We kissed for a few minutes before I feel asleep with my head on his shoulder.

The next thing I knew, I could hear Grant rustling around for his clothes, "What time is it?" I asked him.

"It is 7 in the morning," he hopped on the bed snuggling up to me. I could feel he was dressed already.

"I have to go, we have a tee time for 8:30 at the golf course, have fun shopping, text me with any interesting information my mom and aunt tell you, but not everything they say about us is true."

"Okay, I am going to get up in a few minutes and start getting ready," I said.

We drove to the mall in Corinne's SUV, she had the car valet-parked. She brought the big truck in case we had a ton of shopping bags, which she promised we would.

Corinne asked as we entered the shopping center, "So, girls what are we looking for today, is there something special or are we just shopping?"

I took a deep cleansing breath and said, "I need to get a black semi-formal dress for Preference Night and Pledge Presents Dance, just one dress- I can wear the same one for both events."

She smiled real big at me, "Oh this is going to be fun, only having boys to shop for is so boring! Okay, do you want to go to little stores? I prefer Bloomingdales or Saks Fifth Avenue for what you're looking for today." She didn't wait for my answer, she just took my hand and said, "Saks it is!"

She knew exactly where she was going, leading us to the cocktail dresses, "Okay, so you need a black dress, size what four or six," she was muttering on.

Corinne handed the salesgirl ten different dresses before I had even looked through one display. My eyes were wide like saucers and Heather was laughing at me. Not laughing for long when Courtney took her by the hand and started talking her ear off.

The salesgirl took me to my dressing room, "Do you need a strapless bra to try on the dresses?" she asked me.

"No I will be fine, thank you," I replied.

"Sydney, I will sit out here, please come out so I can see you in each dress," Grant's mom said.

The salesgirl came back a few minutes later with some black high heels for me try on with the dresses. I tried on a dress which went over one shoulder, it was cute but not my favorite, I went out to model for Corinne, she shook her head no. I tried another four dresses, all no. Finally I put on the one; it was strapless, fitted through the bodice, the waistband had wide black silk ribbon folded down on top of each other going all the way around, and the bottom of the dress reminded of a tulip. I walked out Courtney and Heather were standing behind Corinne. I had slipped on the heels the salesgirl brought me.

Corinne jumped out of her seat when she saw me, "Oh this is it, you look stunning," she said.

I paid for the dress, charging it to my parents' credit card because there is no way I could afford it on my own. We went downstairs to look for shoes and accessories. Not finding any we headed out, I was carrying the dress bag over my shoulder, very happy with my purchase. I would be able to wear this dress forever, it was timeless. We started going in and out of every store, seriously, I was tired, thirsty, and my stomach was growling.

"Hungry?" Corinne asked as we headed into Bloomingdale's.

"Yes," I said.

"Okay, lets' eat at Charlie Palmers and it is my treat," she said.

Heather and I were not about to fight with her about it. I needed some serious sustenance if I was going to last the rest of the day shopping with them, they are like shopping warriors never showing any sign of fatigue! The four of us talked non-stop through lunch, they told us funny stories about the boys when they were little, and vacations they had taken.

"The boys were all so cute when they were little, with sunblock on their noses, playing in the sand at the beach. When they took their first surf lessons you would have thought they had found heaven. All of them enjoyed it so much, we had to drag them out of the water everyday," Courtney said with Corinne agreeing.

"How long have you had this beach house?" I asked.

"Well, we used to rent a house for the first few summers, then Kevin and I decided we should just buy one, so I think six years now," she said.

"You know girls, Mr. Wilder and I have a winter home in Vail, that is where we spend our winter vacations," Courtney said.

"No, I don't think either of the boys mentioned a home in Vail," Heather said.

We shopped all day filling the back of the Suburban with at least two dozen shopping bags. I found a beautiful pair of black high heels and jewelry to match at Nordstrom. We stopped off at our house to unload our packages and then headed to the Montgomery's where the guys had ordered pizza for dinner. They beat us home and when we entered the house we found them on the downstairs patio drinking beer and sunburned from not using enough sunblock while on the golf course. They looked like I felt.

"So, who won?" I asked taking Grant's beer out of his hands and taking a drink.

He raised his eyebrows at me, "Long day," he asked.

"Great day," I said.

"Noah won, he always wins, I think he is spending too much time entertaining clients on the golf course," Kevin said.

"Are you girls hungry, we know how shopping works up your appetite?" Curt asked. "Starved," Heather and I said, jumping up to go get some pizza.

We sat around the fire pit talking and laughing with our boyfriends and their parents the rest of night.

Noah asked me, "Sydney, do you have any sorority sisters you can set me up with?"

Grant smacked him on the chest, "Dude you're too old for those girls, go on one of those dating websites or something, my girlfriend is not going to be your matchmaker."

I just laughed, "Noah, I doubt you have any problem finding a date," I said.

"You're right, I don't," he said. I rolled my eyes at him.

We talked about going to the movies on the weekend. Corinne and Courtney were talking about some new movie about male strippers and I could hear their husbands saying "Hell no, we are not going to watch that movie with you two, that is just wrong!"

The rest of the week was busy; working, tanning, reading, and watching our men surf their hearts away. The weekend came and we went to the stripper movie with Courtney and Corinne, while the guys went to see some superhero flick. We had dinner out afterwards and then headed home.

On the way back to the house I asked Grant, "When are you going to tell what we are doing next weekend?"

"I am not going to tell you until we are on our way there," he said with a devilish smile.

"Okay, well I need to go to my parents' house to pick up my boots and hat. Can we go up tomorrow? It is too busy during the week, how about after work?" I asked.

"Sure, maybe we can have dinner with your parents," he said.

Sunday came and we headed to my parents'. When we came into the house my mom and sister were sitting on the couch looking at a magazine together and giggling.

"What is going on in here?" I asked.

My sister stood up, sticking out her left hand to me, screaming, "Look, look what I got!"

On her left ring finger was a giant diamond ring, well maybe not giant, but rather big. I grabbed her hand, holy shit, she is engaged, he proposed, I was shocked.

"So, he finally got the nerve to ask you to marry him," I said.

I gave her a big hug I could see my mom eyeing Grant, who at the moment looked very uncomfortable. Grant gave her a hug too.

"So, when is the big day?"

"We haven't decided but we are thinking of early May of next year before it gets hot," she said.

My sister, Jade Stanton was getting married, unbelievable. I am so glad I will not be here during the planning stages.

"Can you try to pick a date after my finals, so I don't have to worry about studying during your wedding weekend," I requested.

"Yeah sure, we can do that," Jade said.

My dad came in the house a few minutes later with a plate full of steaks. We sat down at the table to eat dinner, making small talk.

"Grant, you know Sydney's mother and I are both from New York, when are you leaving for Yale," he asked him.

"Sir, I will be going to New York about a week before classes start so probably early September or late August."

My dad loving all this "sir" stuff, not offering up his first name to Grant like his parents had done for me.

"So, this is the room you grew up in, your formative years?" he said laughing at me.

"Nice yellow wallpaper!"

"Shut up, I picked it out when I was 12 years old, give me a break."

"You know you could redo your room."

"I am not here enough, this is the longest I have been here all summer." I was inside my walk- in closet looking for my stuff.

"Hey come here, can you reach my hat on the top shelf or else I have to get a step stool," I said.

Of course he could reach it, he was 6'2", he pulled it down and put it on my head, "Sexy... you look good," he drawled.

He pushed me up against the shelves and started to kiss me, "Stop, my parents are downstairs," I said. "So," he kept kissing me.

"You are making me all horny, now leave me alone, let me find my boots then we can go, and once we are home you can have your way with me," I said.

"All-righty then partner," he said speaking with a southern accent.

"You are so weird!" I found my boots on the bottom of my closet behind a bunch of empty shopping bags. They were a deep red, with rhinestones down the sides.

"Wow, where did you get these, I like them?" he asked.

"Come on," I pulled him out of the closet and we headed downstairs.

"What do you need that stuff for?" my Mom asked.

"I don't know it is a surprise," I told her.

"Alright, you two be safe," my parents said. We said our good-bye's and headed back to my house for the night.

The drive back to the beach was nice; we talked about how fun the summer was, I tried to get him to tell me what we were doing next weekend, but he wouldn't even give me a hint, saying the cowboy hat and boots were enough of a hint and he was surprised I hadn't figured it out yet. We parked his car at his house and then headed to mine for the night.

Heather and Curt were in her room, I could her giggling noises coming from under the door. I went in and put the boots and hat away. Grant came in to my room with a look of mischief on his face.

"What's with the look on your face, what are you up to?" I asked.

"Nothing," he said.

"What is behind your back?"

"Nothing."

"Something." I was changing my clothes, not paying him any attention since I knew he was up to no good.

He said, "Close your eyes."

"Why?"

"Just close your eyes Sydney, geez!"

"Okay, they are closed," I heard a funny noise, which I could not place.

He was standing in front of me now, "Keep your eyes closed and open your mouth," I did, I opened my mouth just a little, "Sydney, open your mouth a little wider please," so I did as he asked. "I am going to put my finger in your mouth, close your mouth around my finger," he put his finger in my mouth and as I closed my lips around his finger it was sweet, it was whipped cream.

"Yummy, can I open my eyes now?" I asked.

"No," he lead me to the bed and laid me down.

I was only in my bra and panties.

He removed both and said, "We are going to have a sweet evening."

I could tell by the sound of his voice he was impressed with himself and what we were about to do. He put whipped cream on me, on places whipped cream was not invented to go. Licking his way all over my body, the sensation was exhilarating, I could feel my desire for him coursing through my body. His tongue was heavenly, the way he licked the whipped cream off and then made this sucking noise with his lips, was pushing me to my limit. I still had my eyes closed relishing the warmth in my body, but I could tell he moved for a second. This was my chance I couldn't take any more of his delightful torture on my body. I jumped up quickly and threw him down on the bed.

"It is my turn," I said.

"Okay, okay, I am not going to fight you."

"Close your eyes and take off your jeans," I told him.

He did exactly what I asked, he had taken off his shirt, before he started seducing me. He was lying on my bed, completely naked and the sight of him was making me crazy. I shook up what was left of the whipped cream, drew a heart on his stomach and licked it off slowly, not lifting my tongue from his stomach as I made my way around the heart. He was moaning with delight as I finished.

"Are you going to keep teasing me or are we going to finish this?"

"You teased and tortured me for much longer than this," I said.

"That is very different, I am hard as a rock here, can you help a guy out!?"

"Condom," I asked.

"We didn't use one the other day?"

"You know I haven't been with anyone else, come on Sydney, trust me I don't have STD's, I get tested every six months," he said. I looked at him like that is odd but okay.

I was straddling him, "I see you want to be on top," I nodded my head yes, my breathing had quickened so much I couldn't speak.

I was lowering myself down onto him, he was holding me by my hips and the feeling as he began to penetrate me, was mind blowing the way he filled me, he slid right in with my sex, completely saturated with wetness for him. I began to move my hips back and forth, the way we moved in sequence was unbelievable.

I could hear him, "Sydney, your body is so wicked, what you do to me with it... feel me move inside you."

I could feel him hitting my sweet spot, deep inside of me. I was climbing -my orgasm just out of reach, I could almost feel it. Sweat was dripping down my back and I was panting from the ride I was on.

He could tell I was almost there, "Not yet, let me feel you around me, don't let go yet," he moaned at me.

He took his thumb and began pressing on my clit, the feeling of him inside of me and pressing down on me pushed me over the edge.

"Oh, God, I can't hold on... what you're doing to me..." I couldn't finish my thought, my body was in full release, I was holding onto his chest, my nails digging into him. He was still moving my hips back and forth and grunting out my name, finally I could feel him exploding inside me, his orgasm leaving him breathless. He pulled me down, kissing me.

"Sydney, I love you, God I love you so much, you make me so happy," he confessed to me.

We were cuddling in bed, still feeling the waves of our orgasms, "Hey, what is that hanging on your closet door?"

"Hmm...,"my brain was all scattered, "oh that is the dress I got the other day shopping."

"What is it for," he asked me.

The dress was concealed in the dress bag the department store had put it in.

"You know; Sorority Rush Preference Night, active members wear black dresses when the girls come through the house on the final night of Rush, before we extend out bids for the new Pledges, and I am going to wear it again for the Pledge Presents Formal," I said the end of my answer to him more quietly realizing what that meant.

"Oh, yeah, yeah, I know you girls have to do so much more stuff then we do for Fraternity Rush, when is the formal?" he asked.

"I don't know, we won't find out until we get back to school," I got kind of excited for a minute.

"Why, will you go with me?"

"I would love to take you to the Formal, but it depends when it is, if it is before I leave then yes, we have a date," he said.

"Who will you go with if I can't take you," his voice sounding gruff.

"No one, I will just go with my friends, I guess."

He quickly changed the subject, not wanting to linger on the topic of us being separated. "Oh, umm, what happened to the surprise you got me a while back you know the one that is not chocolate?" Way to change the subject, I thought to myself.

"Oh, I forgot all about that, well I think I will keep a secret a little longer! When you tell me about next weekend, then you can see the surprise," I said smiling at him but still he wouldn't tell me, rats, he is good at keeping secrets!

I got out of bed the next morning, hurried out of the house and headed to work, Grant was still sleeping when I left. I knew he didn't have to be at work until late in the day. The shop was busy of course, traffic was bad, not that I care since I walk to work but tourists were honking their horns. Finally, I was able to take a break, I went to get a slice and tea for lunch at the pizza place. My phone beeped at me.

Monday: 12:21 pm: Grant to Sydney: Hey girlfriend, going shopping with mom, c u ltr.

Monday: 12:22 pm: Sydney to Grant: Hey boyfriend, what are u getting?

Monday: 12:23 pm: Grant to Sydney: jeans for sat. I have a special night planned.

Monday: 12:24 pm: Sydney to Grant: hmmm…special night, tell me about it…

Monday: 12:25 pm: Grant to Sydney: NO! C U late night, luv u!

Monday: 12:26 pm: Sydney to Grant: MEAN…LOL!

I was back at work, the day flying by like they always did. Heather came in on her break and bought a few things.

"What are you wearing Saturday night?" she asked me.

"Either jean mini or jeans, cami, with a grey and white checkered button- down, and my red boots, and you?"

"Not sure, I wish I knew what we are doing, it would make it easier."

"I know, right," I said to her.

"I have to head back to work, see you later, bye," she said.

Grant came over after work, it must have been close to 10:00 when he kissed me, I was asleep on the couch waiting up for him. Heather and Curt had gone out with some people from her work and I decided to stay home and read my book.

I could tell he was tired, "Let's go to bed sleepy head," he picked me up and put me over his shoulder, I didn't care I was wiped out. We climbed into bed and we both slept like logs, no movement all night.

We woke up early, he went to surf and I came down to the beach to watch my man do his surfing thing. I tried a few times and then gave up after I kept falling off the board, when I would stand up? Grant keeps saying you have to practice and to try again. I just laughed, not my thing. I am happy to watch him and read my book. He came out of the water when he was done and we headed to his house for breakfast. His mom said she would be working today with a new client but she wouldn't tell us who, high profile athlete and all, had to be someone local though.

"It is taco Tuesday kids, so come after work and I will make tacos for all of us. I will be back by 4 pm, what time are you done working?" she asked.

"I am working from 10-2," I said.

"I should be off by 3, unless it is crazy busy again," he said.

"My mom makes killer tacos, not like the kind from Taco Bell, she takes a corn tortilla, presses ground beef on half, seasons each one, and then fries them in oil, seriously they are the best, then you can top them with whatever floats your boat!"

I started laughing, "That is my line." Sounds great. I cleaned up downstairs in Grant's room, I was climbing the stairs to say good-bye, when I overheard Grant and his Mom talking.

Grant: *"Mom, thank you for going shopping with me the other day."*

Corinne: *"Grant, it was my pleasure, helping you pick out jeans was aggravating, but picking out the other thing was fun."*

Corinne: *"When are you going to give it to her? She is going to go crazy, I hope you know what you two are doing. What is going to happen when you are separated by 3000 miles."*

Grant: "Mom, keep your voice down, I don't want Sydney to hear us talking and I don't know, I am trying not to think about the 3000 miles and I don't want to bring it up because I know she will get upset."

I pretended like I was just now coming upstairs, "Hey Grant, are you still upstairs?" I yelled.

"Yeah, I am in the kitchen." I came bouncing into the room, giving them each a hug and kiss before heading off to work.

"You two stay out of trouble," I said and was laughing when I left.

My mind was wrapped around their conversation all day, what they were talking about, I tried to distract myself with work. I was attempting to help Rick with the surf stuff because he was swamped, then he yelled at me since I had no idea what I was doing. I switched spots with Russ who was working the register.

"I think Rick is going to kill me if I don't get away from his area of the shop," I told Russ.

"No problem, you work the register and I will help him, he is protective and doesn't want things messed up back there."

Thank goodness the shop was packed all day, Heather was home from work when I got there, I told her about the conversation I overheard and she thought maybe he got me a present. Maybe, sounds reasonable. We went over to the Montgomery's for dinner. Grant was right, the tacos his Mom made were super good.

We were walking on the beach after dinner, holding hands.

Grant asked me, "Who gave you the ruby ring you always wear?" It was a round ruby with diamonds going around the ruby, set in gold.

"My parents gave it to me for my 16th birthday," I said.

"It is nice, what about the diamonds in your ears?" I wore the same diamond studs every day.

"What is this about? My parents gave me the earrings for my high school graduation, if you must know."

"Did Trent ever give you any jewelry?"

"He did, why do you ask?"

"Just curious I guess. What was it, do you still wear it?"

I was getting annoyed with this line of questioning, "He gave me a bracelet, no I don't wear it, I got rid of it over winter break last year."

I looked at him totally aggravated, "What, why are you looking at me all mad?" he asked.

"Because, if you wanted to know if I still wore another guy's jewelry you should have just asked," I said.

"Well, I am sorry, I just wanted to know."

"Whatever," I said with my arms crossed, I had stopped walking.

"Whatever," that is not nice."

I was walking again, he kicked my feet out from under me and caught me at the same time so I would fall in to his arms on the sand. He was lying half on me and half on the sand, holding my hands above my head so I couldn't fight him.

"Let me go," I was trying to fight him but he wouldn't release me.

He said, "You're so stubborn, Sydney Stanton, relax and don't hit me and I will let you go, after I am done kissing you."

He was kissing my lips, then my jaw line and around to my ears, I was giggling from the ticklish feeling he was giving me. Eventually, my body relaxed and he released my arms, so I could wrap them around his neck. The sky was dark and the moon was beaming down on us, you could see stars in the sky. I looked up at the stars and I just wished to myself, just a private wish.

I could feel him gazing at me as I looked up at the stars, "What are you thinking about?" he asked.

"Nothing, just how beautiful the sky looks," I said.

Not wanting to tell him my private wish.

"I think there is more to your story, but I am not going to force you to share your thoughts with the man you love," he said making a sad face.

I turned to him, "You know if you tell your wish, it won't come true, so I can't tell you, it's the rule."

He pulled me up from the sand and we raced back to the house, I tried to race him, but he beat me by a mile.

We were getting ready for bed, he said, "You know tomorrow is Wednesday so only four days until your surprise." His devilish smile plastered on his face

"Come on just tell me," I said.

"I will tell you this much, we are staying at a hotel not far from the surprise."

"Hmmm…do we have our own room," I asked.

"Yes, we all have our own room," he said, smiling from ear to ear and wagging his eyebrows up and down.

"Wow, how did you manage that?" I asked.

"Sydney, my Dad owns a hotel management company, we are staying at one of the hotels he manages, so we are checking in early, we can use the pool and then get ready for the event."

"Why do you keep saying event, what is it? Just tell me," I begged.

"No, go to bed!" he barked at me.

CHAPTER 16

As the next few days came and went, each day I would get a countdown text, or find a sticky note, saying how many days until the big surprise. Finally I woke up and it was Saturday morning, I couldn't wait, I had breakfast and walked down to the beach to watch Grant surfing. Two days off in a row, I was super excited.

After Grant was done surfing, I gave him a kiss by his house, "Sydney, Curt and I will pick you girls up at noon, make sure you have everything you need. I love you."

"I love you too! See you in a little bit."

Heather was running around the house all giddy about our plans. I went to my room to pack, I could see my dress still hanging on the door. Knowing Grant would not be able to take me to the Formal, my wish would not come true. Oh well, seize the moment, I reminded myself.

I was all finished packing; bikini, shorts, toiletries, make-up, boots, hat, jean mini-skirt, red-cami, checkered button down, and my surprise. I had on short shorts, bandeau, and tank top.

"I am all ready, I can't wait to find out our surprise. Do you know what it is?" I asked Heather.

"I think I might, you haven't figured it out yet?" She asked.

"I have no clue."

"Well I think we are going to…" Just then Curt and Grant came in and we turned, looking guilty as hell.

"What are you two whispering about," Curt asked.

"Nothing," Heather said.

"How much stuff do you two need for one night?" Grant asked all flabbergasted with our pile of bags to go to the hotel.

I just shot him a look, "Just put our stuff in your Jeep and let's go, I want to swim and have lunch by the pool, and then have plenty of time to get ready."

It only took us about twenty minutes to get to the hotel, we were minutes from Angel Stadium.

"Hmmm..." I said as we pulled up to the hotel, "Angel Stadium is just right there, I think I will Google on my phone and see what is up there tonight."

"Suit yourself, but you will ruin your surprise if you do," Grant said as he kissed my cheek and hopped out of his truck.

We checked into our rooms, changed, and headed down to the pool. When we came out on the pool deck, Grant and Curt's parents were already poolside having lunch in a cabana.

"Having connections has its advantages," Grant said to me as he placed his hand low on my back and lead me over to the cabana. Greetings were given to everyone.

"We just sat down to lunch, order whatever you want and have them put it on our room," his mom said. I think Grant and Curt ordered just about everything on the menu, I had one margarita with lunch, I didn't want to get to sleepy from lying in the sun and the alcohol.

"Kids, the car is picking us up at 4:20, so we will meet you in the lobby. See you later, your father and I going for a nap and to get ready," with that the two sets of parents left.

"Eew, you know what that means, gross," Curt said.

"What? They have needs too," Heather said laughing, while Curt and Grant both made faces, their bodies shook from the chills. I just laughed.

After I finished eating I laid down on a lounger. I stood a few minutes later and walked to the pool, I slowly walked down the steps, I could feel Grant watching me. I just smiled and dove in to the water. When I came back from swimming one lap, Grant was waiting for me at the bottom of the steps. I swam right up to him under the water and grabbed his ankles. He pulled me up to him from my armpits.

"You look so hot in this bikini, I am not sure I like the other guests staring at you," he told me.

I just giggled, "No one is staring at me, and I wear this same bikini on the beach all the time, what is the difference?"

"I don't know, it just feels different here, like you are on display or something," he said holding me close to him while we floated around the pool.

I told him, "It doesn't matter who stares at me, I only have eyes for you and you know it, so how about we blow this popsicle stand and go take a shower together?"

"Later guys, we are going to get ready, see you in the lobby in a couple of hours," I said to Heather and Curt.

I had a towel from the pool wrapped around my waist, I pushed my sunglasses on top my head as we walked in to the elevator and, before I knew it, Grant had me pinned in the corner, the lightning bolt was pumping through me sending shivers down my spine. His hands were grabbing me from behind.

"Oh my God, it took all my willpower from ravaging you by the pool. You look too delicious in this bikini, it is lethal. When we get to our room I am going to take you so fast and hard you will be screaming for mercy," he gasped to me.

Just then the elevator stopped and he released me, two businessmen got on and pushed their floor. My breathing was very heavy and I was biting my bottom lip to keep myself steady.

We got off on our floor and ran to our room. Before he had the door open I jumped on his back, he carried me into the room, shutting the door behind him with his foot. He dropped me on the big bed, and using the remote he turned on the music station on the TV. I was sprawled on the bed, just my lower half wrapped in the towel.

He crawled above me, "You are mighty fine Miss Sydney Stanton, mighty fine."

I was smiling and laughing at him, he was wearing his board shorts which were at this moment riding very low and I could see his hips and the top of his trail.

"You are a mighty fine looking specimen yourself Mr. Montgomery, why don't you show me just how fine you really are?" I said seductively.

That didn't take much; he had his shorts off in less than a second.

"With this towel wrapped around you, it's like a present I forgot to open on my birthday," he said as he looked down at me.

He was licking his lips and I was biting mine.

"Then what is stopping you, unwrap your present!"

He pushed my bikini top up exposing my aching breasts and took his time licking each one.

Then he unwrapped the towel from around my waist, "I think I love my present," he said as he untied the strings to my bikini bottom.

"Now where is that mole? I need to get a closer look."

It wasn't long before I was begging for mercy, he had two fingers inside me, thrusting them in and out of me, pulling my juices out and sucking them up with his lips, each suck had me arching my back and begging for him to take me.

"Grant, I can't take it, please take me, I am begging you… I want you inside of me," I was gasping for breath and begging for mercy.

"I know you are ready to come but don't, I want to get deep inside you before you do," He pushed in to me with such force I groaned from the pleasure, every time with him was like the first time, him stretching me and me begging for him to get deeper. Thrust after thrust he kept on, I could see by the look on his face he was holding back, waiting until I would scream out his name.

"Damn it, fuck me harder, I want to come," I screamed at him, "Damn you Grant, I love you," I screamed again at him.

His eyes were burning into mine, I could feel him, "Sydney come then… come with me," he groaned back. I was coming so hard and I could feel him bursting inside me.

"Oh, don't stop, God it is so great every time, every single time," he said, leaning his forehead on mine. He was gently kissing my lips; my body was slowly coming down from the high.

We feel asleep for a little while, until the hotel room phone rang. I answered the phone, "Hello," my voice all scratchy from being asleep.

"Mrs. Montgomery, it is 3:00 pm, this is your complimentary wake up call, have a nice day," the lady said.

I sat up laughing.

"What is so funny?"

"Well first off, we got a wake-up call and second, she called me Mrs. Montgomery."

"Mrs. Sydney Montgomery, I like it, it just rolls off my tongue," Grant said grinning from ear to ear.

"Don't tease, that is not nice," I said smacking his arm and getting out of bed.

"I am showering first, because it takes me longer to get ready."

"I thought we were showering together," Grant said jumping up to follow me into the bathroom.

"You go watch TV or something, we will never be ready on time if you take a shower with me," I was pushing him back with my arm stretched out between us.

"You sit here and watch something -anything," I said putting him in the chair by the TV.

"Man, foiled again," he said laughing, "I could just wash your back and maybe your front," he yelled to me.

Shutting the bathroom door, I said, "NO, stay there!"

"Holy hell Sydney, are you ready yet?" Grant was getting impatient.

He had showered, dressed in his new jeans, a crisp button down, un-tucked with the sleeves rolled up, and a pair of Timberland boots.

"Yeah hold on, one minute, I am just fixing my make-up."

"What takes you so long, you looked gorgeous, when you came out just with the towel around you?"

"Well, after I put my clothes on I had to do some last minute touch up."

I walked out of the bathroom, fixing my cowboy hat on my head.

"You take my breath away, you look...you look, gorgeous!"

"Thank you," I was wearing red kick- ass cowboy boots, a low riding jean mini-skirt, red-camisole, with a grey and white large checkered shirt which was unbuttoned and tied at the bottom just above my belly button.

Grant twirled me around, he let out a "Hell yeah, worth the wait, well worth the wait!" he said like he just moved here from Texas.

"Are you going to tell me where we are going now?" I asked.

He pointed out the window to Angel Stadium.

"You got me all hyped up to go to an Angel's game, are you kidding me?."

"No, it is not an Angel's game," from his back pocket he pulled out two tickets for the Tim McGraw/Kenny Chesney concert.

I started screaming and grabbed the tickets out of his hand, "Are you kidding, me this is awesome, thank you so much, I am so surprised!" I was kissing him and jumping up and down.

"Let's go," I was pulling him to the door.

"Wait, I have something else I want to give you," he said.

He went to his duffle bag and pulled out a large square box, a large square Tiffany's box. I took a deep breath as he walked to me.

I was beginning to shake from the unknown, "Sydney, I have wanted to give you something, something special that binds us together no matter where we are, something you can wear every day. Something that every time you see it or touch it, you will think of me, and know how much I love you."

He put the box in my hands; my hands were shaking from the unexpected surprise. I swallowed hard, I pulled on the beautiful white satin ribbon tied around the blue box, I removed the lid of the box, inside was another box, I unsnapped the box and opened it. I looked up at him, tears filling my eyes. It was a Tiffany Infinity Necklace in sterling silver; infinity symbols bound together five in a row, then circles, then five more infinity symbols, then more circles, and it was so beautiful. I was speechless. My whole body was shaking, my tears dripping down my face.

"Grant is it so beautiful, why, when, did you get this for me? I don't know what to say."

"Ask me to put it on you, that is what you can say," he said taking the box from my hands, taking the necklace out and putting around my neck.

He secured the clasp at the back of my neck. I was touching it with my fingers and looking at myself in the mirror. Grant was standing behind me with his hands on my shoulders, smiling his gorgeous smile at me.

My tears falling down my cheeks, "I love it and I love you, thank you thank you so much, it is perfect, I will never take it off."

I turned to face him, he lifted my chin and wiped away my tears.

"Sydney, don't cry."

"I just love you," I kissed him, my heart filled with all the love between us.

"Okay, are you ready to go downstairs, our limo awaits," he said pulling me to the door.

"Yes, this is going to be a great night," I said.

Everyone was already in the limo when we got to the lobby, and Curt was yelling at us to hurry up. I sat down in the limo, Grant following right behind me, and I looked at his mom. She was smiling at me with total approval. Heather almost jumped out of her seat.

"What is that around your neck?" She screeched at me.

"Grant gave it to me, just before we came downstairs," I said.

"Oh my God, it is gorgeous," she said and gave Curt a dirty look.

"Thanks dude, way to send me up the river," Curt said. Everyone just laughed, I didn't care. I held on to Grant's hand and just held on tight.

The limo dropped us off right in front of the stadium, we went through security, went through the ticket entrance and then to our seats. What I hadn't noticed on the tickets was that we were sitting in a suite. Apparently having season tickets could get you some perks for concerts. We made our way to the suite which was pre-stocked with beer and wine. Dinner would be brought in later. We sat down in our seats and listened to the opening bands. After a few drinks, I headed to the restroom.

Grant went with me, "I will wait for you out here, since I know I will be done before you," he said kissing my cheek.

"Okay."

I finished in the bathroom and was looking at my necklace in the mirror.

"Sydney, is that you Sydney Stanton?" The voice was familiar but I couldn't place it. I turned around, Caroline Parker, not my least favorite friend from high school, but not my favorite.

"Wow, I haven't seen you since Graduation, how are you?" she asked.

"Actually, I am great," I said.

"You look great, your necklace is stunning," she said. We exchanged a few more words and then I excused myself.

"Well, it was nice to see you Caroline, take care," I said leaving the restroom. I walked out and my eyes went right to Grant, I started to walk up to him, not noticing anyone else in my line of sight.

"Sydney wow, good to see you."

"Seriously what is going on tonight?" I thought. That voice, it rang through my head and gave me the chills- damn, Trent. He stopped me before I got all the way to where Grant was standing.

He was holding my elbow, "Look at you all dressed up, I should have known you would be here tonight, since you are a huge fan of these guys," he said with a less than pleasant tone in his voice.

Grant came walking up, with no alarm on his face, absolute confidence in his demeanor.

"Sweetheart, there you are, I was beginning to worry," he said, kissing my cheek and putting his hand on my lower back, claiming me.

Trent was to say the least, stunned by Grant. He let go of my elbow, when Grant gave me a kiss. The smile Grant had on his face gave me the confidence to stand my ground in front of Trent.

"It seems it is my night to run into old friends," I said.

Just then Caroline came up to us, putting her arm threw Trent's.

"Caroline, Trent, this is my boyfriend Grant," I said smiling from ear to ear. Caroline's jaw dropped to the floor. She was in awe; I mean he is the most handsome man I have ever seen.

Grant always the gentlemen, "Trent nice to meet you, Caroline."

"Sydney, our party is waiting for us we should really return to our suite," he said. We turned and left, leaving Trent and Caroline completely dumbfounded.

"So, that is Trent?"

"Yes."

The concert was off the charts great; we danced and sang along to all the songs. When they sang their hit duet, "Feel like a Rock Star," the crowd went wild, and so did I. It was the perfect evening. I am so glad we were going back to the hotel. We had drunk quite a bit and I was ready to get out of these boots. The limo dropped us at the hotel. Grant's and Curt's parents went to the bar for a few more drinks. We headed to our room; I wanted to be alone with my man. Heather and Curt went upstairs as well.

I could hear Corinne and Courtney laughing and saying "Oh to be young and in love!"

We said good night to Curt and Heather as we exited the elevator. Once in our room, the music was on and Grant was watching the news with no sound. I went into the bathroom to change.

"Why do you have to change in the bathroom, you know I have seen you naked before," he was laughing at me.

"Geez, can a girl go potty in private?" I said. He was just laughing. He stopped laughing when I came out wearing the black and pink satin set with his necklace around my neck.

I heard his breath catch. He stood up and walked to me, putting both hands on my face, leaning down kissing me.

"You make my heart skip a beat, you are so beautiful."

I walked him to the chair and pushed him back down to his seat. I slowly unbuttoned his shirt, but left it on, pushing the sides away. I straddled him in the chair and began kissing down his neck; his hands were grabbing my ass, kneading it with his fingers. I kissed him and massaged down his chest to below his belly button, I could feel him kicking off his shoes.

He was beginning to moan, "Mmm...you are making me so hot," he said.

I began to slowly remove his jeans, opening the top button, pulling the zipper down, putting my hand inside them and releasing his very hard erection. I finally pushed his jeans to the floor; I kneeled before him, putting his entire length into my mouth, licking him from top to bottom and then back again. I massaged his balls while he groaned with pleasure; I could feel the blood pounding through his hardness.

Grant whispered to me, "Take off your bottoms and ride me."

I wasn't finished with him yet, "No, I am not done tasting you yet."

I continued to suck on him using my tongue diabolically until he was begging me to stop and ride him.

"Your mouth is killing me, but I want to come inside you, come up here and ride me," he demanded. I took off my satin nighty and I climbed up, straddling him, I let his hardness just barely touch my sex.

"Women if you don't let me inside you I am going to go crazy," he groaned.

He put his fingers inside me; I arched my back and moaned out in pleasure.

"Sydney, you are so wet, I have barely even touched you and my fingers are covered in your sweetness."

"I was touching you, tasting you, and this is what you do to me," I rasped out to him.

He removed his fingers and I lowered myself on him, my legs were over the sides of the chairs. He was thrusting up into me and I was moving back and forth, our bodies were sweating from the heat between us. He was deep inside me, I couldn't stop, he kept saying to slow down.

"No I can't... come, I need to come... I am so hot for you," we were madly kissing, his hands were pushing me back and forth.

He pulled my head back, "Hold on, I am going to come."

I moaned, my body undulated, completely moving without my help. We were panting, moaning from the immense pleasure, it was pure ecstasy, pure bliss was flowing between us.

I would never be able to give this up, "Grant you are going to kill me, you are so hard, I can feel you inside me, filling me with your come, I could ride you all day, you make me feel so good," I told him, then I screamed out from the immeasurable pleasure, as I began coming around him.

I stayed on top of him, he was holding me, and we were gasping for breath.

We were covered in sweat, "I'm killing you?" he said kissing my neck.

"I can't control what I say when you are screwing my brains out."

He lifted me up and carried me to the bed, we crawled under the covers. I was running my fingers along my necklace, thinking maybe wishes do come true.

"Sydney, when do you have to be back at school?"

"I think like August 9th or 10th."

"Why?"

"Maybe I could drive you over and help you get settled, what do you think?"

I jumped up on my knees, "Really, you would really take me back to school?"

"Of course, why would you think otherwise?"

"I guess, I really didn't think about it, I just thought we would be saying our good-bye's here."

He looked at me with a sad face and said, "As far as I am concerned there will be no good-bye's between us, I am not giving you up."

I looked at him, my heart swelling with happiness, "I love you Grant Montgomery."

CHAPTER 17

It took us all a couple of days to recover from our weekend at the hotel and concert. I lost my voice from screaming at the top of my lungs. The Montgomerys and Wilders headed back to Arizona a few days later, leaving the house very quiet. Their parents know how to have a good time and it was great getting to know them.

We spent the next few days working and I decided that with only a few weeks before my summer would be over, I would put my mantra of SEIZE THE DAY into full force. Every spare moment I had I spent with Grant; we went bowling one day, miniature golfing another, the movies another.

I also dragged him with me to get my hair cut, much to his dismay, I told him "This is what we go through to look beautiful for our men."

He just laughed at me and said, "I am never doing this again, you will pay me back later!"

I was working as many hours as possible to give myself extra spending money, hopefully enough to get me at least one round- trip ticket to New York. The tourists were never ending, the beach was crowded, the stores were crowded, and the restaurants were crowded.

When Friday night rolled around, I was ready to have a little fun, "Hey, the Captains Club is having 80's night tonight, we should go, we haven't been there in a while," I said to everyone.

Grant and Curt rolled their eyes letting out a sigh. Heather was totally up for it.

"Come on it will be fun, we can dance and they have special themed drinks for the night, come on," I whined.

"Fine, we don't have to dress up in an 80's clothes, do we?"

I started laughing, "No, only if you want to. I don't think it is a costume party, you're a dork," I said.

We went to the club around 9:00 pm, the place was out of control packed. I could hear Madonna's voice, singing "Crazy for You" over the sound system. We found our usual table filled with our friends. We were relaxing, talking, having a beer when the waitress came around with what looked like test tubes in a tray.

"Hey, you guys want a shot of sex on the beach? It's only a $1.00 a shot." The waitress asked.

We each took two since they were so little. The DJ's voice was announcing he was going to slow things down for a few minutes, the song "I'll Melt For You" was playing.

"Come on dance with me, I love this song," I said to Grant.

"You love this song, you weren't even born when it came out," he said looking at me like I was out of my mind.

"My mom and dad listen to it, I have heard it a million times, come on," I pulled him up out of his seat.

We danced slowly, I was singing along, "You really do know this song," Grant said to me.

"I told you I did."

I was in heaven, his arms wrapped around my waist, my arms latched around his neck, we were swaying back and forth.

"You're right, this is a great song," he said into my ear. "I know you don't want to talk about what is going to happen when we are apart, but…"

"You're right, I don't want to talk about it," I said to him. I could feel my heart starting to pound, this was not a conversation I wanted to have with him.

"You can keep putting it off, but eventually we will have to discuss it," kissing my forehead.

"I just want to enjoy our time together without thinking about us being separated," I told him.

When the song ended a dance party song came on, we dropped our arms, and picked our dance pace.

Back at home, we spent the night at Grant's so he could get up and go surfing.

"Sydney, I think…"

"Grant seriously, I don't want to talk about it!" I yelled at him.

"Okay, well I was just going to talk about driving back to Arizona, I was thinking, I will just stay with my parents once I take you back to school. This way we can see each other for a little longer. What do you think?" he asked me.

I turned around, my smile as wide as can be, "What do I think, I think that is a wonderful idea, but are you sure you won't miss the beach and surfing, and what about work?"

"The beach and surfing will always be here, and my job- they know I am leaving; a couple days earlier won't make a difference."

I ran to him and jumped into his arms, "You're the best, I am the luckiest girl, I love you."

"Umm...you know I will busy during the day with Sorority Rush? Hopefully I can see you at night when we are done, though no overnights because I have to be up so early for Rush everyday, okay?" I could tell he wasn't happy.

"Do I have a choice?" I just smiled and shook my head no at him.

The next few weeks flew by, we spent one day on Catalina Island, which was interesting, not that I want to go back. We drove up the coast to Santa Barbara, spent the night at one of the hotels his Dad manages, and came home the next day. We snuggled by the fire pit, talking about everything; growing up, relatives, school. Avoiding at all costs the dreaded discussion of what would happen when I was back at school and he was in New York. Until finally, I relented after he badgered me about it.

"So, how long is the MBA program?" I asked.

He looked at me with bewilderment on his face, "What, you are actually going to discuss it with me? It is two years, as long as I don't fail any classes."

"Fail any classes you're funny," I said. Grant was super smart, getting good grades was not difficult for him.

"Sydney, what do you want to happen, I mean, what do you want to happen with our relationship while we are apart?"

I looked at him touching his face, I could feel tears creeping up into my eyes. I took a deep breath, swallowed and said, "I want us to stay in love, I want us not to lose the lightning bolt that courses between us, I want to know no matter how far apart we are we will be true to each other."

"Oh, is that all? Is there anything else you want to add to that list?" He said smiling, but I could hear the sarcasm in his voice.

I looked away from him, "I just don't know if we will be able to make all those things happen."

I can't believe I told him my concern, would he be mad at me thinking I was giving up before we even tried?

Grant sighed and looked sad, saying, "I know it is going to be hard with school and being so far apart, I just know we have something special, something that you just don't find every day. If we are honest and communicate and try to see each other whenever possible, we can make it work."

With all the technology available, maybe we could make it work, maybe. We were leaving in two days to go back to Arizona. Heather was super grumpy with my leaving and Curt getting ready to head back up north. I was packing some of my clothes, Heather was sitting on my bed.

"Why don't you try to come out this year, you can stay with Kendall and I, it will be fun?" I said. She looked at me with tears running down her face.

"Yeah, I can do that, but this summer has been so out of control wonderful, I never thought we would have so much fun and I never thought I would fall so hard for Curt."

I took her hand and sat across from her on the bed, "Heather, you are only one hour away from him by plane, or a seven hour drive, you can probably see each other once a month. You guys really have a chance, you can make it work, I know you can."

She sighed and let out a deep breath, "You're right, we can we can make it work, what about you guys what are you going to do with Grant 3000 miles away?"

I didn't answer; I just stood back up and started packing.

"Sydney, what are you going to do?" she asked me again.

"I don't know, I guess, our lives will play out however it happens, you know what I mean, I just know he is going to be so deep into his program at Yale, that after a few months, he won't have time for me, even with phones, email, and Skype, it will eventually takes its toll…"

I stopped talking mid- sentence, running my fingers along the necklace he had given me.

"Sydney, I think you guys will make it work, I have never seen two people more perfect for each other, if you guys aren't soul mates then let lightning strike me now," she said, leaning away from the window, just in case. I laughed and threw a pillow at her.

I kept laughing, "Well time will tell, I am just going to enjoy every moment I can with him."

I finished my last day of work on Thursday, said my good-byes to everyone at the surf shop. I asked Russ to mail me my last paycheck and gave him my new address. He told me I could come back and work for him anytime. That made me feel good. My anxiety level was climbing. Leaving the beach was heartbreaking, all the memories I had amassed over the summer were flooding my brain. I stopped by the hardware store on my way back to my house.

"Hey baby," Grant said when I came in the store.

He came up and hugged me, "You look awful, are you alright? You look like you are going to cry."

I just threw my arms around his waist and put my head on his chest, tears were falling down my face, "I am going to cry," I said barely able to spit out the words.

He was stroking my head, "It will be alright, crying isn't going to change anything," he said.

He pulled me away and wiped my cheeks, "Why don't you go home and I will come by and see you when I get off work, maybe in about an hour or so," he said.

I nodded my head yes and waved good-bye to him.

I flopped down on my bed, like the world was coming to an end. In my mind it was; the wonderful summer, wonderful boyfriend, all ending. I fell asleep face down on my bed and woke up to Grant moving my hair off my face and caressing my arm.

"Hi," I said stretching. "What time is it?"

He smiled, "Time for you to get up, let's go get some dinner, the four of us, one last night together," he said.

"Okay, let me just clean up, give me five minutes."

"Five minutes, yeah right, I am going to wait right here, so you don't take all night just to go get pizza," he said crossing his arms. I gave him a dirty look and pushed him away.

We were out the door in ten minutes, the four of us walking all cute down to town to get pizza together. We ate a large pizza and drank a pitcher of beer. We decided to walk down to the pier and then down to the beach before heading home.

I asked Grant, "You know the first night I came down here- the bonfire party night?"

"Yeah, what about it?" he asked.

"If you already knew who I was, why didn't you come up to me and start a conversation, I know you saw me staring at you over the fire?" I asked him.

"I don't know, I guess I was so shocked to see you here, I thought maybe my eyes were deceiving me. Then I could see Heather and the look on her face, you two talking about me, I knew Heather was telling you to stay away from me and well, I didn't feel like trying to prove myself to you at that moment. I was wrong, I should have just come right over and introduced myself to you, then I would have gotten into your panties at least a few days earlier than I did," he started to run away from me when he was finished, knowing I would punch him in the arm for that comment.

"Grant Montgomery, you are such a naughty boy!" I said to him.

He ran back up to me picking me up, lifting me high above his head, he slowly let me slide down him until our lips were touching.

"Now this is what I call delicious," he said and we began to kiss.

Not a hot I want your sex kiss, but a long I love you kiss. Which was making my insides turn upside down with desire for him, I looked him in the eyes. I could see his dark brown eyes were even darker now, his need for me growing.

"I think we should go home," I said taking his hand and leading him back up the beach.

"I think you are right," he said.

He stopped walking about halfway back to the house and pulled me to him, "I don't think I can walk another step without kissing you again," he said to me.

"Well your wish is my command," I said.

I pulled his face down to mine and gave him an out of control take me to your bed kiss that left him panting and his erection almost breaking through his shorts. When we were close to the house he scooped me up and carried me to his bedroom. Shutting the door and locking it behind him, turning on the music, "Honey Bee" by Blake Shelton was playing.

"Oh, this song, it reminds me of you, well everything reminds me of you," I said.

He laid me down on the bed, I sat up on my knees and began taking my clothes off as fast I could, and he was kicking his shoes off, stripping down just as fast. He pounced on me before I had a chance to move. We were kissing like there was no tomorrow. His thigh was in between my legs and I was grinding on him, moaning for him.

"What happened to my wish is your command," he said.

"What do you want then?" I asked.

"I want to sink myself into you, show you what you do to me, and I don't want you to give in to your climax until I tell you to."

"I know what I do to you," I said as I took his bulging erection into my hand.

"I want you to make me scream your name," I said to him.

After that he flipped me over on to my stomach, pushing my chest into the bed. He entered my sex from behind, it was so good I could barely breath. I was screaming out his name in harsh breaths.

"Grant, don't stop, harder, don't stop," I said.

I was losing control, I was pushing back on him, my orgasm climbing. He was thrusting into me, holding on to my hips, pulling me back to him with force in each thrust.

He didn't stop, his desire for me making him push harder, holding on to his orgasm until he was moaning my name, "Don't stop, keep moving back on me," he said.

I could feel him begin to shake behind me, I was waiting for him to let me come.

"I want to come!" I gasped out.

"No Sydney, not yet." What? He was going to come inside me and I couldn't? I felt his release inside me, I was biting my lips. I could barely breath, holding on by a thread.

I screamed at him, "I am going to come!"

"No!"

He pulled out of me and flipped me on to my back. He pushed my hands above my head and put his head between my legs. His tongue was inside of me tasting me, licking up and down my sex. He sucked hard on the bud of my clit, and with one last push of his tongue, he released my hands.

"Now Sydney, come on my tongue." I was screaming and groaning from the pleasure, I was out of my mind from the sensation he had given me. I could feel his tongue, sucking up my cream.

"Grant, oh my…" I could barely speak. I had my hands in his hair, tugging on the ends. My breathing was erratic, I was flying high. My body was beyond ecstasy.

Grant was holding me now, my body still shaking from the orgasm.

"I can't believe what you did to me with your tongue, the feeling was out of this world."

"I wanted you to remember our last night at the beach together, something you would never forget," he said caressing my face.

"Thank you."

We feel asleep holding each other and woke up in the morning all tangled up in each other with the sheets pulled over us.

CHAPTER 18

I didn't want to get out of bed, I wanted to stay here with him at the beach in our perfect summer forever.

He leaned over and kissed my cheek, "Good Morning, we need to get up and get going, so we don't have to drive when it is super-hot. If we leave in the next hour we can be at my parents' just after lunch."

"I know, but if we stay in bed for a few hours or the entire day, we can leave just before dinnertime and get to your parents' late and get right back into bed," I said grinning wickedly.

I could see him thinking about it, "Although the idea is very tempting, we will be stuck in traffic on the 91 Freeway for three hours if we leave any time after 1:00 pm. So get up hot stuff," he said and hit my ass before I could cover it with a pillow. Damn him!

We loaded up his Jeep with his stuff at his house and then drove over to Heather's and picked up my stuff.

He just looked at me with raised eyebrows, "Really you need all this stuff?"

"Well yeah, and I have stuff in storage back at school," I said with a smile on my face.

"Oh damn, we have to drop your car off at your parents', huh? We are never going to get on the road," he was totally aggravated, he hated complications.

"Geez, we have to stop and say good-bye to them anyways or did you think we were just heading out without stopping to see my parents," I griped at him.

"No, no, you're right, but I forgot, we won't make it to my parent's until dinnertime."

"So, are we going to turn into pumpkins or something?" seriously he could be so rigid sometimes, what happened to my cool as a cucumber boyfriend.

"Not pumpkins, but we may shrivel up like raisins in the desert heat!"

I stuck out my tongue at him, "Ha, ha," I said back to him with a snotty tone.

We said our good-byes to Heather and Curt, and he followed me to my parents' house. We pulled up to the house and I parked in the drive way; my dad was in the garage, my mom in the house, and my sister was out doing wedding stuff, Grant was tapping his foot leaning up against his car when I got out of mine.

He whispered to me as I walked up to him, "Don't go in the house, we will never get out of here if you do."

Totally annoyed by his remark, "Alright, calm down, can I just give them a hug and kiss?"

"Hi, Dad."

"Hi, kids all set to go back to school?" He asked.

"Yes, can you get Mom so we can say good-bye to her and get on the road?" I asked him.

"Honey, you run and get her, my hands are all dirty." I rolled my eyes.

"Fine," I stood in the door way, yelling, "Mom, can you come outside? We need to get on the road!"

I was leaning on the door, waiting for her. I saw my Dad walk out to Grant who was waiting by his Jeep.

"Grant, son, let's talk for a minute," he said wiping his hands on a rag and walking with Grant a way from his car.

"Oh my, this should be interesting", I thought to myself. What is he saying to him? Dads can be so embarrassing. My mom finally came outside, I didn't even notice her walk up next to me, I was trying to read their lips, but I was way too far away.

"Oh, jeez," I sighed.

"What is going on down there?" my Mom asked me.

I shook my head, my hands on my hips, "I have no idea, no idea, something mortifying I am sure!"

"Sydney, you are his baby girl and based on the necklace Grant gave you, I would say there is more than a summer romance going on between you two."

"Mom do something, Dad is going to embarrass me," I was begging her.

"Relax, I am sure he is just giving him the standard warning about you being his youngest daughter, being perfect, too good for him, and if he breaks your heart, to keep the hell away from here because he has a gun that has no registration and can't be traced!" She was cracking herself up putting her arm around me.

"That is so not funny, Grant will probably run as fast as possible to New York, this family is so weird," I said shaking my head and sighing with exasperation.

She handed me an envelope with a check and some cash.

My mom started saying, "Sydney, I know you two had an amazing out of control relationship this summer and I am so happy for you, but just be careful, I don't want to see you get hurt again. He is already done with college and headed to New York. Make sure you don't make him feel guilty for pursuing his dreams, he is very sweet and adores you, but you are still so young. Have fun this year and be honest with him, most relationships are ruined by lies, miscommunications, and not saying how you really feel, ok?" she said looking seriously at me.

"Thank you, I understand, I will try to remember your advice when I am crying my eyes out because he is 3000 miles away."

"Oh Sydney, things will work out, don't worry," she said lifting my chin up.

"I love you, you better get on your way before your father talks Grants ear off, call me when you get to his parents' house, okay?" she said.

I gave her a hug and kiss, and then we walked down to where my Dad was lecturing Grant.

I walked up behind my Dad and made my eyes get really big and mouthed "Sorry" to Grant. Grant showed no expression to me.

I could hear Grant saying "Yes sir, I know sir, I will try not to do that sir."

I cleared my throat, "Hi guys Dad, Grant and I really need to get on the road, we are going to get stuck in traffic…"

My Dad looked down at me smiling completely happy with himself, "Oh yeah, okay honey, give me a hug and kiss, we will see you for Parents' Weekend," he said.

We got in the car, waving good-bye, I had a fake smile plastered on my face, talking through my gritted teeth, "Are you super mad at me?" I asked him.

"Mad no, scared shitless yes," he said.

My jaw dropped open a little and I started to laugh at his response.

"It is not funny, your Dad scares the shit out of me, he basically said, I wasn't good enough for his daughter and that if I hurt you in any manner, he has a gun...did you know he has a gun?"

I was still laughing, "Really, scared of my Dad, he is all bark and no bite."

"Well I don't want to find out!"

I looked at him still giggling and said, "I guess you don't have a choice, never hurt me, and if you do- run away." He shot me a look that sent shivers down my back and not the good shivers.

I think we finally got on the road around 9:30 or 10:00 am, we had to stop for gas and snacks.

My phone was beeping like crazy, "Would you turn that thing off or put it on vibrate, the beeping is annoying," he said.

"Geez, what has your panties in a twist?" I asked him.

"Nothing."

"Something."

"I will be fine once we get on the open road, away from all this traffic," he said. I looked around we had just passed the 55 and were headed out on the 91 freeway, there was no traffic, what is he talking about? I didn't say anything. I started to read my messages.

Friday, 9:46 am: Heather to Sydney: so quiet here!

Friday, 9:47 am: Kendall to Sydney: What time RU getting here?

Friday, 9:47 am: Mom to Sydney: hope Grant isn't too mad about his talk with dad.

Friday, 10:05 am: Sydney to Heather: sorry, just heading out of town, miss you!

Friday, 10:06 am: Sydney to Kendall: just leaving oc, b in az by dinner time, spending nite at Grant's.

Friday, 10:15 am: Kendall to Sydney: argh, u know u need to be @ house by 10 on sat. morning.

Friday, 10:16 am: Sydney to Heather: I will b there, did u get my stuff from storage? Y so early in morning.

Friday, 10:22 am: Kendall to Sydney: yes, on ur bed, rush practice @ 10 am.

Friday, 10:24 am: Sydney to Kendall: argh...call u when I get to HBG house.

Friday, 10:27 am: Kendall to Sydney: k, drive safely.

Friday, 10:30 am: Sydney to Mom: mom, grant super grumpy, tell dad thanks a lot.

I sighed and looked out the window, "What time do you think we will get to your parents' house?"

No response from Grant.

"Hello, earth to my grumpy boyfriend. Are you even listening to me?"

"What?" he said biting my head off. Yikes, this is going to be a fun drive.

I asked him again, "What time do you think we will get to your parents'?"

"Oh, if we don't stop, probably around dinnertime."

"Don't stop, are you nuts, I will have to pee at some point, and you know how cranky I get if I don't eat," I said giving him a look. He just shook his head at me in exasperation.

"Is this how you are going to act the whole drive?" I asked starting to get snotty with him.

"What? I am fine."

"If this is fine, I don't want to see you in a bad mood!"

I just looked out the window, pulled out my iPod and listened to some music. When he is ready to talk then we can talk, otherwise I am not feeding into his crabby world. I leaned my seat back a little and shut my eyes. I was semi- awake but not really, I felt the warmth of his right hand on my thigh. I opened one eye just a little, I could see the grim line across his jaw, I closed my eyes and put my hand on his, latching my fingers through the tops of his fingers. I opened one eye just a little again and I could see the grim line starting to soften.

I didn't say anything to him, we drove in silence for a long time, he did turn on the car stereo and was listening to talk radio- sports talk. I sat up when I felt the car slowing down and exiting the highway.

"Hi, sleepy head, want to stop for lunch and we can fill up the tank?" he asked.

"Where are we?"

"Blythe, we are about halfway there," he said.

"Yeah sure, I could eat and use the bathroom," I said.

We got some burgers and used the restrooms, filled up the tank with gas, and were headed out on the road again, I think we stopped for all of 30 minutes. Hopefully this second half of the ride would be better.

We were back on the highway, "Do you want to play the license plate game?" He asked.

"Sure, starting now," I said.

He had obviously relaxed, we played the license plate game for a while.

"Okay, I am done with this game," I told him.

"You're only done, because you're losing."

"You cheat, I can see you looking at the plates of the other cars in the rearview mirror, totally not fair," I said.

"Totally," he said.

"I am glad you are in a better mood, I don't think I have ever seen you that grumpy."

"I wasn't grumpy! I was *NOT* expecting the lecture I got from your father, it took me a while to digest his words."

"Sorry, I didn't know he was going to do that to you." He grabbed my hand.

"It is not your fault, don't feel bad. If I ever have a daughter and she brings home someone, I will do the same thing to him," he said.

"Oh, umm, so you're not mad at me?"

"No, I am not mad at you."

That made me feel better I let out a sigh of relief.

"That was a big sigh," he said.

"I know, are your parents going to let us sleep together tonight?"

"I don't see why not, they didn't care at the beach house."

"Just checking, I have to been at the house by 10:00 am tomorrow," I said with a fake smile on my face. His face dimmed.

"Okay, I will have you there on time, don't worry."

We drove the rest of the way talking about stupid stuff; songs on the radio, why football is such a big deal and why did they always drive up the middle instead of going around the outside to make a touchdown, it made no sense to me. He just laughed at me and I just smiled at him.

My mind was drifting, thinking about everything from classes starting, Sorority Rush to homework, as we passed the desert landscape.

Grant asked, "Do you know your schedule yet?" I looked at him kind of funny.

"You know your classes, do you have classes everyday?"

"Oh yeah, I mean, no. I have classes on Tuesday, Wednesday, Thursday, no classes Monday's or Friday's, nice right?"

"Good job, how did you manage that?"

"It just worked out that way, can't say I am upset about it, every weekend is a four day weekend."

He smiled really big, I mean really big.

"What, why are you smiling like that?" I asked.

He was thinking I could see the way his eyes were moving and his head was tilted.

He said, "Maybe that will allow you to come to New York more often to see me!"

I had been waiting for him to ask me to visit, not wanting to ask if I could come.

"Are you sure, I mean I wouldn't want to distract you from your studies," I said.

"Are you kidding me, all I will be doing is studying and anyway, the kind of distractions you bring are worth it!"

Seriously this is a long drive, I was beginning to get stir crazy from being in the car for six hours. Finally I could see civilization ahead.

"Oh look, how much further to your parents'?" I asked.

"Probably 45 minutes."

"Ugh, another 45 minutes!"

I was like a little kid all disappointed. He just laughed at me because he could see my bubble bursting. Finally we were getting off the freeway, turning, I had never been in this part of town, totally different then by campus. There was the usual; strip malls with grocery stores, cleaners, restaurants, and so on. We drove down past a bunch of homes. Then Grant turned, went down a long road, beautiful landscaping on both sides, I felt like we were driving into a plush resort. We went through a guard gate using a special access button, then passed a few stop signs.

Grant said, "Curt lives down this street," pointing to his right. I looked down at the houses, if you could call these homes houses.

"Oh." We drove a little further, turned left and another left on to a cul-de-sac.

At the end of the cul-de-sac, Grant went up the long drive way, pulled to the right, opened one of the six garages, pulled in, and parked.

I turned to him, "This is your house, the house you grew up in, is there nothing normal about your family?" I said.

My mouth was open as we got out of the car. Inside the garage was a convertible Jaguar, golf cart and I don't know how many bikes-and I think I saw some off-roading motorcycles. I was standing behind the Jeep, there were three more garages with the doors down, I didn't even want to think about what was in them.

He opened the back and starting pulling out all the stuff, I said, "Wait, I only need my blue duffel bag, everything else just leave in here."

"Oh ok, good, you have a lot of stuff, I will just carry my gear in then." He handed me my bag and started pulling out his stuff.

"You have just as much stuff as I do," I told him.

We made our way to the house through a back entrance, the door was unlocked so someone was home, it was almost 5:00. We came in, walked down a small hall and turned right, there was a set of stairs going up on our left.

"Just leave your bag on the steps, we can get to my room from here, let's find my mom," he said.

I put my bag on the bottom step next to his. He took my hand and started giving me a tour. On our right was a powder room, then what looked like a workout room, we took a few more steps and turned to the left. We came out into the biggest Great Room I had ever seen. There was a wet bar in one corner. The middle of the room had an L-shaped sectional with a massive TV and fireplace in front of it. There were French doors leading to the back yard. The kitchen was out of control, large L shaped peninsula, giant island, two refrigerators, double oven, and an industrial stove. Did I mention the kitchen table; round and big enough for eight people.

His mom was standing in the kitchen drinking a glass of wine. She saw us walking up.

"Kids, oh I am so glad you made it here safely," she said coming up and giving us each a hug and kiss on the cheek.

"How was the drive, hot, traffic?" she asked.

Grant said, "No, we made good time, what do we have to drink I am tired and thirsty?"

"Oh okay, everything, check the beverage drawers," she said.

Beverage drawers, I wasn't sure I knew what that meant. "I had been in nice houses before but this was ridiculous", I thought to myself.

"Sydney are you thirsty, do want a snack, I just got home from work, I am going to run up and change and then I will make us dinner, ok?" she said walking out of the room.

I excused myself to the restroom and when I came back, I was standing alone in the middle of this great room. I looked around, feeling a little out of place. I didn't even want to go looking for Grant, I might get lost. A moment later, Grant came up behind me, putting his arms around my waist. Kissing my cheek, I turned around inside his arms.

He gave me a big kiss and said, "Mmm...I have wanted to do that all day. Do you want to go for a swim and relax by the pool after that long drive?"

"Sure whatever, where did you go just now?" I asked him.

"I went to the other bathroom." I just rolled my eyes. "Of course there was another bathroom, a house this size must have 50 bathrooms", I thought.

"Ok, let's go change," he said pulling me back the way we came in. We went upstairs, to his room.

"You can take the back steps, or there are steps by the front door to come upstairs. This is my bedroom," he said as we walked into his room.

He had a king size bed, dresser, desk, two night stands, there were French doors leading out to a balcony, a walk- in closet, and his own bathroom. The room was painted in grey with a couple of those Fat Head giant stickers of different athletes stuck on the walls.

"Seriously, this is the bedroom you grew up in, so not fair."

"What, you don't like it, let me show you the view."

View I thought, spoiled. He opened the French doors and on the balcony were two chairs and a little table. You could see the entire backyard; the pool, basketball court, tennis court, and a grass area.

Oh, and the bbq area, with fire pit of course. I was shaking my head sitting down in the oversized comfy chair in the corner of the room.

"What, why are you sitting in the corner looking a little pale?" Grant asked me.

"Oh, I don't know, you live in a flipping mansion, do you have servants too?" I said with complete sarcasm.

"No, no servants, should we get some?" He asked laughter in his voice.

"Very funny," I said.

"Oh and my parents' room is way down the hall out of hearing range, so when I make love to you in my bed tonight, feel free to scream out my name," he said with a wicked smile.

I rolled my eyes, "You're so..." he cut me off by kissing me.

"I am so, sexy, irresistible, tasty," I was smiling, looking up at him from under my eye lashes. "Sydney Stanton, you want me," he said.

He pulled me to my feet, "I do not," I said, my breathing having picked up a little.

"Yes you do, you get this look, you smile real big, your eyes start to gleam, and your breathing changes," he said all proud of himself for detecting my desire.

"We are going swimming remember, I am going to change," I said.

Walking over to my bag on his bed, I took out my bathing suit- the skimpy bikini he is so fond of, and headed to the bathroom.

"Yet again, why do you have to change in there?" he asked.

"Yet again, a girl has to pee in private!"

"Why, just leave the door open, I pee with the door open all the time."

"I know and you're also a caveman," I said shutting the door but not locking it.

I finished going to the bathroom, flushed the toilet, washed my hands and was naked just about to put on my suit. The door burst open, Grant, standing with no shirt on in front of me, and beating his chest.

"I Tarzan, you Jane, me caveman," He picked me up and threw me over his shoulders, smacking my ass, as he dragged me to his bed.

I was laughing as he tossed me on his bed completely naked.

"Me like what I see," he said beating on his chest again.

"You are so weird, let me put on my suit," I said.

Trying to get up, he yelled and was thumping on his chest again, "Woman stay!" He pointed to the bed, I didn't want to move, not sure what my caveman was up to.

He walked to his bedroom door, I think he was checking to be sure it was locked. I noticed he had closed the curtains and put the TV on the volume raised up. He pounced on the bed like he was tracking his prey. His hands were moving up my leg starting at my feet, tickling me, then he straddled me, I had my arms folded over my bare chest. He pulled them apart and put one hand by each of my ears. He was nibbling down my neck, making me hot with his touch. I could feel my desire spreading through my body, the lightning bolt going right to my sex. I was moaning softly as he moved down sucking on each nipple. He was already in his bathing suit, but I could feel his hardness on my leg. He released one of his hands and went right down to my wet folds.

"Oh, God, you are so ready for me," he mumbled.

His breathing having changed - his words were harder to form. I was squirming beneath him from his touch. He put one finger inside of me and I let out a moan from the feeling, he pulled his finger out and rubbed all around my folds, opening me and massaging until his fingers pressed on my hot spot.

I moaned again, "Oh, yeah," and was arching my back. He put two fingers inside me this time and continued to move them in and out, pressing on my clit until I was fully moaning, begging him to stop.

He didn't stop, I was clawing at the comforter on the bed, my legs were moving and I was trying not to lose control. He started kissing me, with deep hard thrusts of his tongue, I was sucking on his tongue, while his fingers moved inside of me.

"Come for me Sydney," he said to me.

"No, I want you inside of me."

"Later, come on my fingers, so I can taste you." He said.

His words were liquid desire to my brain, I moaned out in agony from the pleasure he was giving me. I could feel my body shake a little, my pelvis moving up and down and his fingers relentless, not stopping from their movements. I bit my lip and I came hard, releasing the tension from our drive. He pulled his fingers out of me and brought them to his mouth, coating his lips with the glistening juices and then sticking his fingers in his mouth and licking them like they were covered in chocolate frosting.

I didn't take my eyes off of him, he just smiled wickedly at me, "My favorite candy," he said, licking his lips and leaning down to kiss me, I could taste myself on his lips.

He jumped up off the bed, "Come on woman, let's' go swimming," he said.

I didn't move, I had pulled the comforter over me and was just lying on his bed. I wanted to bask in the glow of my orgasm for a few minutes. He went into the bathroom, turning on the water, washing his hands and face.

He came out, "Are you still not moving?" he said.

I started mumbling, "You see I was attacked by a caveman and I am still coming down from the rock my world experience I just had, so cut me some slack."

He pulled me out from under the comforter and walked me to the bathroom, "Put your suit on or you can swim naked, your choice," he said.

Just to see what he would do, I said, "Okay, I will swim naked."

I started to walk to the door he jumped in front of me.

"You would really swim naked in my parents' pool?" He said a little scared by my response.

"If you do, I will," I said. He eyed me for a minute.

"You know the gardeners might come, and we have very nosey neighbors, so maybe we can do that at night, when it is dark," he said all nervous.

I tried to be cool, "No problem, I will get my suit on, I don't want the nosey neighbors getting a free show!"

We made our way to the pool; swam, went down the water slide, jumped off the high rocks together.

Then he started doing flips off the rocks, "Show off!" I yelled at him.

Eventually, we sat in the spa, with the jets on. The water was very relaxing, although, I was relaxed before we got into the pool. We were playing footsies under the water, not really talking just kind of looking at each other.

His mom came out a few minutes later, "Are you two enjoying yourselves?" she asked.

"Dinner will be ready in about 10 minutes, your dad just got home and Noah should be joining us too." Noah who was very nice, could be trying on my patience. He tended to just say things without thinking them through in his brain first, Grant says he has no filter between his brain and mouth.

We dried off and went upstairs to change. It was nice being here with him in the home he grew up in. I was looking around his room while I put on dry clothes. There was a huge bulletin board; covered with everything from concert ticket stubs; to a speeding ticket he had gotten, and pictures of him with his friends, brothers, and cousins. His high school and college diplomas were framed and hanging on the wall. There was shelf with about a million trophies on it for water polo, swimming, and basketball. On his dresser was a photo taken of Grant, Ethan, Noah, and his Dad, all in grey pinstriped tuxedos, must have been Ethan's wedding. Grant looked pretty young- maybe- 17 or 18. They were all very handsome.

"What are you looking at?" Grant asked me.

"I was just looking at this photo, Ethan's wedding?"

"Yeah, I look like a dork in that tuxedo."

"No, I think you look gorgeous, you always look gorgeous."

He gave me a kiss, "Come on, my mom will think we are having sex if we don't get down there soon."

"She already thinks we have sex all the time anyways," I said. He just gave me the look that said, move it!

Dinner was great; roasted chicken, string beans, salad, and strawberry shortcake for dessert! I helped clean up the kitchen and put the food away. Grant, Noah, and their Dad went to watch TV, I am sure baseball was on, so they would be happy. I was loading the dishwasher, while Corinne put the food into containers and into the fridge.

"You know Sydney, when Grant leaves for New York, I hope you will still come have dinner with us, or I can always come by campus and have lunch with you. Just because he is going away doesn't mean we don't want to spend time with you," she said.

It was very thoughtful and made my heart warm from kindness.

"That is so nice of you, yes, I would like that."

We sat down on the couch while the guys watched the game. I was thumbing through a magazine, to pass the time. I was leaning on Grants side a little bit, I was starting to fade, I could feel my eyelids closing. Grant moved to pick up his drink and it startled me.

"What time is it, I am exhausted, would you mind if I went up to bed?" I said to Grant.

"Sure, I am going to watch the end of the game and I will be there in a few minutes," he said.

I said, "Okay, good night everyone, thank you again for dinner."

I was sitting up in his bed, watching a little TV, not really paying attention. I realized I had forgotten to text my mom or Kendall when we got here.

Friday, 9:25 pm: Sydney to Mom: Hi, mom, got here safely, busy with rush this week. Love you.

Friday, 9:26 pm: Sydney to Kendall: hi, we are here, C U in am.

Friday, 9:30 pm: Kendall to Sydney: ok, good, I thought you'd be here hours ago.

Friday, 9:31 pm: Sydney to Kendall: got here around 5, swim, dinner, family visit.

Friday, 9:33 pm: Kendall to Sydney: oh, tomorrow long day, drink coffee am.

Friday, 9:35 pm: Sydney to Kendall: argh…going to sleep.

Grant came in just as I was putting my phone down, "Oh, good you're not asleep," he said.

"No, I just sent my mom and Kendall texts, and I am just stretching out here, in your very cozy big bed."

I moved the covers over so he would crawl in next to me. He got undressed and came into bed snuggling up to me.

"What are you watching?" He asked.

"I don't know, some Lifetime movie; murder, sex, lies, you can change it," I said handing him the remote.

"Thanks."

He put on ESPN of course.

"I just want to remind you, starting tomorrow I am not sure how much time I will have or when I will have free time, so don't get mad if I can't be reached or am too tired at the end of the day to go out with you, okay?" I said to him.

"I know, but I am not used to not seeing you every day," he said.

"What do you mean, there were times we didn't see each other every day this summer," he squeezed me closer to him.

"No, not really, it is just going to be an adjustment, I guess," he said.

I was tired now, my eyes closing as I snuggled up to him. He was still talking but I couldn't keep my eyes open. I was out cold. The next morning, the room was still dark from the curtains being shut. I could hear water running in the bathroom, I stretched not wanting to get up but knowing I had too. I heard the shower turn on, I waited a minute and then quietly climbed out of bed, making my way to the bathroom. The door was open just enough for me to push it open without it making any noise. I stripped out of my pj's and stepped into the shower, his back was too me, I put my hands gently on his back. He flinched for a split second. I took some shower gel, lathering it, washing his back.

"This is nice, will you wash me every day?" he asked.

I didn't say anything, I was enjoying the moment. I let my hand move around his tight abdomen to wash him, my hands reaching down his front.

"Well, good morning to you to," I said, when my hands locked on to this erection.

"Did you think I wouldn't be hard for you when you are standing in the shower naked your breasts rubbing up against my back and hands all over me?"

He turned around, his hair was clean and wet sticking up straight, and water was falling down his back. The sight of him was making me drool.

He moved me up against the wall, he began touching me everywhere, his lips were on fire, I could feel his need. He lifted my leg up wrapping it around his waist and put one finger into my sex.

"Good," was all he said.

He pushed himself inside me, the penetration felt so good.

I groaned out, "hmm…that feels good, don't stop."

He was driving into me with the full force of his body, holding me with one arm around my waist with the other hand on the wall for balance. The feeling of him inside of me was divine, his body moving back and forth with each lunge into me, each sensation making me gasp out.

I was holding on to his shoulders, he was muttering, "Oh, God, you are so warm inside, I feel your walls gripping me… keep your eyes open," he said.

His head tilted back, he was ready to explode inside me I could see the strain on his face.

"Are you ready?" he asked me in a deep tone.

I nodded my head yes, not able to get the words out. My fingers were digging into his shoulders and he was groaning, louder sexy noises coming from deep in his throat.

"Grant, don't stop," I said.

He pushed into me harder, letting out a long "Oh…my…" was all I could hear, I was gone, screaming from his penetration.

When we were done, I was leaning against the shower wall, unable to move and he was standing with his arms on the wall on each side of my head. We were gasping for breath.

Coming down from the high, he leaned into kiss me, barely audible, I said, "Every time, you rock my world, every time!"

CHAPTER 19

After our little escapade in the shower, we dressed and went downstairs for some breakfast, his mom and dad had left for work. I put some English muffins in the toaster, grabbed eggs, cheese and some Canadian bacon from the fridge. Grant was making coffee for us. I scrambled some eggs and grilled the Canadian bacon in a pan. I found two plates and served us a hearty breakfast. We finished our breakfast, sipping our coffee together.

"I like this, you making me breakfast, drinking coffee together, and the shower wasn't bad either," he said. I smacked his shoulder.

"Stop it, yes it is delightful," I said.

We cleaned up the kitchen and then it was to time to go. I ran upstairs to get my bag.

"Why are you taking your stuff?" he asked.

"In case I need it, I don't know what time we will be done and I don't want to make you drive all the way to campus late at night," I said.

He was not happy. This week was going to be difficult.

The drive from his house to campus was about an hour. We got to the Sorority House about 9:30 am. He parked and came to open my door.

"Thank you," I said leaning up to give him a kiss.

"Can I walk you into the house?" he asked.

"Yes, but you have to wait in the front room you're not allowed upstairs or down the hall," I told him.

"Sydney I know, it is not my first time in a Sorority House."

"Sorry, forgot you got around," I said giggling.

I opened the front door, there were girls everywhere, Kendall came running up to us.

"I am so glad you here," she said hugging me.

"Holy snap, what is that around your neck?"

Same reaction Heather had had.

Grant chimed in, "I gave it to her, it is the Tiffany Infinity necklace, do you like it?" He asked her.

"Like it, it is gorgeous, I am so jealous, you have good taste in woman and jewelry," she said.

Kendall showed me to our room and gave me my set of keys to the house.

"Sydney seriously, that necklace is unbelievable," she said.

"I know, he went with his mom to pick out for me, he's really a catch," I said.

"Are you freaking out because he is going to be gone soon?" she asked.

"I am trying not to think about too much, so lets' not talk about it, okay? We should go back to the front room," I said.

When we came down the hall, Grant was surrounded by my sorority sisters.

"What are you doing here, I heard one of the older girls saying to him, I thought you graduated?"

I could hear some other girls saying. "Oh my God, who is that hot guy in the front room?"

Kendall and I walked up to him, "Hi gorgeous, put your stuff away?" he asked me.

"Yes, did you bring in the rest of my bags already?"

"No, I was waiting for you, Kendall can you help us," he asked her.

We went outside to get my stuff from his Jeep. I could feel about 20 sets of eyes watching us.

"Geez, is this the way everything is at the house, nosey nellys," I said.

Kendall laughed at me, "Yes, everybody is in everybodys' business!"

Kendall and I dragged all my stuff down to our room, while Grant again waited in the front room. We came back a few minutes later.

Grant said, "I should go, walk me out."

We walked to his Jeep, "Have fun today," he said, laughing.

"Fun, yeah right, stuck in the house all day with 100 girls, practicing for Rush, fun may not be the best word to describe the next week or so," I said.

I wrapped my arms around his neck, knowing prying eyes were watching.

"You know they are all watching from the windows?" he whispered in my ear.

"I know, should we give them a show," I asked.

He took my head in both his hands, leaned down and gave me without a doubt the most amazing kiss, I could feel my toes tingling. When we finally broke apart, I was all smiles.

He put his hands on my ass and I looked up at him, "Really?"

"Just wanting the show to be entertaining," he said leaning down so our noses were touching.

"You are so bad, but I love it, I will text you later, not sure what time, so don't wait on me for dinner, if you want to go see your friends, you should," I said.

I started to walk away; he grabbed my hand and pulled me back flush against his chest. His arms wrapped around my lower waist.

He gave me one more quick kiss on the lips and said, "I love you, see you later."

Smiling at him, "I love you too Hot Bonfire Guy," I said.

"What, you have never called me that before," he said.

"I know, it's what I called you before I knew your name, sometimes I just say HBG for short. Bye." I waved good bye, he wasn't leaving he was watching me walk back into the house leaning with his back on his Jeep.

I came into the house, there was a round of applause and chanting going on. I looked at my sorority sisters, "Seize the moment," I thought to myself, took a bow, and then said, Thank you, you can watch our show again tonight."

I was laughing and giggling with the girls.

"Okay everyone, time to get serious for a moment, Rush is in two days and we have a lot of stuff to do, please leave your phones and/or iPods in the basket on the table, and sit down in the Grand Salon," the Rush Chairman was yelling.

The Grand Salon a fancy term for giant empty room! First there were the rules of Rush, no outside contact with the rushees, no making promises. Second, learning how to vote at the end of each round. Third, singing, so much singing! Finally, lunch break, we went outside where we had lunch prepared by our house mom and alumni.

Kendall and I sat with some of the other girls from our pledge class. We had a great pledge class in our eyes, the best pledge our Chapter had ever had.

Kendall spoke first, "Well it seems you and Grant have quite the connection, would you like to tell us all about it?" she said making me squirm in my seat.

"No," I said and stuffed some food in my mouth.

"Yeah, come on tell us how you met, share. Some of us didn't meet *super-hot* guys this summer," someone else said.

"You guys are bad, but fine, short version, living at beach with friend, working in surf shop, met him, the end," I said.

"No way," Kendall was pushing my shoulder.

"Tell everyone about the bonfire, Catalina, Angels game, concert, necklace."

"You just told them," I said.

My friend Monica says, "Skip all that romantic stuff and tell us how he is in bed, seriously he has muscles all over, does he go to school here?" she asked me.

I was taking a drink of my iced tea when she asked the question and I started to spit the tea out of my mouth, choking.

"Holy hell, you girls are so nosey! He graduated from here in May and is leaving for Yale in about two weeks, enough," I said.

"No, spill," Monica said.

"Yes, he is very, very good in bed," putting my hand over my mouth and laughing, "I can't believe I just said that, I am out of here, no more details you are a bunch of vultures."

"No problem after you have a few drinks will get down to the nitty gritty," Monica yelled at me. They were all laughing as I walked to my room.

I was in my room making my bed, this was such a pain, moving in, we had stuff everywhere, Kendall had been here for a week and still wasn't unpacked. I finished with my bed and started putting my clothes away, we had one big closet to share, our own dressers, and our own desks. The bathroom was community style down the hall. Kendall came in and plopped down on her bed, we had 45 minutes before we had to be back in the Grand Salon.

"Sydney, you are so mean not sharing your details with your sisters," she said giggling.

"Really, I am not going to share intimate details with everyone, I haven't even told you what he can do with this tongue," I said with a super smile.

"Eew, already too much information, you know I don't like to talk about this stuff," she said.

"I know, I just wanted to see you get all uncomfortable," I said laughing at her.

She threw her pillow at me.

Kendall said, "I bet he is really good based on the noises Matt and I heard coming from your room, when we visited this summer."

"Eew yourself," I said to her.

We were both laughing. I had emptied two duffle bags when we heard banging on our door.

"Let's go everyone, be in the Grand Salon in five minutes," the Rush Chairman yelled.

This practicing for Rush was never ending, we had to learn what questions to ask the girls, what information to tell them, and how to decide if they would fit in to our chapter or not. We practiced greetings, remembering names, and how to move the girls around to meet other chapter members. We didn't finish until after dinner, I was exhausted. I hadn't had my phone all day, finally retrieving it from the basket. I looked at the messages, five texts.

Saturday, 4:45 pm: Grant to Sydney: R U done yet?

Saturday, 5:30 pm: Grant to Sydney: I am guessing since I haven't heard from your r not done yet.

Saturday, 6:45 pm: Grant to Sydney: hanging with some friends. Call me.

Saturday, 7:30 pm: Grant to Sydney: WHERE R U?

Saturday, 9:15 pm: Grant to Sydney: NOT HAPPY, GOING HOME!

I read his messages, argh, I thought to myself, rolling my eyes at his texts in all capital letters, that can't be good. I walked into my room, laid down on my bed, took a deep breath and called his number. We didn't really ever talk on the phone since we were together so much. He answered, total annoyance in his tone.

"Hello," he said.

"Hi, how was your day?" I asked as sweet as could be.

"Fine," was all he said.

"I am sorry, I didn't return your texts' they made us put our phones in a basket and I kind of forgot about it until we were done, I just got back to my room," I said.

"Oh, you didn't go out tonight?" he asked me.

"No, where would you get that idea?" I said back to him.

"I just figured since you weren't answering you were out for the evening," he kind of growled it at me.

I was starting to get super aggravated with him. I didn't want to say anything I might regret so, I tried to change the subject.

"So, who did you hang out with tonight?"

"Just some guys from the house, you know there is always a party going on and they are getting ready for Rush too," he said.

"Oh, sounds fun, did you have a good time?"

"Yeah, it was okay, same as always, beer, poker, music, and..." he stopped talking.

"And what? Girls, were you going to say girls?" I asked.

"Yeah, there were other sorority girls at the house, I kept thinking you would walk through the door," he mumbled.

This conversation was not enjoyable.

"Well, I don't know what other houses are doing preparing for Rush, but we just finished. So, don't be questioning what I tell you," I said curtly.

"You're in a pissy mood," he said.

"Well I have been locked in this house all day with 100 girls and my boyfriend sends me mean messages and then questions my whereabouts, yes I am a little pissy," I said back to him in a raised voice, not yelling just about though. I continued, "I am really tired, I am going to go to sleep, we have to be up and ready to work on some Rush decorations at 8 am, good night," I said in a huff.

I hung up before he had a chance to say anything.

I dropped my phone down and closed my eyes, my arm over my eyes, just then Kendall walked in, I was mumbling something under my breath.

"What's up with you?" she said.

"Nothing, just Grant being a butthead is all. Seriously, I am stuck here all day and he is questioning what I was doing, ugh," I said completely exasperated with my phone call to him.

"Maybe he is having separation anxiety, it is probably good, you have the next two weeks to get used to not being together 24/7," she said.

"Why, what do you mean?"

"Well, if he would just fly off to New York, after being together constantly, the anxiety of being apart would be even worse, this way, you are easing into it, only seeing each other a few hours a day or not at all, 'cuz you're not gonna get to see him at all next week," she said.

My lips were raised in disgust giving me a very unhappy look on my face.

"At all, what, not see him at all during Rush week, I don't think I can handle that," I said.

I let out a big sigh, "This sucks, I finally meet this amazing, rock my world guy, and the final two weeks before he leaves for graduate school, I will be locked in this house and then in classes, this really sucks."

Kendall just laughed, "You will survive," she said.

"Easy for you to say Matt is just five minutes away, you don't have separation anxiety."

I left the room to wash my face and brush my teeth. I crawled into bed a while later, looking at the bags and boxes which still needed to be unpacked. I was really missing Grant, not used to not sleeping next to him. I looked at my phone, no messages. A tear dropped down my face.

Sunday came and went, busy all day, and I mean all day, with Rush projects and practice, finally, getting back to our room late. I had left my phone in my room charging, no need to take it with me, since we weren't allowed to have them, even in our pockets, because the phones were a distraction. Kendall and I walked into our room, thoroughly wiped out. I didn't go wash my face or brush my teeth, I just stripped off my clothes, put on some pj's and hopped into bed. I looked at my phone one message.

Sunday, 11:20 am: Grant to Sydney: I am an ass, forgive, me dinner tonight?

Not really wanting to talk to him after our call the night before and knowing he would be mad again, since I hadn't responded to him today.

Sunday, 9:37 pm: Sydney to Grant: Just got back to my room, sorry, I missed having dinner with you. Super busy day, I miss you tons, rush starting tomorrow, not sure when I will be available, maybe late night. I LOVE YOU!

Sunday, 9:45 pm: Grant to Sydney: Do you seriously think I believe u were doing rush stuff all day long. U didn't have 5 minutes, to check ur phone and respond. I am out anyways, see u whenever.

Sunday, 9:51 pm: Sydney to Grant: I told you last week, it would be like this…hope ur having fun.

The next morning Rush officially started, we were busy all day, only getting about 30 minutes to have lunch. "Don't eat anything heavy", the girls in charge told us, you will be sluggish during the rush parties. Seriously, bossy doesn't even sum it up. When we were finally done for the day, had dinner, cleaned up and prepared for the next day it was close to 10:00 pm.

We went to our room, "I just want to put my feet up, these shoes are not comfortable enough to wear for 12 hours a day!" I said. Kendall and I laughed. I went to check my phone.

Monday, 10:15 am: Grant to Sydney: call me.
Monday, 1:38 pm: Grant to Sydney: R U going to call me?
Monday, 7:15 pm: Grant to Sydney: seriously.
Monday, 9:50 pm: Grant to Sydney: going to bed, who r u with?

I was too tired to even deal with his bullshit, I will text him in the morning. What happened to my easy going boyfriend who trusted me? Maybe he never really trusted me.

Tuesday, 7:45 am: Sydney to Grant: heading into rush parties, busy all day, I will try to call u 2nite, super tired, miss you. I told u it would be like this!

Tuesday and Wednesday were like a blur, I didn't even know which day it was, I was sleeping, eating, talking sorority. All the girls were starting to look the same. The closer we got to bid day the more intense the voting for new pledges became. Fighting about why or why not someone should be part of our house was daunting.

When Kendall and I got back to our room each night, we didn't even talk, we went right to sleep. Not even checking our phones.

Thursday finally, we would finish early today, when I got up, I looked at my phone for the first time in two days- unbelievable I know, but the truth. I cringed when I saw the messages.

Tuesday, 5:15 pm: Grant to Sydney: movie 2nite?
Tuesday, 9:25 pm: Grant to Sydney: what the...where ru?
Wednesday, 10:11 am: Grant to Sydney: out of sight out of mind, it has been 5 days, without seeing you. 2 days since we spoke.
Wednesday, 9:28 pm: Grant to Sydney: I AM GOING OUT!!

My phone had 3 voice mails, taking a deep breath, I started to listen. The first message, I could hear music playing. It sounded like "Payphone" by Maroon 5, but I couldn't be sure that was it. The second call was Grant mumbling, and I could hear someone yelling at him to hang up the phone and stop drunk dialing Sydney. The third call well that was a doozy, he was wasted -his words slurring when he spoke, my stomach churned.

"Yeah, Sydney, this is your boyfriend, you know Grant, or have you forgotten, me already, I haven't even left yet and you are out and about doing whatever, I know you are with someone, who is it?" Then I heard, *"Damn it, give me the phone,"* click.

I listened to the message again, I couldn't believe it, how could he talk to me like that, your true feelings come out when you're drunk. He didn't trust me. My heart was beginning to crack. I started to think, I was deceiving myself to believe this relationship would work, it must have been wishful thinking. I sent him a text.

Thursday, 7:30 am: Sydney to Grant: got ur voice mail this am, sorry u have no faith in me, maybe u should look in the mirror, maybe it is u who has no faith in himself. Don't try to contact me today, I will be busy with RUSH!

The day seemed to drag on forever, I just wanted to be done with this. We spent all day getting ready for the final night of Rush, the biggest night. It was formal, active sorority members wore black dresses with our pins above our hearts. We finally finished the voting, extending bids to 35 girls. Tomorrow we would have a new pledge class. Thank goodness, no more Rush for a year.

I collapsed in my room, I had worn my pretty new dress that I bought with Grant's mom during the summer. Hanging it back up, I was sad. I knew he would be gone soon and not see me in this dress or take me to the formal. Tears were burning my eyes, I didn't even want to check my phone. I am sure there would either be some mean, nasty text from him, or a voice mail saying unkind things to me. I couldn't deal with who Grant was turning into. Was he always untrusting of me or only when I returned to school did this version of Grant appear?

I didn't want to fight via text with him so I just didn't even bother texting. I was tired and didn't have the energy for his insecurities. I went to sleep. I was dreaming or so I thought, my phone was ringing, our room was dark, reaching for my phone on my desk which was right next to my bed. I knocked it to the floor.

"Damn," I picked it up, "Hello," I said with a sleepy voice.

No one answered I could hear a lot of noise and what sounded like "Somebody I Used To Know" by Goyte playing right into my ear.

Then I heard him, "No, I am not calling her, Grant give me the phone don't drunk dial Sydney, you are going to make an ass out of yourself." Click the phone went dead.

A few minutes later, my phone rang again, now I was completely awake it was after 11:30 pm, "Hello," I said again, "Grant is that you?" I asked, no response.

"Sydney, I haven't seen you in days, I can't do…thisss, it is too hard, not being with you," he said slurring his words.

Oh he was out, and he was drunk.

"Grant where are you?" I asked him. "Hey man, where am I? Oh, where, oh, okay, thanks man," he said to someone else.

"Yeah I am at the Finish Line, what are you doooing?" He asked me.

"I was sleeping, do you need me to come get you?" I asked him.

Then I heard "Shit, Grant give me the phone, Sydney, is that you?"

"Yeah, who is this?"

"It is Noah, sorry Grant is drunk, I tried to keep him from calling you, but well I took my eyes off him for one minute and sorry he woke you," Noah said.

"Can I talk to him for a minute?" I asked Noah.

"I don't think that is a good idea, just talk to him tomorrow, he is going to say something to upset you and you know, I'd rather not be responsible."

"Okay, good night," I said.

I lay in bed tossing and turning unable to fall back asleep. Worrying about what he said. What did he mean he can't do this? I wouldn't get a chance to talk to him until after lunch. I finally dozed off around midnight, hoping my phone wouldn't ring again. We woke up early to get ready for Bid Day, the girls who accepted our bids would be arriving by 9:00 am.

Friday, 7:45 am: Sydney to Grant: hope u r not to hung over, I will be done @ 1 pm, come pick me up, please.

I didn't expect a response so early in the morning. I put my phone in my back pocket on vibrate. The morning went super-fast, all the girls we extended bids to, showed up. After the formal greetings we were free to go, yes! My head was pounding from the idle chit chat, hunger and of course, my lack of sleep. I walked up to my room, checking my phone, no messages from Grant. I dropped my head, tears welling in my eyes, I thought this was going to happen, I just didn't think it would happen this fast. In my heart, I could feel the crack getting bigger. I was sitting on the end of my bed when Kendall came in.

"What is it, what's wrong?"

"I don't know, Grant called me drunk last night, and was muttering on about not being able to do this, and then his brother took the phone away from him. Noah apologized for Grant's behavior but I still haven't heard from him today. I sent him a text this morning, but he hasn't responded to me."

Kendall just gave me a hug, "Guys are stupid, you know that, he probably has a hangover and feels like idiot, he will call don't worry, come on- we can walk over to the burger place and have lunch," she pulled me to my feet.

Maybe a change of scenery would lighten my mood. I doubted it!

We were walking back to the house, I was ready for a power nap, tonight we were going out.

"Hey Sydney, I think your Mr. Wonderful is waiting in front of the house for you," Monica said as we got closer.

"Yeah right," I said.

"Yes, look isn't that him leaning on that white Porsche?" she said.

He was leaning on the back of the sports car, faded red shorts, white t-shirt which emphasized every one of his dazzling muscles, his hair was perfectly spiked on top of his head and he had on aviator sunglasses. I could feel my heart skip a beat, the tingling sensation running through my body. I took a deep breath as we approached. Kendall and Monica said hi and bye and went inside.

It was difficult for me to stay mad at him, but I was mad very mad. He stood up from the car when he saw me walking towards him, putting out his hand.

"Hi, gorgeous, you look scrumptious," he said.

I don't know about that; my hair was down, I had on jean shorts, with a cami on underneath my tank top which had my sorority letters across my chest. He pulled me up to him, hugging me and taking a deep breath by my neck.

"You smell good," he said his words make my head spin.

"Nice to see you," I said to him.

"How are you feeling?"

"I feel great, now that you are in my arms, I have missed you so much," his voice cracking a little as he spoke.

"You have a funny way of showing it," I said.

"I know, Noah said I kept drunk dialing you last night and he had to take my phone from me, sorry," he said sheepishly.

I pulled away from him a little bit, "I sent you a text this morning, why didn't you let me know you were coming to see me?"

"I didn't know what to say, I felt it was better to take my chances and just show up here," he said smiling at me.

"Do you remember anything you said to me when you called me last night or the other night's voice mail," I asked him.

"No, why, what did I say?"

"Well um, never mind, we can talk about it later, I am just glad you are here."

"Your chariot awaits," he pointed with both hands to the car.

"Whose car is this?" I asked.

"My car is getting an oil change, so I borrowed my Dads, do you like it?"

"No, I hate it, of course it is super sexy! You look superhot just standing next to it," I said and winked at him, my desire for him boiling a little.

It was a white, convertible sports car, with the top down.

"I thought you might like it," he said.

"I was thinking we could head out for a drive and maybe stop somewhere for a drink, are you game?"

"Sure," I said.

He opened the door for me, climbing in, and buckling my seat belt. Grant started the car and I could hear the engine purr and feel the power. The stereo was blaring, "Whistle" by Flo-rida, when we pulled away from the Sorority House. Grant was singing along to the radio. He took off up the freeway heading to downtown, my hair was blowing all over the place, he was smiling at me laughing about my hair, I started to pull it into a ponytail, and I could feel his hand caressing my thigh. I felt lightning bolts exploding inside my entire body, I have missed his touch, it was almost a week since we had seen each other. We drove for a while and then pulled in front of a small Mexican restaurant, it looked like a hole in the wall, a place only locals would know about.

"Where are we, have you been here before?" I asked.

He smiled real big and leaned over giving me a mouthwatering, heart stopping kiss on the mouth. I wanted to say screw the food, let's go get a room somewhere.

"This is my favorite Mexican Restaurant, I have never brought any girl here, you are going to love it."

I raised my eyebrows at him, "Okay, if you say so, but I just ate."

"What did you eat two bites of a burger and ½ a French fry?" He helped me out of the car, we went inside, ordering at the counter, he ordered for us both, six carne asada tacos, taquitos, and chicken enchiladas, with rice and beans, and two Coronas. The restaurant was super small- just a few tables with pictures of different Mexican beers on the wall.

"I hope you know I am not going to be able to eat all that food," I told him.

"You need to keep up your energy level up for what I have planned," he said smiling salaciously. I walked away from him shaking my head and found a table.

Grant came and sat down across from me handing me a beer with a lime wedge in it. The waitress brought over some chips and salsa, and then a few minutes later our food was brought to the table. Grant didn't lie, the food was yummy. We ate almost everything, my stomach was hurting from all the food.

"Do you want another beer?" he asked me.

"Sure, why not?" I was planning on going out tonight. We each had one more beer, the tension was thick between us, I could tell he wasn't being himself and I was hiding how mad I truly was with him.

"Okay, then should we head out, do you want to go back to my house and hang out for a while and then I will take you home?"

"Yes, that is a good idea."

We were sitting in the parking lot, before he started the engine, I put my hand on his.

"We need to talk, um, your behavior the last few days has um…been very hurtful," I said scared of his response. I could see him start to tense.

"You don't trust me, we had this amazing summer and I didn't think we had an issue with trust but apparently we do," I stopped talking.

His face was getting more and more grim, his jaw line completely strained.

"The voice mail you left, which by the way I saved so you could hear what you said to me, was rude, obnoxious, and beyond out of line. Then the text messages making unfounded accusations and then last night's drunk call, I don't know who you are, how could you say all those things to me?"

He was not comfortable with me being so direct, which surprised me since his mom was a therapist.

"I don't know what to say, I don't know why, just the last few days being apart has been more difficult than I had anticipated," he said.

"So, why didn't you just tell me that instead of making unfounded accusations and snide remarks? What are we going to do when we are separated by the whole country, a three hour time difference, and weeks at a time, if you can't even handle one week?"

I just looked at him, tears filling my eyes, he wouldn't look at me.

"I don't know, I just don't know," he said.

"What does that mean?" I asked. "You don't know what? You don't know if our love is real enough, you don't know if you can trust me or yourself, what, what do you mean?" I yelled at him.

He started the car, I was crying now, he wasn't answering me, he just started driving.

"I think you should just take me home," I said.

"It will just hurt even more if we are together and then we repeat the cycle over and over with the text messages and phone calls which only make things worse," I said with no expression on my face.

I didn't look at him the rest of the way home, I leaned on my hand looking out the window, wiping my tears. He pulled up in front of the Sorority House, the sky was dark like a monsoon was coming. I jumped out of the car before he could say anything, and started at a fast pace for the front door. He was chasing after me.

"Sydney stop, stop please!" he jumped in front of me.

"What?"

My hands were on my hips, I was no longer crying, I was furious with him. I could feel the steam rising in my body, I wanted to smack his face and tell him to just leave now for New York.

I was yelling at him, "Just leave me alone Grant, this is all your fault, when you are ready to be a man and tell me what is going on with you then give me a call, otherwise I don't think we should talk anymore!"

My own words were cutting through my heart, I could feel the crack, all of this was breaking my heart. This is not what I wanted, I didn't want our relationship to end, but I didn't want to play games. He started to recoil from me, I was seething with anger. He had created this mess with his jealousy and insecurities.

"Are you breaking up with me?" he asked.

I was yelling at him, "Isn't that what you want, no ties when you head to Yale, you won't have to worry about what I am doing, it is for the best, what we had was great... just not strong enough to handle one week apart let alone months at a time or the two years you will be gone!"

I unhooked the necklace, putting it into his hands.

"Why are you doing this, it is not what I want, you should keep the necklace," he said giving it back to me.

"This is what *you want*, you can't explain to me why you have become so possessive and jealous, when I have given you no reason for your insecurities. This is your problem to resolve and I don't want any reminders of what we had, it is too painful, just go," I said to him.

Putting the necklace back in his hands, I ran into the house before he could say anything else.

I figured we would break up, I just didn't expect it to happen only a few days after returning to school. I walked into my room, Kendall was on the phone with Matt.

"Oh shit, I have to call you back," she told him.

I was shaking, putting my head in my hands, I didn't say anything, she hugged me.

"Oh Sydney, what happened?"

I told her about him picking me up, going for the drive, dinner, and then when I tried to discuss his behavior he was unable to tell me anything, he didn't even want to fight with me, not even try to save our relationship.

"I guess it meant more to me than him, he never really loved me, it was just fun for the summer, a fling for him," I cried out.

"Do you really believe that Sydney? I think you are being overly dramatic, I know he loves you, you can see it his eyes," she said.

"Are you defending him to me, is this how you treat the person you love, if he loves me then he should trust me and fight for me?" I stood up from her bed, wiping my eyes.

"I need some aspirin and I want to go out, I am not going to cry one more tear over any guy!"

My heart was broken. Shattered into a million pieces. I hadn't told anyone yet, it was too painful, only Kendall knew and Matt too I am sure. I am not going to sit in my room again this year, not going to parties or talking to other guys. If he thought I was cheating on him, I might as well go have some good college fun! We dressed and headed out to fraternity row, all the Fraternities were having parties. We stopped in a few places, I knew we would end up at Matt's house before long.

"Hey let's check out this party before we go see Matt," it was raging.

We found a bunch of our friends inside. We hung around, drinking, dancing and I was having a great time. This was definitely helping me release my pent- up frustrations caused by my now ex-boyfriend Grant Montgomery! The more intoxicated I got, the better I thought I was feeling.

A bunch of us headed next door to Matt's house, which was Grant's house too.

"Shit," I said, my words were slurring.

"Oh Kendall, I love you, you are the best, but if that asshole Grant Montgomery is in there, I am going to kick his ass and then yours for making me come to this party."

I was cracking myself up. I was laughing so hard when we walked in the Fraternity House.

"Sydney, get a hold of yourself, do you want me to take you home?" Kendall asked me.

"No, I want to have fun and I don't want to talk about HBG, or whatever his name is…"

We walked up to Matt, Kendall whispered something to Matt.

"Don't whisper in front of me I am drunk, not an idiot," I said.

"Sydney, we just want to keep an eye on you, don't drink anymore you are going to get sick or pass out."

Matt asked Kendall, "What is up, I have never seen her this drunk?"

"She broke up with Grant because he was being an asshole," Kendall told him.

Well, I wasn't about to listen to Kendall and Matt, I figured I was in the clear, no sign of the jerk. I made my way with Monica for another drink. We got a beer and headed out to the dance floor. We were dancing with everyone not one person in particular. I felt someone dancing close behind me, it was a new pledge, I could see his pledge pin.

"You're cute," I said.

"Dance with me, our bodies move nicely together," he said to me.

I started to laugh, "Was that your best pick up line?" I said, my words slurring.

I could see Matt watching me from the other room. I rolled my eyes at him, I kept dancing with Pledge Boy, I had no idea what his name was. He put his arms around my waste and pulled me in closer to him, my hands were around his neck, I was still holding my beer. The music hadn't slowed down but this guy was really putting the moves on me.

Then out of nowhere, I could feel it, the hairs on the back of my neck stood straight up,

"*SHIT*," I said out loud.

Pledge Boy looked at me.

"What?"

"Nothing."

I was looking around but didn't see him. Maybe my tingling feelings were off because of the alcohol. We kept dancing but the feeling was becoming more intense, I could feel his eyes, burning through me. I stopped looking for him, it was over and I was not going to waste my time on him. The next thing I know, some guy is talking to Pledge Boy.

"Oh, I didn't know," he said.

"Sorry, I have to go, pledge duties," he said.

I was left standing there in the middle of the dance floor like an idiot. I shook my head. Grant was here somewhere.

I stomped off the dance floor, it was really a cement patio. I walked over to Matt and Kendall.

"Where is he?" I asked Matt.

My eyes and mouth all bunched up- I was about to have a hissy fit.

"I know he is here, watching me, he is too much of a chicken shit, I hate him. I hope I never see him again, I wasted my summer with him, he filled my head and heart with lies, Heather was right, I should have never gotten involved with him. He is an asshole!" I turned around to leave.

He was standing in the doorway listening to me rant on about him.

"I am an asshole, you are right, you should never have fallen in love with me, I used you to pass the time this summer, now everyone knows it. Should I tell the pledge how you like it, so when you have sex with him he will know exactly how to get you off?"

Before he knew it I slapped him as hard as I could across the face. He was shocked.

Kendall was ready to jump in to protect me but Matt wouldn't let her.

"She needs my help, I am not going to let him talk to her like that," Kendall said to Matt.

"Wait, I will protect her from him if it gets anymore out of hand, I wouldn't let Sydney get hurt," Matt told Kendall. People were starting to watch this drama unfold. I was so mad- furious would be a better description.

"What are you even doing here, you didn't come to any parties last year and now you have to rain on my parade, go to New York, leave," I said.

"You're wasted," he said to me.

"I am not your responsibility...I am not anything to you, you just made that very clear and your actions this week were the nails in your coffin," I said.

I tried to step around him to leave, he wouldn't let me pass.

"You are not walking home from here alone," he said grabbing my arm.

"Don't touch me," I said gritting my teeth at him.

I looked him right in the eyes, "I hate you, I wish I would have never met you, go to New York, just go," I said.

I pulled my arm away from him.

I turned back to him, "This break up is because of you...we are not all like Ashley," I said and walked out heading home.

Kendall and Matt came running after me. I was ranting about what a fool I had been and who did he think he was dealing with? Kendall and Matt just followed behind me. By the time we walked back to the Sorority House, I was much calmer. I was still totally drunk, but now I was a calm drunk.

"You two should go back to the party, thank you for making sure I was safe, you are the best, both of you," I said.

I walked in and went down the hall to my room. I collapsed on the bed face first and didn't move until the next day.

When morning came I was just lying on my bed not moving, my right hand was throbbing and so was my head. I sat up, no Kendall, she must have slept at Matt's. I looked at my phone, 10:30 am, I never sleep this late. It was Saturday, at least I think it was Saturday. I looked at myself in the mirror. I looked awful, my eyes were puffy and bloodshot. I just stood looking at myself and flashes of the night before came streaming through my brain, like a little play. Fighting with Grant in the car, getting ready to go out...hitting two or three parties before our last stop. A lot of beer, lots of beer. Dancing with some kid, Pledge Boy, I remember calling him Pledge Boy, not that I could tell you what he looks like now. Grant, Grant was at the party, a yelling match, me smacking him. My eyes began to fill with tears again, I looked down at my hand. Damn him, he said vicious things to me, I am so gullible.

231

Heather was right from the start I should have steered clear of Grant Montgomery, he was the bad boy in the crowd. No good ever comes out of falling for the bad boy in the crowd. I was sitting on the floor leaning against my bed, holding my right hand because it was seriously stinging. I had let myself fall in love with Grant, knowing the risks, telling myself all along it was fun for the summer and whatever happened at the end didn't matter, because it was always only for the summer.

I had been the one fooling myself, not Grant, I played right into his hand, allowing myself to fall under his spell. If it was only for the summer, why did he give me the necklace, which meant forever and why spend so much time with his family? Only Grant could answer those questions and I was not about to call him and demand answers. We had said everything last night. I am sure the gossip in the kitchen was going to be Sydney Stanton, completely drunk girl, smacks hot boy.

I crawled back into bed after taking some aspirin and drinking a large amount of water. I had nowhere to go and no one to see today, so I could wallow in self-pity all day. Kendall was probably afraid to come home to a blubbering idiot. I really was glad I was alone, giving me some time to rest and clear my mind. I really didn't feel like rehashing everything with anyone. I was staring at the ceiling, my stomach was growling. Fine, I got up, got dressed, and went to clean up in the bathroom. I put sunglasses on over my puffy eyes and went out into the scorching sun.

"Holy hell, it is hot out here," I said to myself as I walked down the street to get a bagel and coffee.

So, it was 2 in the afternoon, bagels were an any time of day kind of food. I think I should get a part time job to fill the free time I have, maybe something on campus, in the Registrar's Office or Library or something.

CHAPTER 20

I had classes all day Tuesdays, Wednesdays and Thursdays, giving me every Monday and Friday off, so I found a job in the student book store on campus. I worked Monday's and Friday's and every other Saturday. It was actually working out well, it got me up early, and I was always done by 6:00 pm no matter what shift I worked, because the book store closed every day at 6 pm.

Time was moving, it was almost midterms, so we had been in school for more than 5 weeks. I was enjoying my class schedule, but my social life was severally lacking. I mean, I went to the parties but I was never comfortable. Pledge Presents Formal was awful, the wish I had made during the summer of Grant being there to take me, didn't come true. Instead, I went with the other single girls, had a good time, but not as much fun as I would have had if Grant and I were still together.

I hadn't heard from him since our fight at his Fraternity House, I knew he was leaving for Yale at the end of August because his classes started in September. I spoke to his Mom a few times, but it was just too hard. She tried to convince me to call him, but what was the point? She had said he was just being stubborn, that all the Montgomery men were stubborn, but that did not ease my pain. I told her if his feelings for me were real, he would have never let me walk away from him. I turned down every date when I was asked out. My heart was still in a million shattered pieces and I was not ready to put it back together, just to have it shattered again.

I went home for Thanksgiving, it was nice to be away from school, Heather asked me to come down to the beach to go out with her on Friday night, but I declined. Everything there would remind me of Grant. The world was revolving around my sister's wedding.

She dragged me to at least six bridal shops, "Why do we have to go to all these shops, they all have the same dresses, pick one!" I yelled at her.

"Don't yell at me because you are all pissed off about your choice in men. First Trent and then Grant, their names alone screamed bad news. Find yourself a guy who treats you well and is not a womanizer," she said back to me.

Jade was right, I sucked at picking men, I should let my mom fix me up, I started to laugh to myself, snorting a little. I was not going to keep walking around like I was a widow. I just barely turned 19, what the hell was I doing?

"You know you're right, I do pick the wrong men, I think I will let Mom find me a date," I told my sister.

She looked at me and I thought she was going die of laughter.

We were both laughing when my mom walked over.

"What is so funny?" she asked.

"Nothing," we both bit our lips.

I flew back to school Monday afternoon and was walking through the airport in Arizona feeling much better about myself. Getting away for a few days gave me some perspective. I was coming back to school with a new attitude and a new haircut. I chopped my hair off into a bob! I didn't need to stop to get my luggage because I only had a carry- on. So I was heading to the arrival pick up area, where Kendall was meeting me. I had to pass the departing flights. As I walked through the terminal my stomach felt queasy, I went into the bathroom to splash some water on my face. I looked at myself in the mirror, thinking to myself, that was a strange sensation. Maybe I need some water. I went to one of the overpriced snack kiosks, to buy a bottle. Thinking maybe I am dehydrated from the flight, that never happened before, it is only an hour. I shook my head, maybe I was getting sick. I paid for my water and was leaning against the wall, tipping my head back taking a drink. I felt a tingling at the back of my neck. I slowly lowered my head keeping the water bottle at my lips. I began to survey my surroundings. I didn't notice him right away, but he was sitting with his back to me waiting for a flight.

I couldn't move, I was paralyzed with the sight of him. I watched him, he was reading something, I couldn't tell what. Then I almost got sick, a beautiful brunette came up to him, she leaned down and kissed him. Did my eyes just deceive me…no she sat on his lap. Running her hands through his hair and kissing his cheek. I could feel the bile coming up my throat. My shoulders slumped and I could tell my tears were about to fall over the side of my eyes. I was never going to escape the reminders of him. Now this scene would replay in my mind over and over again. I was still leaning on the wall, I heard the announcement of a departing flight for JFK International Airport. Passengers were grabbing their bags to get in line to board the plane bound for New York. The girl hopped off of his lap, Grant stood up, and as he stood he turned looking straight at me. I could feel the tears start to drop down my cheeks. Luckily, a crowd of people walked between us and our eyes never met.

I didn't know what to do, I moved as fast as I could to get out of the building. I could feel the devastation surging through my body. I headed for the exit, I knew Kendall would be circling waiting for me. I felt like I had been slapped repeatedly across the face. Everything he had ever said to me was a bold faced lie, except at the end. The parts about using me to pass the time had been true, how else could he move on so easily. I was walking around broken- hearted and he was already bringing home a new girl. I needed to throw up. So much for not wallowing in self-pity, this just made everything worse.

I didn't tell Kendall about seeing Grant in the airport. I didn't want her to feel sorry for me anymore. I threw myself into my studies and work. I went to all the parties, I accepted almost every date, well- not every date. I was going through the motions, hoping something would make me feel better. But nothing did. When another guy would kiss me, I could barely kiss him back. I had no connection with them. The hairs on my neck didn't stand up all tingling. My stomach never got excited by their look or touch. Some of them actually made my stomach churn in the opposite direction.

I was in my room studying, Monica knocked on the door, "Sydney, you have a visitor," she said.

"I do, who is it?" I asked.

"I think she said her name is Corinne."

What, what is she doing here? I looked haggard; I had been studying for finals, doesn't she know it is finals?. I was wearing sweats and an oversized sweatshirt; actually it was Grant's sweatshirt, which I had kept. I shook my head and walked down the hall. My mind was racing, I couldn't figure out why she had come to see me. She was standing by the door, looking perfect as usual.

"Honey, you look like you could use a break, will you take a walk with me?" She Asked.

She hugged me and said, "Oh, you cut your hair. I miss seeing your beautiful face, we all miss you," she said as we walked out the front door.

We were walking towards the park, "Mrs. Montgomery, why are you here? I am in the middle of studying for finals, what could you possibly want from me?" I asked her.

I could feel my tears threatening to fall down my cheeks.

"Sydney, I am worried about you," she said.

"Why would you be worried about me? Grant and I broke up months ago, he has moved on with someone else..." I stopped talking.

"How do you know there is someone else in his life?" She asked me.

"I don't... I just assumed, he is handsome and smart, girls fall all over themselves to go out with him."

"Sydney, remember I told you to come to me- if you ever needed my help that you could talk to me about anything?"

I looked at her with bewildered eyes.

"Umm...that was a long time ago."

"Sydney, you should have come to me, when you and my son, who is a stubborn jackass, started fighting." I laughed at her comment about Grant.

"Why would I do that, he didn't want me, he said terrible things to me and then...then he said he just used me to pass the time, that he never loved me?"

I could feel the tears coming down my face, seriously it had been months, when was I going to stop crying over him?

"I am so pissed at you Sydney."

"What, you're mad at me...why I didn't do anything? He accused me of cheating, I stood up for myself and told him if he couldn't tell me what his real problem was, that I didn't want to be with him, he couldn't even come clean with me, he didn't even try to fight for me."

I was trying not to yell, but I was having a hard time controlling my emotions.

"And then over Thanksgiving everything became clear to me, it was time for me to give up on him ever coming back to me, I was ready to stop acting like a widow. And then I saw him in the airport."

"You saw him, did you talk to him?" She asked me.

"No," I said.

"You should have gone to him and told him how you felt," she said.

"Are you crazy…he was with another girl. She was sitting on his lap and kissing him, it was awful, I was ill for days from what I had witnessed," I told her.

"Who is she?" I asked Corinne.

Mrs. Montgomery looked dumbfounded, "I don't know who she was, he didn't come home with any girls and when I asked him if you two had settled your differences and made up, he got mad at me and barely spoke to me during his visit."

"Well, I am sorry; I don't know what to tell you. Grant didn't trust me, no matter what I said, he assumed the worst. My last words to him after I slapped his face were something about Ashley and that not all girls were like her."

She smiled at me, "You slapped him…good for you!"

She was so weird.

"You are happy I slapped him, why, would you be happy about that?" I asked her.

"Look there are some things you don't know. Grant, well I had never seen him so happy. You brought out everything wonderful about him and didn't put up with his bullshit. Montgomery men are stubborn and arrogant as hell, but when they fall in love they love hard, and when Ashley betrayed him in such a cold calculating matter, he was a mess. I feared he would need serious intervention. He started drinking heavily, his grades- well he almost flunked out and he didn't care who he went out with. He eventually got on track again, stopped partying, brought his grades back up, got in to Yale and didn't go out with anyone forever, well until you I think."

I didn't know what to say.

"Corinne, I don't know what to tell you, I have to go back to study, I have finals in two days and then I am going home for winter break."

"You need to talk to him," she said.

"I don't have the energy to talk to him, he is mean, and my heart is broken into a million tiny pieces, I can't bear going through any of that again. He doesn't love me, it was all a farce. You should go, thank you for coming to check on me, but I am fine."

I started walking back to the house. I felt defeated, all of the emotions coming back.

"Sydney look, we are going to Vail for winter break, why don't you come with us, then you two will be forced to resolve your differences?" she said.

"Are you nuts, I am not going anywhere near Vail or him. That is a terrible idea. I don't play games and I would only be setting myself up for a world of hurt, why do you care so much, we were only together for three months, that is hardly anytime at all."

"I am a therapist, I see this crap all the time and what I see in your eyes and what I saw in his over Thanksgiving, and when I went to visit him last week is such sadness, you are in love with each other-stop fighting it," she said.

"If he is in love with me, why hasn't tried to contact me, email, text, even snail mail and why did I see him with another girl, she was kissing him in the airport, none of this makes sense, I have to move on I can't keep myself wishing for his return," I said.

"I am going to find out about the girl in the airport, don't you move."

Pointing at me to stand still, she pulled her phone out of her purse. It was 6:00 pm in New York. She put her finger over her lips so I would be quiet. Like I wanted him to know I was standing here while she was on the phone with him. I had my hand on my forehead, what the hell was I doing, I could feel a headache growing inside my brain and the tension in my neck was fierce.

"Hi Darling, its Mom, hold on I am going to put you on speaker, my Bluetooth is not working and I am driving," his mom was good at this.

Then I heard his voice and I almost gasped, I had to cover my mouth, "Hey Mom, what's up? You don't usually call me in the middle of the week. Is something wrong?" he asked.

"Well now that you mention it, I wanted to ask you something, I ran into…" my eyes got all big please don't say Sydney. "I was getting my hair done, and I was talking to Tony at the salon and he said he saw you kissing some girl in the airport over the Thanksgiving Holiday, you know when you came home," she continued, "I was hoping you were going to tell me you and Sydney had made up and were working things out," there was silence.

"Mom, your source is way off base, it wasn't Sydney- that is over, she doesn't want anything to do with me," he said.

"How do you know, have you even tried to contact her? What are you so afraid of honey, she is your soul mate and you are letting her slip through your fingers," she was chastising him.

"Shit Mom, I can't believe you are doing this to me again, I was horrible to her, I said awful things to Sydney and embarrassed her in front of her friends and the guys in the house."

"Grant, don't be so stubborn, do you want her to fall in love with someone else, marry him and have babies with him, babies that should be my grandchildren. Get off you fucking ass and call her, fly here and beg her to take you back. You are going to regret it if you don't, mark my words you will regret it."

He didn't say anything for a minute.

"Mom, do you know something? Is Sydney in love with someone else? Mom tell me, I know you, you can find anything out," he said. I could hear the desperation in his voice.

"No, I don't know anything. I know she has been dating, but I don't think she is in love, why do you care if you are not still in love with her?" she asked him.

"It is not that simple. Listen I have to go study," he said.

She took him off speaker phone, "Grant I want to know who you were kissing in the airport," she asked him again.

I could still kind of hear his voice, even though he was no longer on speaker.

"Mom, it is better if you don't know, you will be mad, really mad."

Corinne took a few steps away from me so I couldn't hear him at all. But I could hear her perfectly, I don't know what he said, but her response was loud.

"You are a fucking idiot, don't you dare get involved with her, do you hear me, don't even..." she stopped talking when she turned around and saw the look on my face.

"We are not done with this discussion, I will talk to you on the weekend," she said and then hung up.

I didn't say anything I just walked back to the Sorority House and went back to studying, well trying to study. I couldn't concentrate, my tears wouldn't stop, they kept coming. I knew who he had chosen over me, Ashley, that's who he was with in the airport. The reaction Corinne had when he answered her question made it perfectly clear. He had chosen the woman who betrayed him over the woman who loved him. He didn't bring her here from New York, he hooked up with her at home on his home turf. He went to her, instead of me. Now I really feel sick.

I had taken up running a few months ago, it made me feel better, the ground beneath my feet as I ran was like floating above the earth. I would put my ear buds on, pump up the music and run 3 or so miles a couple times a week depending on my schedule, or if I was super upset. When I felt upset I would go for a run, a way better way to deal with some emotions than eating ice cream. All though ice cream had its moments too. The upside to running so much, was that I was in the best shape of my life. I had one more final to take, I was going to run off some steam, shower, eat, and head to my last final. We were going out tonight to celebrate and then tomorrow, Kendall and I were driving home for winter break.

I finished my run and was stretching out my muscles in the park and cooling down. Since the hot, hot days of summer were over, the days were beautiful, cool enough to wear jeans during the day without sweating your ass off ,and the during the evening hours a light jacket would cover all the bases- December in Arizona was perfect, no wonder all the old people moved here for winter.

I was in deep thought, talking to myself.

"Hi, I have seen you running a few times, my name is Jason," he said extending his hand.

He had just finished a run as well, sweat beading down from his forehead and neck, he looked like he had just run 10 miles, his shirt was drenched and he was breathing heavily.

"Hi Sydney," I said, turning off my iPod, shaking his hand.

There it was, a spark, when our hands touched, not a lightning bolt but definitely a spark. I blushed.

"Oh yeah, I think I have seen you too," I said.

"Are you done with finals?" he asked me.

"No, I have one more in about two hours, then done!" I said smiling.

"I, um, well I have wanted to ask you out for a long time, do you have plans tonight?"

I was surprised by how quickly he had asked me out.

He said, "I am sorry, I am not usually so forward, but, I have been trying to get the courage to approach you for a while."

How sweet, how honest.

"I do have plans tonight, I am going out with my friends, maybe you could meet us," I said to him.

"That could work, what are you up to tonight?" he asked.

"Have you been to The Barrelhead? It is the country bar on 7th Avenue."

He started to laugh a little, "You don't have a southern accent, do you like country dancing?" he asked me.

"Well, I have always loved country music, but had never experienced country dancing before, one my friends is from the South and she turned a bunch of us on to it, it is really fun. Come you will have a good time, that is where I will be tonight, and tomorrow I will be headed home," I told him.

I raised my eyebrows at him as if to say, if you're really interested you will come.

"Okay Sydney, I will see you at The Barrelhead," he said smiling and running off.

I walked back to the house and down the hall to my room, I was all smiles when I walked in to my room. Kendall was studying at her desk, she looked up at me.

"Wow, that is a big smile on your face, did you have an orgasm during your run or something," she asked. I looked at her scrunching my face together.

"Eew, no, I just got asked out by a cute guy, Jason. I think he said his name was Jason."

"When are you going out with him?" she asked.

"Well he asked me what I was doing tonight and I said I had plans, but he could meet us at The Barrelhead."

"Nice, smooth, Sydney, see if he can dance, I like it," she said.

"I know, okay I am going to shower and then we can eat?" Kendall and I have only one class together and the final was today. It was a statistics class, we both hated it but it was a requirement for our General Ed.

We were walking back from the final.

"So, what does this Jason, look like?" she asked.

"Umm, he was cute, dark skin, dark eyes, short black or maybe dark brown hair, I don't know he was a sweaty from running, you will see him tonight if he shows up," I said.

"I am sure he liked what he saw, when he looked at you in one of your skimpy running outfits," she said laughing.

"You're bad, I am ready for a serious power nap before we go out tonight, what time do you want to leave?" I asked.

"I don't know about 8:00."

We both lay down and rested. It felt great to be done with finals and things were looking up- Jason could be a nice distraction. He was the first guy to truly spark my interest since Grant. Maybe I was finally ready to move on. I hadn't cried about him in a few days, since Corinne had been by to talk, hopefully the good feeling rolling inside me would continue.

We drove over to The Barrelhead around 8ish, there were about 6 of us going, we crammed into Kendall's car. Matt and some of his buddies were meeting us. I had on my kickass red boots, tight low riding jeans, cami, with a short sleeved plaid button down on over it. It could get seriously hot, when you are burning up the floor country dancing. My hair was still in a short bob, my cowboy hat pulled down just slightly. I looked good and I felt great!

We found a high pub table and sat down, the waitress came over and we ordered a round of beers, thank goodness for fake ID's. Music was playing and a few people were dancing together, but the line dancing hadn't started yet. We were sipping on our beers, when Matt and his friends came in to the club. They were all standing around our table waiting for the waitress, we were talking, having fun. Then I saw Jason come through the door with a buddy. I waved to him and they came over.

He introduced me to his friend and I introduced them to my friends, "Don't worry you don't need to remember all their names, just these two," I said pointing to Kendall and Matt.

"Kendall, Matt- this is Jason," I said they shook hands and Matt and Jason started talking about how bad the football team had done this year.

Kendall and I exchanged glances, "Nice," she mouthed to me. I laughed and took a drink of my beer.

Finally, the DJ's voice could be heard, in a southern accent he said, "Okay, everybody put your drinks down and get out on the dance floor, we are going to start this night off with a little Luke Bryan, I know you all love this song."

We headed to the dance floor, Jason was right next to me, I smiled at him, "Can you dance?" I asked him.

"We will find out," he was laughing when he spoke.

"Country Girl (Shake It For Me)" came blasting through the sound system. The crowd burst out in cheers.

"Okay, let's start this night out slow for the beginners in the crowd, we are going to do the Boot Scootin' Boogie," the DJ announced.

It was a super easy dance and Jason had no problem keeping up. We danced the next three songs in a row.

He leaned over to me, "Can we take a break and get a drink, I am parched," he said.

"Okay, partner if you are parched, let's get you a drink," I said laughing.

He took my hand in his, I could feel myself blush. He ordered us each a beer and we went to the table to sit down.

We sat talking for a very long time, the usual questions, where are you from, how old are you, what year in school, what sorority/fraternity are you in? We had gotten through the basics, he was from San Diego, a Junior, just turned 21, and was in a fraternity, thank goodness not the same as Matt's. Matt and Kendall joined us when the line dancing started to get too fast for Matt to keep up. We were laughing about I don't know what, we had had a few beers and a round of shots. I wasn't paying attention to the dancing, my eyes were focused on Jason. He is super cute.

"Are you staring at me?" he asked almost giggling.

"No, not staring just taking in your cuteness," I said giggling to myself.

"I think you're cute too," he said.

"Can I kiss your cheek?" He asked.

"Yes," I said.

I could feel Matt and Kendall watching our exchange.

"Oh, look our Sydney got her first kiss, I am such a proud father," Matt said, laughing, wiping a pretend tear from his eye.

I shot him a dirty look and threw my napkin at him.

I stood up, "I am going to the restroom, Kendall, do you need to go?" I said with raised eyebrows.

"Yeah," she responded. Girls always go to the restroom in twos.

Once inside the sanctity of the restroom...Kendall said, "He is adorable, I couldn't believe he asked to kiss your cheek- that is so cute, just take it slow with him."

"I know, we are leaving tomorrow, it is one night and well, I haven't had this kind of feeling about anyone since Grant, I am not going to say the feelings are as intense, but there is definitely something there," I said.

"Good, I am glad," Kendall said.

"Can we pee now, my bladder is about to burst?" I asked her. We both laughed. We headed back to the table, it was very busy, hard to walk a straight line, weaving around all the people inside the club. As we approached our table, Matt was standing up talking to someone.

"Oh, here they are, look who is here tonight," he said. Matt's eyes were huge.

Now we had come here, I don't know how many times, and never, I mean never, seen Mr. and Mrs. Montgomery. My eyes got really big, I smiled.

"Oh, my gosh, it is nice to see you," I said.

Kendall and I both giving them hugs. Jason was looking very uncomfortable.

"Corinne, Kevin- this is Jason," I said introducing him to my ex-boyfriend's parents.

My heart was racing from the odd situation.

"Nice to meet you," they both said to him.

"Are you kids done with finals and heading home soon?" Corinne asked.

"Yeah, Kendall and I are driving back to California in the morning," I told her.

"Well, it was great seeing you," I said to them.

I turned to Jason, "Jason would you like to dance with me?" I asked him.

He smiled, stood up, and took me out to the dance floor. Chris Young's song, "You" was playing, perfect I thought a nice slow song, he wouldn't be able to see my face as we danced. We were dancing close, each with an arm around our waists and our hands clasped together in an informal manner. I laid my head against his chest, he wasn't as tall as Grant, but not short, maybe 5'11". The Montgomery's were still talking to Matt and Kendall, I was watching them, they were all shaking their heads, and of course I was trying to read their lips. I could only see Kendall's face clearly.

I was completely focused on her, reading her lips she said "No, they haven't talked, no she just met him, this is their first date."

Mr. Montgomery was rubbing Corinne's back. She looked upset, they both turned and looked at me dancing with Jason. I diverted my eyes so they couldn't see me watching them.

Another slow song came on and Jason pushed me away from him and twirled me around.

I smiled, "You do know how to dance, you were holding out on me," I said laughing.

"Yes, my mom made me take dance lessons, telling me girls adore boys who can dance," he told me.

My smile was big, he was nice, very nice. He pulled me in close, both hands wrapped around my waist, my arms around his neck.

"So, who are they the Montgomery's?" he asked.

I sighed and took a deep breath, looking up at him from under my eyelashes. I couldn't lie, why it was not worth lying about.

"They are my ex-boyfriend's parents."

He looked down at me, "Oh, no wonder you were so uncomfortable," he said.

"How did you know I was uncomfortable," I asked him.

I thought I had been all cool about the awkward moment.

"Well, you had an odd look on your face when you came back from the restroom and were moving back and forth from foot to foot when you were talking to them," he explained.

"Sorry," I said. He tilted my chin up to him, looked into my eyes.

"We all have a past, I didn't think you had been locked away in tower somewhere for the last 19 years."

I laughed, "You're funny, thank you, and you are very observant."

The night was fun, before we left The Barrelhead, Jason asked for my phone number and we talked about getting together over winter break.

Kendall and I woke up in the morning, threw our stuff in the car and headed home, glad the semester was over. It took us more than seven hours to get home because of an accident on the freeway. We talked the whole time. The subjects we avoided were Grant, and Jason: I didn't want any lectures from Kendall, she and Matt had the perfect relationship, it was disgusting how perfect they were together.

CHAPTER 21

Kendall dropped me off at home, my dad was on a business trip, sister at work, so it was my mom and I. A quiet Saturday afternoon, I found her cleaning out her closet when I got home.

"Hey Mom," I said jumping onto her bed, "I am home," she came out of her closet.

"I am so glad, how did your finals go?"

"Good, I think I might get a 3.5 GPA this term," I said with pride.

"Great, hard work pays off," she said grinning at me.

"So what is on your agenda while your home?" she asked.

"Not much, just relaxing, but I don't want to spend my vacation planning Jade's wedding," I said to her with a grim look on my face.

She was back in her closet, "Sydney, have you and Grant made up yet? I know you don't want to tell me what happened, have you spoken to him?"

Seriously, was this the only question everyone could ask me? I didn't want to have this hanging over my head all vacation with her asking me a million questions about what happened.

"Mom, that shipped has sailed, he has moved on, or backwards, I am not sure, but I have met someone," I said.

That statement had her walking out of the closet.

"What do you mean you met someone?" she asked.

"You're not even over Grant," she said with a sour look on her face.

"Yes, I am. Grant is not a part of my life anymore, anyways, his name is Jason and he lives in San Diego, we are going to try to get together over vacation."

My mom was annoyed, thinking I had totally given up on Grant, she rolled her eyes at me.

"Mom, did you just roll your eyes at me?" I asked her laughing.

"Yes, you didn't invent eye rolling you know," she said.

She continued, "I am not going to lecture you, but if you really believe you are over Grant and you have no feelings for him, than by all means start dating this Jason, but don't lead Jason on if you are still in love with Grant."

My mouth fell open at her words. My heart was still broken, I wasn't looking for a hot romance like I had with Grant just someone nice to spend time with and have a good time with, I deserved to be happy.

Jason called me late Sunday night, "Hi Sydney, it is Jason," he said.

"Hi," I said.

"Would you like to meet me in Temecula and go wine tasting?" he asked.

"Yeah that sounds fun, when?" I asked him.

"How about Tuesday late morning?" He asked.

"Okay, sounds good," I said.

"I'll text you the address, see you there around 11:00 am."

Wine tasting sounds fun, I had never done that before. Monday I relaxed and did laundry. Heather text me, she would be in town until Christmas Day and then was meeting Curt in Vail, spending the week with him, and then she would be back. That hurt a little. Not going there, I thought to myself. Heather was applying to Berkley, hoping to get in so she and Curt could be together.

I put the address of the winery into the GPS in my mom's Lexus, I turned on the music, and headed out to Temecula. All my favorite songs were being played; this would be a nice ride. I followed the directions the GPS was barking at me, this was far- I wouldn't want to live way out here, I thought as I was driving. My phone rang, I answered, through the car's blue tooth.

"Hello, you have reached Sydney Stanton, I am getting ready to go wine tasting, who may I say is calling?" was how I answered the phone.

I knew it was Kendall, I was just goofing around.

"You are a serious dork," she said.

I was laughing, "What's up?" I asked.

"Who are you going wine tasting with?"

"Jason."

"Is he with you?"

"No, we are meeting at the winery. Sounds fun right?"

"Yeah, listen I was thinking for New Year's Eve, we could go to the party at the Country Club?"

I must have made a grunting noise, as if to say boring.

"Listen, it sounds fun, poker, black jack, a palm reader, dancing, come on it will be fun and it is free," she said.

"Fine, is Matt coming out for it?"

"Yeah he will be here a few days after Christmas. Sydney, have you heard from Grant?"

I was rolling my eyes.

"Why does everyone keep asking me that, no, no, no, he is with Ashley again. I saw them together in the airport after Thanksgiving, he made his choice, I really don't want to get in to this conversation when I am about to meet Jason."

She was yelling, "What do you mean, you never told me about seeing him in the airport, what did he say to you?"

"I didn't talk to him, I just stood there watching them together, I almost got sick in the middle of the airport, it was right before you picked me up."

"I knew something had happened, you were all pale that day when you got in the car, damn I should follow my gut instinct."

"You know it is a very long drive to Temecula, remind me not to do this again. Heather is going to Vail with Curt, so I am sure she will come back with all kinds of information about Grant, probably more than I will want to hear about."

"Hey, I need to go, my exit is coming up and I don't want to get lost, I will talk to you tomorrow."

"Ok, fine, but we need to talk about you and Grant," she said before hanging up.

I pulled in the parking lot of the winery. Jason was waiting for me in front. He looked handsome, I smiled at him, he leaned in and gave me a hug and kiss.

"Oh good."

"What?"

"You are as cute as I remember," he said laughing.

I giggled and he took my hand leading me in to the building. We tried four different kinds of wine, with cheese and crackers and then had lunch out on the patio overlooking the vineyards.

"This is lovely, thank you for planning a wonderful day, can I kiss your cheek?"

"I would rather you kissed my lips," he said grinning at me.

So I did, I kissed him on the lips, it was a long sensuous kiss. It was nice, I could feel the tingle going through my body, it was a slow warm feeling. I smiled at him after our kiss.

"That was nice," he whispered to me.

"Would you like to walk around the vineyards?" he asked me.

"Are we allowed too?"

"Yes, there is a walking path we can take."

He paid the bill and we walked hand in hand, talking, laughing, stopping for the occasional kiss.

We said our good-bye's after a few hours of getting to know each other, we made plans to meet in Carlsbad in a few days. I drove home, the long long drive home, thinking about Jason, it had been a wonderful day. He planned everything perfectly and our conversations were great, no awkward silences or misunderstood comments. The kissing was nice, not hot, just nice, safe. I needed nice and safe, safe was good. Less likely to get my heart broken again with safe. It was just, he wasn't Grant, my eyes filled with tears, I missed Grant so much, just thinking about him made my chest ache with pain. I tried to shake all thoughts of him out of brain as I drove, I put on the radio, hoping the music would distract me. That only made it worse, every song reminded me of him. By the time I got home I was emotionally wiped out. I cried the whole way home, tears streaming down my face with no stopping.

I went to bed that night feeling defeated about Grant and not knowing what lay ahead with Jason. Jason called me the next morning, thanking me for a wonderful day and looking forward to Saturday in Carlsbad. Christmas was on Sunday, so we planned to have lunch and do some shopping at the outlets together. Jason almost always called, very rarely texting. He said he liked hearing my voice and being able to get to know me. He was so nice. I didn't want to bring him to my house, nor did I want to go to his, meeting parents was way far away, I wanted this to go slowly really get to know him before anything substantial happened. Sex was out of the question, no sex until we knew each other very well.

We met in Carlsbad, the place was packed, outlet shopping is a big deal. We ate lunch to help us keep our energy up during our shopping.

"Sydney, would you like to go skiing next week, I mean if there is snow in the local mountains?"

"Sure, I am not very good at skiing but we can go for the day."

"Well, it is a long drive, I thought maybe we could spend the night up there," he said innocently.

I wasn't buying the innocent routine, but I played along.

"What day were you thinking?"

"Whenever, we can just decide and go, no big planning."

"Let me see what is going on at home, and I will let you know."

We finished lunch and went in to every store, I was exhausted, my hands were hurting from all the bags we were carrying.

He walked me to my car, I put my bags in the back seat and closed the door. He was leaning on the car, he pulled me up to him by my waist.

"I really like you Sydney and I think we are very good together, we can talk for hours without stopping," he said.

Giving me a kiss on the lips, a pretty heated kiss based on the reaction I was having, and the reaction he was obviously having.

"I like you too Jason, I would just like to keep this going at this slow pace. I don't want to rush into anything when I am not emotionally ready to commit," I said to him.

I could see the disappointment in his eyes, "I understand, you were hurt and you don't want to be hurt again, I get it Sydney, but you can't hold it against me, I am not like your ex-boyfriend, you are going to have trust me," he said.

That sounded familiar, too familiar. I kissed him, not wanting to discuss this anymore, kissing was a good distraction.

"Yummy, you give good kisses."

"What else is that tongue good at?" he asked.

I was completely blushing, "Jason," I said.

"Sydney you turn me on, I can't even walk right now I am so turned on by you," he said.

I was laughing and he was holding me close, I could feel his erection.

I wiggled my eyebrows at him, "Yes I can feel you on my stomach," I said.

"Give me a minute while I recite the Pledge of Allegiance to get this bad boy down," he said.

I was laughing at him. Is that what guys did to get an erection down, think of the Pledge of Allegiance. I was driving home, another good day with Jason. We had fun together and the chemistry was there between us, just…he wasn't Grant. I was comparing everyone to Grant, I have to stop comparing Jason to Grant. There was no comparison, Jason was nice, safe and made feel warm inside. Grant was all those things, and more, and he still held my heart. Shit my mom was right, I can't move on without finding out if my feelings were still true about Grant or was I just holding on to what could have been with him.

I declined Jason's next invitation to go skiing, knowing what ultimately would happen if we spent the night together in the mountains. I told him we could get together after New Year's Eve. He wanted to spend New Year's Eve together, but I told I had made plans with my family and I wasn't ready to introduce him to my parents yet. I had no problem being honest with him I just told him exactly how I felt.

It was New Year's Eve, we would be heading to the Country Club around 9 pm for the party. I was meeting Kendall and Matt, we always had a good time together and there would be other members there our age, kids we had grown up with. It was taking all of my willpower to keep myself from texting Heather, I totally wanted to know how Grant was, if he had brought anyone with him to Vail. I was in my room getting dressed for the evening, pacing back and forth like an idiot. Trying to convince myself not to do it, not go down that path again. Weighing the pro's and con's of why I should or shouldn't text her. I finally succumbed to my weak self. I grabbed my phone and before I could stop myself I had sent a text to Heather.

Monday, 7:01 pm: Sydney to Heather: hey, how is Vail, good skiing.

I sat on the end of my bed waiting for her response, what a dumb question, you should have just asked about Grant. They were probably out for the evening, I mean, it is New Year's Eve. My phone vibrated.

Monday, 7:03 pm: Heather to Sydney: skiing is good.

That is it, nothing more, I was going to have to pull the information from her, argh.

Monday, 7:05 pm: Sydney to Heather: can u elaborate? Crowded, super cold, anything else u might think I want to know about...

Monday, 7:07 pm: Heather to Sydney: yes, slopes crowded, house beautiful, family great, wish you were here with me, miss you!

Monday, 7:10 pm: Sydney to Heather: are u having fun? what r u doing 2nite?

Monday, 7:12 pm: Heather to Sydney: yes, very fun. Staying in 2nite. What r u doing 2nite? Do u have a date?

Monday, 7:14 pm: Sydney to Heather: going 2 country club, poker, black jack, free drinks and fortune teller.

Monday, 7:15 pm: Heather to Sydney: who r u going with? R U going to ask the fortune teller anything?

Monday, 7:17 pm: Sydney to Heather: kendall, matt, family. Maybe, what should I ask?

Monday, 7:21 pm: Heather to Sydney: ask about Grant?

Ask about Grant, I was already thinking about it. She was being very strange in her responses. I wonder what she is not telling me. I didn't respond right away, I went to take a quick shower.

Monday, 7:43 pm: Sydney to Heather: went to take shower, why should I ask about him, do you want to share anything with me. Is he there with someone?

Monday, 7:44 pm: Heather to Sydney: no, not here with anyone. I know he misses you, and regrets what he did. Maybe you should talk to him.

Did she just encourage me to talk to him, she must be drunk already.

Monday, 7:46 pm: Sydney to Heather: did he tell u he misses me? did he say he was sorry for his behavior for breaking my heart? Did he tell you he was back with Ashley? He picked the

girl who betrayed him over the one who loved him, I can't talk
to him, it hurts too much.

Monday, 7:50 pm: Heather to Sydney: y do u think he is
back with Ashley?

Monday, 7:51 pm: Sydney to Heather: I saw them together
@ airport when I came back 2 school after turkey break.

Monday, 7:53 pm: Heather to Sydney: oh, maybe he was
looking for comfort.

Comfort…What does that mean? She is out of her mind tonight!

Monday, 7:55 pm: Sydney to Heather: COMFORT r u for
real, what comfort do u get from a girl like that? they deserve
each other.

Monday, 7:57 pm: Heather to Sydney: they are NOT
together, I told you that already.

Monday, 8:00 pm: Sydney to Heather: u never said, they
weren't together, u said he wasn't in Vail with anyone. I have
to go get ready, I will text you back in a few minutes it doesn't
take me long since I cut my hair.

Monday, 8:02 pm: Heather to Sydney: u cut u r hair? When?
Why?

I went to dry my hair, I could text and put on my make-up at the
same time but not dry my hair and text, and I still needed to figure
out what I was wearing tonight.

Monday, 8:10 pm: Sydney to Heather: u know I cut my hair
over turkey break, r u drunk?

Monday, 8:11 pm: Heather to Sydney: sorry, I forgot! Who
will u kiss @ midnight?

Monday, 8:13 pm: Sydney to Heather: LOL, my hand I
guess! U r lucky to have curt, I am jealous. I wish things would
have turned out differently and I was with you guys in vail.

Monday, 8:15 pm: Heather to Sydney: what about the guy
from the barrelhead? Y r u not with him? if he begged would u
take him back?

Monday, 8:16 pm: Sydney to Heather: LOL, he would never
beg, he doesn't care enough to beg. He didn't even try to fight

for me, begging not in his repertoire. How did u know about Jason?

Monday, 8:21 pm: Heather to Sydney: his mom made a big deal about seeing u out on a date with him at country western club.

Monday, 8:22 pm: Sydney to Heather: how did grant react? I am sure he didn't care.

Monday, 8:23 pm: Heather to Sydney: he cared, he punched a hole in the wall, his mom had to take him for stitches. R U still seeing the guy, y R U not with him 2nite?

Monday, 8:25 pm: Sydney to Heather: shocking, why does he care? he hasn't ever tried to contact me. He doesn't want me but he doesn't want me to b with anyone else. He is an ass! Yes, went a couple dates, it was nice.

Monday, 8:27 pm: Heather to Sydney: is he a good kisser? Have u, u know been with him?

Monday, 8:30 pm: Sydney to Heather: NO! I have not, rude. Yes, he is a good kisser but...he is not grant. He is a nice guy...he is safe.

Monday, 8:31 pm: Heather to Sydney: LOL, is that what you want to be safe? Oh, safe is good.

Monday, 8:35 pm: Sydney to Heather: u r weird 2nite, is everything ok, you seem not ur self. Safe is the only thing I can handle...my heart is still broken, I cried after each date with Jason.

Monday, 8:36 pm: Heather to Sydney: why, why cry?

Monday, 8:38 pm: Sydney to Heather: My heart it aches for him, I don't want to talk about this anymore. Give curt a hug for me, c u when u come back. I have to finish getting ready, I want to know what fortune teller knows about my future, hopefully something good...Happy New Year!

I finished getting ready, Heather was odd tonight, she must be hiding something, she was asking a lot of questions. I went with my family to the country club party, Matt and Kendall were already inside, playing black jack. I got a drink from the bar, my mom gave me the evil eye.

"What?"

"You shouldn't be drinking," she said.

"Get a grip it is New Year's Eve and I am having a drink, probably more than one," I said to her.

"I am going to the fortune teller, this should be interesting," I said to Kendall.

"Okay, let me know what she says."

"I will," I said.

I waited my turn and then went into the private area.

She looked me over and then asked, "Do you want me to read your hand or your Tarot cards?"

"Can you do both?" I asked.

"Sure," she said.

She pulled my cards, I was watching her, not really believing what she was about to tell me.

She looked at me and then the cards.

"These cards show you with a broken heart, the one you love is far away, he is the only one who can mend your heart, he is your soul mate. Do you know who the cards are talking about?" she asked me.

My throat had closed up, tears were in my eyes, I was unable to speak, I was nodding my head yes!

"Let me see your palm?"

She requested my right hand. She looked at me again.

"There is another man, waiting for you, waiting for your heart to mend, but he is not the one for you, the one who broke your heart he is the only one for you," she said.

I pulled my hand back really fast. I was feeling sick, I needed some fresh air. I was freaking out, "Thank you," I said as I left her.

I was standing on the patio, my body was shaking from the reading by the fortune teller. I pulled out my phone to check the time. It was nowhere close to midnight, I headed for the bar.

"I need a shot," I said out loud to myself.

Kendall and Matt were standing at the bar.

"Oh good, I am glad you are here, I didn't want to have a shot by myself," I said.

The bartender lined up three shots of Patron; we did the salt ritual, sucked down the shot, and stuck limes in our mouths.

"One more?" I asked.

"Sure."

"Okay, one more round," I said to the bartender.

Three more shots were lined up and down the hatch they went. I was feeling no pain. I went and played some black jack, then danced a little with some of our friends.

I walked out on to the patio to look at the stars and make a wish, not that any of my other wishes had come true, but what the fortune teller had told me was making me crazy. I looked at my phone, it was almost midnight, there was one text.

Monday, 11:57 pm: Jason to Sydney: Happy New Year, Sydney, looking forward to seeing you in the New Year.

I was reading the message from Jason and my phone rang, it was Heather, how nice, I thought.

I answered her call, "Hi, shouldn't you be getting ready to kiss Curt and not calling me," I said laughing.

"I don't want to kiss Curt at midnight...I want to kiss you...I want to hold you, Oh, God, Sydney, I miss you so much, I am so sorry," his voice cracked as he spoke...it was Grant.

COMING SOON

Want to know what happens with Sydney and Grant? Look for the second book in the Wishing Series; see what becomes of Sydney and Grant's relationship. The second book *Not Another Wish*, will tell you all you want to know. Find out why Grant behaves the way he does, and is the fortune teller right? Is the one who broke Sydney's heart the only one to mend it? Will Sydney forgive Grant for his horrible behavior or will Sydney move on with someone else? Look for the final book in this series on Amazon.

THE AUTHOR

This is the first novel by the author, S.P. Wilcox, born and raised in Southern California. She has been married for 16 years, has four kids, 3 boys and 1 girl. She decided to write a book after her husband suggested she should write her own book. So she did. She spends most of her time, chauffeuring her two youngest children around town to school, dance class, sport activities and their friends' houses. She loves to read and has read probably all of the same books you have including, Avoiding Commitment, the Thoughtless series, 50 Shades of Grey, Beautiful Disaster, The Marriage Bargain, Pushing the Limits, Taking Chances and so so many more.

You can visit the author on Goodreads and on Facebook, just look under S.P.Wilcox.

Website coming soon!